Withdrawn

"Terry Brennan meticulously crafts stories of intrigue and action. His ability to weave archaeological and historical detail into a riveting plotline is simply amazing. Both *The Sacred Cipher* and *The Brotherhood Conspiracy* could step off the front page of any newspaper tomorrow. You'll find them captivating!"

—MIKE DELLOSSO,
author of *Fearless* and *Frantic*

"*The Brotherhood Conspiracy* weaves a beautifully intricate web of intrigue and suspense. Painstakingly researched with powerful characters, it takes the reader on an exciting and thought-provoking adventure. Brennan brilliantly meshes an internal struggle of faith with an epic story about a world on the brink."

—DAVID E. STEVENS,
former Navy commander and F-18 fighter pilot, author of *Resurrect*

THE
BROTHERHOOD
CONSPIRACY

A NOVEL

TERRY
BRENNAN

Kregel
Publications

The Brotherhood Conspiracy: A Novel
© 2013 by Terry Brennan

Published by Kregel Publications, a division of Kregel, Inc.,
P.O. Box 2607, Grand Rapids, MI 49501.

Published in association with the literary agency of WordServe
Literary Group, Ltd., 10152 S. Knoll Circle, Highlands Ranch,
CO 80130. www.wordserveliterary.com.

ISBN 978-0-8254-4317-6

Printed in the United States of America
13 14 15 16 17 / 5 4 3 2 1

To my sisters, Pat and Kathie;
And to my brother, Butch—
your years were much too short.

ACKNOWLEDGMENTS

There is no greater partner, encourager, editor than my best friend and wife, Andrea, who not only lived *with* me through the trials, tribulations, and occasional joys of writing this book, but who also walked with me over the four long years it took to bring this sequel to completion. Sweetie, I couldn't have done it without you.

I owe a large debt of gratitude to our daughter, Meghan, who is a deft editor but, more importantly, helped me keep my female characters real and relevant to twenty-first-century women. Thank you also to her husband, Azizi, who was supportive of Meg's time, and to our son, Matt, for his encouragement.

Thank you to the great team at Kregel Publications, and particularly my editor, Dawn Anderson, whose probing questions always drive me nuts (what do you mean, *motivation?*) but always make the work so much better. Miranda and Cat—you are missed. And thanks to Greg Johnson and the team at WordServe Literary who have supported me from the beginning.

Without the Stephen Schwarzman Humanities and Social Sciences Library on Bryant Park in New York City, many of the pages in this book would be blank. Breathtakingly beautiful in its style and scope, if it's not in the NYC "main" library, it probably doesn't exist.

I can't forget those who helped me get started: Marlene Bagnell, Wanda Dyson, Kathryn Mackel, Angela Hunt, and Nancy Rue. Thanks for giving me a good foundation—and hope. And to Mike Dellosso, Tim Shoemaker, and Adam Blumer—other writers who offered encouragement and support along the way.

Lastly, to my "guys"—Fred, James, Michael, and Mike—who regularly put up with my anxiety and insecurity but always impart wisdom; and to Michael O'Neill, who more than once helped me understand how to be a better man.

PROMINENT CHARACTERS

The team that discovered the Third Temple of God
hidden under the Temple Mount:

Tom Bohannon. Executive director of the Bowery Mission in New York City; former investigative reporter.

Joe Rodriguez. Curator of the Periodicals Room in the New York Library's "main" building on Bryant Park; married to Deirdre, Tom Bohannon's sister.

"Sammy" Rizzo. Director of the book storage and retrieval system in the Humanities and Social Sciences Library on Bryant Park at 42nd Street in New York City; colleague of Joe Rodriguez; a small person, a tad over four feet tall.

Dr. Richard Johnson Sr. Managing director of the Collector's Club in Manhattan; former chair of the Antiquities College at Columbia University; fellow of the British Museum.

꼭꼭꼭

Abu Gherazim. Foreign minister of the Palestinian Authority; a moderate Muslim leader.

Annie Bohannon. Tom's wife of thirty years; photographer.

Avram Levin. Commander of the Aleph Reconnaissance Center in Jerusalem; known to his men as "the Hawk."

Baqir al-Musawi. President of Syria.

Bill Cartwright. Director of the Central Intelligence Agency; President Whitestone's longtime friend and accountability partner.

Brandon McDonough. Provost of Trinity College, Dublin; expert in biblical archaeology and Richard Johnson's boss at the British Museum.

Chaim Shomsky. Chief of staff to the prime minister of Israel.

David Posner. Deputy director of Mossad, Israel's international intelligence and special operations agency.

Eliazar Baruk. Prime minister of Israel; lives in Tel Aviv.

Holy One, or Effendi. Old man of the desert; reclusive leader of the Prophet's Guard.

Jonathan Whitestone. President of the United States; Republican; evangelical Christian, from the state of Texas.

Kallie Nolan. Masters candidate in biblical archaeology; friend of Sammy Rizzo; assisted the team in finding the Temple.

King Abbudin. Ruler of Saudi Arabia, sixth of the Saudi kings.

Leonidas. Informer, selling secret intelligence to radical Islamists.

Levi Sharp. Director of Shin Bet, Israel's internal security force.

Lukas Painter. Director of Mossad, Israel's relentless and feared international intelligence agency.

Mehdi Essaghir. President of Iran.

Moishe Orhlon. Israeli defense minister.

Ronald Fineman. Messianic rabbi and custodian of Jeremiah's Grotto.

Rory O'Neill. Commissioner of the New York City police department.

Sam Reynolds. Career diplomat of the U.S. State Department; assisted the team that found the Temple.

Moussa al-Sadr. Imam; founder of the Lebanese militia that became Hezbollah; after thirty years in hiding, emerging leader of the Muslim Brotherhood.

PROLOGUE

1978

The night air smelled of dead fish and diesel. The waves of the Mediterranean falling against the dingy gravel beach muted the faint sound of running feet. No moon marked the team's passing. Their lives depended on being invisible.

This was blood work. Close, messy, fatal.

They ran through the shadows between the Esso refinery's flashing scarlet lights and the dark parade ground of the women's military college, best known for training Qaddafi's female bodyguards.

They were four, covered head-to-foot in black, only their eyes visible through the holes of the hood. The leader had cold, blue eyes.

No insignias, no uniforms, no ID, no names. If they were caught, or killed, they would not be identified.

They ran under an oasis of palm trees, across a vulnerable, flat, open space, and then stopped short of a small parking lot, a stone garage protecting them from view of anyone on the other side.

Thirty minutes total. This close to the Libyan coast, the sub wouldn't wait any longer. Get it done and get out, or get dead.

The main building was on the far side of the parking lot, across a stretch of lawn. The director's wife grew roses, surrounding the mansion with sweet perfume.

The refinery director and his family were on a hastily arranged holiday.

Qaddafi had commandeered their lovely home once again—far from prying eyes in the capital—to celebrate his son's birthday with those he trusted, and those he wanted to influence. He was here, tonight.

Pointing to the right, the leader broke his team into two pairs, each inching toward a corner of the garage. Night birds sang in the treetops, French tamarisk wrestled to mask the power of massed rose bushes. The leader and his partner approached the left corner of the garage and raised their silenced Glocks.

And came face-to-face with the muzzle of a rifle.

The other soldier must have hesitated for a moment . . . only a split second . . . surprised by these two ghosts in black. The leader put a bullet between the soldier's eyes before he could blink. They ran through the small parking lot, clogged with stretch limousines, as the other team came around the right side of the garage and snapped C-4 incendiary devices to the gas tanks of the parked limos.

Through a grove of date palms and carob trees that blocked the garage from the view of the main house, they ran up behind a shoulder-high hedge of Phoenician juniper. Across an expansive, manicured lawn sat the director's mansion, about a hundred meters away, the rear terrace aglow from the multi-colored paper lanterns surrounding its outer edge.

Joined by the other two soldiers, the squad edged along the hedge until they had a clear view. There were three groups of men on the terrace, all—with the exception of one man—wearing kaftans and kaffiyehs, the robe and headdress common to Arab men. One group was seated in a semicircle, the other two groups stood at each side. In the middle of the seated group was Qaddafi, a thin, ascetic-looking man dressed in a long, flowing, golden robe, with a small, embroidered, round golden cap on his head.

To his left, in stark contrast, sat a black-robed imam, a black turban on his head, his jet black beard visible against Qaddafi's golden splendor, even at this distance. Their target—not Qaddafi, but Imam Moussa al-Sadr, religious leader of the Shi'ites of Lebanon, founder of Amal, meaning *hope* in Arabic, the four-teen thousand–strong militia wing of al-Sadr's Movement of the Disinherited . . . enemy of Israel.

Their orders were simple. Kill al-Sadr. Across the Mediterranean, twenty-five thousand Israeli troops poured into southern Lebanon as part of Operation Litani. The invasion was both in retaliation for the thirty-seven Israeli citizens massacred four days earlier by eleven Palestinian terrorists who hijacked a bus in a daring, daylight raid near Tel Aviv, and to root out the terrorist base camps, like those of Amal, that spawned these agents of terror.

The Israeli commando leader didn't know why al-Sadr ventured into the lair of Qaddafi, his bitter enemy. It didn't matter. He had his orders, to snuff out the life of this enemy. He would obey. Or die trying.

The team's two shooters extricated and assembled the pieces of their Remington M40A1 heavy barrel sniper rifles from their backpacks. Silencers would decrease the accuracy of the rifles. Night-vision scopes, the light on the terrace, and the training of the shooters and their spotters, would help. Still, the leader would have preferred another fifty meters closer.

Two muzzles were pushed through the branches of the juniper hedge.

Just as children came running onto the terrace.

There were dozens of them, swarming around and through the three groups of men, some being lifted by waiting arms. In the midst of the seated group, three children, two boys and a girl, came forward and crawled up onto the lap of the man in the golden robes, bringing a radiant smile to his face. A fourth, another boy, slower than the rest, stood at Qaddafi's knees and looked back and forth for a place to sit. But there was no more room on his lap or in his chair.

As the commando leader raced through his options, the black-clad cleric reached down, picked up the boy, and brought him close to the others on Qaddafi's lap. Qaddafi reached out his hand and stroked the boy's head.

The leader looked, left and right, at his shooters. They shook their heads. At this distance, even without the silencers, there was no shot without great risk of killing one or more of the children.

The clock was ticking. The incendiary devices, intended as a diversion for their escape, would explode in ninety seconds. The plan was to get the shot, then run—without concern for stealth—for the darkness of the parade ground, getting there as the cars exploded in the parking lot. With luck, attention would be diverted long enough for the team to reach the beach and the inflatable. If Libyan defense helicopters weren't in the air quickly enough, they had a chance of reaching the submarine.

"If we don't take the shot now, we're out of time," came a whisper from his left. The orders were clear. Eliminate al-Sadr. At all costs. The leader decided to wait. Ninety seconds and the bombs would go off. The children would be scared, they would run.

His men all looked in his direction. The leader held up his hand, flat, palm out. Wait.

In the silence, punctuated by the distant, muffled laughter of children, a soft breeze drifted off the Mediterranean, tasting like the sea. They waited for the explosion—the light, the noise, the confusion, the scrambling—to get their shot. They waited . . .

There was no audible or visible alarm. No claxon sounding, no searchlights reaching into the darkness. But from each side of the mansion, a dozen heavily armed soldiers came running—pinching in, straight toward their location. They were discovered . . . perhaps the dead guard was missed. At the same moment a phalanx of tall, beautiful warrior women ran onto the terrace and surrounded Qaddafi, rushing him from the terrace toward the house.

The shooter on the lieutenant's right took a shot at al-Sadr . . . the one on his left responded. But the imam was moving. He put down the boy, and the first bullet ripped above his head. At the sound he dropped into a crouch as two bodyguards surrounded him. One spun to the ground in a death dance. And al-Sadr was gone.

The leader tapped his partner on the shoulder, sending him into the dark to cover their retreat as the shooters squeezed off four shots each, emptying their magazines. Five Libyan soldiers fell to the grass. The leader tapped them on the shoulders and they followed the first soldier, leaving the unidentifiable sniper rifles in the top branches of the hedge, grabbing their Uzis as they ran.

More soldiers were joining the attack from the sides of the mansion and, while some of the first group dropped to a knee to return fire, the rest were rushing headlong toward the hedge. The leader swept the advancing soldiers with two bursts from his Uzi, then spun around and ran toward the parking lot. Which is when hell came to visit Libya.

Even the leader was surprised at the viciousness of the blast and the ferocity of the fireball that consumed the limos in the lot, blew the front off the garage, and sent a shock wave through the copse of trees that nearly knocked him off his feet. In the shock and blinding light, the leader pursued his retreating team, running as fast as his legs and his lungs could bear.

There was a pause in the shooting coming from the Libyan soldiers, as he hoped. Then the fireball fell back to earth, its bulbous, burning mass cut by two-thirds, and the resultant loss of light intensified the blackness of the night. In this momentary eclipse, the leader burst from under the trees and raced across the open space toward the parade ground. He knew one of his men was covering his retreat while the other two rushed on to free the inflatable and get it in the water. Perhaps they would make it.

First he heard shouts, then shots as bullets began buzzing past him like lethal bees released from a deadly hive. The bullets were too close.

In a split-second decision, he cut hard right, away from the parade ground. The sound of the Libyan's automatic rifles seemed more distant. He ran harder. After only a few strides, he cut back to his left for an all-out sprint to the darkness. Then his body was ripped by a spray of bullets. Across his chest. From ahead of him. From his own.

I turned too quickly.

It seemed like a long time as he fell to the earth. Enough time to think of his wife, Tabitha. Their two sons—his sons—now without a father. He thought of his father, Chaim, who begged him not to take this risk so close to discharge. This risk . . . this job . . . unfinished . . . and he skidded into the dusty ground, thinking of his family, his life pouring into foreign soil he would never leave.

PART ONE

PROPHET'S CALL

1

THE PRESENT · TUESDAY, JULY 21

Open-mouthed, Tom Bohannon, executive director of the Bowery Mission in New York City, watched as an earthquake in Jerusalem changed the future of the world.

Television news helicopters hovering a few hundred feet over the yawning chasm of the Temple Mount broadcast a surreal scene. From the center of the crater came billows of white, smokelike, limestone dust. As if released from a subterranean faucet, torrents raged from both ends of the ragged "V" that cleaved the Mount in two from east to west. New rivers swept through the Kidron Valley from one end of the cleft and into the streets of Old Jerusalem from the other.

Bohannon stared at the television screen in mute shock. Moments before, he had watched the first ritual sacrifice in a Jewish temple in more than two thousand years—a temple that was hidden under the Temple Mount for a millennium, a temple that he had helped discover. Now, the Dome of the Rock and the Al-Aqsa Mosque had disappeared into the spreading cleft of the Mount's platform, the flat stone base, supported by Herodian arches, upon which the Dome and the mosque once stood. Bohannon felt decades older than his fifty-eight years. His normally straight, strong six-foot frame sagged at shoulder and waist as huge slabs of the platform fell into the crater's black maw.

Unseen, deep in the bowels of the Mount's underground caverns, the Third Temple of God lay crushed under tons of stone and debris.

"It's gone."

Jerusalem

With the first shockwave, Captain Avram Levin was thrown off his high stool overlooking the banks of television monitors in the Aleph Reconnaissance Center. He crashed onto his right shoulder on the hard concrete floor. Pulling against the railing with his left arm, he was on his feet when the second shock hit. This one buckled the room in the middle, then a wave of movement flowed through the room, cresting as it hit the buckle. Half of the Aleph Center slipped away to the right amid a hail of sparks, taking screaming men and crashing equipment with it as it dropped into a crevasse where once was solid ground.

Levin's left hand throbbed as he squeezed the rail with all his strength, his feet trying to find purchase on the wildly dancing floor. Bile rising in his throat, Levin willed his eyes away from the ragged opening that had just consumed his men. He turned his gaze to the few monitors that were still transmitting. A gaping cleft spread across the Temple Mount, swallowing everything in its wake.

⟞⟝⟞

Eliazar Baruk was on his feet, stunned at the swiftness of the destruction, his eyes still glued to the now blank television screen. His right hand grasping the corner of his desk for support, the Israeli prime minister felt the eruption of random shifts ripping at the foundations of his office on Kaplan Street in Qiryat Ben-Gurion, between the Bank of Israel and the Ministry of the Interior.

Screams . . . shouts . . . running feet . . . crashing metal.

A massive chunk of concrete fell from the ceiling, crushing a corner of Baruk's desk. The door to his office splintered and snapped clear from its hinges. Andrew, his most trusted protector, clawed at the splintered wood trying to reach the prime minister. But Andrew was bulled to the side as the massive bulk of General Moishe Orhlon, Israel's defense minister, pressed through the shattered door.

"Moishe, call up the reserves . . . all of them," Baruk said. "Good God, what have we done?"

Damascus, Syria

Imam Moussa al-Sadr tore his kaftan from neckline to hem, fell to his knees, and pounded his fists into his chest. "May Allah forgive us," he whispered to the carpet.

Rocking on his haunches, his gaze went back to the carnage on the television screen filling the far wall. Disgusted with the so-called peace to which the Palestinians and Egyptians had capitulated, al-Sadr's rage overflowed during the Jews' sacrilegious blood sacrifice. Now, as he watched the Dome of the Rock swallowed by the abyss on Temple Mount and the Al-Aqsa Mosque crumble into dust, his fury erupted with the killing heat of molten lava.

"Fools!" al-Sadr screamed. "Traitors!" He pointed a long finger at the screen. "May Allah's curses be on you and your children." Falling to his knees again, he beat his fists into the carpet. "Fools . . . such fools . . ."

Minutes passed as the heaving in al-Sadr's body subsided. Then he rose—rod straight, face like flint, his eyes blazing with the fervor of a fanatic. He turned to the two men who were sitting with him on the floor rug. When he spoke, his voice was dead . . . cold. "Such fools. What did they expect they would receive from embracing peace with the infidels and the Jews? Look."

Al-Sadr shook his fist at the television screen. "Is this worth peace? Never. Never, at any price. But, now, these fools and their friends must pay the price of their treachery. Come, this is our time."

Washington, DC

"Walk with me," President Jonathan Whitestone said, grabbing the arm of the CIA director as he stepped through the French doors of the Oval Office and turned left into the colonnade on the west side of the White House.

"Well, Bill, we just watched the end of a very short-lived peace in the Middle East," said the president, pulling Director Cartwright closer to his side. "This Temple Mount disaster can ignite into World War Three at the whiff of a match. I don't trust the Israelis or the Arabs to keep their hands off the Mount. The Bavarian peace treaty is as shattered as the Mount itself."

President Jonathan Whitestone stopped abruptly and spun Bill Cartwright so they were face-to-face. "Bill, what is happening here? The Arab world is blowing up around us and now this fragile peace just got swallowed in an earthquake. Most of the time, it's the Jews and the Arabs that scare me, Bill. God knows what they're going to do about this political mess. But I'm even more frightened about what we just witnessed happening to the Mount. What do you think it means?"

The two men participated in a Tuesday evening Bible study in the White

House residence and had known each other since both served on the deacon board of Trinity Baptist Church in Dallas, fifteen years before.

"Mr. President, we both know that ritual sacrifice in the Temple started the clock ticking. Nobody knows how much time is left in these last days—maybe a year, maybe one hundred years, maybe a thousand. But the clock is ticking. And I believe that changes everything."

"Everything?"

"Yes, Mr. President. We can debate the biblical meaning and implications, but our job is to understand the political and military implications of what we've just seen. We can't trust what we trusted before. The world has changed on us. And we need to figure out how it has changed, who it has changed, and what we need to do about it."

Whitestone shoved his hands deep into his pockets, his head bowed. "God help us, Bill. We've just left the era of history and entered an era that will be orchestrated by biblical prophecy. It's hard to believe, but we've got to understand where this will take us." The president lifted his head and put his right hand on Cartwright's shoulder. "Find out for us, Bill. Get together whomever you need. But keep a tight lid on it. Find out where we're headed . . . before we get there."

THURSDAY, JULY 23

New York City

Tom Bohannon wandered helplessly in the darkness beneath the Temple Mount. He was alone, shivering, lost. Every few steps, he called out for Doc or Joe. Where had they gone? Just then, from the corner of his eye, he saw a dark figure emerge from the inky blackness. The barest glint of metal registered in his consciousness as a razor-sharp blade pierced his neck, inches from his carotid artery.

Like a drowning man being pulled from the bottom of a swimming pool, Tom Bohannon's eyes were wide open, his heart pounding, his lungs devouring oxygen, his body half out of bed as his mind flailed for a grasp of reality.

He was at home, in bed. Safe.

But his body and mind were raging with alarms. What ripped him from his sleep at three in the morning?

He sat up, tried to calm his breathing and avoid waking Annie, and listened to the dark. Something was wrong. Every cell in his body flooded with adrenaline. He felt the firm grasp of fight-or-flight fear. Someone was in his house.

Bohannon wrestled to still the pounding of his heart that reverberated through his ears. He probed the dark for memory of the sound that yanked him awake. And he listened.

Something . . . someone . . . is here.

Bohannon swung his legs from the bed and gently rested his bare feet on the polished walnut floor. Rehearsing every creaking floorboard, he padded to the doorway of their bedroom as if snakes were sleeping in the dark. He willed his hearing into the hallway, down the steps. There was a dead calm to the air. No breeze through the open windows. But Bohannon felt a stirring in the house, a shiver of presence that froze the pores of his skin.

Fear of what he might see strangled his throat, grasped his shoulders, and clamped his feet to the floor. He forced himself to the open doorway and held his breath as he peeked around the doorjamb and into the hallway. Nothing stirred the shadows. Still, the warrior in him begged for a weapon.

Stepping quietly over the boards at the door's threshold, Bohannon eased across the hallway to a closet on the far wall, caressed open the door, and reached into the left front corner for what he knew rested there. A polished, black oak climbing stick purchased in Switzerland years before. Its head was carved into the sweep of an eagle's wing, curved in the middle to fit a man's hand, with a thin edge milled at its end. The bottom of the stick was cut to a point and covered with an overlapping, hardened steel cap that extended into a sharp point for piercing the earth. It could be lethal.

Bohannon hefted the stick, held it in the middle, ready to use either end to defend his home, and began searching for the cause of his fear.

Had they come back, the killers with the amulet—the Coptic cross with the lightning bolt slashing through it on an angle? Those relentless stalkers, the Prophet's Guard, who murdered Winthrop Larsen, tried to kidnap his daughter Caitlin, twice attempted to murder him and Doc Johnson?

In his late fifties, Bohannon was still fit and strong. At six feet tall, possessing the imperfect face and physique that was uniquely masculine, he had proved his courage and tested his strength in the bowels of the Temple Mount—and more recently lost some of his extra weight during long, high-impact bike rides he took with his son, Connor. There was fear—the Prophet's Guard had proven they were to be feared—but there was no hesitation. He would stand between his family and any threat, no matter the cost.

The moon was down. Only the wash from the street lamps, shaded by the trees on their front lawn, weakened the blackness of the night, but failed to pierce the myriad shadows. Bohannon drilled his vision into the dark and took a step forward.

My cell phone! It was back on the top of the dresser in his bedroom. Backward was not a direction he wanted to go.

Pressing close to the wall where the floorboards were less worn, Bohannon edged down the hall. Terror gripped him as he stopped and looked over his shoulder, expecting a shadow specter to move behind him, a threat to his sleeping wife. Nothing moved.

He turned his face and peered down the second-floor hallway of their hundred-twenty-year-old Victorian home. Every corner harbored a threat. Connor's and Caitlin's rooms were down that end. So was the bathroom. Bohannon crept along the hallway. As he approached the bathroom door, he crouched low and readied the hiking stick to strike. His breathing stopped. He heard a noise downstairs, a muffled scrape of something against the wooden floor.

Perspiration soaked the curly hair at the back of his neck. His family was in danger. He was their protector. He would give his life to save theirs.

Bohannon turned on the balls of his feet, picked his path, and moved toward the top of the stairs. He held his breath as he peeked through the banister and down the steps, only half of which he could see. There was no other sound.

This was the most threatening part. The stairs. Every one groaned and cracked with the wear of years. His breathing was rapid and shallow. Could he reach the telephone? Should he use it? He stepped down, keeping his feet to the very side of each stair tread. One-by-one. He reached the landing. No light penetrated the large, stained-glass window. He searched the darkness below.

Halfway down the bottom flight he stopped and peered around the edge of the wall to his left. The parlor was still, quiet. The front door was closed, secure. Through the open pocket doors the dining room was a blackened shroud. Someone could be in there, watching, and Bohannon would never know.

He nearly stumbled, fumbling with the walking stick weapon in his hand, as the scraping sound sliced through the silence once again, from his right.

The kitchen. The back door.

He shifted the walking stick to his left hand, stepped over the middle of the stair tread to the other side and rested his hand on the banister for balance. He was breathing in short, rapid strokes and desperately tried to remain silent.

Bohannon edged down the final stairs. The telephone stand was on the other side of the stairs, tucked into a corner. Out of the question. He stood immovable, as he threw all his senses at the doorway to the kitchen, probing around the corner. He hefted the stick in his hands, slipped his grip down the shaft, and raised the heavy, sharp-edged head.

Silently he slipped off the final step and sidled to his right . . . the laundry room, to the butler's pantry, and into the kitchen from behind. Each step took an eternity. Each step pumped more adrenaline into his system as he frantically looked both forward and over his shoulder to his unprotected back.

Entering the butler's pantry, Bohannon saw a dim light shimmering from the kitchen. Only moments had passed, but he felt he was stalking this prey for hours. His calf muscles ached, every muscle taut. Were his reflexes fast enough? Would he have an advantage . . . surprise, weight, desperation? Would he survive?

Bohannon set his jaw, tensed his arms, and eased his body to the threshold of the kitchen.

Connor looked up from the screen of his laptop, a half-eaten sandwich and a glass of milk on the wooden table, and pulled out his earbuds.

"Hey, Dad," he said, his face puzzled. "I dropped the milk. Did I wa— What's wrong?"

Dayr al Qiddis Oasis, Egypt

Racing over the hard sand and gravel flats like so many Arabian stallions at full charge, with red-on-green flags of a scimitar moon snapping, the six midnight black Land Rovers—windows as dark as their intent—barreled forward in a chevron formation kicking up clouds of sand behind them. The spearhead of black hurtled forward through the Wadi Abu Gerifat to the southwest, closing quickly on the large tent compound gathered along the edge of the Red Sea Mountains, far from the sight of the road to the oasis Dayr al Qiddis Antun.

Charging out from the compound, a troop of mounted riders spurred their real stallions into a collision course with the phalanx of Land Rovers.

The horse-and-rider troop, dazzling in their white kaftans and carrying huge war banners of dark green, split in half and swarmed down both sides of the Land Rover formation. Their war cries of welcome echoed off the mountain flanks to the east, drowning out the whine of the engines. The welcoming party escorted the vehicles into the midst of the tent compound to the portal of a huge, green tent.

Men came running from all directions, joining the riders in a rising tide of throaty warbles, shouts of triumph, and beating drums.

Imam Moussa al-Sadr stepped from the foremost vehicle and was immediately surrounded by the black-robbed entourage that poured out of the other Rovers.

Clothed in the simple black linen robes of the Shi'ite clergy, al-Sadr's once pampered body was now lean and hard, carrying the stamp of thirty years on the run, in hiding. He was smaller and thinner than the image which hung in mosques and homes throughout Lebanon, revered as the heart and soul of Hezbollah. The once jet-black beard was now streaked with gray and his long fingers were misshapen. But his dark intentions blazed hotter than Daniel's furnace.

Al-Sadr was led into a small, dark room in the middle of the green tent. Patterned carpets hung on the walls and covered the ground. Two small lamps hung from the ceiling, their light muted by red glass panes. A small, low table separated two cushioned wooden chairs. A silver tea set sat atop the table, a hookah positioned at the table's flank. Goats bleated in the distance, and somewhere meat sizzled over an open fire.

Al-Sadr was led to one of the chairs by the silent attendant. He sat, and waited.

Moments later, the old man arrived. His kaftan was the color of sandstorm, his sandals as wrinkled and aged as his skin. Only his face was visible. That was enough. His skin was dark, heavily creased by sun and wind. And his eyes were mismatched—one yellow and one brown. The mark of Allah.

Al-Sadr assessed this man, the one spoken of in whispers, never named. He was older, more frail, than al-Sadr himself. Yet there was life in this spirit that belied the age of the flesh. Al-Sadr could not escape the magnetism of the old man's eyes. Fierce, feral, consuming, they sang a song of jihad, a song echoed in his own heart. They called him to great sacrifice. They embraced him with ancient hate.

The old man bowed from the waist. "Welcome, my brother." His voice sounded like silk in a breeze. "Allah be praised for your safe arrival."

Al-Sadr rose, and returned the bow. "I am honored, Holy One, to be in your presence. Thank you for your kindness in granting me audience."

The older man sat, waving al-Sadr back into his chair. "It is I who am honored to have you here in my tent. I beg you to forgive the poverty of my humble home. Would you honor me by sharing some tea?"

Al-Sadr inclined his head and, out of the shadows emerged a bull in a man's shape. Arms as big as thighs, an angry, sweeping crescent scar connecting the corner of his mouth to the lobe of his right ear. Al-Sadr could not miss the amulet—a Coptic cross with a lightning bolt slashing through on the diagonal—hanging from his neck as the bull-man poured the tea, then disappeared once more into the shadows.

"My brother, I beg your forgiveness for being so rude," said al-Sadr, "but I come today not for your blessing, but for your help."

"How can I help the heart of Hezbollah?"

"Holy One, I believe we can help each other."

Al-Sadr's spirit began to swim in the beckoning of the old man's eyes. His mind fought against a sudden riptide of malice.

"You seek a scroll, I believe," said al-Sadr. "And the scroll holder that protected it."

The old man moved not a muscle, but power shimmered around him in waves. "You are correct . . . in part. And you seek the blood of the Jew and the infidel."

"Yes, Effendi . . . and we both seek that which has been stolen from us and destroyed by the Zionist pigs—the most holy Dome and the mosque of the Haram. Help me, Holy One, and I promise you . . . not only will al-Haram al-Sharif be restored to Islam, but the mezuzah and scroll will be restored to you."

Silence hung in the air and mixed with the stale smell of powerful, old smoke.

"The scroll was deciphered." The old man spread his hands, palms up. "It is no longer of any use to us."

"Then I will bring you the blood of those who have defiled your scroll and murdered your followers."

"Why would I need you for that task, my brother? There are many who wear the slash of lightning, many who would be blessed to give their lives to restore what has been stolen."

Moussa al-Sadr leaned forward, resting his right elbow on his knee, turning his right hand palm up. "Holy One, I am offering you the power and reach of the Muslim Brotherhood."

"Is it yours to offer?"

"Soon, Effendi . . . Soon the resources at your disposal will be unlimited."

Al-Sadr could feel the power of the man's presence pressing into him, searching for weakness, for duplicity.

"What is it you seek from me, Lion of Lebanon?"

"I seek nothing, except your wisdom, your support, and your counsel as I fulfill my promise." From beneath the black folds of his kaftan, al-Sadr withdrew two pieces of paper. He raised his hands in front of his body, holding his prize in front of him. "And I bring you gifts."

"Allah, be praised," said the old man.

"The first is a list of student dissidents in Cairo. We have infiltrated their groups, their meetings, and have helped to awaken their anger and frustration at Kamali and his insatiable government. They have raised their voices in protest, but they remain dry grass . . . waiting for a spark. Waiting for your spark."

Al-Sadr showed the old man the second sheet.

"A numbered account in a Swiss bank. There are two million dollars there. Use what you need. There is more if necessary."

The old man's eyes narrowed. He took measure of al-Sadr once more.

"Where does this abundant gift come from? And what is required?"

Al-Sadr laughed. There was no mirth in his laughter, only mayhem. He raised his arms to heaven. "Praise to God . . . the money was raised by the Holy Land Foundation in America and now is being raised by its new offspring. How sweet to use America's dollars against their own self-interests."

"*Allahu Akbar*," whispered the old man.

With the reverence of ritual, al-Sadr passed the documents to the old man. "Begin the revolution, Holy One. Use these gifts to raise the voice of jihad from the sands—raise it so that it will be heard throughout the world!"

"*Allahu Akbar!*" the old man shouted. And his cry rang death.

Washington, DC

Flashing lights from the four escort choppers barely pierced the polarized, bulletproof windows of Marine One. Surprisingly, all of the bullet-proofing and strengthening of the VH-3D Sea King failed in one key regard—sound. The presidential helicopter boasted leather seats and other comforts, but the thirty-year-old Sea King still rattled the eardrums.

President Jonathan Whitestone sat very close to CIA director Bill Cartwright on the short jump to Camp David. And not only because of the noise.

"Khalil is scared to death that the Iranians and the Israelis are about to start throwing nukes at each other," Whitestone said of the Jordanian king who waited for him at the secure Maryland retreat. "He's convinced it was Mossad that assassinated the two nuclear scientists in Tehran last month."

"He's right on that," Cartwright said above the clatter. "Iran doesn't have the weapons-grade plutonium for a warhead. But they're getting close."

Whitestone leaned back in his seat. He knew Cartwright was right. Intelligence briefings continually measured Iran's march toward nuclear weaponry.

President Mehdi Essaghir's determination was inexorable. And it had to be stopped.

"Am I doing the right thing, Bill?"

"I don't think you have any choice, Mr. President. The Arab Spring has created an incredible power vacuum in the Middle East and the Iranians are certainly going to try to take advantage of the opportunity. Egypt is the glue that holds together a fragile Mideast peace. Now we don't know what we have in Egypt, the Saudis are scared to death they'll lose control, and we took Iraq out of the game. For all his faults, at least Saddam kept the Iranians bottled up. Right now, the door is wide open for the Iranians to step in and dominate the region."

"And if Essaghir had nukes? God help us all," said the president.

"Israel will not tolerate a nuclear Iran," Cartwright responded. "If we don't work with them on this, we will likely see mushroom clouds in the desert. And once the Israelis unleash their nuclear weapons, who knows who will follow suit. No, I think we have to convince King Khalil to keep pushing for peace, for a moderate agenda, and keep that as our public policy position. But, pragmatically, there is really no other choice for us but to help Baruk pull off this scheme."

"We have to keep Stanley out of this," Whitestone said of the secretary of state. "It's just you and me, Bill. And it's got to stay that way. Compartmentalize everything. Clandestine is not to get a whiff of what we're doing in the financial sector."

"Yes, Mr. President."

"I'll talk to Baruk tomorrow. Make sure his part is ready to go."

Whitestone looked out the side window as the five identical Marine helicopters orchestrated another high-speed shift in formation, what the Marine pilots called "the presidential shell game," mixing up the four decoys with the presidential craft. "I'm worried about this, Bill," he said, his eyes still on the chopper ballet outside. "The stakes are so high, and the margin of error is so slim. This could cost us the presidency."

"Yes, sir. But," Cartwright leaned close again, "doing nothing nearly assures a nuclear war in the Mideast. Your presidency might survive, but I don't think Israel would. And neither would the U.S. economy. There would be no oil. The country would be devastated. We just can't allow that kind of chaos."

Whitestone closed his eyes and said a short, silent prayer.

"I'm surprised," said Cartwright, "that the Israelis didn't accuse the Iranians of causing the earthquake."

The president opened his eyes and looked at his CIA chief. "What kind of shape is Jerusalem in?"

"Could have been worse," said Cartwright. "The damage was localized to Jerusalem—a very limited area of Jerusalem—even though the quake was very strong."

"Troubling, that, isn't it?"

"Yes, sir. Still, one-tenth of the city has been opened up, as if chopped with a meat cleaver. More than five thousand people died and up to twenty thousand refugees are living in a tent city in the Hinnom Valley. Jerusalem hasn't erupted into civil war—yet."

"As if we needed another flashpoint for potential trouble in that city."

"So far, they're treating each other with respect. Neither the Israeli government nor the Waqf have been able to figure out what to do with the Temple Mount. But the Israelis have been able to make their quarantine of the Temple area stick—too dangerous to let anyone near it—so that's probably kept tempers quiet. And it appears as if our far-right Fundamentalists have worn themselves out with dire predictions about the end of the world. It's relatively quiet and . . . that scares me more than anything," Cartwright concluded.

"Me too," said Whitestone.

The president looked out the window once more, to the west, where the sun was setting. "Seems like we're moving much faster toward Armageddon than we are toward Camp David."

———◁∿▷———

Six men disembarked from the transatlantic container cargo ship *Adelaide*, just as four of their brethren did a few months prior. Sea bags slung over their shoulders, dressed in the nondescript clothing of merchant seamen, these six dark-haired, dark-hearted men descended the gangplank in full daylight, undistinguished from the score of shipmates who preceded and followed them to shore at the Staten Island Cargo Ship Terminal.

Merchant ships were still the simplest and safest way to gain unnoticed entry into the United States. Airports were far from impenetrable, but increased levels of security and screening left too much risk of unwanted questioning. Getting on a ship leaving Egypt was no problem. Making it through connections in Europe was becoming more difficult. And America . . . who knew what the Americans would do next?

Tarik Ben Ali raised a hand to bid farewell to his brothers . . . brothers in the faith; brothers in the hunt. Each one knew his assignment. Each was sworn to secrecy, sworn to success, or sworn not to return.

3

FRIDAY, JULY 24

New York City

Something hit Tom Bohannon in the chest as he walked out the front door of the Bowery Mission, something as angry as the drivers trying to navigate the snarled traffic and double-parked delivery trucks on the Bowery. Still jumpy, he jerked back and looked down for the blood on his shirt, but saw only the meaty finger of a protester, who stepped forward and began thumping his chest again.

"You destroyed the Temple, you brought destruction on the Temple Mount and the Western Wall," railed the thick-set, muscular man, his face contorted with hate as a New York City policeman stepped in and dragged him back behind the police barrier in front of the Bowery Mission. "Fool . . . you have placed Jerusalem at risk!"

Feeling the eyes of the world on his back, Bohannon looked down at his shoes and willed his feet to move forward. But they remained frozen to the concrete sidewalk. In spite of the tumult behind the barrier and the horns of impatient taxi drivers, he could hear the shouts from across the street of the people bussed in from the Lower East Side mosque: "Free Temple Mount. Free Temple Mount. Free Temple Mount."

Stew Manthey took Bohannon's arm and steered him around the shouting throng and through the narrow passage being held open by the police. "It's been like this every day," Manthey said. "When is it ever going to stop?"

Bohannon's despair bent his neck—its intensity matched only by the depth of his confusion. His body moved in response to Manthey's urging, but it had no direction or destination of its own.

Manthey, CFO of the Bowery Mission, pulled Bohannon to a halt at the corner of Bowery and Stanton. "You don't need lunch, you need some peace. And you need to talk. C'mon," he said, steering Bohannon down Stanton Street, "we're going to the park."

―――∽∿∩∼――

Officially it was called Sara D. Roosevelt Park. But the long, thin strip of paved basketball courts, fenced in soccer fields, and community gardens that stretched from Houston to Canal between Chrystie and Forsyth streets had always been known as Chrystie Park to Bohannon. The gate to the community gardens was open. Manthey and Bohannon entered and found a park bench shaded by an overhanging red maple.

They sat in silence for a moment, breathing in the heavy perfume of peach-colored roses and the honeysuckle that covered the chain-link fence to their backs.

"You know, Tom, I thought you were distracted before the four of you took off for Jerusalem," said Manthey. "But since you've gotten back . . . well . . . it's like you've hidden yourself in some deep place . . . locked yourself in a room and refused to open the door."

Bohannon felt Manthey turn toward him.

"Tom, you've got to talk about this," Manthey said. "What happened over there? What's changed you so much?"

Stew Manthey looked a bit like Grizzly Adams. In the final year before his retirement, the Bowery Mission's CFO defied the perception of his colleagues by growing a thick beard that was speckled with gray and nearly covered the lower half of his face.

The change in appearance didn't change the CFO's effectiveness. For more than twenty years, Manthey astutely guided the Mission through seasons of financial change, challenge, and growth. Outside of his job description, for the last twelve years Manthey served as Bohannon's mentor, the CFO's integrity and character providing wise counsel for the mission's VP of operations.

It was counsel Bohannon desperately needed. And a listening ear he could trust.

"I don't know, Stew," Bohannon said, running his hand through the curly, copper-colored hair that grew long on his neck. He stared out over the beds of geraniums and remembered planting the same kind of flowers with Alexander Krupp at his Bavarian estate after he, Joe, and Doc escaped from Jerusalem. That seemed so long ago, so far in the past. Yet only weeks had passed.

"This whole experience has been so confusing. When we first found the mezuzah in Louis Klopsch's safe and discovered the scroll inside, it felt like I was on such an adventure. That Charles Spurgeon had warned Klopsch about the importance of the scroll gave the quest a sense of gravity. Trying to understand the scroll, figure out its message, figure out the code it was written in was thrilling—like the adrenaline rush I used to get when I was in the middle of an investigative piece for the *Bulletin*. Even though we knew there was this group trying to prevent us from deciphering the scroll . . . well, you know . . . it felt like we were destined to be part of this. Remember? I felt like this was something God was instructing me to do. We were on a mission. It was so exciting . . ."

Bohannon fell silent as he looked out over the garden. He loved gardens. Whenever he had dirt, he planted flowers and vegetables—anything to get him outdoors and in the soil that was his therapy. Normally, sitting among this living green landscape, the heady dankness of composted loam filling his nose, Bohannon would have felt a restorative peace. Not today. His face, imperfect but handsome, looked as if he had lost his best friend. His eyes, normally a glimmering blue, were lifeless and distant.

"We felt we had to go to Jerusalem to see if the message on the scroll was true. I know *I* had to go. It was like a calling." He paused, trying to sort and organize his memories with his feelings. "Then Winthrop was killed . . . murdered . . . when the car bomb blew apart his van outside the Collector's Club.

"How could we go on after that?" Bohannon asked the trees. "How come we didn't just give it up . . . turn all the information we had over to the government and let them deal with it? Right now—I wish we had. Yet . . ." He bowed his head. "Yet, I still thought I had to go to Jerusalem. We all did."

A soft breeze rustled the leaves of the trees, caressing Bohannon's cheek.

"You were called," Manthey said with a reverence often reserved for church buildings. "I have no doubt that God chose you to be part of this. I don't know why. But I know it's true just as much as we're sitting here right now."

Bohannon rubbed his palms against the knees of his pants. "C'mon, let's walk."

They strolled along the paths of the garden, past the seldom-used bocce court.

"You know what I'm ashamed of?" Bohannon asked. "I'm ashamed that I felt like I was living a movie in Jerusalem . . . and I was loving it. I was Indiana Jones and James Bond and Jason Bourne all rolled into one. The hero beating off the bad guys in the name of world peace. And all the time I was playing with our lives. Now, today, it seems so irresponsible. Then . . . well . . . I guess I was caught up in the thrill of the chase."

Bohannon stopped and looked at Manthey. "You know, Stew, I never thought we would get under the Temple Mount. I mean, that was impossible, right? But there we were, wandering around in the tunnels, crossing underground lakes, pursued by Israeli soldiers and Islamic terrorists." Bohannon shook his head. "And we found it . . . we found the Third Temple, hidden there for a thousand years. Then, it was one miracle after another. Krupp's crew was there, repairing the collapsed Eastern wall; they got us on their plane, and, within hours, we're in Krupp's Bavarian estate trying to figure out what to do with the evidence of the Temple's existence."

Bohannon started walking again, shaking his head, oblivious to the colors and aromas all around him. "Everybody thought it would mean war—the president, the Israelis thought news of the Temple would drive the Arab states to war. But peace? Peace, Stew. They signed it . . . they all signed the treaty and decades of war and death were over."

Bohannon found himself at the gate leading out of the garden. He stopped, and turned around to see where he had been.

"For a month. They had the hope of peace for one month, and a signed peace treaty for a couple of hours," said Bohannon. "Then the earthquake hit and everything above and below the Temple Mount was destroyed—along with the peace. Now"—he turned back to face Manthey—"the Middle East is worse than ever. Winthrop is dead. Thousands have died in Jerusalem . . . for what? Why? What was the point? And, you know what? It's my fault. I'm the one who was 'called,' who felt I was on a mission from God. I'm the one who didn't want to give up, to quit, because I was having so much fun. I was the hero . . . Now what am I?"

He sensed Manthey was searching for a suitable answer. None came.

"I just want to get back to normal," said Bohannon. "I thank God this is over. That we all got back here in one piece—Joe, Sammy, and Doc. I just want to get back to normal again."

They came to the traffic light at Chrystie Street. "Just plain old Tom," Bohannon said as they crossed the street and walked under one of the ubiquitous sidewalk bridges—protective scaffolds—that was being erected over the sidewalk along Rivington Street. "But, you know what?" Bohannon turned to face Manthey. "I don't know if I'll ever be normal again. I just can't seem to shake—"

Bohannon felt Manthey's hands on the shoulders of his shirt before it could register in his brain what was happening. His back slammed against the wall of the building to his left as one of the steel, bracing beams from the overhead scaffolding flashed past his ear, swinging like a pendulum at the end of a long chain. As the beam swung upward, it pierced the plywood flooring of the completed section of the sidewalk bridge, and stuck there, sending a violent shudder through the rest of the structure.

Stew Manthey still had both fists wrapped up in his shirt as Bohannon glanced up at the rogue beam. "See," Bohannon said, "I need to get back to normal before I walk into a truck."

4

SATURDAY, JULY 25

"Don't tell me it can't be done." Gideon Goldsmith pounded his fist against the map on the wall. "You tell Baruk that it must be done. The city of Jerusalem has been decimated. Five thousand people are dead and tens of thousands are living in tents. And he's worried about political repercussions?" The mayor of Jerusalem, as small and nondescript as his position, pounded the map once again, as if noise would add to his argument.

"My city needs healing. My people need healing. Leaving this city with a gaping wound in its heart only invites more disaster. We must rebuild the Mount."

General Moishe Orhlon, Israel's defense minister, empathized with the mayor and shared his grief for Jerusalem and its citizens. He felt sorry for Goldsmith as well. But not that much. The man was a fool if he thought he could pressure the government into a decision about the Temple Mount.

"Mr. Mayor." Orhlon's sonorous voice was as soothing as a lullaby, but as final as a father's last word. "You may repair your streets. You may inspect your buildings. You may invite people to return to their homes as soon as they are deemed safe. You may even demolish those buildings that are a hazard . . . with prior approval, of course. But you will not go near the Mount. Not even close."

Thin, bald, embittered by years of insignificance, Goldsmith's face burned crimson as he looked at the men and women around the table for support of any kind. None was offered.

"But the Wall," he pleaded, abandoning any pretense of power. "The rabbis are demanding we do something about the Wall."

For once, you're right. Orhlon turned from his pity for the mayor and half-pointed to a man across the table, the half-hearted gesture the only physical evidence of the exhaustion that sapped strength from each of his cells. "Avram, how long before you are ready?"

Captain Avram Levin, commander of the Aleph Reconnaissance Center, which covered central Jerusalem, including the Old City and the Temple Mount, looked up from the legal pad on which he was writing. "All of the cameras have been replaced or relocated," he said, looking only at General Orhlon, his ultimate commander. "The Aleph Center is now in a secure building. Our monitors and computers have been replenished and the men I lost—"

Levin's voice caught for a moment, confirming once again Orhlon's confidence in Captain Levin as an exceptional leader of men.

"—the men we lost have been replaced with well-trained veterans. All that remains is completing the fiber optics to link the cameras to the monitors. Two days."

Orhlon's gaze swept the recovery task force sitting around the table in Central Command. "All right, then . . . Mr. Mayor, you have Krupp's crews for two more days. After that, you will have to continue the recovery with the police and reserve units at your disposal.

"Captain Levin . . . as soon as Aleph Center is operational, we will divert the Krupp Industries crews to the Temple Mount. Since Mr. Krupp was kind enough to offer his unlimited support, and the service of his engineers and laborers from the refinery site, we will take him up on the offer. Combining our engineers and equipment with Krupp's support, we will rebuild the walls of the Mount, starting with the Western Wall. But only the walls. We'll get the stones back in place, repair the breach, and make sure the perimeter is secure—but that is all. And no one goes near the walls until we are ready."

"But—" Gideon Goldsmith tried to interject, but was immediately stopped by Orhlon's raised hand.

"And you, Mr. Mayor, take care of your wounded, your homeless, your streets and houses. And leave the future of the Mount to those with a clearer, more complete vision."

Damascus, Syria

King Abbudin of Saudi Arabia reluctantly yielded the floor to his wild-eyed adversary across the conference table. Even here, among the leaders of the Muslim Brotherhood—the long-standing, but little-known, ruling body of global Islam—Abbudin no longer enjoyed his unquestioned leadership of the past, nor the ability to squash a dissenter like a ripe melon. Not any longer.

During most of his reign, Abbudin felt a match for any Arab usurper. Years earlier his influence withstood a challenge from President Baqir al-Musawi of Syria, that Alawi Shi'a dog who used fear and his secret police to suppress the Sunni majority of his country. Of course, to keep their two Sunni populations at peace, he needed to marry one of al-Musawi's cousins, making her one of his thirty wives.

Abbudin was the sixth of the Saudi kings, all sons of Abdul Aziz al Saud, the first Saudi king. In 1902, twelve years after the Saud family was driven into exile by the Al Rashid dynasty, Abdul Aziz recaptured Riyadh with just twenty men. Raider, plunderer, and charismatic leader, Abdul Aziz overcame family feuds, tamed the nomads, and, in 1932, completed his unification of the Arabian peninsula into one Sunni nation—with the help of millions in British pounds sterling. Six years later, oil was discovered under the desert sands. And the House of Saud took permanent control of the Saudi throne—and its oil fields.

One of Abdul Aziz's thirty-seven sons from sixteen wives, Abbudin officially succeeded his half-brother, King Fahd, in 2005. He was regent, and defacto ruler of Saudi Arabia since 1996, when Fahd was incapacitated by a major stroke. Thus it had been Abbudin who deftly maneuvered the Saudi kingdom through the rise of Islamic radicalism, the second Gulf War, and the emergence of domestic unrest that slithered unseen into the nation's consciousness.

Round of cheek and jowl, wet sandbags under his dark, questioning eyes, Abbudin was unlike the four brothers who preceded him. He possessed neither the passion for financial and social reform of Faisal, the royal bearing and statesmanship of Khalid, nor the political deftness of Fahd, who supported both Palestinian and American interests in the Middle East. Where his predecessors were successful in maintaining Saudi wealth and power, Abbudin dealt with a changing world, one that consistently nibbled away at the edges of his kingdom.

Now eighty-four, still shrewd and calculating behind his rimless glasses, Abbudin bent with the winds of change, giving room but never giving way.

Soon, this Shi'ite anarchist sitting across the table would feel the sharpness of his teeth. But, today, in this council, he must yield. The time for revenge had not yet come.

Other than those around this table, King Abbudin knew that few in the world were aware that Imam Moussa al-Sadr was the true leader of Hezbollah, the deadly militia which now controlled not only the land but also the government of Lebanon. Fewer still were aware he was alive.

Imam Moussa al-Sadr was the founder of the first armed paramilitary force in Lebanon, the Lebanese Resistance Brigades Movement—or Amal—a lethal group of trained assassins. A member of a prominent family of Shi'ite theologians, Moussa al-Sadr was appointed the first head of the Supreme Islamic Shi'ite Council. The Resistance Brigades, and the Shi'ite Council, were the birthplaces of Hezbollah.

Al-Sadr mysteriously vanished in 1978 during a trip to Libya to meet with Colonel Muammar Qaddafi. His disappearance was a meticulously planned, flawlessly executed rescue, necessary to protect him from the Israeli spies who sought his life. Most of the watching world thought he had been assassinated by Qaddafi, his bitter enemy. The Islamic world mourned him as a martyr.

Now, after thirty years of leading Hezbollah from the shadows, al-Sadr stood before the leaders of Islam still fueled by the fires of religious fervor.

"My good friend," al-Sadr said, slowly waving the back of his bronzed hand toward the Saudi king, "we are all aware of your inestimable wisdom and we are indebted to your thoughtful leadership through this dreadfully disorienting period in the history of Islam. The Arab world has benefited richly from the intelligent guidance of the House of Saud."

Abbudin's jaw clenched, causing a momentary thrust of the dark beard perched at the end of his chin. But Abbudin bided his time. He would wait for his moment of revenge for these barely veiled insults that slipped so softly from al-Sadr's lips.

"I, for one, refuse to believe that any true Muslim would fail to join in the call to jihad. Perhaps," al-Sadr insinuated, inclining his kaffiyeh ever so slightly in the Saudi king's direction, "in the past, there may have been economic or political or religious differences that kept us divided. But now . . . now . . . how can we be anything but united?"

Al-Sadr's burning gaze swept around the table.

"The Haram al-Sharif has been desecrated, the beautiful Dome has been destroyed. Our Al-Aqsa Mosque no longer exists. And the Zionists refuse to allow us access to either bury our dead or save our holy sites. Who knows what rape they are perpetrating within the Haram."

Moussa al-Sadr's power and influence within the Muslim Brotherhood grew exponentially when Hezbollah's heavily armed and well-trained militia humbled the vaunted armies of Israel, forcing the Jews to scramble back across their fortified borders after an ill-advised invasion of Lebanon in the summer of 2006.

But it was the Americans who had led Abbudin to this precipice. Foolishly, he believed the younger Bush would be as wise as his father. Abbudin lived with deep regret for the younger Bush's weakness, his hatred for that madman in Baghdad, hatred that absorbed his good sense and blinded him to prudence. There had been no weapons of mass destruction. But misguided and misdirected intelligence had led the West into an endless land war in Asia.

As a result, America reinforced its image in the Arab world as the Great Satan, the Shi'a religious fanatics in Tehran were racing joyously toward nuclear war, and King Abbudin, the once undisputed leader of the Arab world, felt as if he no longer led anyone. This was a world which had no place for Abbudin's calculated, self-serving version of moderation.

"As Protector of the Two Temples, the family Saud is also dedicated to protecting Islam's revered al-Haram al-Sharif," Abbudin said to the assembled members of the Brotherhood. "But, what can be protected that has already been destroyed? This earthquake was an act of God. The Israelis are only trying to stabilize a dangerous situation. An act of God is no reason to call for jihad."

Abbudin remained regal in bearing, the power of his wealth radiating through his long, embroidered robes. But few around the table appeared to be impressed.

"Your esteemed majesty must be correct." Al-Sadr's words slithered across the table like a viper on the prowl. "The Zionist pigs would never do anything to benefit themselves at the expense of their Arab brothers. As the king of the Saud claims, we can all put our trust in Israel's protection of Islam's shrines."

Silence filled the spacious room.

"Fool!" Imam al-Sadr leapt to his feet. "Puppet! You have placed your trust in the Americans rather than your own people, and what have you reaped? Personal wealth, and the enmity of all true Muslims. We have already waited too long."

Abbudin watched as others got to their feet. "The Zionists continue their aggression—Gaza, West Bank, Jerusalem, and now the Haram al-Sharif itself," al-Sadr raged. "Arabs must no longer bow to the yoke of Zion. And we must no longer wait for the weak to find their strength."

Al-Sadr's right arm rose, a specter in black, a gnarled finger pointing at King Abbudin. "It is time we wipe the world clean of Zion," he shouted, as those around him pounded the table with their fists. "And all those who give succor to the pigs of Israel. It is jihad, and nothing less, that will restore the Haram and the holy city into our hands."

Jerusalem

Style eluded him, no matter how hard he tried. Keeping up with the example set by the prime minister was beyond his level of competence.

Chaim Shomsky purchased only expensive suits. All his shirts were hand-made, his ties from Venice.

Yet he always looked like a schlump.

Shomsky spilled over the edges of the leather chair in the prime minister's makeshift office, trying to find the crease that once defined his pants. His clothes were disheveled, as always, but his mind was precisely tuned to the times.

Eliazar Baruk's chief of staff since the early days of Baruk's first campaign, Shomsky held the pulse of the prime minister's office firmly in his flabby hand, another of the misleading dichotomies that populated Shomsky's life and work.

Shomsky was no schlump. He was the architect of Baruk's surprising run to the prime minister's office and was the glue that held Baruk's ruling coalition together, although that unity was often purchased with promises yet to be repaid.

Shomsky rubbed a handkerchief over his perpetually perspiring bald head. The droplets ran alongside his eyes—black and lifeless like those of a shark—and over his round, reddened cheeks.

"Elie, you've got to get control of these situations, or they will destroy you," said Shomsky, staring down Baruk. "The wolves are out for blood—and it's your blood they want. Thank God the earthquake damage was limited to the area around the Mount. Still, you've got thousands of refugees living in tent cities out in the fields, hospitals are packed with the injured, hundreds of the buildings in the city need to be inspected to see if they are structurally sound, and the Arabs are apoplectic about the Temple Mount. All of that," Shomsky said, waving his hands in the air, "and the newspapers are still running stories about campaign financing. We have to get their attention off our contributors. And we must devise a solution to the Temple Mount."

Baruk was no pushover. Shomsky learned that on the campaign trail. But Baruk had also evolved into a pragmatic politician, which gave Shomsky the edge he needed for manipulation. One of Baruk's hot buttons—the prime minister's fatal flaw—was his desire for a legacy of greatness.

Shomsky often played to that desire in order to exercise power.

"The prosecutor has interviewed Meyer Feldberg," said Shomsky.

Baruk twisted uncomfortably in his chair, grimaced, and set his hands on the desk in front of him. "You said they would never get to Meyer."

It was difficult to suppress the grin. Shomsky loved these moments when he could exert some control over the prime minister. Tall, thin, and unflappable, Eliazar Baruk had come to his position from an unusual direction, the first lawyer to serve as PM. Dean of the school of law at Tel Aviv University, Baruk projected a patrician's disdain for the mundane. But, now, with the campaign finance investigators at his heels, the fastidiously polished exterior was beginning to show some cracks.

"The prosecutor I can't control," said Shomsky, shrugging his massive shoulders with a sigh, the movement bunching the expensive suit jacket into a ball behind his back. "And our friend the banker, I'm afraid, has left too many loose ends. Which is why you must act quickly on the Mount."

Baruk picked up a pencil from his desktop and began absently chewing on the eraser.

Good, now I've got him worried.

Baruk took the pencil from his mouth and waved it vaguely toward the ceiling.

"There is no solution to the Mount," said Baruk. His words had all the life of gray clouds.

Shomsky shifted himself closer to the desk, casting a glance over the top of wire-rimmed glasses that perched precariously on the down slope of his giant, splayed nose.

"Exactly," said Shomsky, tapping a pudgy finger on the desktop to pierce Baruk's growing anxiety. "There is no solution to the Mount. So we make a solution that solves our problems, as well."

Baruk's hand stopped in midair, the pencil failing to reach his mouth. "How?"

Shomsky smiled, and a chill entered the room.

"We make you a hero of Israel . . . and indispensable to the future safety of the nation."

"Again . . . how?"

Shomsky had waited patiently for the past hour, waiting precisely for this moment. Now was the time to push the button.

"First, you announce that the Temple Mount will be rebuilt."

"And then?"

"Then you tell the Arabs they're not coming back."

Baruk dropped the pencil and firmly grasped the edge of his desk. Shomsky felt the full weight of the prime minister's formidable personality.

"That would mean war."

Shomsky shrugged. "We could sneeze and it would mean war. We have fought them seven times, and we will fight them again. War with the Arabs is inevitable, someday. We just need to make it on our day. But no, Eliazar . . . denying the Arabs access to the Temple Mount would not mean war, at least not right away. The Arabs will erupt, yes. All of our enemies—Russia, Iran, North Korea—will scream threats. Even the Americans will be distressed. But it will buy us time, Elie. Time we desperately need to sweep away this investigation while the country, the world, looks elsewhere. Look, we tell the world that we're just trying to make the Mount safe, stable once again. That's where the earthquake did its worst damage. So, we'll rebuild the Temple platform. But, for the time being, the Arabs are not coming back. Nobody builds anything on top of the Temple Mount until we are certain that it is safe. Who could fault us for that?"

Baruk looked down at the top of his desk as he reached for another pencil. This one he tapped against the top of the desk. The pink eraser bounced off the wood. "That's a tactic, not a solution," said Baruk. "It's an explosion in waiting."

"Oh, I have a solution," said Shomsky, sliding back into his chair. "A solution that will earn your mark in history."

Shomsky saw just the hint of a smile cross Baruk's face. A hardening of the eyes. And Shomsky knew he had pushed the right button.

Tel Aviv, Israel

Another long day and night, turning into morning, and this one was still not over for Eliazar Baruk. Home in Tel Aviv, in his secret communications room, the strain of eighteen-hour days was draining him of energy and damaging his hope. Now, on top of everything else, was this. Baruk looked once again at the "eyes only" Mossad report in his hand, the one he'd read dozens of times thus far.

"They intend to take advantage of the situation, exploit the moment," said Baruk.

"Your information is solid?" asked the American president.

"Painter is already sending all our information to Director Cartwright's secure line. Check it out with your own assets. It's solid, Jonathan. The Iranian madman is going to make his move sooner than we expected."

Baruk watched over the encrypted video link as Jonathan Whitestone, his elbow perched on the bare desk deep in the cellars of the White House, rested his head in the palm of his right hand.

"He blames me . . . he blames you . . . he blames the world for the loss of the Dome of the Rock," said Baruk. "But let's be honest, Jon, he doesn't need an excuse. His Supreme Council of fanatics will believe anything and do anything President Essaghir says. Believe me, the Iranians are preparing to inflict catastrophic damage on the world's oil supply and, at the same time, to launch a preemptive strike against Israel. Three weeks from now, during Ramadan."

Sleep deprived, Baruk tried to will his body to remain alert, pushing against the gathering gray in his mind as a janitor tries to rustle dust balls into a manageable herd. Even he wondered if he were thinking straight.

"Are you sure you can take them all out?" asked Whitestone.

"Sure? Are you kidding? You want a guarantee of certainty, Jonathan?" Baruk could hear the weary edginess to his own voice. "Look, Jon . . . what is certain is the devastation that will result from this Iranian aggression. And we can both be certain of this, also . . . Essaghir must be stopped. How certain am I that our plans will succeed?"

Baruk threw his shoulders back, desperately trying to shrug off his exhaustion. This job was going to kill him.

"What other choice do I have? We must strike the Iranians first. And, if we are to strike, it must be decisive and debilitating. Besides you and me, only three of my men know of this plan—Orhlon, Painter, and Sharp. They are confident it will work. We will use their own weapons against them . . . irradiate their nuclear research facility, their petroleum production and pumping facility, and their gold reserves . . . all in one night. No missiles, no smart bombs. Nothing to use as proof on the world stage."

On the screen, Whitestone shook his head. "Men on the ground? You believe you can inflict this kind of damage with men on the ground and escape undetected? How, Eliazar? I need to know how you believe your men will get close to these installations."

Baruk understood. He was asking the American president to take a great risk and he needed some assurances.

"Because we have already been there—at all three locations—unnoticed. And we have planted assets at all three. It will be done, Jonathan. But we need you to put a lock on the rest of their funds. We will destroy their capacity for war. We need you to destroy their economy."

5

SUNDAY, JULY 26

New York City

The Collector's Club is closed each Sunday. So Richard Johnson normally had the whole place to himself. He liked it that way. Sunday was the day when he got most of his work done—there were no interruptions. Which is why he was startled this Sunday morning by the interruption sitting on the front steps of the club's building on East 35th Street.

"Brandon?" Johnson stood rooted to the sidewalk as he tried to register the unreality of this short, elderly man planted on his steps. An eccentric shock of white hair, as wild as the white-capped surf at the Cliffs of Moher, rioted defiantly on the top of the man's skull and tossed in the breeze.

"Ah . . . good morning, Richard. I was hoping you would soon pass by. As me sainted mother would say, 'Lose an hour in the mornin' and you'll be looking for it all day.' And it's getting a bit hard on me keister, sittin' on this stoop."

Brandon creaked to his feet and absently brushed the back of his pants with his left hand. He took a step toward Johnson, his right hand extended.

Dr. Brandon McDonough, provost of Trinity College in Dublin, lecturer emeritus of biblical archaeology. McDonough's signature facial feature was a nose that wrote the story of his life: flattened by a few too many bustups with the O'Reilly twins; twisted like a mountain highway by too many seasons of rugby; its point painted with an array of purple blotches from too many bouts with "the drink."

But neither his iconic Irish appearance nor the heavy brown rims around his glasses could hide the penetrating intelligence that radiated from McDonough.

Johnson's boss when the two men spent their summers at the British Museum, he was one of the few men in the world whom Johnson considered a mentor. Now, here he was, in his ever-present brown tweed suit, his brogue as thick as Irish wool, on a stoop in midtown Manhattan.

"Brandon, what are you doing here?" Johnson grasped the small man's warm, gnarly hand. "I'm stunned. Is everything all right?"

"All right? Good Lord, Richard, everything is lovely." McDonough, his face the shape of a harvest moon, and his perpetually red cheeks pushed up by the amused smile that seldom left his face, moved forward and placed his left hand around Johnson's right elbow, not releasing his handshake. "I'm here, my lad, to tell you personally that you have made me so proud. What you accomplished, what you found, 'tis certainly a miracle of the Almighty. My, my, Richard, a wonderful accomplishment." McDonough's firm grip delivered more affirmation than any Hallmark card.

Affirmation that Richard Johnson was incapable of receiving.

"A wonderful failure, if you were to ask me," said Johnson, prying his hand from the Irish professor. "Here . . . come inside. I'll make some coffee and we can sit and talk in comfort." Johnson steered McDonough up the steps of the Collector's Club, unlocked the door, and, once inside, shifted the building's highly sophisticated security system from nighttime surveillance to daytime occupancy. No one ever turned security off at the Collector's Club. "Come, we'll go upstairs to my office."

"Thank you, Richard. But, lad, tell me," McDonough said, searching Johnson's face for understanding, "why is it you believe this great discovery was a failure?"

—∿∿∿—

Ali Suliman looked over the *New York Daily News* he held in front of his face. He sat in the early morning sun on a bench outside the bistro on Madison Avenue at 35th Street. Suliman wasn't there for the sun outside or the Sunday brunch inside the bistro. He was watching the two men who stood huddled together in front of the impressive building on the far side of 35th, across from where he sat.

The building was his assignment. The men, his prey . . . if they got in the way.

Suliman put the newspaper on the bench, got up, and walked into the shadows, away from the Collector's Club. He would be back.

—∿∕∾—

Johnson led his visitor through the ornate entry hall with its marble floors and columns and into the elevator in the middle of the building.

There was just enough room for the two men in the antique lift, one of the accoutrements added when Stanford White redesigned the five-story, baroque-style building in the late nineteenth century.

"It was a failure because the Temple was destroyed before we could truly examine it." Johnson opened the door at the fifth floor, led McDonough to the front of the building, and unlocked his office.

"Is that it, then?" McDonough shook his head and turned to Johnson. "Surely that was a bit of bad luck, I admit. But you didn't cause that earthquake. What you accomplished was remarkable."

Dr. Richard Johnson Sr., former chair of the Antiquities College at Columbia University and fellow of the British Museum was now—in his retirement—managing director of the Collector's Club in Manhattan. The club was one of the most influential in the world of stamp collecting and housed perhaps the most extensive philatelic library on the planet.

For a man of such lofty credentials and stately bearing, Johnson's office occupied a lovely but unpretentious space. It contained the obligatory hardwood floor and rich oak bookcases. The weathered, welcoming leather chairs he loved. And a unique, blue Persian rug. But there were no trappings of power. Johnson's desk was utilitarian. No trophy pictures adorned the walls. No glitz or glamour. It was an academic's office—in a constant state of barely controlled chaos.

Johnson was tall, lean, crowned by a thick, silvery-gray mane swept back from his considerable forehead and curling around his ears and shirt collar. Today, his day off, he was wearing a pink, Ralph Lauren golf shirt, well-worn Levis, and a pair of weathered, Bostonian penny loafers. He guided his old friend to one of the leather chairs while he busied himself with brewing the coffee, the velvet enticement of a rich Arabica flirty with brazen promise.

"Brandon, it sounds so absurd to say this out loud to someone I've known for such a long time, but, my colleagues and I . . . we risked our lives while we tried to decipher the message on the scroll." Johnson turned away from the coffeemaker and took a seat opposite McDonough. "And we risked our lives in a more dramatic and direct way when we did what I can only categorize as a wildly foolish escapade—traveling to Jerusalem to find this lost Temple. We were stalked by a sect of assassins, hunted by Israeli security forces, and targeted by a radical Islamic group hell-bent on protecting the Mount. Just outside this building, one of the finest men I've ever known was blown to bits by a car bomb. How the rest of us escaped with our lives, I have no idea."

"Aye, and sad it was," said McDonough. "I know it must—"

"No. That's just it, you don't know," snapped Johnson. Anxiety was beginning to claw at his chest. "After all we risked, after all we endured, and after all we found . . . to have it all completely destroyed just weeks later has been devastating. I've got to admit to you, Brandon, I am frightened to my soul by what I did, and my heart and spirit have been crushed by losing what we fought so hard to gain. For me, it was a disaster. A disaster of epic proportions. I thought . . ."

Johnson shook his head, emitted a deep sigh, his eyes searching for an answer in the designs of the Persian rug. "I thought, for once, I might help make history." He looked blankly at the palms of his hands and lost consciousness of the man sitting across from him. "But that's all gone now. Gone. Destroyed in a breath.

"And what do I have now?" Johnson said to his hands. "Nothing. I have nothing. Except regrets."

Johnson was suddenly aware of someone at his side. Dr. McDonough, with a cup of coffee in his right hand. His left hand he placed on Johnson's shoulder.

"Surely, now, that is why I am here, my friend." McDonough handed the coffee to Johnson, who stared into his wise hazel eyes. "My boy, not for a second do I believe you have failed. As me sainted mother would say, 'Don't be breaking your shin on a stool that's not in your way.' I believe you have triumphed. And your greatest triumph may yet be achieved."

Johnson steadied the cup in his hands. "I'm sorry, Brandon, I don't understand. What can you mean, triumph?"

McDonough crossed the carpet and picked up his own coffee mug. "Richard, I truly understand your grief, because an Irishman has an abiding sense of tragedy which sustains him through temporary periods of joy. But, believe me, this should be a time of joy.

"What was Abiathar's purpose . . . his father's purpose? What did they intend to achieve?" McDonough asked, perching himself on the edge of his chair. "They wanted to restore ritual sacrifice in the Temple of God, either on, or in, the mountain of God. This priest, Abiathar, he and his father and scores of others put their lives at risk, for many years. Such excruciating work, in such difficult circumstances, was it not? Do you think, after all they endured—twice exiled from Jerusalem, years laboring in the bowels of the earth, eating and breathing limestone dust, praying over their brothers buried under collapsed tunnels—after all that, do you truly believe this Abiathar would leave the existence of a Third Temple simply to chance? To the chance that his message would travel hundreds of kilometers, through Christian and Muslim armies, and come to rest in the hands of the one man who could read it? What, honestly, are the odds of that happening in 1099? Are you with me there, love?"

The designs in the Persian rug began to swim before Johnson's eyes, a mirror image of the confusion in his mind.

"Richard . . . tell me, son, how closely did you examine the outside of the mezuzah? The container which held the scroll for so many years . . . how closely was it inspected, eh?"

"What are you talking about?" The words came out like a rebuke. "We were interested in the scroll, in its language and structure, in its message," snapped Johnson. "What of the mezuzah?"

"Richard, ancient mezuzahs were often inscribed on the outside with messages of equal importance to the scroll within.

"What was Abiathar's Plan B?" he asked. "Surely, these men would have had alternatives in play. What if the Temple under the Mount was never found? It appears Abiathar's message never reached the man in Egypt to whom it was sent. Is this the only message he would send? Or, more likely, what if his temple was destroyed by some earthquake or flood or other natural disaster? What would they have done then? Just give up? I think not, Richard. Me sainted mother used to say, 'Brandon, you'll never plow a field by turning it over in your mind.' This was a man of action. He would not have simply shrugged his shoulders and hoped. What else did Abiathar try to tell us? Are there other messages, besides the one on the scroll?"

———

Johnson pinched the edge of the cloth and peeled away the flaps of acid-free cotton embracing the metal tube. There was little light inside the vault of the Collector's Club, but enough to reflect off the bronze surface and snag the glint in McDonough's eyes. He watched as his colleague's face shifted through a gamut of expressions . . . wonder coming back again and again.

"Is it inside?"

Johnson turned within the vault and reached over to a wide, thin, stainless steel drawer. The drawer slid open silently. "No, we didn't want to roll it again once we got back to the States." Johnson lifted the drawer off its soft rollers and placed it on the table alongside the mezuzah. He flipped a catch and opened the stainless steel lid against the hinges on its back rim. "We're all concerned, not just for its safety but also about the effects of our weather on the scroll itself. This vault was designed to preserve the precious stamps that fill these drawers. No moisture. No humidity. Temperature controlled." Johnson lifted the thin tissue paper covering, exposing the scroll to low light. He stepped back.

An inhale caught in McDonough's throat as his left hand came up and clutched the lapel of his jacket. "Holy Mother of God . . . 'tis beautiful," he whispered. "Wonderfully preserved."

"Ha!" Johnson leaned back against the inside of the vault. "You would have been appalled at the way we treated this treasure in the tunnels under the Temple Mount. Carrying it around like a letter to Uncle Phil. We swam across an underground lake with it; can you believe that? It's only dumb luck that kept it from being destroyed."

"Or, perhaps a spot of divine intervention?"

"What?"

"Nothing . . . nothing, my boy. A slip of the tongue, 'tis all," said McDonough. "The letters are beautiful, eh? Artfully sculpted. So much more defined than those on the Rosetta Stone. An amazing find. And this," he said, pointing to a small circle at the bottom of the leftmost column, "this is the mark of the high priest?"

"Yes," said Johnson, joining his friend at the side of the table. Johnson rested his right hand on McDonough's left shoulder and leaned over the table. "It's hard to see with the naked eye, but inside the circle are two Phoenician letters, *aleph* and *resh*—the hallmark of Abiathar, high priest of the Jewish community that first fled from Jerusalem to Tyre when the Seljuk Turks captured the Holy City. Abiathar . . . builder of the hidden Third Temple under the Temple Mount and author of this coded scroll."

McDonough turned his hand over and ran a fingernail lovingly over the aged parchment. "He must have been quite a resourceful man, this Abiathar."

Returning the scroll to its hermetically sealed new home, Johnson picked up the rewrapped mezuzah from the table. "Let's go up to my office. We'll be more comfortable and have more light to see if our friend Abiathar left us anything else."

Back on the fifth floor, Johnson stalled at the threshold to his office, as he had so many times since his return from Jerusalem. The workmen had completed the job admirably. The bow window overlooking 35th Street was not only repaired, but was now restored to the elegance envisioned in Stanford White's original design. The scars on the room's walls and woodwork, caused by the blast, were plastered and painted or repaired. But the scars on Johnson's heart were livid and throbbing with hurt. He loved Winthrop Larsen like a son. Like many fathers, Johnson grieved at the words he never said. Winthrop's body was gone, torn to shreds by the bombers of the Prophet's Guard, but his memory lived within these walls. With a reverent sadness, Johnson stepped across the threshold and into his place of grief.

"We'll have good light by the window," said Johnson. He crossed to a large table, up on its edge like a drafting table, various arms flayed out to its sides. Johnson pulled out a spring-loaded dowel and lowered the face of the table to a horizontal plane. Placing the wrapped mezuzah on the table, he reached for one of the hinged, metal arms and pulled a bright light over the table surface.

Johnson motioned McDonough to a high stool, but the scholar was oblivious to the gesture. His eyes were riveted to the bronze cylinder on the table. Pressed against the side of the table, McDonough stretched out his right hand and traced some of the etched designs in the air above the mezuzah.

"Now, let's see what you have to say for yourself."

McDonough pulled down one of the metal arms attached to the sides of the table, the one suspending a powerful magnifying glass surrounded by a high-lumen lamp. He carefully positioned the magnifying glass over the bronze mezuzah and switched on the lamp.

As Johnson watched McDonough caress the cold metal tube as if wooing a lover-to-be, his heart warmed. The memory of many long hours in the caverns of the British Museum flashed across Johnson's consciousness, he and McDonough working together as they tried to pry secrets from cold stone or inhospitable metal. Those were happier times, times when—

"Where do you think the mezuzah originated?" asked McDonough. "In Jerusalem or in Egypt?"

Johnson felt his mind cloud over. It was a question he hadn't considered, one apparently without an answer. "I . . . I don't know."

"Do you recognize this?" McDonough asked as he swung the magnifying glass around so Johnson could observe what he had discovered.

Johnson turned his head to the right, bewildered by what he saw. "Is that a *tau*?"

The tau, an ancient Egyptian symbol of truth—the symbol pressed against the lips of each Pharaoh when a king was initiated into the Egyptian mysteries—looked like the letter *T*, or like three pieces of a Templar's cross with the top, vertical piece missing.

"Yes . . . three, side by side. But, what is that beside the taus?" asked McDonough.

A small circle beside the three tau symbols, a circle containing two letters—aleph and resh, Abiathar's signature. "Well . . . I'll be . . ."

"Yes, you are," said McDonough. "But that's not the point. Your friend Abiathar was communicating with a compatriot in Egypt, was he not?"

Johnson's mind began to focus. "Yes . . . Meborak, the Exilarch of Egypt, was his ally in a plan to overthrow a usurper to the leadership of the Egyptian Jewish community."

Johnson stepped away from the table and crossed to the bay window overlooking 35th Street. "It was this mezuzah, with the scroll message inside, that Abiathar sent to Meborak for safekeeping." Johnson turned his back to the window and faced the room. "But we also discovered there were other, earlier messages between Abiathar and Meborak . . . messages that originally created the Demotic language code that Abiathar used in the scroll's cipher. So, it's really not that strange that we would find an Egyptian symbol connected with Abiathar's hallmark."

"Perhaps," said McDonough, resting against a stool. "But, why would Abiathar combine his signature with an ancient, pagan symbol like the tau when he could have used any number of other symbols . . . symbols from the Torah? Even if they were concerned about keeping their little conspiracy a secret, why select the tau?"

Without warning, Johnson's innate curiosity was overrun by a rising surge of anger. He felt it, but couldn't stop it. Slamming his hand onto the drafting table, his voice erupted. "This . . . this is what Winthrop died for?" He made a fist and slammed it again on the table. "Playing stupid children's games of hide-and-seek . . . solve the puzzle . . . win the prize."

Johnson grabbed onto the edge of the table like a vise clamp, steadying himself as he brought his voice under control. "There's no prize here, Brandon," he whispered. "Just silly men, playing stupid children's games . . . games that cost the best of us his life. Who cares? Who really cares what the stupid thing means?"

Johnson stared blindly at the mezuzah. He felt McDonough's hand upon his shoulder.

"Richard, with the first message, you discovered the Third Temple of God, an event that I believe has changed the course of history."

Johnson tried to close his heart against the words. *No. It wasn't worth it.*

"Finding Abiathar's hallmark on the surface of the mezuzah, I'll wager there must be a second message here, a different message that Abiathar tried to communicate through the symbols on this mezuzah?"

I can't. I can't. It's my fault that Winthrop is dead. I killed him just as surely as if I placed the bomb in his van. No more. I can't take it. I couldn't bear it if someone else were hurt . . . someone else were killed . . . just because I wanted to follow the thrill of the chase. No . . . I can't.

"Richard." The voice was soft, pleading, close to his ear. "This message was meant to be found. Whatever it is, Abiathar's purpose was that someone—this Meborak most likely—would find it and understand it. Richard . . . now that the door of the mezuzah has been opened . . . if you and your friends don't discover its meaning, others will. Others who may not be so—"

"But, what if someone else is injured, or killed?" Johnson shook his head, slowly, back and forth. "I don't think I could survive."

"Richard, lad," said McDonough, "I don't think you have a choice."

Johnson looked for escape. But there was none.

6

MONDAY, JULY 27

New York City

"Do you think we're still in the mystery-solving business?"

Sammy Rizzo sat behind his custom-designed desk in the bowels of the Humanities and Social Sciences Library at Fifth Avenue and 42nd Street in New York City, frustrated that his "great adventure" may have ended, throwing Nerf darts at a large bull's-eye hanging on the wall.

"I don't think so, Sam. I think our treasure hunting days are over."

Joe Rodriguez, Rizzo's friend and curator of the library's Periodicals Room on the main floor, was sprawled in a chair across from Rizzo, his six-four frame extending in all directions as Rizzo failed miserably at his target practice.

"What are you—the Gentle Green Giant Wuss? What about the phone call?" said Rizzo, spinning in his chair and whipping a dart over his left shoulder. "What about the inscription Doc and his leprechaun friend found on the mezuzah? Do you think Tom's asked us all over to his house tomorrow night to watch *American Idol?*"

Leonard Antonio Rizzo, a short, muscular Mediterranean-looking man, standing just a tad over four feet tall, with a dense shock of jet-black hair and thick, black-rimmed glasses, had come to the New York library system with a degree in library science from NYU and a chip on his shoulder. With a long-deceased father named Leonard, an uncle named Leonard, and two cousins named Leonard, he also came with a nickname. Sammy started in the stacks, but he didn't stay there long. He was a master of organization, had a memory to die for, and soon ruled the world of book retrieval that operated in obscurity in the depths of the miles of stacks that extended beneath Bryant Park.

Now, Sammy Rizzo was master of the digital-age Dewey Decimal System. He was the sorter, slicer, dicer of the Humanities and Social Sciences Library, keeping its ten million items in perfect order, available at the swipe of a pencil on a request slip. It was a world Sammy ruled from the flight deck of his custom-designed office desk. Even when he wasn't watching.

"I don't care what Doc found," said Rodriguez. "It sure seems to me that Annie and Deirdre have made up their minds that we're not going anywhere."

"Well, what if the Prophet's Guard is still determined to gets its hands on the scroll and the mezuzah?" Rizzo was not giving up without a fight. "It may not matter what Annie and Deirdre want," he said, whistling his last dart toward the Velcro target. "Our butts may still be on the line."

"You know, I can't blame Annie and Deirdre," said Joe. "We were crazy to risk our lives over in Jerusalem and we'd be crazy to get involved again."

Sammy Rizzo hopped off his chair and began collecting the errant Nerf darts.

"Josey, baby," he said, tossing one of the darts to Rodriguez, "who are you trying to kid. I know you, and I know you got a rush from all our adventures. Tell me you wouldn't want to get back in the game."

Rizzo watched his friend's face contort, wrestling with conflicting emotions. "I don't know," said Rodriguez. "I think Deirdre would kill me for even thinking about it." Then his face brightened. "But it sure sounds interesting what Doc came up with."

"Well, if we're still looking for clues," said Rizzo, climbing back into his chair, "I've had a question bugging me ever since we decoded Abiathar's scroll. Did you notice anything odd about Abiathar's message?"

"You mean, besides the claim that he built a Jewish temple under the Temple Mount?"

"Yeah, Sherlock, besides the most obvious." Rizzo whizzed a Nerf dart past Rodriguez's ear. "Just one day, I'd like to get some respect."

Rodriguez raised his hands, palms outward. "Hey . . . Sammy . . . no offense, okay? What are you thinking?"

Rizzo began to rock back and forth in his specially designed chair, adrenaline coursing through his body like a drug, elevating his heart rate and kicking his fingers into a steady percussion on the desk. He admitted this secret only to himself, but he had never felt more alive than on the quest for the meaning of the scroll and their search for the hidden Temple. He was a member of the team . . . an equal member . . . and it brought him back into Kallie's world. Perhaps, if their destiny was still tied to the scroll and mezuzah, there might be another opportunity to prove his worth to Kallie. As a man, not as a clown.

Rizzo took a deep breath to slow his heart. "In Abiathar's letter to Meborak, near the end, he wrote something that was out of character with the rest of the letter. He said, 'Look to the prophets for your direction.' Everything else in the letter was very concrete—about his history, why and how they decided to build the Temple. But then, near the end, he includes this cryptic comment. What does it mean, 'Look to the prophets for your direction'? What prophet is he talking about? What direction?

"And, that was it." Rizzo waved his knobbly hands in front of his face. "No other mention of prophets in anything else we've found. But it must have had some significance to Meborak in Egypt. Otherwise, why include the reference?"

Sammy braced for a sharp retort, readied his own zinger for return. But Rodriguez, as was his habit, surprised him.

Rodriguez pushed himself forward in the chair to face Rizzo head-on. A question framed his eyes and tickled the corners of his mouth. "But . . . you're right. Geez, Sammy, you're right. We need to go back to the beginning here." Rodriguez jumped to his feet and began to pace the length of the office. "We've all been so caught up in everything that's happened to us, we haven't taken any time to go back and think about how all of this got started."

His long frame shuddered as it came to a halt at the far end of the office, as if he had just walked into a doorpost. Rodriguez swiveled on his heel.

"We didn't get any directions from the prophets," said Rodriguez.

Good . . . it's finally starting to dawn on him.

"We cracked the code, went over to Jerusalem, found the hidden Temple, but— but we never got any direction from any prophets that I know of. What—"

"What does it mean?" Rizzo asked, spreading only a thin layer of rebuke on his words. "It means we haven't scratched the surface yet. Maybe Abiathar's got a lot more to tell us. And I'm wondering what it is."

Sammy watched as Rodriguez raised his hands to both sides of his forehead, then ran his fingers through his nappy, salt-and-pepper hair. "Oh . . . I am going to be in so much trouble."

7

TUESDAY, JULY 28

New York City

"I don't care who he is, or what he had to say," said Annie Bohannon, pacing back and forth in front of the windows. "You guys are not going to get mixed up with this again. Over my dead body, Tom Bohannon."

"C'mon, Annie . . ."

"Don't Annie me, Tom. Are you crazy? Where is Winthrop Larsen? What happened to Caitlin on the Fordham campus? You, all of you"—she swept her hand in the direction of Doc, Joe, and Sammy—"are lucky to be here alive. And now, because some bonehead Irishman that Doc knows has a theory about the mezuzah . . . This is crazy, even to be talking about it. We already decided to get that thing out of our lives. And you're not going back. Do you hear me, Tom? You're not going to get involved with this madness again."

Bohannon survived attacks from the assassins of the Prophet's Guard, escaped the murderous designs of fundamentalist Muslim jihadists, and was spared from a lethal, clandestine Israeli commando strike force. Still, he must admit, Annie did intimidate him—particularly when the Italian side of her ancestry popped to the surface of her emotions.

"Annie . . . all we're doing is talking about what this guy—"

"Dr. McDonough," interjected Richard Johnson. "Brandon McDonough, my superior at the British Museum."

"—what this Dr. McDonough has to say about the mezuzah. And Sammy's come up with a very valid question about the message on the scroll. Look, we're just kicking this around. It's a fascinating theory, after all."

"Theory, my petunias," Annie snapped. "I know you guys well enough. I could hear it in your voices when I came into the room. I can see it, feel it, smell it in this room already—the thrill of the hunt; the sense of adventure. Well, stick a pin in it, because, Tom, you're not going anywhere. Our entire family was terrorized for more than a month because of that stupid metal pipe. You were gone for two weeks. Thank God they kept your job for you last time. Can you imagine what people at the Mission will think, what the library will think of Joe, if you go back in and ask for more time to chase down another secret message? Probably fire you and lock you up in the looney bin."

Out of the corner of his eye, Bohannon noticed Rizzo holding an imaginary noose around his neck, pulling it tight, his tongue hanging out the corner of his mouth. *Geez, Sammy . . . not now.*

"But that's not it," said Annie. Her long blonde hair was pulled back in a ponytail, a testimony to hours in the kitchen. A short-sleeve, loose-fitting blue-checked blouse was tucked into tightly fitted jeans that still caught Tom's attention and caused his heart to skip. Her face was a bit fuller than when they met thirty years ago, but her blue eyes still flashed with life and her skin was soft and flawless, the color of peaches in high summer gleaming from her rounded cheekbones. When she smiled, life warmed. But there was no smile today.

She looked at Tom like a jury foreman with a verdict. "Tom, I'm not ready to be a widow."

Bohannon opened his mouth to respond . . . to defend . . . but her look stopped him cold.

"I want you to be here when our daughter gets married, when our son needs your advice for starting his own life. I want to grow old with you and spoil our grandchildren together.

"It's a miracle you—all of you—came back alive." She crossed the room to Tom and stood over where he sat in the stuffed armchair. "I won't live like this anymore," said Annie. "I can't."

Washington, DC

"Tell me what else you know."

"We've been digging around on both sides of the pond, pulling in favors," said Cartwright, throwing a file stamped TOP SECRET on the table between the two presidential sofas. "It looks like there's been some kind of power play among the Arabs. Nothing definitive, but there are rumblings that somebody new has entered the picture and is consolidating power and influence."

"The Iranians?" asked President Whitestone. "The last thing we need is Essaghir grabbing another handful of power."

"No, sir," said the CIA director, "not the Iranians. As far as we're being told, there is a new voice being followed in the Muslim Brotherhood."

"Abbudin's out? Well, I'm not surprised," said Whitestone, sitting on the sofa opposite Cartwright. "Somehow he held on to his influence after the Iraq war, but now, after the earthquake . . ."

"He's too close to us," Cartwright finished the sentence.

Whitestone, like his predecessors, believed the Saudi king was Washington's greatest ally in the Islamic world. A man of principle and understanding, and a man who loved his petrodollars, Abbudin was committed to moderate cooperation with the West. His hand upon the helm of the Muslim Brotherhood had thus far averted a Mideast conflagration.

"Bad for us . . . bad for the world, maybe," said Whitestone.

New York City

Tom wanted to avoid the traffic on 254th Street. Even on a Tuesday evening in sleepy Riverdale, in the very northwest corner of the Bronx, cars were up and down the street to the Metro North train station. So he turned left on Independence Avenue and walked in the direction of Bingham Road and the entrance to Wave Hill, the former home of Mark Twain, now a public garden.

It was Johnson who suggested the walk after dinner. After Annie's impassioned plea.

"So, what did you need to talk about, Doc?"

Old trees covered the road like a green canopy, creating a tunnel of shade and shadow spackled with bright splashes of slanting sunlight. There was no sidewalk, but now, with Wave Hill closed for the day, Independence Avenue was a solitary street. Doc Johnson walked to his right, to the inside of the street, and seemed to be consumed with avoiding the numerous potholes at the edges of the macadam.

A lazy breeze came off the Hudson River and stirred the tops of the trees.

"Doc?"

Johnson shook his head and half turned toward Bohannon. "Oh . . . yes.

Well, Tom, you may find this request a trifle odd, to say the least, but . . . I . . . umm."

Johnson went back to studying the various levels of decay in the roadway.

Tom found a short stretch of isolated sidewalk fronting a large, gray Victorian home, guided Johnson onto the sidewalk and into the shade.

"Okay, Doc . . . what's this all about?"

With no road to survey, Doc finally looked Bohannon in the eyes.

"Tom . . . what's happened to you?" asked Johnson. "When we were in Jerusalem, it was your faith that kept us together, that got us out of some tough spots. It was your prayers that showed us the way, over and over again. You were so confident that God would intervene and answer your prayers. But now, lately, you've sounded like a different man."

Now it was Tom who searched the ground for an answer. "Well, Doc . . . you know. I am different now—"

"No, wait, let me finish," Johnson interrupted. "For the first time in my memory, in Jerusalem, I had a sense of God's existence, his presence. And I witnessed your confidence in God's presence in your life, and how it led you. And circumstances didn't change that faith. You've been through a lot, like your daughter's heart surgery. But those things only made your faith stronger. Your relationship with God was very winsome, Tom. It was interesting, attractive, and confusing at the same time. But it's been on my mind ever since."

Tom knew Doc had long searched to satisfy a longing he could barely define. Johnson lived most of his life in the rarefied air at the pinnacle of academia. But, for all his intellectual accomplishments, Doc often saw himself simply as a frustrated sixty-eight-year-old man with an unfulfilled pursuit. In addition to secrets and treasures, Johnson also spent his life in pursuit of meaning and purpose. Sadly, despite his earnest attempts, Johnson found no peace in atheism, Eastern mysticism, or New Age philosophies. With all his knowledge, he was still a man seeking truth.

"I wish . . . I was hoping I could find your kind of faith. Maybe that would help me deal with the anguish and remorse I feel over Winthrop's death. In the past, your faith has given you a place of comfort in the midst of crisis. I've seen it. It's something I'd like to find. But," Johnson leaned over and picked up a small stone, tossed it in his hand. "I don't see that comfort in you now. I can understand my doubts about what we experienced, but it's alarming to see you lose faith." Johnson flipped the stone into some bushes on the far side of the street. He frowned and looked up at Bohannon with pleading eyes. "What has happened?"

Bohannon tried to keep his face placid to mask the turmoil in his emotions. Part of him was angry at Doc for putting words to his own disappointment with God, part of him felt guilty for his anger at God, and part of him just wanted to find someplace to curl up and hide from all the stress that continued to build in his life. He was conflicted, confused. If this was a time for fight or flight—his emotions were on the cusp of running as fast as his feet could carry him. But that was the old Tom. The Tom who would run and hide from his problems; the Tom who would unplug and withdraw from the life around him. Like his father, the Tom who would isolate his consciousness from the pressures of life and the world around him.

The old Tom . . . who was dying, but whose character flaws still hung around like cantankerous weeds that randomly pushed their way into a well-tended garden.

The new Tom took a deep-breathing sigh, trying to break the knot in his chest.

"Doc," he began, finding it difficult to tie his thoughts to his tongue, "I was so sure we were doing something good."

Tom shook his head. The thoughts and feelings pounding through his nervous system felt like a wild, white-water ride down a swollen river. "I . . . I just don't get it." Tom turned on his heel and paced away, his hands holding his head, fingers tangled in the curls at the nape of his neck. "If this so-called adventure of ours was God's will, how could so much evil come from it? Not only Winthrop's death. My daughter was nearly abducted. Kallie lost everything. Shoot . . . thousands of people died during that earthquake in Jerusalem. That was good? That was God's plan?"

Tom spun around. "I feel like a fool!"

Bohannon's confession echoed up to the height of the trees providing them shelter. "A fool who endangered my wife and my children. A fool who nearly got us all killed. Who am I to think that God speaks to me? Just an arrogant, self-centered . . ." Bohannon threw up his hands, out of words. He inspected a tree trunk.

"Self-pity doesn't become you." Doc's voice was as soft and gentle as the gathering evening—without a hint of accusation.

"I have flagellated myself with the same self-recrimination. I feel personally responsible for Winthrop's death and every bit as foolhardy as you do. But there is something that you are forgetting. Something that you cannot deny, that Brandon helped me to see. What happened under the Temple Mount was real. I've been on plenty of digs, uncovered some remarkable artifacts. But I never experienced anything like what all of us experienced under the Mount. It was more than amazing . . . it was miraculous. And you and I lived it. There was some power at work that is beyond us. You call him God—and you prayed and he answered.

"If God exists, then he is not capricious. Your God, the God of the Bible, is not like the ancient gods of the Greeks, or the Sumerians, or any number of people groups, who were so fickle and unpredictable that men could never figure out what was coming next. The Christian God is the great creator, the one who brought order and beauty out of chaos. If you believe, he's the one who sent his Son as a sacrificial offering to wash away the sins of those men who believe. That's in your book. So, Tom, that God is not a puppeteer who is impulsively pulling your strings. If he is the Creator God, who brings order, then it is not in his character to bring chaos."

Bohannon was stunned by Johnson's theological insight. "Do you really believe that?"

"It is my belief, Thomas, that you will need to reconcile the dichotomy you perceive as God. Either he is a good God who cares for you . . . who leads you in prayer . . . or he's an unpredictable and erratic creature who can't be trusted. I don't see how you can have it both ways."

Well groomed, impeccably dressed, Doc was an anachronism sitting comfortably on that rock. And Tom, without conscious effort, found himself once again considering the depth and progress of Doc's spiritual journey. But Doc wouldn't let him off the hook.

"I believe you are experiencing what is called a crisis of faith?" Johnson said with a question at the end, a smirk wrestling with a smile. "And how you deal with your dilemma will determine the rest of your life. And, I believe, will have a profound impact on mine.

"Come along." Doc rose from the rock, reached out, and grasped Bohannon's elbow. "The light is beginning to fade and I don't want to break an ankle on this sad excuse for a street."

Tom's mind was scrambled like the stones at the crumbling sides of Independence Avenue as the evening gathered around them. Doc was leading, picking his way along the left side berm, head down, intensely focused, as they came to the crest of a small rise. Tom heard it first. A rumble. He looked up. Over the rise launched a black SUV, no lights, spitting stones as it rode the side of the street. There was no thought. Had he thought, they would both have died. Tom's right hand flashed out, latched onto Doc's shirt between his neck and right shoulder, and pulled with all his strength as he dove headlong into a hedge of forsythia bushes that lined the side of the street. Bohannon could feel the heat of the engine on his back, his body jolted as fender or running board rapped the sole of his retreating shoe. His face felt like it was at an acupuncture convention, but the huge SUV continued careening down the street, the driver apparently unaware of the two men he sent diving into the bushes.

Suspended in the shrubbery like some tossed-away rag doll, Tom groped with his left hand, looking for something solid to use for leverage, and then realized he still held Doc's shirt firmly in the grasp of his right fist. "Doc?"

"Yes . . . yes, I'm all right," Doc croaked from within the bush. "Punctured and bruised, yes, but alive."

Bohannon released Doc's shirt and pushed against the bush, trying to regain his feet. "Stupid kid, probably joyriding in his father's gas guzzler." His right foot scrabbled in the stones, then got traction. "Probably never saw us." Bohannon stumbled to his feet . . . and saw Doc staring at him. The force of Bohannon's rescue had pulled Doc to the left, but also backward, dragging Johnson into the bushes on an angle, his face still pointing out to the street.

Bohannon pulled Johnson from the prickly embrace of the forsythia, then held him at arm's length.

"You didn't see him?" Doc asked, his question dripping with warning.

Tom felt a shiver ripple up his spine. "No . . ."

"Black hair. Prominent nose. Skin the color of the desert," said Johnson. "He was looking directly at us. And he wasn't happy that he missed."

8

SATURDAY, AUGUST 1

Damascus, Syria

The sun hammered hard against the al-Shaab presidential palace situated on a hilltop overlooking the drab, dusty streets of Damascus. But in the bunker, far below the soaring fountains and white marble porticos of the palace, the dim lighting and heavy air-conditioning obliterated any thought of sun or sand.

It was a small band, but some of the most powerful men in the Arab world, that met around the polished maple table. The president of Syria was the ostensible host, but even his presence was trumped by that of Rahim Kashmiri, the ruthless leader of the mafiocracy that ruled Syria's economy and kept the president on a short leash. Across from Kashmiri sat Muhamed Nazrullah, the visible head of Hezbollah who carried Lebanon in his back pocket. Facing the president sat a short, thin man with a round head, a wispy beard and—at least in public—an unrelenting smile. A man who looked more like a school teacher than the president of Iran—Mehdi Essaghir, public enemy number one of the United States and Israel.

But the power behind this meeting—the true leader of Hezbollah and the Muslim Brotherhood—stood at the head of the table, holding the others in rapt attention.

As usual, a black kaftan covered Moussa al-Sadr's thin, bony frame and a black turban covered his head, leaving visible only a wild mass of gray-streaked beard and two eyes that sang of fanaticism.

"This is our moment," said al-Sadr. "The Saudis are of no importance. Abbudin has been neutralized by this lie of Islamic unity . . . this farce of the

Arab Spring . . . as if we would actually trust that fat, Sunni fool." His voice was as low as the lighting in the sealed bunker. "We hold the heart and hope of Islam in our hands. Kamali will not survive in Egypt, where the Brotherhood is consolidating its power. When we rise up, all Arabs will join us in the battle. Jihad will call to them from the sands of time."

"We don't need speeches," said the criminal Kashmiri. "What we need is action."

Al-Sadr leaned forward, his thin hands supported by the edge of the table, the withering force of his will projected at the overflowing bulk of the thug, Kashmiri. *You, too, will earn justice.*

"There is only one goal, my impatient friend." Al-Sadr's voice dripped honey, but his eyes overflowed with hate. "The restoration of the Caliphate. Just as Islam ruled the known world one thousand years ago, so Islam will rule the known world today. For that momentous event to occur, we must break through the Israelis' illegal blockade, reclaim the Haram al-Sharif before the Zionist pigs can seal up the Dome of the Rock and the Al-Aqsa Mosque with their plans to rebuild their so-called Temple Mount. There can be no Zionist presence to desecrate the holy hill. Now is the time to strike. But with wisdom, not foolhardy bluster. Our attack must be swift and decisive. We must give the Americans no time to respond."

"The Americans are fools."

Al-Sadr looked down the table and was surprised to see it was the Syrian puppet who spoke. "You have some insight to share, Baqir?"

The president held a small knife in his right hand and was seemingly absorbed in cleaning his fingernails. "The Americans are fools," he repeated, his gaze fixed on his fingers. "They have no idea what to expect from us. One day I received one of their senators, and the next week I received the Russian president. No, venerable one, the Americans are confused. They don't know who is their friend or their enemy, except"—Baqir al-Musawi bowed to the Iranian president—"for our fearless brother. The fools even believe I have stamped out the Muslim Brotherhood here in Syria. No, my brothers, our concern remains how to neutralize the Israelis."

Al-Sadr nodded his head in agreement. "Yes, Baqir. Someday the long-arm threat of Iranian nuclear warheads will prevent Israeli aggression. But, for now, the fighters of Hezbollah will once again neutralize the weak-willed soldiers of the Jews, but this time on their soil. Is the heart of Amal prepared to strike?"

"The army of Hezbollah moves at your wish," said Nazrullah, who was heavier and younger than his mentor, but who wore the same clothes, grew the same beard, and nurtured the same hate.

"Then begin inserting your men across the border," said al-Sadr. "They will not engage the Israelis in any way, even if it costs them their own lives. Put them in place, then await my word."

Al-Sadr pointed to a map on the wall behind him. "Tunisia, Yemen, Bahrain are the dominoes that will fall first. And when our Brotherhood stirs up the fury of the poor and oppressed in Egypt, Kamali will receive justice."

"Yes, yes . . . we know all that, Moussa," said the Syrian president with a dismissive wave. "Kamali upholds that blasphemous peace with the Jew and has poured billions into his own bank accounts. He bent his knee to the American dollar. He will receive a just reward for his sins. And the family Saud? They have prostituted themselves for the petrodollars that fuel their debauched lifestyle. Abbudin is a traitor to the faith. We must wipe his family from the face of the earth, yes. But why Qaddafi? Why our friend and ally?"

The force of al-Sadr's hatred swept through the room like a stampede—pushing against dissent. "The king of all kings of Africa?" he mocked. "The man who was the West's greatest enemy when he had courage? Where is he today? Not this whimpering dog who creeps to the door of our enemies for their blessing. This man is your ally? This effete pretender who takes his blonde, Ukrainian 'nurse' with him wherever he goes, flouting the chastity of Islam? This is your ally?"

Baqir waved the back of his hand. "Moussa, we all know you have a vendetta against Qaddafi. It was thirty years ago, if it even happened. With you, it's personal with Qaddafi, it's not political."

Imam Moussa al-Sadr leaned across the table. An old, frail man, yes, but also a physical force of threat and revenge. Baqir moved back in his seat.

"You may unleash your disrespectful tongue and your well-equipped army against your people," al-Sadr said. "You may insult your servants, even your wives, Baqir, but do not believe you can insult me without consequences. You are only president by the will of others—and not the poor, oppressed people of Syria whom you rape every day."

The imam looked long and hard at the president of Syria, then backed away. "My personal interest in our esteemed colonel is a poor cousin to the wrath of Islam. Yes, many years ago Qaddafi's ego was unequaled. He was my enemy then, he is my enemy now. But his attempt to assassinate me is not the reason Libya must fall into our hands. We must control Northern Africa and the Suez Canal to cut off the supply of energy to the West, the oil and gas, even the hope of energy. We must be prepared to defend against an attack from the West, but we will also have the bases from which to launch our attacks against Israel. Libya must fall into the hands of the Brotherhood. Qaddafi is a prancing fool . . . an embarrassment."

"Qaddafi may be a prancing shadow of the man who once defied the West," said Kashmiri, the power behind the Syrian president, "but he will not run. He has nowhere to go. More importantly, he truly believes he has been anointed by Allah as king of Africa. Blood will run deep in the streets of Tripoli—in all the streets of Libya—before Colonel Qaddafi will leave his bunker."

"That bunker will be his grave," snarled al-Sadr. "The Brotherhood will control the Red Sea, the Suez Canal, the Mediterranean from Gibraltar to the Bosporus. The Jew will be surrounded with no help from outside. All will fall under the blade of jihad. All of our enemies, Baqir." Al-Sadr pointed a crooked finger across the table. "All of them. And the world will tremble at the rise of Islam. A friend of our enemies is our enemy, Baqir. It would be wise of you to remember that. Qaddafi has not."

Smiles greeted him from around the table, but they were the smiles of predators waiting to pounce. The smiles warmed what little heart remained in Moussa al-Sadr's chest. One last strike against the Jew. Many paid the price for his hate. But his blood lust remained. More would pay.

9

SUNDAY, AUGUST 2

New York City

Tom loved An Beal Bocht, the revered Irish pub nestled up against the Manhattan College campus in the Riverdale section of the Bronx. It spoke to him of his ancestors . . . of his grandmother, Mary McStravick, who, at the age of nineteen, left behind her family and her life on the farm in Derryclone, County Armagh and sailed to a new life in Philadelphia. Mary was married, had five children, and was widowed within fourteen years of stepping foot in America. And she lived into her nineties. He was from hearty Irish stock.

"I'm glad you gave up," said Connor Bohannon as they left their bikes locked in the sidewalk rack and walked into the pub.

Tom sat down heavily in the corner booth against the front window. "And who was gasping for breath coming up the hill? I was just taking pity on you."

"Sure, Dad. I could tell. Your face was brighter red than the traffic light."

"You have no respect . . . oh, hi, Bronagh," Tom said to the sometime bartender, sometime actress, full-time mom and wife who came to their table. "How about two glasses of cold water, two pints of Guinness, and . . ." He turned to Connor. "Beef stew? Okay, thanks, Bronagh."

The Bocht was quiet. There were still a few hours before musicians showed up for the traditional ceili and Tom soaked in the silence and the joy of just sitting with his son. Connor was twenty-two, two years younger than his sister, Caitlin, and followed his father's legacy by graduating from Penn State a few months earlier. But there were few similarities between Tom and his son, except for how much they looked alike. Connor was long and lean, five inches taller than his father, and wore both his hair and his beard significantly longer than Tom. But his hair was the same coppery red with golden glints, his eyes the same pristine blue, and his smile held the same welcoming warmth.

"Are you going to give this thing up?"

Connor's unannounced question caught Tom by surprise. "What thing? The Guinness?"

"Dad, I'm serious."

Connor swiveled on the bench that sat up against the front window and turned his body to face Tom head-on.

"This whole treasure hunting adventure thing . . . are you going to give that up?"

Tom turned his back into the corner of the booth so he could face his son. Connor's face had the look of someone trying to talk a daredevil out of jumping his motorcycle over the Grand Canyon.

"I think we already have, Connor. I wouldn't be surprised if Doc doesn't send the mezuzah and scroll off to the British Museum with Brandon McDonough."

As if chiseled in granite, Connor's expression didn't change. "You're kidding yourself, Dad. I think all of you are kidding yourselves."

"I don't understand."

"Maybe you don't. Maybe you don't see each other's faces when you talk about the message, when you talk about Jerusalem and the scroll," said Connor, his voice betraying an uncharacteristic urgency. "Maybe you don't hear the excitement in your voices or the palpable burst of adrenaline that rushes through each one of you when you talk about what happened over there. Yeah—you're discouraged by the outcome. You're upset that your discovery brought so much destruction and death when you thought it would bring peace. But it's not over. Not for you, not for the others. You're not ready to give it up yet. You still think you're on some great adventure."

Tom was taken aback, both by the words and by Connor's passion. "Where is this coming from?"

Connor's eyes turned to forged steel, hard and cold.

"Mom's been begging you to quit, to get out of it, to give it up, and you treat her as if she's some child, patting her head and telling her not to worry. Mom's worried, Dad. We're all worried. And we have reason to be worried. There are people out there who will kill you, kill us, to get their hands on that mezuzah and scroll. But I don't think that registers with you."

"Connor, that's all over."

"No! Not really. You talk about our safety, like it matters, but you don't do anything about it. You tell us you want to keep us safe, but you don't throw away the one thing that keeps us all in danger. You're just lying to yourself and to us."

Tom's heart was pierced and his stomach knotted both by his son's accusations and the realization that they were true.

"I . . . I don't . . ."

"You're not willing to give up this so-called adventure. I can tell. Mom can tell. And it makes us feel as if we're not important. As if the only thing that's important is that stupid mezuzah and a message nobody cares about."

Bohannon felt a shiver go up his spine. How could Connor . . .

"But, Connor . . . it is important."

"Important!" Connor slammed his fist against the table. "You still don't get it. What's important is that Caitlin refuses to go back to Fordham at night because she's still afraid of being abducted and that she can't sleep because of the nightmares. What's important is that Mom stares at her coffee cup each morning as if she's a million miles away. What's important is what you are doing to your family and you don't give a . . . awww, what's the use?"

Connor pushed the table away, got to his feet, and was out the door before Tom could think of something to say. He was about to get up and run after him when he saw Bronagh standing at the other side of the table, two steaming dishes in her hands and a look of disbelief on her face.

"Beef stew?"

10

THURSDAY, AUGUST 6

"Do you have any idea what you're requesting?"

"Certainly." Chaim Shomsky tried to appear relaxed, confident. But his confidence was as rumpled as his suit. "We're asking for funds to mount an operation that must never come to the attention of the government, the press, or the Arabs. Even though we believe we know where to look, finding the Tent will be a challenge. But once we get it here and get it set up, any Arab hope will be blocked. We'll be in control of the Mount, and all Jerusalem, once again."

When Shomsky first met him, Meyer Feldberg's eyes were a glittering, glacial blue—the color of the diamonds Feldberg's slaves pulled from the earth of South Africa. That was when the money Feldberg poured into Baruk's political ambitions was fairly clean. But Feldberg's heart later became as black as his tactics and his shadowy associates, and the money became more tainted, with more strings. Polluted by years of cigar smoke and infected with the poison of greed, Feldberg's eyes were now clouded deeply gray, surrounded by bloodshot fractures, tongues of damnation fire flickering in their midst. Feldberg—clearly comfortable in his position, his advantage, and his five-thousand-dollar suit—easily pierced Shomsky's well-honed outer coating of disdain. Once again Shomsky felt the menace of wealth and power in the hands of the ruthless.

"Where did this brainless idea come from?"

"I was talking to a rabbi after the Temple's discovery," said Shomsky, his anger restrained by the bonds of prudence. "He said, 'Next thing you know, someone will find the Tent of Meeting.' And I thought, *why not?*"

"You make it sound so simple," said Feldberg, fit and muscular in his fifties, his bald head as smooth as a baby's cheeks. "Clearly, ignorance is bliss. Sadly, your ignorance of Scripture is legion."

The insult penetrated the folds and rolls of Shomsky's flesh, mixing with the tide of perspiration that flowed beneath his shirt. Shomsky hated meeting in Feldberg's study. It was safer than either man's office, but Feldberg kept his home like a hothouse and Shomsky left each meeting feeling like, and looking like, a well-used dish towel.

Shomsky absently attempted to restore the crease to his pants leg. "You, Meyer . . . you read the Scriptures?" he said, raising his eyes.

Meyer Feldberg picked a cigar from the humidor on the desk, rolled it between his thumb and index finger, lifted it to his nose, and inhaled deeply. His eyes were closed, drinking in the deep aroma of Cuban tobacco. "Choose your words wisely, Chaim. Push the wrong button and"—he picked up the large, gold cigar scissors next to the humidor and neatly sliced the tip off the Cuban—"you might lose something you find precious."

A shiver of ice ran up Shomsky's spine. He'd witnessed the outcome of Feldberg's displeasure firsthand. This man, whose wealth held Eliazar Baruk in bondage, was not one to trifle with. Diverting his gaze to the window, he straightened his tie and squared his shoulders.

"No offense, Meyer. Your knowledge of the Talmud just surprises me."

"There is much about me that would surprise you. If Baruk were more a scholar than a lawyer, he might understand that what he is asking would take a miracle."

Feldberg sat down behind his desk, now a bulwark between him and Shomsky.

"Look," said Feldberg, "there are two monumental problems, at least, facing anyone who hopes to find the Tent of Meeting. First, it's fallen off the face of history without a trace. Second, even if it existed, even if it were found, getting it secretly into Jerusalem—let alone on top of the Temple Mount—would be next to impossible."

Shomsky cursed Baruk, silently, for putting him in this office in the first place. Feldberg's power and arrogance were palpable, and Shomsky always felt like a child in the principal's office, waiting to hear the litany of his sins, each time he was forced to sit across from Feldberg.

Feldberg placed the unlit cigar on the desk and spread his hands apart.

"The Tabernacle was the portable structure the Israelites constructed in the desert, to the specific instructions and dimensions that God gave to Moses on Mount Sinai, and it housed the Ark of the Covenant and the great bronze altar," said Feldberg, as if instructing a child. "It was a huge structure built of wood and hides and it protected two rooms that were built inside the Tent: the Holy place, which was the site of the altar and ritual sacrifice, and the Holy of Holies, where the Ark of the Covenant was kept. The entire Tent was often referred to as the Tabernacle. It was led by the pillar of fire by night and the pillar of smoke by day. This is the structure that Baruk is talking about when he refers to the Tent of Meeting.

"Our number one problem, then, is that no one has seen the Tent for thousands of years. Which makes me doubt whether you or Eliazar could possess any real idea of where the Tent may rest."

"That's it?" With effort, Shomsky managed to sound affronted. "I tell the prime minister, sorry, we've decided that it doesn't exist?"

Feldberg fingered the brass letter opener lying on top of his desk. It brought a smile to his face. Shomsky could visualize its point pressing hard against his throat.

"Look, Chaim, do you want the truth, or do you want some fairy tale? The Tent disappeared from history; it's as simple as that. After the Israelites entered the Promised Land, they eventually set up the Tent of Meeting and the Tabernacle in Shiloh, where the Ark of the Covenant was kept, presided over by the priesthood. In the time of Eli the priest, the Philistines routed the army of the Jews. So the elders decided to bring the Ark from Shiloh and send it into battle with them, expecting God to destroy their enemy. He didn't, the Israelites were defeated, and the Philistines captured the Ark. They didn't keep it long. Supposedly, God sent a plague and the Philistines begged the Israelites to take the Ark back."

Feldberg was still toying with the letter opener, but his eyes were on the cigar. He picked it up and rolled it between his thumb and forefinger. Shomsky could tell keeping it unlit was a true struggle. "So, what happened to the Tent?"

"After the Ark was captured, the Tent of Meeting was taken down and removed to the city of Nob. Remember the story of David eating the shewbread? Scripture says David went into the house of God to eat the shewbread. That was the Tabernacle at Nob. Sometime after that, no one knows when, the Tent was moved from Nob to Gibeon. And it remained in Gibeon until Solomon completed the first Temple.

"And that's where history loses track of the Tent," said Feldberg. "We're told that, when Solomon dedicated the Temple in Jerusalem, he brought up the Ark and the Tent of Meeting and all the sacred furnishings that were in it. And that's the last word recorded in the Scripture about the Tent of Meeting's existence. Not surprising, since the Tent of Meeting was, in effect, the sanctuary that moved with them. With Solomon's Temple constructed, there was no longer any need for another Tabernacle. And it disappears from history. Gone. Poof."

Feldberg was intently studying the tawny richness of the Cuban cigar between his fingers. Slowly, he raised his eyes and bathed Shomsky with a look of thinly veiled contempt.

"So, that's the first challenge. Find it. And I can tell you that we've already started moving on that front. What's the second?"

Feldberg picked up the letter opener. He idly tapped it against his index finger then pointed its tip toward Shomsky's rumpled body. "The second challenge, my strong-backed friend, is picking it up."

He took the unlit cigar, deposited it into the inside pocket of his impeccably tailored suit jacket, pushed himself to the front of the chair, and rested his elbows on the edge of the desk.

Once again, Shomsky felt like he was playing catch with a scorpion. A stab of adrenaline barely masked his fear.

"Because the Tent of Meeting the Israelites carried through the wilderness probably weighed over ten tons . . . twenty thousand pounds. It took six heavily loaded wagons to move the Tent. And the six treasures of the Tabernacle, such as the Ark and the golden altar of incense, were carried on platforms on the shoulders of the Kohathites—eight thousand men. So, tell me, how do you plan to smuggle the Tent and the Tabernacle into Jerusalem, even if you do find it?"

"We plan to bring it in by truck . . . make it look like building material for the Mount."

Feldberg nodded his head. Shomsky could almost see him calculating the angles.

"That might work," Feldberg said. Once again he fiddled with the letter opener. "And I've got a lot invested in Baruk already. I think it's a fool's errand . . . but tell Eliazar he will have his money and he can mount his search."

Shomsky unfolded himself from the chair, anxious to be out of the billionaire's presence.

"But . . ."

He stopped on his way to the door, knowing what was coming next.

"When I have need of a favor," Feldberg said with the silken smoothness of a serpent, "many favors . . . Eliazar would be wise to accommodate my requests. Is that not right, Chaim?"

Despite the suffocating heat in the study, Shomsky shivered as he opened the door.

New York City

Tim Maybry pulled Bohannon into the Bowery Mission chapel. "C'mon, Tom, I know you've got a board meeting," the construction manager argued, "but I need you to look at this. It will only take a minute—and you'll thank me afterward."

The Bowery Mission's renovations had continued during Bohannon's absence in Jerusalem, Maybry's capable leadership and a willing group of workers performing miracles with the old, once dilapidated-looking building. With the precise care of world-class surgeons, not only did they remove decades of paint from the mission's façade, revealing a startling number of architectural wonders hidden for years, but they also came up with an inventive solution for presenting a unified look to the three side-by-side, disparate, different-age buildings that were built with four styles of brick: pink mortar. Mixing red coloring with the mortar, the bricks of each building were re-pointed with the pink mortar, effectively blending the different styles and shades of brick into a cohesive whole.

This morning, Maybry clearly had another goal in mind. A head shorter than Bohannon, Maybry looked more like a school teacher than a construction company owner— slight of frame, tightly trimmed hair, horn-rimmed glasses constantly sliding down his nose. But he had earned his stripes with a string of arresting church buildings. This man knew his stuff. And Tom trusted his opinion.

"We're just about done with repainting the vault roof," Maybry said as they walked, hitching a thumb toward the arched ceiling of the chapel. "We were ready to reinstall the organ pipes—they did a beautiful job of restoration, by the way—when we found a real problem. Here . . . this is shorter."

Maybry swung up on a ladder propped on the chapel's altar. The ladder disappeared into a hole in the ceiling and Bohannon followed Maybry up the rungs. He knew where he was going, even though he wasn't happy about being this high off the floor. Heights were fear-filled. Now he was anxious about more than the board meeting.

Bohannon emerged into a dusty space behind the organ pipes. "Tim, what's wrong?" But Maybry had already crossed the small room, ascended newly constructed stairs, and unlocked an unfinished wooden door. He waited for Bohannon.

They stood together on the top step.

"Look at the floorboards under the safe," said Maybry.

But Bohannon already recognized the problem. The room was the office of the mission's first president, Dr. Louis Klopsch, hidden for nearly one hundred years. On the far side of the room was a massive safe. When the office was discovered during the early stages of the renovation, this safe—more than eight feet wide, five feet high and a good three feet deep—yielded an incredible treasure trove of ancient, museum-quality books, manuscripts, and pamphlets, including the scroll—sealed inside an etched, brass mezuzah—that ultimately launched Bohannon and his motley team of secret-seekers on a quest that tested their courage, character, and faith.

"The boards under the safe have bowed into an unstable arc. The last time I was in here, two weeks ago, they were fine. Something we did when we were shoring up the old organ supports—we needed to do that to keep the organ pipes secure and make sure that one of them didn't suddenly eject itself into the chapel—something caused a shift . . . something changed."

Now Bohannon had another item for the board's agenda.

"The safe has to come out," Bohannon said. Then he looked at the size of the door, the steep steps, and the size of the hole in the floor. "This is going to be interesting."

Bohannon turned to face Maybry. "I'm curious to see how the inventive talents of your crew will solve this problem," he said. "I guess we'll be talking more after the board meeting."

He shot a glance into the small room, and said a prayer that the safe stayed right where it was until they figured something out. At least until the meeting was over and the board members left the building.

11

SATURDAY, AUGUST 8

Tel Aviv, Israel

It often dismayed the prime minister that his beautiful, sprawling home in Tel Aviv had been turned into a virtual fortress. Even the damage done by the recent earthquake disturbed him less than the loss of his idyllic retreat. When Baruk's Kadima party had shocked the political pundits and secured the highest number of seats in the Knesset, Eliazar Baruk woke to find himself prime minister of Israel, titular head of a fragile coalition government, and a prisoner in his own home.

At least that's how it felt now, looking out over the electrified fence, past the armed guards, and beyond the fortified security barrier that separated his long driveway from the rest of the street. He knew the security was necessary, but it stole the serenity from his home.

Baruk was on the veranda, rubbing a cold glass of iced tea against his brow, captured by the velvet aroma of gardenia rising from his garden, when his wife, Shakirya, escorted his guests into the warm afternoon sun.

"Levi . . . Lukas." He shook their hands. "Thank you for coming. Some iced tea?"

Baruk guided his guests to chairs under the trellis as his wife filled their glasses from the pitcher on the sideboard. "Thank you, Shakirya."

Baruk sat across from the two men, measured their unease, and weighed his words. These were trustworthy, proven men of action, not politics.

"We are going to rebuild the Temple Mount," Baruk announced, without preamble. "But I am determined that, unlike the aftermath of the '67 war, Israel will not relinquish its sovereignty over the Mount. To ensure that sovereignty, Israel must allow no political vacuum for the Muslims to exploit. Our sovereignty over the Temple Mount must be clear and unquestioned."

Evaluating the effect of his words, Baruk studied the men sitting in the dappled shade across from him. Clearly, they waited for instructions.

"There is only one thing that would ensure Israel's control of the Temple Mount," said Baruk. "The existence of the Temple in its rightful place atop Mount Moriah. But, should we attempt to begin construction of a new temple, the Arab states would never allow us the time to complete its construction. They would try to stop us. They would call for the world to stop us. We need another solution."

Baruk held their gaze. No one flinched.

"I want you to find the Tabernacle Moses brought through the wilderness. I want you to bring it to Jerusalem, secretly, and be prepared to erect it atop the Temple Mount as soon as the reconstruction is complete."

Baruk sat back in his chair, drank from his glass, and saw surprise register on the faces of Lukas Painter and Levi Sharp as they looked first at each other and then back at the prime minister.

Lukas Painter was director of Mossad, Israel's relentless and feared international intelligence gathering force. Painter was as formidable as the organization he led. The gray stubble that covered his head gave accent to the chiseled cut of both his sculpted muscles and rock-hard jaw. Painter, a battle-scarred warrior, served four different prime ministers over the past fifteen years and still there was neither an ounce of doubt about his duty, nor an ounce of fat on his body.

Levi Sharp was director of Shin Bet, Israel's internal security force, and the polar opposite of Painter. Sharp was recruited as a spook out of university and dispatched to Harvard where he earned his master's in political science. During those summers, Sharp was an invited observer first at FBI headquarters in Washington and then at Interpol headquarters in Paris. Where Painter was larger than life, Sharp was nearly invisible. Slim, bland in appearance and dress, introspective by nature, and quiet by choice, Sharp tended to blend into the background. Only his eyes gave testimony to the Zionist zealot who flirted with fanaticism.

Baruk waited for their barrage of questions.

With a slight nod of his head, Sharp allowed Painter to ask the question. "You know where to start looking, don't you?" asked Painter.

New York City

It was tough for Sammy Rizzo to find anyplace where he could be eye-to-eye with Kallie. Restaurants? He would need a kid's booster seat. And forget going for a walk, or sitting on a park bench.

But Sammy was resourceful and determined. He would engage with Kallie on her own level, no matter what it took.

Plan. Adapt. Plan again. That was Sammy's constant effort. New York City . . . Manhattan . . . was a tough enough place to survive. But for a little person who barely reached chest level on an average guy, New York was a challenge on the scale of Mount Everest. The only beneficial result of the Americans with Disabilities Act was that the city owned a fleet of kneeling buses, but even those were purchased not to help little people get on the bus but to make it easier to get wheelchairs onto the lift ramp.

Normally, these were annoyances that Sammy's cultivated caustic personality would overcome and spit back in the face of the Big Apple. But now, with Kallie, all that had changed.

Size wasn't a problem when they first met—Kallie Nolan doing research in the library on Bryant Park for her master's in archaeology and Sammy ensconced in his specially designed library office where everything was designed to bring him to eye level. That's how they first met . . . on equal terms. Sammy possessing the knowledge and resourcefulness Kallie required.

Now, living on a level plane with Kallie was of utmost importance to Sammy. When they were alone together, he even shed the wise-cracking clown persona that had served him so well since his childhood.

Sammy pushed the plastic container of cheese, crackers, and fruit back across the small, green metal table in Kallie's direction. They were sitting in glorious shade, under the trees along the pathway on the downtown side of Bryant Park, that rectangular oasis of green grass and mature trees that brings grace to Manhattan's manic midtown. Though out of the sun, they were still oppressed by the summer's heat and humidity. The bite of charcoal smoke invaded the shade from a street vendor's food wagon and the voices of many tongues floated between the leaves.

Sammy was perched atop a low brick wall, in just the right relationship to Kallie, who was sitting on one of the park's green, wooden slat chairs.

Kallie picked at the grapes as if they were petals on a daisy. "Sammy," said Kallie as she plucked a plump, green orb, "tell me about us."

Sammy nearly fell off the wall, frantically grabbing for the edge of the stone cap.

"What?" he croaked.

Kallie twiddled another grape. "Us. Tell me about us." She tilted her head over her shoulder to bring Sammy within sight.

Sammy didn't know whether to speak or to breathe. He didn't think he could do both. Kallie shimmered in the dancing shadows of the tree's shade, her bright yellow, sleeveless sundress rivaling its namesake. Her presence, her beauty, always overwhelmed him, dulling the barb in his tongue and bringing to rest a mind that moved with the frenetic pace of an Italian tarantella. He sat, stalled . . . unable to process his next thought. A burst of laughter floated across the broad, central lawn.

"Us? . . . Well, I thought we were friends," said Sammy, trying to evade the question.

But Kallie threw a grape and hit him square in the chest of his new shirt, a proper blue, broadcloth, button-down topping a pair of clean, neatly pressed khakis. "Talk to me, Rizzo," she demanded.

Truth . . . could he tell her the truth? What would happen then? Ooohh . . . There was no escape.

Sammy ducked his head to avoid Kallie's gaze. "I like you, I like you a lot. You're very important to me, Kallie. But I'm not a fool. I'm not blind. I see how men look at you, then look at me, then look back at you with an unanswered question on their faces. *What is she doing with him?* How long? How long could you live like that—companion to a man who some people think belongs in a circus?"

"Look at me."

He processed a long sigh, then forced his eyes to hers.

"You're precious to me, Sammy Rizzo." Her eyes searched his face. "You saved my life . . . yes, I knew it was you who threw your body on top of mine when the bullets were flying as we escaped from the kibbutz . . . and you rescued me from jail. You have comforted me, quietly, without demands, as I grieved the loss of my profession and my adopted country. You've treated me with respect and honor . . . rare among some of the other men I've known."

"Then? . . ."

"I don't know *then*," said Kallie. "I only know *now*. Now, it's a privilege for me to walk beside you. It's a pleasure to spend time with you. And I'm grateful

that you trust me enough to allow me to see inside the jokester. But, Sammy
. . . I don't know if this, us, is going anywhere. Not because you're short. But
because I don't know where I am. Or where I'm going."

Kallie put her right hand on his.

"I don't want to disappoint you or hurt you," she said. "I don't want you to
expect something, hope for something, from me that I just can't give right now.
Please understand. My life came to a crashing halt. I was thrown out of my
home without a moment to think about it. I don't know what I'm feeling right
now or what I'm going to do."

Sammy could hear the pleading in her voice, the sincerity of her emotion.

"I want us to be friends a long time. Something else? I don't know. But
. . . but, this I do know. You are one of the finest men I've ever met, Sammy
Rizzo—no matter what charade you play on the outside. I respect you, your
courage, your heart. I don't care about how tall you are, Sammy. I care about
the size of your heart. I don't want to wound that heart."

Kallie stood up. "Friends. Can you accept that?"

Sammy looked at Kallie. "Sure," he said, and his voice didn't crack.

12

Washington, DC

"You're back . . . don't you spend any time over at Langley?"

The bright afternoon sun flooded the Oval Office windows, washing Jonathan Whitestone's back with warmth and causing Bill Cartwright to squint and turn his head to the side. "I don't have any good news for you."

"Why am I not surprised?" the president said absently. "When was the last time we had any good news, Bill?" Whitestone signed the last of the stack of documents and passed them to the aide waiting beside his desk, gesturing the young woman out of the Oval Office. Whitestone rose from behind the *Resolute* desk, walked across the carpet woven with the presidential seal, and fell into one of the facing sofas. "C'mon, Bill, sit down. This sounds like it may take awhile."

The CIA director sat in the sofa facing the president and rested three manila folders on the table between them.

Whitestone liked Cartwright because he was a no-nonsense, pragmatic veteran of both business and government. Whitestone trusted Cartwright because the two had been prayer and accountability partners for two decades. Right now, Whitestone needed both Cartwright's counsel and his integrity. The president could see dark days ahead and believed Cartwright was not going to dispel any of that darkness with his report.

"Baruk has decided to rebuild the Temple Mount," Cartwright said.

Whitestone felt the bottom drop out of his stomach. Even in the August heat and humidity, Whitestone kept his office air-conditioning to the minimum. He liked it warm . . . it kept his muscles from tightening any more than necessary in the pressure cooker of the Oval Office. Still, he felt a chill ripple across his shoulders and a half-breathed sigh escape his lips.

"Whose bright idea is this folly? Don't tell me . . . Shomsky, right?"

"Seems like he's convinced Baruk that this is the prime minister's moment in history . . . his chance to make history," Cartwright replied.

"His chance to stop history."

"There's more . . . they're—"

"Wait—Shomsky doesn't know about the raid, does he?"

"As far as we know, only Baruk, Orhlon, Painter, and Sharp know of the plans."

Whitestone's hands came up in front of him as if his fingers were asking a question. "Then what is Baruk doing? How can he pull a stunt like this when we're already—"

"Mr. President . . . that's not all," said Cartwright. "They're not going to let the Arabs come back to the Mount. In fact, they're not going to allow anything to come back to the Mount. They plan to rebuild the platform in the name of safety and then allow it to remain empty."

Whitestone felt confused. "What?" He pushed himself to the edge of the sofa. "What's the point? Why rebuild the Mount and then enrage the Arabs by not allowing them to rebuild the Dome or the Al-Aqsa Mosque? That doesn't make sense, Bill, not even for Shomsky. What are they planning? Baruk's not stupid. He must know what he's doing."

"Yes, sir. The Israelis have a plan for the Mount. They're just not making it public."

The president held his breath and held his tongue. *Oh, Lord . . . what?*

"The Israelis are searching for the Tent of Meeting. They're already planning an incursion into western Jordan to search Mount Nebo . . . the place where the book of Maccabees says Jeremiah buried the Ark and the Tent. If they can secure the Tent of Meeting, Baruk intends to erect the Tent on Temple Mount . . . I guess he figures he can get it up before any protests hit. With the Tent on the Mount, the Israelis, Baruk believes, will have a legitimate claim to sovereignty over Temple Mount."

Whitestone settled back into the corner of the sofa. His silver hair was perfectly cut, his navy blue suit impeccable. But he felt panic fighting to emerge from his calm exterior.

"But, the *Tent*? Come on, Bill, how can we—how can anyone—believe that the Tent of Meeting still exists? There's not been a mention of the Tent of Meeting in, what, two thousand years?"

"Three . . . three thousand," said Cartwright.

"Right, three thousand years without a word. The existence of the Tent of Meeting is about as close to impossible as you can get. Even if Baruk and Shomsky have thrown themselves into this fool's search, this is not something we seriously need to concern ourselves with. Right?"

Cartwright held the president's gaze. "The existence of the Tent is as close to impossible as keeping a secret Temple hidden under the mountain for over a thousand years. It's about as close to impossible as a handwritten copy of the book of Jeremiah surviving for fifteen hundred years in a clay jar near the Dead Sea. Mr. President, who is to say what's impossible if we are truly in the final season of God's plan for mankind?"

A subtle twitch. It was deep inside his chest, to the left. Barely discernible. The president felt it, and knew he had felt it before. Too much stress. *God, what am I doing?* Whitestone felt tired, worn down to the marrow of his bones. But anger pulsed life into his body. Baruk had betrayed his trust.

"This is insane," said Whitestone. "Forget the Tent. If Israel rebuilds the Temple Mount and forbids the Arabs from coming back, the Muslim nations will go berserk. Baruk is just asking for a war."

"Yes, sir. And it couldn't come at a worse time. Abu Gherazim has, indeed, been appointed foreign minister of the Palestinian Authority. He's planning a major speech for next week, from Amman, with the Jordanian king at his side."

"Great . . . we finally get a Muslim moderate leader who's willing to speak out for peace, for compromise, for benevolent coexistence between Palestinian and Jew, and Baruk is ready to blow up any possibility for peace in the Middle East." President Whitestone raised his piano-player fingers and rubbed above his top lip. "How did Gherazim manage to get himself appointed? That's a bit of a shock, too."

Bill Cartwright opened the top manila folder, extracted a photograph, and passed it to the president. "Seems like somebody found out about the family heritage Gherazim has worked so hard to hide."

Whitestone had seen the photo before . . . two young men in black kaftans and turbans, gazing seriously into the lens, standing in front of an unidentified mosque. "I guess having a brother who was the founder of Hezbollah finally paid a dividend. Is Gherazim thinking of turning his name back to al-Sadr?"

"Not anytime soon," said Cartwright. "I'm sure he's going to be Abu Gherazim for the foreseeable future. He hates the memory and the legacy of his brother. Realistically, he remembers al-Sadr as a terrorist and murderer. I don't see how he's been able to walk that tightrope over there . . . he's really a target for both sides . . . but, for now, he's the only voice calling for the reformation of Islam from the inside out. We need Abu Gherazim, Jon. We need him for any possibility of peace in the Middle East."

Once again, the president felt the weight of the world settle on his shoulders. His shoulders, literally, were beginning to ache from the load.

The president looked up. "What do we do now?"

Cartwright opened the second manila folder, extracted another photograph, and passed it to the president. Whitestone looked at the picture of an etched, bronze mezuzah. "You think there's something here?"

"It's possible," said Cartwright. "If the mezuzah and scroll led to the Third Temple, who's to say they might not also lead to something else . . . something like the Tent of Meeting? The priest, Abiathar, was a resourceful man. Perhaps there are some clues here we could use. And we need something to get us out in front of the Israelis . . . either to convince them to abandon this reckless plan or to intervene in some other way. Like find the Tent first. That's why we need all the help we can find."

The president shook his head at the implied suggestion.

Whitestone turned the photo over, as if there might be a surprise clue on its reverse side. "Bring Bohannon and his team back into this? Why? Why do we need them, and why would they come? They're civilians, Bill. Good grief, they almost got killed the last time. Why don't we just leave them alone and see what we can find out on our own?"

Cartwright was shaking his head as he opened the third manila folder. This one contained several pages of paper containing what looked like a series of images, accompanied by a single sheet of paper. The CIA director passed the sheets with the images to the president.

"When I started thinking about Bohannon, there was something nagging at the back of my mind," said Cartwright. "So I asked our boys in the satellite room to make a few passes over the New York City area. Without a direct threat, we don't usually shoot visuals over the States, but we do get residual infrared. Our guys dialed in on the area around Bohannon's home in Riverdale."

On the sheets were three thermal images—like photo negatives—taken around a house. The image was only in tones of gray, but it was remarkably clear. The president could easily identify the shapes of bodies in each image.

"They come and go at different times," said Cartwright, handing over the last sheet of paper. "It's random, sporadic, not always the same number."

The president scanned down the page. So many dates and times.

"We went back over the last few days and pulled up what we could. This has been going on for a while. Somebody has been watching Bohannon's house. And I'll bet they're wearing lightning-bolt amulets.

"We've alerted NYPD," said Cartwright, "and they're stepping up patrols . . . will try to keep an unmarked car in the vicinity. But, even though it's still the Bronx, that part of Riverdale is very suburban—heavily wooded, houses spread out, long, deep, wild areas along the Hudson. Nearly impossible to control."

President Whitestone looked at the thermal images once more. "Oh . . . Oh, God help them."

New York City

The solution was up instead of down.

The Bowery Mission's main, five-story building, fronting on Bowery, was constructed specifically for the mission in 1909. Directly behind that structure was a three-story building, fifty years older, that was originally the location of a casket maker. Flanking the 1909 building which housed the chapel, on the uptown side of Bowery, was the oldest structure, a Federal-style, two-story building that now housed the mission's kitchen and dining hall.

Three days after meeting with Maybry, Bohannon stood atop the casket maker's building and watched as a long-necked crane, with Louis Klopsch's ancient safe suspended in a reinforced pouch from its tip, began to retract from the hole in the building's roof.

It was a good time to move the safe. Activity around the mission was at its lowest point on a Sunday evening, minimizing the risk to others. Traffic should be cooperative, and there was still plenty of daylight remaining to complete the move. The safe itself was mammoth, heavy, and dangerous. Huge double doors spanned the entire front of the steel safe, still painted a flat black with decorative stencil designs at the corners. Maybry at his side, Bohannon watched as the crane drew itself back into Freeman's Alley, a frighteningly narrow right-of-way behind the mission. With the care of a porcelain maker, the crane operator lowered the safe onto the waiting deck of a flatbed truck.

While teamsters scurried around the truck, securing the safe, Bohannon and Maybry made their way down the fire escape.

"Too bad you guys couldn't just get rid of it," said Maybry. "This is costing a mint."

"It's part of Bowery Mission legend now, part of our history," said Bohannon. "And not to forget, the assortment of books and manuscripts that were preserved in that safe—most of them—earned six million dollars for the Mission."

They reached the ground, slipped past the crane, and circled the truck, testing the tautness of the cables and straps that held the safe in place—just as the teamsters had done three times already. "Well, they'll take good care of it at the library," said Maybry. "That will be a sweet, little exhibit commemorating your trip to Israel."

"You make it sound like we went on vacation."

Maybry shrugged and walked over to the driver as he began to climb into the cab. "This truck is awfully narrow."

"Hey, Mack, that's all that would fit up this alley."

"Okay . . . okay," said Maybry, holding up his hands. "Just take it easy, okay? That's a lot of weight there and not a very wide base to carry it."

"Don't worry about it, Mack," said the driver as he started up the diesel. "Once we get out of here, and around the corner on Bowery, it's almost a straight shot to the library: right up Third Avenue, one left-hand turn on 39th Street then two rights to come up alongside the library at Bryant Square. They're waiting for us to put this baby in place. It's as good as home. What you should be worried about is that hole in the roof."

〰〰〰

Tarik Ben Ali sat in a stolen taxicab at the corner of Third Avenue and Fifth Street, opposite Cooper Square, his "Out of Service" lamp lit, as he surveyed the traffic coming up Third Avenue.

There had been little time to prepare. Only by watching the mission had they discovered the safe was being moved. Only two hours ago they learned, from a talkative truck driver, where the safe was going and how it would get there. Now Ben Ali hoped they had made the right decisions.

St. Mark's Place at Third Avenue was the target. That was an easy decision. The intersection was a major crossroads of both vehicular traffic and pedestrians—crowded, confusing, at almost all hours of the day and night, with cars and people constantly jostling for position to get across the street. Two of Ben Ali's team sat at an outdoor table of Ray's Pizza, just off the corner. They were ready to move as soon as he signaled.

Earlier, looking at their map, they planned the best route to the warehouse in Queens. With Allah's good favor, they should be well hidden before anyone knew the truck was missing.

———

The flatbed inched up Third Avenue. Not because of traffic . . . the traffic was light this time on a Sunday evening. But more because the driver was concerned about shifting weight. The safe was securely strapped to the truck. It wasn't going anywhere. But the relative size of the safe, calculated against the narrow width of the truck bed, made every bump in the street, every pothole or sinkhole, an adrenaline-pumping adventure.

A cab crossed two lanes of Third Avenue without signaling and jerked to a stop in front of the truck.

"Yo . . . Mack," the driver shouted as he laid heavy on his air horn.

Shocked by the horn blast, a lady with a little white dog jumped into the cab and it took off up Third Avenue.

"Crazy cab drivers will drive me nuts," the truck driver muttered to himself as he slowed for the busy intersection at St. Mark's Place.

———

Tarik Ben Ali watched as the truck with the safe nearly collided with a taxi cab just short of the intersection with Fifth Street. The truck's horn blast made him jump in his seat. He picked up the cell phone and speed dialed the number.

———

Gil, the truck driver, eased to a stop at St. Mark's Place. This was not a bad spot to catch a red light. Lots of NYU coeds lived in the dorms a block away and the parade this evening kept his attention from the taxi that came up close on his left.

Before the light turned green, the taxi driver hit his horn, bulled his way through the pedestrians, and suddenly pulled the cab across the right-most lane, right in front of Gil's truck.

"What are you, nuts?" Gil roared, leaning forward on his massive steering wheel as he tried to get a better look at the cab. Pedestrians trying to navigate the street crossing were shouting, gesturing at the taxi as they poured around it on both sides. "Get outta there. You're an idiot!"

He didn't hear the door open, but he sensed the movement to his right. He turned to see a dark-haired man climbing into his truck cab. Words formed on his lips, action flexed in his biceps. But, before he could react, he heard the door open behind him, a searing pain throbbed through the back of his head, and the lights went out.

———≈∽∼———

Ben Ali opened the back door of the taxi as Mustafa steered the semiconscious man toward it.

"Hey, what are you doin?" someone asked.

"We need to get him home," Mustafa said as they poured Gil into the back seat. "Too much to drink."

Mustafa ran back to the passenger side of the truck and jumped in. As the traffic light turned green, Ben Ali turned the taxi back up Third Avenue, followed closely by the hijacked vehicle. Both the taxi and the truck traveled the short distance to Stuyvesant Street and turned right, taking the diagonal street over to Tenth. Ben Ali tried desperately not to speed, even though his adrenaline was pumping. They both got through the traffic lights at First Avenue and Avenue A, but the lumbering truck caught the red at Avenue B and Tenth. Ben Ali pulled the taxi to the curb on the far side of the street. He jumped out, ran around the taxi, pulled open the rear door, and dragged the half-conscious truck driver out of the back seat and across the sidewalk. As he planted the driver against the stoop of a walkup, between two trash cans, he pushed the button on his cell phone.

"Drive beyond me and I will fall in behind. It will be easier for me to follow. Make a left at the next street, Avenue C, and go straight. You will see the entrance. Don't miss the road. We need to get across the bridge quickly."

———∼∼∼———

At least the truck was moving more quickly now. They crossed 14th Street and drove under the raised highway, taking the slight left onto the access road for FDR Drive. As he drove up the ramp, Ben Ali stole a quick glance at the truck in front of him, then at the map on the seat beside him. Good . . . the FDR would take them directly to the 59th Street Bridge, which would deposit them safely in Queens.

The truck was not speeding, by any means. Ben Ali had given strict instructions that they be very careful with the heavy load but, most of all, that they remain below the posted speed limit. So why were so many of the cars on this road honking their horns at the truck . . . many of the drivers gesturing toward Mustafa. He didn't understand.

They came to the tunnel that carries the FDR under the United Nations Plaza and, for a moment, Ben Ali was afraid the safe wouldn't clear the tunnel's low entry. He took a breath as the truck made it into the tunnel, but froze when a white NYPD cruiser raced by on his left, its lights flashing like an alien apparition.

The police cruiser closed on the truck and pulled up alongside.

"Pull the truck over," he could hear through his open window.

The truck began to increase speed, the exit for the 59th Street Bridge just ahead.

"Pull the truck over . . . now!" came the order from the police car as it added its sirens to its array of flashing lights.

The truck closed rapidly on the exit, a big, sweeping, left-turning curve. Ben Ali's eyes opened wide. As the truck careened into the exit's curve, the safe began to shift to the right. The truck bed settled down on the right tires and the left tires looked as if they were about to leave the ground. The police cruiser braked heavily to get behind the truck and away from the safe. Ben Ali's tires were screaming as he jammed on his brakes to avoid both the police car and the dangerously listing truck.

At what seemed like the last moment, the truck straightened out. But the exit curve did not. The truck slammed into the concrete barrier on the outside of the curve, pushed it aside, and continued on into the ramp of oncoming traffic exiting from the downtown side of the FDR.

It was mayhem. As oncoming cars slammed into each other trying to avoid a collision with the flatbed, the truck crossed the far ramp, ran up onto the sidewalk, and came to rest in a small park beside a veterinary hospital. The safe sat at the edge of the flatbed, then, as if it were rising from sleep, the truck rolled ponderously over onto its right side, the safe gouging a huge chunk of grass out of the park.

The police cruiser, pulled over to the berm of the exit curve, sat empty, its doors open, as the two uniformed officers, guns drawn, zigzagged through the mangled cars toward the truck.

Shaken, but not panicked, Ben Ali eased the taxi around the stopped police cruiser and slowly inched his way onto 61st Street. The carnage was behind him, but his eyes were on the flatbed truck, and the two police officers who were staring into the empty cab, already calling in for help.

Allah be praised. They will know where to meet me.

―⁓〰―

Once the city's Parks Department cleansed Bryant Park of its drug dealers, pimps, prostitutes, and most pickpockets, and renovated the broad, green expanse on 42nd Street between Fifth and Sixth avenues, New York City gained its most beautiful midtown oasis. Gravel walkways under broad shade trees bordered the well-tended grass rectangle that welcomed luncheon picnics, sunbathers, and Monday Movie Nights several times during the summer.

To rid the park of its darker element, the city installed lights—lots of them—antique-looking, copper patina lampposts with frosted-glass globes. Cosmopolitan cute, they gave off plenty of light, enough to dispel most shadows, even under the trees.

Which left Kais and Aziz little cover. There was even less shadow surrounding the massive Humanities and Social Sciences Library that fronted Bryant Park along Fifth Avenue. There was no way to be invisible.

It was late Sunday night. There were a few strolling couples crossing through the park. Traffic on 42nd Street was a trickle of its normal deluge. A light breeze carried the smell of pizza across the lawn and gently mussed the leaves on the plane trees. It was quiet.

On their third circuit around the perimeter of the park and library they identified their best chance of entry. At the back corner of the library building, on the northwest side of the park along 42nd Street, there was a prewar, stone public restroom, now closed. Behind the stone restroom, which stood on its own, separated from the shuttered restaurants along the library's rear terrace, was a dark, sheltered space to store trash. Behind that, toward the back of the library building, was a small, wooded plot that was relatively isolated. Across a wide gravel walkway from the plot, a set of stone stairs dropped down from the building's surrounding wall into the darkness of the library's northeast corner. The stairs were guarded by a locked, wrought-iron gate.

And a security guard, sitting on the wall, having a smoke.

Kais looked at his watch. Time spilled from his window of opportunity.

He tapped Aziz on the arm, and they slipped around the far side of the restroom, ducked into the shadow surrounding the dumpster, then crawled through the darkness of the wooded plot, toward the gate and the guard. Coptic cross amulets—with the lightning bolt slashing through on the diagonal—dangled outside of their shirts.

Kais crossed the gravel path, hesitating in the shadow of a large bush that flanked the gate and butted against the wall. He could smell the guard's body odor.

Thrashing loudly, Aziz emerged from the darkness of the wooded plot onto the sidewalk of 42nd Street and immediately captured the guard's attention. As the guard tossed away his cigarette and motioned in the direction of Aziz— "Hey, you"—Kais slid to the side of the bush away from the guard's vision. A two-sided blade in his right hand, Kais placed his foot on a jutting piece of the wall and drew his arm back.

A brilliant shaft of light exploded in the night, bathing Kais in its blue-white illumination, the knife poised to swing into the sitting guard's neck.

"Don't move . . . not an inch."

Kais's eyes shifted to the left, to the gravel walkway, and traveled down the shaft of light. He heard the guard dismounting the wall as he saw a blue-uniformed New York policeman emerge from the shadow of the wooded plot, a service revolver resting across the arm that held the flashlight. Kais began to raise his hands, then shoved off his left foot and rolled his body to clear the wall.

He heard the noise and was spun around like a rag doll by the pain that incinerated his chest. By the time his body hit the sidewalk, he heard no more.

⌇⌇⌇

The darkness was intense on the western side of the building, in the small alleyway between the Collector's Club and the apartment building at the corner of 35th Street and Madison Avenue. At 3:30 on a Monday morning, New York's streets are mostly abandoned, silent strips of asphalt. An occasional taxi. A bus. Then the unnatural quiet.

Ali Suliman—dressed entirely in black, his head and face, except his dark eyes, covered by a black hood—edged down the side of the building, feeling for the service door he knew was cut into the stone foundation. In his right hand he held the "scrambler," a high-powered, microwave-impulse transmitter designed to confuse and countermand any electronic security system, converting its programmed security code to a new code supplied by the scrambler device. Suliman located the touch pad beside the service door, positioned the scrambler under it, and triggered the intense impulse. He took a deep breath, punched in the counterfeit code, gingerly pushed against the heavy metal door, and waited for any telltale sign of an alarm.

The door swung easily inward. Suliman stepped quickly into the dark of the building, disappearing into the shadows, out of sight of the closed circuit cameras. He saw the blinking red and green lights of the building's internal security apparatus on the wall to his right, placed the scrambler against the face of the metal box, just below the keypad, and triggered a second pulse. The lights all burned green, and steady, and Suliman breathed once again.

━━∿∽━━

So much for electronic gadgetry. The ornamental wrought-iron gate guarding the Collector's Club vault and archives was secured not by digital electronics but by a much more fundamental security system. A padlock . . . a huge padlock, its hasp girded with strips of wound steel, a half-inch tempered steel shackle, impervious to bolt cutters, holding it in place. Suliman shrugged.

He placed the black duffle bag in his left hand on the marble floor, unzipped the top, and withdrew a device about two feet long, a muffled electric motor at one end, attached to two steel arms, side-by-side, with flat, spade-shaped, grooved pads at the ends. Suliman positioned the arms of the device between two of the wrought-iron bars, pushed a button on the motor, and watched the arms swing outward until they touched the bars. Then the bars began to move, pushed apart by the small, but powerful, arms of a miniature version of the Jaws of Life.

Twenty minutes later, Suliman squeezed through a ragged, two-foot-wide opening in the wrought-iron gate. He ignored the priceless archives of the world's rarest stamps arranged in wooden bins and cabinets to his left and moved with purposeful haste to the vault on the right, behind the proctor's desk, hidden by thick, dark green velvet drapes. His heartbeat quickened as he eased the drapes aside and stepped up to the face of the vault. His right hand rose, fingers out-stretched toward the metal vault, but stopped in midair.

He saw this style vault once before, when the Prophet's Guard attempted to break into a secure diamond deposit vault in South Africa. This was not what he was told to expect. The vault door was imprinted with the highest level Swiss Security rating, UL3. A fingerprint scanner he expected to be able to deal with. But this? The fingerprint scanner on this safe required a unique customer code and a biometric hand scan before access was permitted to the fingerprint scan. Worse for Ali Suliman was the seismic alarm which would detect any vibration in the walls, floor, or ceiling of the vault. Neither his skill nor the scrambler would overcome this vault's security. A bomb would fail to move the double-plated, welded doors.

Suliman stood before the vault, absently fingering through his black shirt the amulet that hung around his neck. This vault was an unexpected impediment, a barrier to overcome. Somehow, he would discover a way to fulfill his mission.

Suliman moved away from the vault as if it were a sleeping infant. And his eyes fell on the ragged hole he had ripped in the room's wrought-iron gate. Only, now, the task had become much more difficult.

⟨⁓⌣⁓⟩

There were only five of them now, huddled around a table in the back corner of Berket, a twenty-four-hour Middle Eastern gyro and hummus fast-food eatery on Houston Street on the Lower East Side.

The chagrined driver of the flat-bed truck had his arm, broken from the whipsawing steering wheel, in a makeshift sling. Mustafa, the right half of his body darkened by the ground-in dirt from their abrupt encounter with the park, held a wet towel, filled with ice, against the purple knot growing above his right eyebrow.

The other two sat slackened in their chairs, with the vacant look of unbelief, so common to disaster victims, imprinted upon their faces.

Tariq Ben Ali felt the same sense of despair and desperation as the others. Yet he could not mentor these men in doubt. They had been chosen for this task, set apart by their leader. Ben Ali would not allow them to fail. Yet . . . what to do?

"We will not break into the vault," said Suliman. "Never. And soon they will know we were there."

Ben Ali turned to face Aziz.

"Are you sure Kais was dead?" Ben Ali was not mourning. He wanted to ensure there was no chance they were betrayed.

"His back came apart like a ripe melon," said Aziz, his eyes on the dirty floor. "I saw it before I ran into the park. He was dead."

Ben Ali nodded his head. "In a few hours they will realize the mistakes they have made. They will know we are here. As long as the scroll is inside that vault, it is out of our grasp. But the mezuzah . . ." Ben Ali scratched the stubbly beard that vainly tried to cover his chin. "They may not realize what it is we seek. Perhaps the mezuzah is also lost to us . . . unless they are fools. We will wait to see what kind of fools they are."

13

MONDAY, AUGUST 10

New York City

The dirt-and-grass-covered steel safe was too big to fit into an evidence locker. So the officer on duty directed the freight haulers to put it into a corner where he sealed it off behind some spare cyclone fencing attached to rickety wood slats, wrapping the whole thing in overlapping layers of yellow crime-scene tape.

"We got lucky that they were driving a truck illegally on the FDR," said Rory O'Neill, commissioner of the New York City Police Department. "It took awhile for the precinct captain to get the mess on the FDR cleaned up and gather the reports of all the officers involved. It was late when he saw the incident report about the shooting on 42nd Street. But he's a good man. He picked up the connection right away and immediately contacted the duty officer at Central Command. They had patrol cars outside the mission, the library, and the Collector's Club within ten minutes. The club was dark and quiet. There were no alarms. It was only this morning, when they opened, that the break-in was discovered."

Tom Bohannon wrestled with the panic that held his life in bondage. "Nothing was taken?"

"No," said O'Neill. "But . . . we know the stamps weren't the target."

It was whispered, almost a thought. "Then it wasn't a drunk driver."

"What?" asked O'Neill.

"The black SUV." Eyes closed, pulling air into his lungs, Bohannon turned away from the safe, toward O'Neill.

"They're back," he said.

"'Fraid so," said O'Neill.

"I thought . . . maybe it was over." His words fell from his lips with a weight as heavy as the safe.

Jerusalem

"One of the assassins is dead. The others have vanished."

He could sense outrage rising in the silence.

"How do you know such a thing?"

Leonidas thought the new imam a fool. His laugh was an intended insult.

"Because I know more than you, and because what I tell you is true. That is why you pay me such exorbitant sums."

"We pay you for information, Mister Leonidas, not for insults."

"It's not *mister* anything. Just call me Leonidas. And you pay me to keep Shin Bet off the necks of the Northern Islamic Front. You pay me in order to have the freedom to operate, the freedom to exist. Without me, you and your faithful would be in jail tomorrow. You don't pay me for information. You pay me for disinformation. The information I throw in for free."

Leonidas allowed the silence on the cell phone to build. "I do it because it amuses me," he said. "That is why I have returned."

Once again, he let the tension and the silence build. This imam—the arrogant, half-wit brother of the murdered imam Leonidas originally engaged—might bully his ignorant followers in En Sherif, his splinter group from the Northern Islamic Front. But Leonidas would buy none of his bluster. This imam was, of course, a fanatic. But he was also a fool. As a fool, he would not survive long against Israel's internal security forces, the Shin Bet. Leonidas needed to extort as much money from this man as quickly as possible. He wouldn't be around long. Neither would Leonidas.

"So," said the imam, properly chastened, "the Prophet's Guard did not succeed?"

Better, thought Leonidas. *Better.*

"No, they did not succeed. The Americans still have the scroll and the mezuzah. But, be assured, the Prophet's Guard still has men in New York who are both determined and ruthless. Their attempts at recovering the scroll, or destroying those who possess it, are not over."

"Good . . . good," said the imam. "I am pleased. It would grieve me deeply should the Prophet's Guard succeed."

Leonidas believed it was only a matter of time until the Prophet's Guard did succeed in fulfilling its quest. Those men were relentless, and single-minded. But, let the fool learn that for himself.

"You still have your opportunity. Take it if you can," said Leonidas, uncertain of the imam's ability to exact any revenge. "I'll be checking my account. You know the number."

He hung up before the imam could respond.

Perhaps a month . . . perhaps two. Then he would find a place to hide in the South Pacific. He would hide well. He already knew that secret.

Washington, DC

It seemed to President Whitestone that his heart was racing all the time now, ever since the earthquake in Jerusalem changed everything. As he closed the door to the Oval Office, he laid a hand against his chest, and the racing beat forced him to take in a deep breath before he turned to face Bill Cartwright once again.

"You're sure these guys were Prophet's Guard?" asked Whitestone.

"Yes, Mr. President. They hit the library, the Collector's Club, and tried to hijack the mission's safe, nearly all at the same time. And the one who was shot wore the amulet."

"Why?" asked Whitestone. "Why are they still after the scroll?"

Cartwright crossed the Oval Office and looked out the windows to the Rose Garden. It appeared to the president that his CIA chief was leaning heavily on the wood frame of the door. "I don't think it matters why," said Cartwright, his voice low, speaking almost to himself. "Sir," he said, turning back to the room, "Reynolds will be here soon. We need his help." He walked over and sat across from the president before continuing.

"You and I are pretty confident that God has been using Tom Bohannon in a powerful way recently. Someone else may have been able to decipher that code. But not only did Tom—and his friends—decipher a code in an extinct Egyptian language, they then followed the clues in the message, evaded Israeli intelligence agencies, survived attacks and three days under the Temple Mount, and found the key to a stunning, regional peace in the Middle East. For two librarians, a retired academic, and a guy who runs a homeless shelter, that's quite a feat. How could they have accomplished all of that—and survived—on their own strength, their own ability?

"But," said Cartwright, "if God's hand was in this, then it probably still is. If God has a plan he's working out through Tom Bohannon, I don't think that plan has been completed. Do you?"

"No," said the president, "I guess not."

"Then we need Bohannon's help. We need Reynolds on board . . . I believe he can carry the message."

A knock on the door . . . and Sam Reynolds stepped into the Oval Office.

Whitestone got up from the sofa and turned toward the door. "Sam, thanks for getting here so quickly."

"Of course, Mr. President."

"Sit down, Sam. Bill?"

Cartwright wasted no time. "Last night there was a break-in at the Collector's Club in New York City, an attempted break-in at the Humanities and Social Sciences Library, and the Bowery Mission safe—the one that held the mezuzah and scroll—was hijacked while it was being moved to the library. The safe was recovered."

Reynolds moved his gaze from Cartwright to the president, and Whitestone could read the question in his eyes. "It was the Prophet's Guard," said the president. "One of them was killed by a policeman. He was wearing the amulet."

"They're back?" asked Reynolds, shaking his head. "How's Tom, his family?"

"Pretty shaken, I'm sure," said Cartwright. "They're okay, but I'm also sure Bohannon hoped he was done with all this, that somehow this cross would pass him by and leave him to live his life."

Whitestone hated this part. But he knew it had to be done. They had to be sure.

"Sam," said the president, "I want you to go see Bohannon. Seems the Guard is awfully hot to get the scroll back. We need to know why. We need to find out if there is anything else that Bohannon knows that we don't . . . anything about the scroll that we should know . . . that might help us deal with the situation in Israel. We need his help."

The president watched as one question after another flashed across Sam Reynolds's face. He was encouraged when Reynolds didn't ask any of the obvious ones.

"Excuse me, Mr. President, but I don't understand. The Middle East has exploded, but not because there was a temple discovered under the Temple Mount. Hezbollah has taken over the government in Lebanon and they still have forty thousand rockets sitting in the Bekaa Valley near the border and pointed at Israel; corruption and riots have crumbled the government in Tunisia, the Muslim Brotherhood engineered an overthrow of President Kamali in Egypt, Qaddafi is dead and buried, and Libya is in a shambles. All of it part of this so-called Arab Spring that is spawning revolution in nearly every Muslim capital in the region. Al-Musawi is butchering his own people in Syria, and we're sitting on the brink of a third land war in Asia. So why do we care about a temple that's now destroyed? Why do we need Bohannon? We've got enough on our hands."

"All very true, Sam," said the president. He moved to the edge of the sofa, rested his arms on his knees, and stared hard at Reynolds, trying to take stock of this young man—a career diplomat from the State Department who had the chutzpah to lay his career on the line when he thought it was the right thing to do.

"Whoever is behind this reincarnation of the Muslim Brotherhood has a lot more planned than the overthrow of an oligarch in Egypt. The sands in the Middle East are shifting so fast we don't know where we stand. But let me tell you something that you and the State Department don't know. Baruk has not only decided to rebuild the Temple Mount, but he's also got both Mossad and Shin Bet looking for the Tent of Meeting. He thinks, if he can find it—a big *if*—he can erect the Tent of Meeting on the Temple Mount and solidify Israel's claim of sovereignty."

Reynolds looked as if someone had offered him a gold Rolls Royce, for free. Both surprise, and unbelief.

"The Tent of Meeting . . . but that can't exist. It was hides and wood and would be thousands of years old. That doesn't make any sense."

"Neither did a temple under the Temple Mount," said Cartwright. "Listen, Sam, we are scrambling right now trying to keep the Middle East from erupting into an all-out Islamic revolution that would overthrow all semblance of order as we know it. If the Egyptian president can be taken down, who's to say the Saudi king might not be next. And you know what that would mean to our economy and our security presence in the Middle East. If access to our military bases in the Middle East is cut off, Iran and Russia will own that part of the world. And we might as well kiss Israel goodbye. We're at a tipping point right now. This unrest sweeping North Africa has all the trappings of an Islamic revolution against governments that supported peace in the Middle East and were our allies against terrorism. A change like that, in the hands of radical Islamists, could threaten the economic stability of every nation in the West. Somehow, we've got to prevent that from happening."

Whitestone joined in. "Baruk's decision to rebuild the Temple Mount and keep the Arabs away is bad enough. But if the Israelis find the Tent of Meeting, and try to erect it on the Mount . . . we could easily see all Islam rise in a holy war. Sunni and Shi'a banded together to destroy the West. If that Tent exists, we can never allow the Israelis to get it to the Mount. We need to know if there is any clue to a Tent on that scroll and we need to know it *now*. That's where Bohannon comes in."

"All right . . . yes, Mr. President, I'll call him," said Reynolds. "The reason we're pulling him back in . . . sir, do we want to share that with Bohannon?"

Whitestone smiled inwardly. *Smart . . . I'm glad his job was salvaged . . . him helping Bohannon get out of Jerusalem alive was not such a bad thing after all.*

"Sure—tell him it's a very simple reason," said the president. "And, actually, it's true." Whitestone cast a glance at Cartwright, picked up a folder with thermal satellite scans of Bohannon's neighborhood, and handed it to Reynolds.

"Sam, this has only just begun," said the president as Reynolds scanned the images, his mouth tightening. "Somebody else might be able to look at that scroll, or that mezuzah, and help us. But, for whatever reason, I think Tom and his friends have been divinely called to be in the middle of . . . well . . . of what may be the most climactic period in human history." Whitestone reached his left hand across the coffee table between the sofas and placed it on Reynolds's arm. "My father often told me, 'Son, you don't want to get between God and his purposes.' It's not only that we likely need Bohannon's help as we try to navigate our way through the international minefield we're facing. But a higher power may still have a part for him to play. And we've got to ask him to play that part."

Reynolds met the president's gaze without a flinch. "At any cost?"

"At any cost, Sam," said Whitestone. "We may all be asked to make the same investment. But we need to know if there is any more information on that scroll, or that mezuzah. And it appears Tom Bohannon has been selected."

New York City

Hell's Kitchen was getting almost as trendy as the Meat Packing District. Manhattan's continuing renaissance swept through the warehouses of the West Side, and now joined forces with the immensely popular Hudson River

Greenway that stretched the length of Manhattan Island. But in this corner, along 11th Avenue, industrial buildings stood their ground.

The sun was still hard to the east. Bohannon needed to cup his hand over his eyes to shade the glare as he and Commissioner O'Neill emerged from the NYPD evidence storage facility. O'Neill stretched out his hand to say goodbye.

"Listen . . . can I buy you a cup of coffee or something?" asked Bohannon.

O'Neill looked at Bohannon then glanced at his watch. "You've got something to tell me?"

"Well . . . sort of."

The commissioner reached out and grasped Tom's elbow. "C'mon, I've got a few minutes."

O'Neill waved off the two linebacker-size plainclothes officers and led Tom across 11th Avenue to Jimmie's Coffee Shoppe. They found a booth in an empty corner as the two linebackers came in and sat down by the door.

A round man with a two-day growth of beard called from behind the counter. "What'll it be, gents?"

"Corn muffin and coffee regular," said O'Neill. Bohannon thought even that was courageous in Jimmie's.

"Hot tea with lemon . . . that's it."

O'Neill tapped a bent spoon on the laminate tabletop. "Tom, you understand, right? These clowns haven't stopped. And they're not going to.

"Look, I don't think you have to worry about the Northern Islamic Front, at least not here in the U.S. To be honest, from the intel we're getting, the leaders of the Islamic Front are still after your blood. They blame your group for the death of their imam, and for the deaths of hundreds more under the Temple Mount when it collapsed. But they're not the immediate problem.

"No," said O'Neill, "clearly it's the Prophet's Guard you have to worry about. You still have the scroll and the mezuzah in your possession, artifacts they protected for over eight hundred years and still consider their birthright. I'm convinced they won't stop until they possess the mezuzah and scroll again. That puts you square in their crosshairs."

Tom shook his head. "The mezuzah's been opened, we broke the code of the message on the scroll. The secret they protected is no longer a secret. Why come after us now?"

"I don't know," O'Neill admitted. "But, clearly, they're after the scroll and mezuzah. And there must be a reason. So, what's on your mind?"

"Yo . . . here you go, gents." Jimmie slid the cups and the muffin, wrapped in plastic, across the top of the counter. Tom watched closely where Jimmie put his hands—what side of the cup he touched—as he got up and rescued the order, including a plate for O'Neill's muffin.

New York City's police commissioner only came up to Bohannon's shoulders, but he was a compact, solid ex-marine under a bald head and a face that carried the well-being of eight million New Yorkers in every crease and wrinkle. O'Neill, thought Bohannon, was part of this adventure since the night Winthrop Larsen was blown all over 35th Street by a Prophet's Guard car bomb. But Bohannon had known the Commissioner for many years prior, as O'Neill and his wife made regular trips to the Bowery Mission to help feed the homeless. And Mrs. O'Neill was a driving force behind the renovations at the Bowery Mission's Women's Center.

O'Neill was an honest straight shooter who often revealed true concern, compassion, and consideration—considerable qualities in a man so accustomed to lawlessness and violence. This was a man Tom had learned to trust.

"Two weeks ago, I got a call from Doc Johnson. A colleague of his from the British Museum had come to visit. He asked Doc if our guy Abiathar could have created a Plan B—something that might give additional hope to the Jews for a reestablished Temple. So Doc and this Irishman, Brandon McDonough, closely examined the scroll and the outside surface of the mezuzah. They found some symbols on the mezuzah. I don't know what they are or what they mean but, now . . . after last night . . ."

Rory O'Neill leaned over the table, bearing in on Bohannon. "Why go after the safe? There must be something in there they want. Or they think there's something in there they want, something in addition to the scroll and the mezuzah. There must be more than we know. But why go after the safe?" O'Neill unwrapped the plastic and ripped a crumbling chunk from the corn muffin. "Look, they can't believe we left the mezuzah in the safe, can they? Otherwise, why break into the Collector's Club, why try to break into the Bryant Park library? There must be something else in the safe that they want."

Over the rim of his coffee cup, O'Neill eyed Bohannon. "So, what is it, Tom?"

Bohannon twirled the tea bag in his cup. "When we first discovered the safe, and Joe and I were cataloguing its contents, there were three small drawers on a shelf in the middle. The center drawer was where we found the mezuzah, wrapped up in the red silk purse. The other two drawers were locked. We never found a key to open those drawers. Then, with everything else that was happening, I guess we forgot about the drawers. Now . . ."

The corn muffin had disappeared. O'Neill threw down the last of the coffee. "Let's go find out."

Washington, DC

The connection was far more sophisticated than Skype—the video more precise and sharp, the sound flawless like the two men were in the same room. Still, Jonathan Whitestone felt like a fugitive from an old Flash Gordon movie when the Israeli prime minister's face came up on the screen. Deep in the caverns under the White House, Whitestone was in one of the few rooms he knew was safe from all outsiders. Neither surveillance cameras nor the White House taping system were permitted in this small room. Nothing said here would ever appear on any record. Which was a good thing.

"What in God's name do you think you're doing, Elie?"

His head and shoulders pushed back into his chair, Eliazar Baruk visibly retreated from the screen.

"Are you out of your mind?" Whitestone's rage sent shards of pain through his chest. "How can you hatch a plan like this without letting me know? You and I have bargained our souls on what we've planned and, now, you could jeopardize it all for the purpose of some stunt? And you don't even talk to me about it?"

Baruk pulled himself closer to the screen. "Jon . . . do you tell me everything regarding America's security? It's our sovereign right to protect our land."

"Holy heaven, Eliazar. Rebuilding New Orleans is our sovereign right, but it won't incite anyone to declare war on the United States. But you . . . if you rebuild the Mount, the Arab world will explode. Are you going to let them excavate the Dome of the Rock first? Are you going to allow them to rebuild their mosque, their shrine to Muhammad?"

"It's not safe," Baruk replied.

"Not safe? Don't play with me. It'll be safe enough for you to erect the Tent of Meeting, won't it?"

Baruk smiled—guilt masked as relaxed calm. "Cartwright is very good. Give him my compliments."

"This is a fool's game, Eliazar. And it's likely to endanger everything you and I have been trying to accomplish."

Baruk leaned even closer to the camera and the screen. "Put away your sanctimony, Jon. You and I have been trying to accomplish something that will be condemned in every capital in the world. So don't preach to me about the sanctity of the Temple Mount to the Muslims. It is a much more sacred place to my people, and we've been forbidden to even walk on its surface for the past thirteen hundred years. The Mount is in our hands. The future of the Mount is ours to decide. We . . . I . . . am determined that Israel will establish lasting sovereignty over the Mount, once and for all. Get used to it, Jon. We're not giving it back, and the Arabs are not coming back."

President Whitestone's anger roiled like thunderheads on the horizon. But his lot was cast with Baruk, and there was no turning back now.

"Jon, listen, it's not going to affect anything we've planned," promised Baruk. "We do need to rebuild the Temple Mount. It is dangerous the way it is now . . . who knows what could fall next? As far as the Arabs are concerned, we're just making the place safe. Our Muslim brothers think they have us in their grip . . . promise peace talks, speak of friendly coexistence, while the Muslim Brotherhood topples one government after another and Essaghir is hatching his own plot to control the world.

"We will not wait for the Arabs to move," said Baruk. "We will never again stand by and watch our people murdered by madmen who want to wipe us from the earth. We will destroy this threat, Jon. Our plans are still in place. Our commandos are already safely in northern Iraq. The Kurds don't even know they are on the ground, but they are in prime position. It's only a short jump into Iran. We will succeed. We must succeed."

Whitestone opened a mental cupboard and stashed both his anger and his anxiety inside. They weren't gone. They were just set aside until he was ready to unleash them and prove to Baruk that no one sandbagged the president of the United States without being wounded in return. He pulled himself up straight in his chair and slipped on his presidential aura.

"I want you to allow Kallie Nolan—the archaeologist who helped find the Temple—to return to Jerusalem—"

"I can't allow her—"

"Just wait, Eliazar," Whitestone snapped. "Give her permission to return to Jerusalem. Nolan's put in three years of study and research to write her thesis as a doctoral candidate at Tel Aviv University. The thesis is finished, submitted to her readers and review board. But it all goes to waste is she fails to stand for her dissertation in front of the faculty in Tel Aviv. I need you to open the door."

"Why?"

"Because I'm asking."

Baruk spread his hands in surrender. "Of course, Jonathan. After all," he said, "if we can't trust each other, who can we trust?"

New York City

Standing in front of the battered safe, Bohannon now noticed that it was not standing straight. It was slightly cockeyed, twisted and torqued from the lower left to the upper right corners, where a long, green stain marked the safe's crash landing on FDR Drive.

Tom approached the double doors on the front of the safe. He swung to the side one of the large, floral-design ornaments that covered the combination dial, then retrieved the combination from his BlackBerry. He dialed it in, heard a faint click, and pulled on the door's handle. It didn't move. He pulled again, harder, with both hands. The door didn't even twitch.

O'Neill gestured and his two bodyguards stepped forward, each grabbed a handle of the side-by-side doors. There was a good bit of groaning—from the cops, but not from the doors—before they gave up, defeated by the stressed metal.

"Those things are not budging," said one of the bodyguards. "We could burn it with acetylene, or take a sledge and a wedge to drive them open."

Bohannon winced at the thought.

"No need for that," said O'Neill. "Tom . . . the department has an expert on safes who we use as a consultant. But we just sent him to Syracuse to help with an investigation. He won't be back for at least a week."

Tom ran his hand over the painted decorations on the front of the doors. Curiosity and anxiety filled the spaces that weren't occupied by dread. "Couldn't we find somebody else?"

"Not in here," said O'Neill. "This is the last place you want to invite an expert on locks. We'll wait for our guy. Nobody is going to be getting inside that safe, anyway."

"Yeah," said Bohannon, "but I sure would like to see what's inside those drawers."

Three swarthy men, dressed like construction workers, sat in a booth looking out the front window of Jimmie's Coffee Shoppe. Their eyes followed Rory O'Neill and his bodyguards to the black, unmarked SUV that waited by the sidewalk. The commissioner shook hands with Tom Bohannon and got in his car. Bohannon walked off down 29th Street toward the faraway subway stop at Penn Station.

"Do you think they know?"

The leader watched Bohannon walk into the distance. "We can't wait to find out," he said. He turned to the others at the table. "We come back tonight."

14

TUESDAY, AUGUST 11

Philadelphia

He walked with the long, loose gait of a hoops star returning to campus, trench coat hanging from his left arm, right arm swaying in balance to an inner rhythm. The color of golden sand in twilight, his hair was cut to the length of a businessman and pampered like that of a movie star—as perfect as the crease in his tan slacks and the cut of his sport jacket. His face was punctuated with a smooth, genuine smile that rarely left his lips. Sam Reynolds radiated warmth that put everyone at ease.

Except Tom Bohannon, who felt a sense of dread as Reynolds approached his table in the upscale sports bar tucked into a corner of Philadelphia's main Amtrak station flanked by Market Street and the Schuylkill River.

Bohannon was introduced to Sam Reynolds by NYPD commissioner Rory O'Neill, not long before Bohannon and his team embarked on their mission to Jerusalem.

It was Reynolds who arranged for their eclectic assortment of unique gear to be airlifted, through Turkey, to a secure area at Tel Aviv Airport, where it was separated into FedEx and UPS trucks for innocent-looking delivery. And it was Reynolds who was their lifeline under the Temple Mount, who risked his career to keep their mission alive, who served as their witness, over a secure satellite phone, as Bohannon and his team transmitted live video feed of their astounding discovery . . . the Third Temple of God, secretly constructed under the Temple Mount by a Jewish priest and his followers, over one thousand years ago.

And it was Reynolds who called yesterday and asked Bohannon to meet him halfway between Washington and New York, in Philly's 30th Street Station. No explanation. Just a time of arrival.

Bohannon stood and offered his hand.

"Hi, Tom . . . I'm glad to see you're still in one piece."

"So am I, although it looks like we're still in the crosshairs of the Prophet's Guard."

Reynolds motioned toward their chairs. "I know. That's one of the reasons I'm here today."

"I'm not surprised," said Bohannon. "But I was really glad to hear you survived. I know there were some pretty angry people down there in Washington and the first scuttlebutt was that you were treated pretty roughly—about to be tossed out on your ear with no pension. But then Rory told me you held on to your position. How did you pull it off?"

"Trade secret, my friend . . . trade secret." The easy smile spread across Reynolds's face, warming the air around their table. "Let's just say a day dawned when emotions calmed, friends had a chance to whisper in some ears, and ten years of exceptional service finally carried some weight. I got slapped on the wrists, hard, for being off the reservation with you guys, but it didn't take long before the office realized we were in a lot more trouble now and that State needed all hands on deck."

The conversation was put on hold while the waitress came and took their orders.

"Thanks, Sam. I don't know if I'd be sitting here if you hadn't covered our backs. I owe you a debt."

Reynolds stopped the spoon he was spinning on the top of the table.

"Good . . . that's just what I need," said Reynolds, who smiled like the guy who had snatched the last cookie. "I've got a favor to ask."

Jerusalem

Leonidas was startled when the cell phone rang. A blocked number. He was expecting no calls. But . . .

"I'm told I am to call you Leonidas," said the shapeless voice. "I'm told you have been of great service to the imam of the Northern Islamic Front. I'm told that, for a price, you have been a distinguished provider of information. I'm told—"

"Enough of what you've been told," Leonidas snapped. "Who are you? Who gave you this number?"

"Ah," said the voice, "unfortunately, our beloved imam has chosen to embark on a prolonged pilgrimage. We are not aware if he is expected to return any time soon. So, my dear Leonidas, the responsibility of maintaining this relationship has fallen to my unworthy self."

Leonidas calculated the prudence of severing the connection and destroying the cell phone. He tortured his brain for any crack in his façade, any hint he had been careless.

"You wonder if you have been compromised, yes, my friend? Rightly, you wonder who I am. Most likely you are preparing to end this communication and destroy the only thing that connects us. So, my fine friend, allow me to offer you an overture of security.

"First, if we remain connected until we complete this conversation, you will find one hundred thousand dollars deposited into your account tonight. Second," said the voice, not waiting for a response, "I will introduce myself and I will inform you how to contact me . . . most definitely a risk on my part. Once you have assured yourself of my identity and that the money has, indeed, been deposited, perhaps then we can do business."

The addition to his account would be welcome. Still, Leonidas was more than wary.

"Money does not buy trust," said Leonidas. "You will never have contact with me again unless I can verify who you claim to be—and if, at that time, I am interested in continuing this conversation. So, my friend, to whom am I speaking?"

For a moment, Leonidas wondered if he had called the man's bluff. Then the silence was broken.

"Find my dossier," said the voice. "My name is Imam Moussa al-Sadr. I am the founder of the Amal in Lebanon."

"Do you think I'm a fool?" growled Leonidas. "Whoever you are, our conversation is over."

"Stop!" Even through the phone, the command of the voice was powerful, arresting. "Look in the dossier. When I disappeared from Libya in 1978, the world assumed I was dead. But there are two things that were never revealed. First, Lukas Painter dispatched a Mossad assassination team into Tripoli that was ordered to eliminate me and lay the blame at the feet of Qaddafi. Second, the Mossad team was intercepted by Qaddafi's security and one of the team was mortally wounded—sadly, by what is often called friendly fire. The name of that operative was Lieutenant Hillel Shomsky, the son of—"

Leonidas snapped the cell phone shut and held it in his tightly balled fist. The rules of the game, he now knew, had irrevocably changed.

─────※─────

Lukas Painter looked at the map of western Jordan displayed on the LCD screen in Mossad's operations center. Touching the screen, he rotated the image, exposing the southwestern flank of Mount Nebo.

"What do you think?" he asked over his shoulder.

"I think I'm glad this is Mossad's mission," said Levi Sharp. "But I'm also thinking that you certainly don't have to lead it. I wouldn't want to go that way . . . not having to cross that road. Whoever is given this assignment should go up the other flank, through the little valley to the northeast."

"It's a fool's journey, if you ask me," said Painter.

"Then don't do it."

"But nobody's asking *me*," Painter responded. "And if it is a fool's journey, I'm not sending my men somewhere I'm not willing to go myself. We have our orders . . . get to the top of Mount Nebo and see what we can find. *Find.* If there was ever anything hidden on Mount Nebo it was probably stolen long ago." Painter turned away from the LCD display and sat down at a nearby desk. Sharp pulled up a chair next to the desk.

"It's the only clue we have, Lukas."

"Some clue . . . a verse from Scripture that says Jeremiah hid the Tent of Meeting and the Ark in a cave on Mount Nebo. First of all, assuming this clue isn't just a fable, tell me how Jeremiah got all that stuff up there. The Tent was huge. And where has it been hidden for three thousand years that it's not been found yet? People have been digging all over Mount Nebo for generations looking for the grave of Moses. Why hasn't some good-intentioned archaeologist stumbled over the Ark of the Covenant?"

The gentle hum of air purifying equipment laid a hush of white noise over the room.

"We don't have any of those answers, Lukas. What we know is that we have to start here. So, how do you plan to get thirty kilometers into Jordan, climb to the top of Mount Nebo, search through the tombs, caves, and monastery, and get home without being seen or discovered? That's the answer I'd like to have."

Painter rubbed the gray stubble covering his head and looked back over to the LCD screen. "I don't know. Even with satellite pictures, infrared scan, and low-level drones, we need to get an asset on the ground over there. But, sooner rather than later, somebody is going to take that long walk. And it will not be easy."

Philadelphia

"There's one key thing that most people don't understand," Reynolds said to Bohannon. "These guys don't need a reason to hate us. The Muslim Brotherhood has been around for eighty years and for eighty years their purpose has been the same . . . to establish an Islamic world order. They get it. We don't. It's a battle for survival—our survival or theirs. There is no middle ground. There is no *moderate* position in a war for survival.

"We've got to wise up in the West. Islam has, at its core, an unshakable conviction that Allah will only be served when all of mankind worships him and follows the way of Muhammad. That conviction is served by a foundational belief that if violence is the only way to bring about world domination by Islam then violence is not just acceptable, it is required.

"The only possible way Islam will be able to coexist with the West is if Islam changes from the inside out. Islam needs a reformer, somebody like Martin Luther, who will bring about a fundamental change in the Islamic faith that will expunge every precept that encourages violence, whether that precept is cutting off the hand of a man who steals, or stoning an adulteress, or encouraging terrorist attacks that kill thousands of people in the West.

"But a change like that . . . a change like that will take a lifetime. It took a lifetime after Luther for Protestants and Catholics to stop killing each other in the name of religion . . . many lifetimes in Northern Ireland. First, a Luther needs to emerge from within Islam—a true, genuine, sincere reformer. A reformer who can stay alive long enough to promulgate his message."

As Bohannon nodded his head, Reynolds continued. "The odds are pretty heavy against that kind of reform ever taking hold in the majority of Islam. Not that every Muslim is our enemy—that is far from true. The majority of Muslims want to live in peace and would be content to live in reasonable coexistence with the West. But the radical Islamic movement worships what is one of the core beliefs of the Islamic religion—one core belief that requires the destruction of Western culture."

Reynolds prodded the remnants of the turkey club sandwich lying in tatters on his plate. "How much do you know about the Muslim Brotherhood?"

"They were an outcast political party until Kamali's overthrow," Bohannon said. "Now they won the election and the president of Egypt is one of their guys. Isn't that right?"

Reynolds sluiced a pair of limp steak fries through a mound of ketchup and tossed them in his mouth without a drip of red spoiling his crisp, white shirt.

"The Muslim Brotherhood is the world's oldest, largest, and most influential Islamic group," said Reynolds. "The Brotherhood's credo is 'Allah is our objective; the Qur'an is our law, the Prophet is our leader; jihad is our way; and death for the sake of Allah is the highest of our aspirations.' On the Brotherhood's English language website, they describe their principles as including the imposition of Islamic Shari'ah law as 'the basis for controlling the affairs of state and society' and liberating all Islamic countries from foreign imperialism."

Bohannon waved down a waitress and ordered a cup of tea. "That doesn't sound like any political party I'm familiar with. I thought these guys were pretty moderate."

"You judge," said Reynolds, leaning into the table. "The Muslim Brotherhood was formed in Egypt in 1928 by a teacher who believed the purity of true Islam was being polluted by the corruption of Western culture and morals. His desire was to bring about a more pure form of Islam. The Brotherhood now operates in nearly every country throughout the Middle East and Northern Africa, and many in Western Europe. It's been active in the U.S. for nearly fifty years. By the end of World War Two, the Brotherhood had over two million members. Now, that number is hard to calculate because it operates under so many different names.

"For example, in Jordan, the Brotherhood formed its own political party, the Islamic Action Front, and now holds the largest number of seats of any party in the Jordanian parliament. The Brotherhood also operates in Israel, as the Islamic Movement. The northern, more radical branch boycotts Israeli elections but the southern branch holds two seats in the Knesset."

Bohannon got his hot tea with lemon. "That's nuts," he said.

The smile was gone from Reynolds's face, his lips pressed tightly together.

"The Muslim Brotherhood in Palestine is the controlling organization behind Hamas, which is correctly called the Islamic Resistance Movement. And the Holy Land Foundation here in the U.S. is the primary fund-raising organization for Hamas.

"Until a few years ago, the Holy Land Foundation was the largest Islamic charity in the U.S. Read their literature . . . the HLF presents itself as one of the foremost advocates of moderate Islam, an Islam that seeks to peacefully coexist with the rest of the world, including Israel and the United States.

"From 1988 to 2001," said Reynolds, "the Holy Land Foundation funneled more than fifty-seven million dollars from U.S. donors to Hamas. It raised thirteen million in the U.S. in 2000 alone. The Department of the Treasury began to investigate the group and believed it was using the funds it raised to support schools that served Hamas's ends by encouraging children to become suicide bombers and to recruit suicide bombers by offering support to their families.

"The Foundation's assets were frozen in 2001 and seven leaders were indicted on forty-two counts of providing material support to a foreign terrorist organization. The government also named over three hundred U.S. organizations and individuals as unindicted coconspirators. The case went to trial in 2004, resulted in a hung jury and mistrial in 2007 . . . a terrible blow to counterterrorism efforts here. But we learned a lesson about how to present a complicated, terrorism financing case. There was a retrial at the end of 2007 and late in 2009 all defendants were convicted on all counts."

Reynolds reached for his coffee cup, but it was empty.

"So, what's the point?" Bohannon asked. "We all know that Hamas are bad guys. What does this history lesson have to do with me?"

Reynolds was trying to make eye contact with the waitress. "There's been a fundamental fracture in the Arab world for decades, a fracture that runs along both religious and political fault lines.

"On one plane is the ongoing religious conflict between Sunni Muslims and Shi'ite Muslims, essentially a difference of opinion about who was the legitimate heir after Muhammad's death and therefore the legitimate leader of Islam.

"On another plane is the battle between Arab nationalists like the Palestinians, who would accept a political solution to their conflict with the Israelis, and the Islamic activists like the Muslim Brotherhood, who are committed to overthrowing all of Western civilization and replacing it with the reestablishment of the Islamic Caliphate—an empire stretching from Spain to Indonesia."

Bohannon could smell the coffee before the waitress appeared over his left shoulder. "That's a little far-fetched, isn't it?"

"Thanks," Reynolds said to the waitress. "I'll likely need it filled again." He raised the cup and appeared to relish both the heat and the aroma. His eyes closed for a moment as he sipped and savored the dark, black liquid.

"Remarkably good, for a sports bar, I must say." Reynolds set the coffee cup on the table and turned his attention back to Bohannon.

"Since the earthquake, there has been a fundamental shift in the Muslim leadership in the Middle East. Suddenly, we see signs of unity . . . between Shi'a and Sunni; between Hamas and Hezbollah; between the Muslim Brotherhood and the Palestinian Authority . . . unity under a new leader. We don't know who he is. Our intelligence is stumped. But we know what he wants."

Reynolds leaned in toward Bohannon. "We believe the Muslim Brotherhood, or this new leader—or both—are behind all of the political unrest in the Middle East today—the overthrow of the governments in Egypt, Libya, and Tunisia, the riots in Yemen and Bahrain, and the civil war in Syria. Even the peaceful—so far—overthrow of the Lebanese government by Hezbollah, something that could never happen without the support and approval of Syria and Iran. Old enemies are working together. That's the seed of Islamic revolution being planted all over the Middle East."

This was more than an intellectual treatise for Reynolds. It was a reality he confronted every day.

"Recently, a very unusual thing happened. Hamas and Fatah—the Palestinian militant groups that slugged it out over control of the Gaza Strip—signed a reconciliation agreement ending years of bloody conflict . . . on the very same day that the northern and southern factions of the Islamic Movement declared their reunification. The very same day. Hamas and Fatah signed their agreement in Cairo, under the mediation of the Muslim Brotherhood.

"And this new leader, this phantom who appears to be guiding an Islamic unification, one of his targets is control of the Temple Mount—as a symbol of Muslim power—and the reconstruction of the Dome of the Rock and the Al-Aqsa Mosque. And if the Israelis don't give up control of the Mount, then this new leader wants holy war . . . jihad.

"Thing is, the Israelis are not about to budge. In fact, the Israelis are searching for the one thing that could give them legitimacy over a rebuilt Mount."

Bohannon felt a flush of confusion. "Another temple?"

Reynolds shook his head. "No . . . not a temple," he said. "A tent."

The space around the table seemed to close in, as if the eyes of the world were telescoping in on him. Bohannon's breathing came in short, shallow gulps.

"Tom, I have a proposition . . . a proposition from the president."

"No . . . no . . . no. Come on, Sam. There are so many reasons why I can't do this." He could barely hear his own voice. "I'd be risking my life, my family's safety, again. I can't do that. I'm a civilian . . . I run a rescue mission. Get some of your spies or commandos and do it yourself."

Tom heard the chair squeak as Reynolds leaned back into its leather depths.

"Kallie Nolan can go back to Israel," Reynolds said. The words set off warning bells in Bohannon's head. "She can have the time she needs to stand for her dissertation, finish her PhD. Not have all that time and money she invested in her degree just get wiped out. And she can gather her belongings, close up her apartment, and resolve any issues with her job."

Bohannon looked across at Reynolds who was seated comfortably, one leg crossed over the other, his fingertips tapping together in a recycling rhythm.

"Better yet, one of my colleagues at State has convinced his counterpart in Jerusalem to review Nolan's case. To reconsider her expulsion."

Pressure increased in Bohannon's temples as his options evaporated.

"All you need to do is agree to help us . . . look at the scroll. See if you can find anything. And, if you do, help us to follow the clues."

Reynolds's cell phone rattled to life. He pulled it out of his jacket pocket and handed it to Tom.

"And you should answer this call."

New York City

"They're going to let Kallie back into Israel? Why would they do that?" asked Annie as she paced across their living room. "Sam Reynolds asked you to meet him in Philadelphia just so . . ."

She turned to face him. Bohannon was sitting in the antique Morris chair that occupied the bay window in their Victorian home. He was physically tired and mentally exhausted from his trip to Philly, his discussion with Reynolds, the message from Rory O'Neill that somebody, probably the Guard, had failed to break into the evidence warehouse the night before . . . and now he had to confront his wife with the one thing she didn't want to hear. Annie's fierce gaze pierced his heart.

"What else?" Her voice barely rose above the background sounds of their neighborhood, but it dripped with cold fury. "What else, Tom? What does Reynolds—what do those bloodsuckers down in Washington—want in return, eh?" She took an offensive step toward him, her fists squeezed into tight weapons. "Tell me!"

Tom Bohannon hadn't shirked a righteous fight at any time in his life. Not when he was threatened by one of the most powerful politicians in Philadelphia to back off an explosive story when he was an investigative reporter for the *Philadelphia Bulletin*. That crooked politician was still in jail.

But Bohannon became very cautious when Annie's anger erupted to the surface. It was a well-learned lesson. Good judgment comes from experience—and experience comes from bad judgment. Tom tried to pick his words carefully.

"There is a problem," he said. "A problem that has to do with Jerusalem."

"Oh . . . God," Annie breathed.

"You know Krupp has been rebuilding and strengthening the walls of the Temple Mount since the earthquake . . . and they're just about done. But, now, the Israelis are planning to rebuild the Temple platform, but they are not going to allow the Muslims to come back. No Dome of the Rock . . . no Al-Aqsa Mosque. Reynolds told me the Israelis are trying to find the Tent of Meeting. They plan to erect the Tent of Meeting on the Temple Mount and claim it for themselves."

Annie remained stock-still in the middle of their living room, her fists now turning white. "That may be the most stupid thing I've ever heard. Regardless, what does that have to do with you? Aren't there enough people in the State Department and the CIA to worry about Israel and the Arabs? What did Reynolds want with you, Tom?"

A stab of anger overwhelmed his weariness. Before he knew it, Bohannon was on his feet.

"Do you think I *want* to be part of this again?" Regret and remorse punctuated every sentence. "Don't you understand that I'm sick of being frightened to death that something is going to happen to you or the kids? Looking over my shoulder every time I go out the door. I'm not made for this kind of life. I've seen enough death. Enough! I don't need any more. I don't want any more. Don't you get it?"

Annie set her jaw, withered Tom with a menacing gaze, then walked to the oak secretary desk in the corner. She opened the glass doors that fronted the top half of the desk and ran her fingers across the spines of the bright yellow magazines stacked like soldiers on the bottom shelf. Her fingers stopped and she pried loose one of the yellow spines.

She looked at the cover of the *National Geographic* magazine for a moment, turned, and walked b`ack to her husband, the magazine held out in front of her.

"I do get it, Tom. You've made a decision. You're going back. Well, I've made a decision too," said Annie. "I'm also going back."

Only desperation rattled around in Tom's empty stomach. In front of him, Annie held the magazine—its cover one of the most iconic images in photo-journalism: *The Kurdish Rebel.*

The young girl stared boldly into the camera, an epic written into her gaze. She stood outside a mud-brick, one-room house, its whitewashed walls a stark backdrop. She was dressed in the traditional garb of Kurdish women, a heavily embroidered, purple, flowered dress, covered by a black robe, a wide, golden sash around her waist. A white headscarf, draped over her burnished brown hair, along the side of her head and around her neck, created a stunning frame to world-weary, piercing emerald eyes that stared boldly back at the camera. While her eyes were riveting, what made the photo such an iconic image was what the young girl was holding. Twin cartridge belts crisscrossed her chest. In her right hand she held a Kalashnikov automatic weapon, its butt resting against her right thigh. In her left arm she cradled a child—a young boy of about two or three years, who also gazed at the camera with sparkling emerald eyes. One of the boy's hands clutched the shoulder of the woman's robe. The fingers of his left hand were curled around the tapered end of a .39-caliber cartridge in one of the belts.

"You gave this up a long time ago."

"I called Larry yesterday," she said. "I told him I was willing to give him one more shoot. A photo story of the thousands of Muslims and Jews now living together in a refugee tent camp outside Jerusalem—a city where for a thousand years they hadn't figured out how to live together. Another refugee camp. Another kind of war. And I would do everything I could to give him another cover—another image that would capture the attention of the world."

Bohannon looked up from the face on the cover of the magazine to the determined face of his wife. "The last time you did this . . . it broke your heart.

It almost broke your spirit. I don't think you've picked up one of your cameras since."

He took the magazine from Annie's hands. The world-famous image was taken in a Kurdish refugee camp high in the mountains between Turkey and Iraq, during the Kurdish rebellion of 1988. Annie was covering the desperate plight of these Kurdish rebels, under attack from the government forces of both Turkey and Iraq. The Kurds were pleading for help from the outside world. But these Kurds were *peshmerga*, guerrillas of the PKK—a radical, nationalist movement tagged as a terrorist group by the United States—and no one was coming to their aid. They were dying by the thousands.

"I didn't kill her. I know that now."

After the cover photo of *The Kurdish Rebel* was published, Annie's professional career took off. She was riding the rocket of success, named one of *National Geographic*'s chief photographers, when she got the news.

In a desperate attempt to regain power over the mountains controlled by the Kurdish rebellion, Saddam Hussein unleashed the ferocity of the Revolutionary Guard. Sweeping through one rebel camp after another, often using poison gas, the Guard murdered indiscriminately. Except in one instance.

An Iraqi general—Ali Hassan al-Majid, Hussein's cousin—recognized the rebel girl in the purple dress from the cover photo. He would give these Kurds something to remember. The general stood the girl in front of a whitewashed wall, facing a firing squad. There were two photos the Revolutionary Guard nailed to huts in every Kurdish village they captured—one of the girl, and her son, staring into the camera; another of them crumpled on the ground, the whitewashed wall stained red. It was over a year before Annie learned of the young woman's fate.

"You blamed yourself for her death for years. Why, Annie? Why now?" Bohannon searched his wife's face. But Annie turned away and stood looking out the window.

"I wasn't sure if I would do it . . . until a few moments ago." She turned, the light to her back, and faced her husband. "Now you can experience what I've lived with for the last two months. The overriding sense of dread that filters into every moment of time when you're out of the house. The panic that rises in my chest when the phone rings and I'm the only one home."

Annie took a step toward him. "You don't have to do this, Tom. If you really are so sick of this, just let the government handle it."

Tom crossed the room and took Annie's hands in his.

"Annie," he whispered, "do you remember how we talked about this at the beginning? That we thought God was at work in our lives . . . that following the clues on the scroll seemed like something God was calling us to." Annie stiffened even more. "Well . . . they think if God worked through us once, he may want to work through us again. Just like Brandon McDonough, they are wondering if there are any other messages, any other clues, either on the scroll or on the mezuzah. Maybe something that only we can decipher."

Annie pulled her hands free and stepped back.

"Reynolds has no right asking you to risk your life again."

Bohannon stepped closer to his wife. He lifted her chin and looked into her blue eyes. "It wasn't Reynolds who asked. It was President Whitestone."

⸺⌇⌇⸺

Annie had stormed off to bed. Bohannon was back in the Morris chair, trying to remember every word of his earlier conversation.

"Mr. Bohannon . . . please hold for the president."

Bohannon had nearly dropped the cell phone. *"Tom? This is President Whitestone."*

"Good afternoon, Mr. President."

"Look . . . Tom, I know the last time we spoke it was not a very pleasant conversation. Can you—"

"No, sir, it wasn't very pleasant. Please allow me to apologize for my rudeness."

"No offense taken, Tom. It was a tough situation. You did what you thought was right. That's pragmatic. It's what we do everyday—take a look at all the possibilities and then do what we think is the right thing to do. That's why I'm speaking with you today."

"Yes, sir."

"Tom, Sam can fill you in on all the details . . . what's going on and how we think you can help us. But this is the important point, for me at least. You know I'm a man of faith, Tom."

"Yes, sir."

"Well, I'm convinced that God used you, and your compatriots, to find and reveal the hidden Temple under the Temple Mount. I don't know why. But I believe God's hand was in this . . . was with you. You and your friends deciphered a message

that our computers are still trying to duplicate. The full force of the Israeli security apparatus, and a group of deadly serious radical Muslims, failed to stop you from finding the Temple. And you escaped to share your findings with the world. I don't know what the odds were against your success and survival, but they must have been astronomical.

"Well, as Sam will tell you, this situation is far from over. And I believe that God's purpose for you in this situation is also far from over. We need your help, your connection. We need you to go look again at the scroll, the mezuzah, for anything that might help us avoid the spark to World War Three. And we need you to listen . . . listen to God's direction, follow his lead, see if you can find what has been lost for so long—find it before it's too late."

Silence. Bohannon had heard the question, but his mind could find no answer.

"Can you do that? Can you do that for us, Tom? Are you willing to allow God to use you again?"

15

THURSDAY, AUGUST 13

Jerusalem

"You should be dead."

The voice on the other end of the cell phone was hollow, lifeless. *A good sign*, thought al-Sadr.

"Yes . . . many times," he said. "Yet, I am still here."

Al-Sadr allowed the silence to linger. It was the other man's move.

"You are who you claim. And I received the funds."

"Ah . . . good," said al-Sadr. "Avarice. What a fine foundation for a business relationship. I would like you to—"

"You don't have much time."

Startled, al-Sadr waited for the man named Leonidas to continue.

"The Israelis are looking for the Tent of Meeting," said Leonidas. "If it can be found, they intend to erect it once the platform on the Temple Mount is completed."

"Never! We will rise against—"

"You have no time," Leonidas interrupted, life and anger coming back into his voice. "There is a passage in the book of Maccabees that claims the Tent of Meeting and the Ark of the Covenant were taken by the prophet Jeremiah and hidden in a cave on the top of Mount Nebo in Jordan. Mossad is planning an incursion . . . tonight . . . to search the caves on and around the mountain, seeking for any clue that might determine whether this fable is true."

Blood rage pumped through al-Sadr's temples, his hand slowly crushing the cell phone.

"If the Tent of Meeting exists," Leonidas whispered, "and if the Israelis manage to erect it on a rebuilt Mount, the Haram al-Sharif will be nothing but a memory. You pay me for information. What you do with it is your own concern."

Jordan

Five men. It was all Lucas Painter would allow himself to risk. Including himself, a team of six. Baruk protested Painter's involvement as too risky, but General Orhlon, Israel's defense minister, understood. This mission was critical. And Painter was fearless . . . and lucky.

The morning before, two of his men crossed the Allenby Bridge, southeast of Jericho, driving from Israel to Jordan. They were dressed as businessmen on their way to Amman, with all the proper papers for doing business in Jordan. Three others mixed with the pilgrims streaming down the road to the double horseshoe switchbacks of the Jordan River—the place where tradition says Jesus was baptized. They lost themselves in the throng. The Jordan, little more than a stream at Bethabara, was easily breached in the falling dusk.

Painter could take no such risk. He was too well known, on both sides of the border. So he climbed into the false bottom of a bakery truck just before dawn and rode in that cramped, hot space for hours while the driver made his deliveries.

Shrouded in darkness blacker than a swindler's heart, Painter now lay in a deeply cut defile on the flank of a dry wadi in the desert of Jordan. About one kilometer to the east, along the dry riverbed of the steeply walled wadi, was an olive grove with storage sheds and maintenance buildings. Even at two o'clock in the morning, it was an area to be avoided. Fifteen hundred kilometers above him was the monastery at Syagha atop Mount Nebo, thought to have been erected above the burial place of Moses. Somewhere in that collection of ancient buildings, crumbling ruins, and deep caves could also be the hiding place of Jeremiah's Tent of Meeting.

Painter nudged the sergeant at his side. Only a shadow moved. Painter nodded his head upward and the shadow moved again, slithering up through the deep cut in the canyon walls. Four other shadows followed his lead. Painter, with night-vision glasses, watched his team, covered in black from head to foot, melt into the darkness of the barren landscape. There was no moon. His men were nearly invisible.

The sergeant stopped just short of where a footpath crossed through the gully. Painter, on the side of a rise, looked for light or movement. No one was on the hill.

"Go," Painter whispered into the voice filament tucked inside the full-face hood worn by each member of the team. Four men vanished. Painter climbed through the darkness and joined the sergeant at the top of the gully. Silently, they edged up the western ridge of the mountain, the side closest to the road. The other teams skirted a cliff face and moved along a shallower ravine, gaining the crest on the eastern edge of the compound.

━━∿∩∿━━

With his night-vision binoculars at full illumination, Captain Hamid followed the progress of the shadows as they ascended the flank of Mount Nebo. Hamid and his snipers were spread in a twenty-meter arc about one hundred meters higher than the olive grove compound, hidden by an outcropping of rock. Below them, three teams—one on the eastern side of the compound, two on the western side—moved swiftly across an exposed section of rock face, like the shadows of clouds racing before the moon, circling the walls of the compound.

This is the way I would have come.

Hamid's plan, with four additional men on the far, eastern flank as backup, allowed for no combat with the Israeli commandos. Engagement was foolhardy. Israeli special forces were like black death—silent and lethal.

He held up one finger, pointed to the watch on his wrist, then turned a thumbs up. The men on his right and left sighted through their night-vision scopes. Each had a designated target. Each had a silencer attached to the muzzle of his sniper rifle.

━━∿∩∿━━

Moving independently, Painter and his partner made for their target, as he knew his other teams would close on theirs. After studying the fly-over photos and infrareds, Painter decided to ignore the compound of buildings surrounding the sand-colored church with the huge brazen serpent monument on the crest of its roof. Target of too many archaeologists . . . picked over too many times . . . it was an unlikely hiding place. No, Painter instructed his teams to move higher on the crest of Mount Nebo, away from the monastery, to Khirbet Al-Mukhayyad, where the tombs of a local population dated to at least 2000 BC.

They would have thirty minutes on the mountain, no more. A single click on their radio earphones would mean someone had the information they sought, or the thirty minutes had elapsed. Two clicks meant to leave—quickly. From his review of the aerial photographs, Painter had identified twenty-six caves. They would have to search quickly.

⸻

Hamid counted off the seconds in his mind. Training convinced him the others were counting at the same, methodical rate. Eighteen . . . seventeen . . . sixteen . . . fifteen . . .

The crosshairs in his sight remained locked on a spot between the temple and the ear. His target stopped.

⸻

It wasn't a sound, or a smell, or a feeling. It was thirty years of combat and training. Painter stopped in the lee of a large boulder, disappearing into its cleft. The night was silent. He reached up the hill with his senses and his night-vision binoculars, searching for the source of his hesitation.

⸻

Six . . . five . . . four . . . three . . . Hamid's finger caressed the trigger.

⸻

Painter slowly eased to the edge of his sheltering darkness, raised his left hand to the radio transmitter at his right shoulder. He didn't like the feel of this. It was time to . . . The first bullet hit before his hand could toggle the radio switch to signal retreat. It hit just above his left ear, drove skull fragments and brain tissue before it, and smashed out the other side of his head, ringing off the rock to his right. Painter was dead before the second shot tore through his chest and pierced his heart.

The target was driven into the rock by the force of the two bullets.

Hamid lifted his head from the scope. To his left and to his right, eight other Syrian-trained soldiers held up their right thumbs.

Hamid pulled the night-vision binoculars to his eyes. All six bodies were sprawled in varying poses of death.

The night was silent once more.

16

Friday, August 14

"Eliazar, face it, we have a leak." General Orhlon's voice had the vitality of an invalid on life support. "There is a traitor."

Orhlon was simply worn out. Every ounce of his strength and reserve was sucked dry. Weeks of standing on high alert, moving from crisis to crisis, had dissipated even his bulk and resilience. But this? This was too much. Even the legendary Bull of Benjamin felt crushed in his spirit, discouraged to the point of despair. Only his anger fueled his flagging body.

"And he is close," said Orhlon. "He is someone we trust."

General Moishe Orhlon lost his struggle to sit straight before the prime minister. The weight of the last few hours was so heavy. His shoulders sagged, his head drooping and shaking back and forth. Six men dead. Executed. Lukas Painter, the dependable warrior, the steel ramrod of Mossad. Lukas, his right arm and comrade for so many years, through so many battles—those hidden and those revealed.

And he would not even be honored with a public funeral. *Lukas . . . my friend.*

"Their bodies?"

Baruk sat across the table from Orhlon in the conference room of Central Command's Operations Complex. To Baruk's left sat Levi Sharp, director of Shin Bet. None of them slept that night. Nor had anyone else at Central Command. These men were oblivious to the sun rising over Israel.

"Dumped out of a truck before dawn on the Allenby Bridge, just short of our guard post," said Sharp. "Whoever is responsible didn't want to acknowledge the dead bodies, either. To the world, this incursion never happened."

"Who do we repay?" the prime minister asked. "David?"

Orhlon held his breath waiting for the answer. Lieutenant Colonel David Posner should be neither star-struck nor awed by the other men in the room. As deputy director of Mossad, he accompanied Lukas Painter on countless operational meetings and briefings. He was present when Aman, the branch responsible for collection of intelligence within the Arab world and along Israel's borders, shared its briefing on the Jordanian incursion with the senior staffs of Shin Bet and Mossad. He understood the risk of the mission. But Orhlon wondered if, in fact, he knew whom to punish.

"We don't know, Mr. Prime Minister," said Lieutenant Colonel Posner. "We're confident it wasn't Jordanian military. So that leaves unofficial sources. Perhaps Palestinian Islamic Jihad, who are trained well enough. This attack was carried out by a well-disciplined group. The shooters were gone before we could identify them by satellite. The truck was nondescript military. The Syrian 14th Special Forces Division is stationed outside Dar'a, only a kilometer from the Jordanian border, and could have deployed a tight unit to Mount Nebo in a few hours. What we do know is that, whoever they are, they were in place when Director Painter and his squad pushed off."

Orhlon felt the prime minister's eyes on him. It was Orhlon's chief of staff who ran Aman and so Orhlon himself carried the responsibility for their failed intel. Struggling with the burden of his guilt, the general lifted his head to meet the prime minister's gaze.

"Which supports your conclusion, Moishe," said Baruk. "One of our trusted friends is a traitor. Whoever executed Painter and his men responded rapidly and from short distance based on some inside information received at the last minute. Someone within our inner circle condemned those men to their deaths."

Eliazar Baruk was wearing an open-collared, short-sleeve shirt that hung limply on his bone-thin frame . . . not one of the usual finely tailored Italian silk suits which were his trademark. Still, as he leaned into the table, he commanded all the respect due a prime minister. "Moishe," he whispered, "you were betrayed. We have all been betrayed. This is not your failure."

Baruk looked around the table.

"It is all our failures. We all failed Lukas. But, one of our number killed him. That one, we will find, and we will extract our revenge."

Orhlon felt a current of malice race up his spine and into his resolve. *I will find you.*

"Moishe," said the prime minister, "rebuild the command structure."

Orhlon noticed the prime minister's eyes flick toward Posner and he nodded.

"David," said Orhlon, "as of this moment you are promoted to the rank of colonel and installed as acting director of Mossad, pending approval by the Security Committee of the Knesset. Choose your deputy director."

Posner didn't miss a beat and Orhlon was affirmed in his decision, knowing the new colonel had prepared himself for all eventualities before entering the conference room. "I'd like to request Major Evan Mordechai. I know he's Shin Bet, but I've known Major Mordechai since officer's training. He is one of the smartest, well-briefed officers I know. He's a great leader of men. And . . . well, sir, I would trust him with my life."

"Very well, Colonel," said Orhlon. "Major Mordechai will be assigned to Mossad and installed as your deputy. Levi?"

"Avram Levin's served Shin Bet well for years," said Sharp. "He's more than ready. It will be a seamless transition from Mordechai to Levin. I'll process his promotion to major."

Orhlon pointed his finger at Posner. "But one thing without fail, Colonel. Whether it's Mossad or Shin Bet . . . find this traitor. Find him quickly. Or more men will die."

Balata Camp, Nablus, West Bank

From the sky, Balata refugee camp looked like a solid white postage stamp pasted to the terrain on the western end of Nablus, the Palestinian city sprawling out of the narrow, steep cleft between Mount Ebal and Mount Gerazim in the tinderbox known as the West Bank.

Balata, the largest refugee camp in the West Bank, crammed over twenty-three thousand people into a space smaller than New York City's Central Park. The streets between its one and two-story, flat-roofed, concrete block houses were so narrow that an overweight person could not pass through them. During the second Palestinian uprising against Israeli occupation—the Al-Aqsa Intifada in the first five years of the century—the Israel Defense Forces invaded Balata, a hotbed of Palestinian militants, by "traveling through the walls" . . . blowing holes in the walls of one house after another, advancing down a street with the homes used as shields against the Palestinians firing from the roofs.

Imam Moussa al-Sadr had no need for subterfuge. This was his turf, these were his people . . . home to Islamic warriors loyal to al-Sadr's Hezbollah army. Still, with the unpredictability of the IDF and its incursions, it was wise to exercise discretion. Al-Sadr's aged, crooked body moved silently through the darkened streets of Balata, his black kaftan billowing in his wake. One heavily armed, masked bodyguard preceded him, pausing to ensure that crossing each junction was safe, while the one behind walked backwards, his Kalashnikov trained on the darkness they had vacated.

They stopped, the bodyguards flanking a flat, unmarked door, nearly invisible along the vast expanse of whitewashed cinder block. Al-Sadr rapped his arthritic knuckles against the wooden door. It swung open and they disappeared into the blackness.

—∿∽∾—

"Now the Israelis will know that we have someone inside."

Al-Sadr detected a hint of censure in the voice of the commander of the Al-Aqsa Martyrs' Brigade. Two candles on a table burned in the corner of the damp, lower room of the safe house. He closed the distance until his beard nearly came up under the commander's chin, like a scimitar against his jugular. "You question me, commander?"

Every angle of Youssef's body was chiseled, hard as granite and with as much compassion. He towered over the stooped shape of Imam al-Sadr. Youssef murdered on order, sent his men on suicide missions without remorse, and had cut the heart out of his cousin who was suspected of being an Israeli spy. This rock shuddered before al-Sadr, as if an earthquake had shaken its foundations. His eyes searched the mud floor for refuge.

"Forgive me, Holy One," he whispered, his scarred face turned to the ground. "I meant no offense."

Al-Sadr's silence hung in the air. He stared at his commander's supplicant form, then slowly turned away and walked toward the light.

"I do not care if that whore of a traitor is discovered," al-Sadr said softly. "He has his reason to hate the Zionist pigs, but he would sell his mother as food for the jackals if the price was right, and he would sell us out to the Israelis if it suited his ends. He has been of some service, but he can never be trusted. And there was no choice. Those Israeli commandos had to be stopped. We haven't finished our search of Mount Nebo . . . though I doubt anything will be found. No . . . there was no choice. Leonidas must fend for himself."

Al-Sadr turned from the corner so the candles were at his back. Darkness veiled his face, but not his fire.

"Commander, you will begin infiltrating tonight. Immediately. I want a thousand trained soldiers of the Martyrs' Brigade under and around the Haram al-Sharif as soon as possible. We must be ahead of the Israelis, ready to strike before they can mount any claim of sovereignty." Al-Sadr stepped forward. "Who knows what atrocity they are perpetrating upon the sacred stone. No . . . we must restore the Dome of the Rock, rebuild the Al-Aqsa Mosque. You, Commander"—a withered, bony finger rose in the gloom—"will rescue the Haram and save our sacred shrines. Or," he whispered, "you will all die—on the Mount, or at my hand."

New York City

The house that George Steinbrenner built, the new one-point-three-billion-dollar Yankee Stadium that opened in 2009 in the Bronx, was one of the most expensive ballpark visits in the nation. Bleacher seats—those in the sun, with no back on the benches—were fourteen bucks. The most expensive seats in the new Yankee museum—the high-backed, faux-leather, blue easy chairs with teak armrests, stretching in an arc close to the field from first base to third base—cost twenty-five hundred dollars for each game. Buyers were required to sign four- to ten-year agreements on the seats to simply acquire the right to pay twenty-five hundred dollars a ticket. When half of those seats remained empty through much of the 2009 season, the Yanks cut the price to only fifteen hundred dollars a ticket.

In the new economy of baseball, two suite seats would cost the normal man a month's wages. So, in the new economy, five-dollar tickets and the New York Yankees just didn't compute.

But there they sat, in the upper deck along the first-base line—with a great view of the field and the omnipresent, distracting, five-story high Diamond Vision LED scoreboard—for the livable price of five bucks. The promotion covered about a dozen night games against poor-draw teams—powers like Baltimore, Kansas City, and Seattle. For Joe Rodriguez, who was priced out of his Saturday season package with the move to the new Yankee Stadium, the five-dollar seats were a godsend.

"When I was a little kid," said Tom Bohannon, who sat next to Joe, "I remember going to Connie Mack Stadium in Philadelphia and paying fifty cents for a bleacher ticket."

"Yeah, but that's when baseball gloves were three-fingered, horses pulled trolley cars, and Edison was still trying to figure out the light bulb, right?"

"Very funny," said Tom. "But it was a simpler time . . . a better time, I think."

On this night, in a not-so-better time, it wasn't the woeful Orioles who were failing to keep Rodriguez's attention. His mind was a riot of conflicting thoughts and emotions. He felt trapped, a man whose fate was being decided by unknown men in unknown places.

Joe seriously considered just giving away the tickets to the game. But this was one of the few places he knew he could get Tom alone. Yeah, odd to think they could be alone in the midst of a crowd of forty-five thousand Yankee fans. But the strange reality was that—if you preferred and if you kept your voices down—two people could engage in a private conversation in the midst of a great throng. And Joe needed to talk to Tom . . . alone.

"When you were a kid you could buy a new car for less than four thousand dollars," Rodriguez responded. "A loaf of bread cost a quarter and you walked four miles to school every day . . . in the snow . . . with cardboard in your shoes."

"Okay . . . okay," Tom said with a chuckle. "You got me."

Joe looked at the men on the field, in their white, pinstriped uniforms, and had no comprehension of what was transpiring in the game itself. "Time changes things," he said, his voice hollow. "Time changes people, too. Not always for the better."

Somebody got a hit. Bohannon's eyes were on the field. "Yeah, except for Jeter. He seems to be getting better with age."

Rodriguez pulled in a long breath, the smell of hot dogs and mustard drifting up through the stands. He turned his head toward Bohannon. "I'm not talking about Jeter."

When he left high school in Washington Heights, Joe Rodriguez stepped away from the Catholic religion of his Puerto Rican parents. Too much hypocrisy, he thought then. Rules that didn't make any sense for a modern world. Massive, marble-filled, gold-laden churches that lay empty ninety percent of the week while the neighborhoods around them surrendered to poverty, drugs, and despair. For him, it didn't add up. So he took his muscular, six-four frame and passion for basketball to Rutgers where he failed to make the traveling team for two years and walked away from hoops. But he got some scholarship help in return for working part time in the school library. So he took his boundless energy to the stacks and soon found a world he loved more than a layup. The church . . . he left that in the dust of the past.

Four years into his career with the New York City Library, Rodriguez literally ran over a red-haired young woman as he pushed his way into the kitchen during a house party on the Lower East Side. Joe quickly forgot about the beers he had been sent to fetch when he picked the poor girl up from the floor. He was aware that she was attractive. He remembered the cut of her pastel green dress and the cool feel of her creamy white skin. But the image that burned itself into his memory were the swirling sabers of combative fury that burst forth from her deep blue eyes and refracted from her red curls. An imposing man known to have an edge to his New York attitude, Rodriguez had taken a step back in the face of this Irish warrior . . . and knew he had met his match.

Deirdre Bohannon married Joe Rodriguez a year later, but her prayers for Joe started the night of their first meeting. For the last ten years Joe knew of Deirdre's desire to bring him back to God and her born-again Christian church. He admired her tenacity and was grateful for the respect she showed him by not beating him over the head with her faith. In all those years, Joe never felt the call. Until he witnessed Tom Bohannon's faith. Now . . . well . . . now he was just confused in his heart. But his mind knew what to do.

"Look, Tom, I know you're having a tough time. I know you're taking this thing pretty hard—all the things that seem to have gone wrong since we started on this crazy chase. You take it harder than the rest of us, I think, because you feel responsible. You were the one hearing from God; you were our leader. You had the vision of what we should do next. And we followed that vision . . . all of us."

"I never asked to lead anyone," said Tom, trying to keep his eyes on the game.

"Do you know why, Tom?"

"Why what?"

"Do you know why we followed you?"

Rodriguez watched Bohannon's shoulders sag with resignation as he broke away from the game and stared at the seat-back in front of him.

"Because we believed in you," Rodriguez said, his voice rippling with a whispered urgency. "We believed in your relationship with God, and with the power of prayer in that relationship. Not all of us have that kind of a relationship—but we all believed in you and your relationship with God. Why? Because we could see it. We could see it in the way you walked out your faith. When things got tough, you went to God for guidance and support. Not out of some kind of responsibility, but because you were confident God would answer you, help you, guide you. There was a pureness about it. A healthy vitality of faith and spirit that I think all of us were caught up in . . . even Doc and Sammy. We could see your faith, and we all believed because of your faith."

"I wish I felt about myself the way you feel about me."

"And that's my point, Tom," said Rodriguez. "I do feel that way. I do believe in your faith in God. And I believe that God has faith in you . . . faith that you will stand up for what you know is true, no matter how you feel. Faith in you to do the right thing at the right time for the right reason. Faith in you to follow him, no matter what he says or where he asks you to go. I saw it, Tom. I saw it under that mountain. I saw it when all our lives were at risk and one misplaced decision could have been disastrous for all of us. You consistently went to God and God consistently answered you. Do you really think any of us could have missed that?"

"So . . . so what? Everything is changed now."

"No . . . that's just it. Not everything has changed. You still have a faith that the rest of us respect and envy, and a faith that God responds to. It's still in there, no matter how you feel. No matter how much you feel like you've failed. It's still in there. And, you want to know something else?"

Bohannon's chin was pushed forward, his lower lip pushed up against his top teeth, his lips cemented shut like he was about to be force-fed a hot dog that had lived on the floor beneath their seats since the last home stand. "What?"

"I'm not going to let you lose it." Joe stretched out his hand and placed it on Tom's left arm. "Tom, you carried all of us under the Temple Mount. Your faith and your dedication to that faith carried all of us when we should have given up all hope. Now, it's my turn to carry you . . . I believe in your faith. I believe in your relationship with God . . . shoot . . . I wish I had that kind of relationship with God. Maybe. Someday. But now— now, Tom, I'm not going to let you give up. I'm not going to let you sink under a riptide of self-recrimination and self-pity. We need you—now more than ever. And you need me now. In fact, you need all of us now. And Doc and Sammy are with me on this. We've already talked about it. God saved our lives in Jerusalem, in Germany. God watched over our families and kept them safe. Your God, Tom.

Your God who watched over you and walked with you. Now, you doubt. You're discouraged. You feel despair, thinking you've failed. Well, Bohannon, I've got something to tell you."

Tom planted his right elbow on the metal armrest separating their seats and rested his chin in the palm of his right hand. His look confirmed everything Joe feared.

"I'm watching over you now. I'm walking with you. We all are. And, if you need help getting over this responsibility you feel for all the death and destruction—getting through this burden of failure you think you need to carry—then we're here to help you carry it. And, you know how we're going to help you? We're not going to let you forget. We're not going to let you forget how we prayed and you got the idea for making a raft out of our waterproof sleeping bags. How we prayed and you actually saw the way to find the shaft that led us to the hidden temple. How we prayed and God gave us all the courage to send out the video of what we found to every library in the world . . . a step that led to a real, signed peace between Israel and the Arabs.

"So the peace treaty didn't last. So what? Do you think, if God had a plan for all that was happening, that his plan suddenly ended with that earthquake? Look, Tom, something else is going on here—or it's all a continuation of what started when we found that mezuzah in the Bowery Mission."

Bohannon shook his head. "What's your point?"

"Don't you get it? I'm your brother. And I love you," said Rodriguez, squeezing Bohannon's arm. "And I'm not going to let you try to walk through this alone . . . try to carry this burden alone."

Forty-four thousand, nine hundred and ninety-eight fans jumped to their feet and cheered wildly, sending chills down Rodriguez's spine—until he realized all the hubbub was only for an A-Rod homer. Joe caught his brother-in-law's eyes and poured his heart into Bohannon. "Tom . . . we're not leaving you. And God hasn't left you. I don't understand it and I know you don't understand it, not after all that's happened. I don't know about my faith, but I believe in your faith. And I'm going to hold you up as long as it takes for you to see that faith, and God's presence, show up again in your life and in your heart."

Bohannon pulled his arm free and turned back to the game. "No, Joe. This is not your fight. It's not your struggle. This is something I've got to figure out. This is not a burden that you need to carry."

"Tom . . . that's what brothers are for!"

Another cheer rocked the House That Ruth Built. Cheap seats or fancy suites, they were all Yankee fans, they were all of one heart and mind.

Joe reached out with his right hand and placed it behind Bohannon's head, rustling his hair. "Come on . . . let's see what's going on and get our five bucks out of these seats."

17

Saturday, August 15

"I'm sorry, Eliazar. Lucas Painter was a good man. A loyal warrior. I know you and your country will miss his wisdom and courage."

President Whitestone wished he was in the same room with the Israeli prime minister. It would be so much easier to read him—his body language. What the president could see across the secure video transmission, he didn't like. The man on the screen was drawn and distracted, gray shadows surrounding eyes that were devoid of energy or spark. Whitestone began to fear their plans may begin to unravel.

"One of my own, ambushed, butchered," Baruk said. "He was like a son."

Whitestone gripped the table. "Last week you challenged me because of my doubts. The threat from Iran is closer to reality every day that goes by. We must act. If we don't, millions more will die, as you know well. Innocent people. People just trying to go about their lives in peace, in your country and in my country. The Iranians are determined. The leaders of their government are madmen, particularly that fool of a president. If we don't cripple them now, if we don't destroy their capacity to strike, they will be standing at our doorstep with death in their hands."

Baruk lowered his face and shook his head.

"If we stop them," Whitestone continued, "then it will be worth even the life of Lukas Painter. If not, your nation will be their first target."

Whitestone waited while Baruk ran a hand through his hair. Then the prime minister seemed to be suffused with resolve, like a dry sponge soaking up water. He squared his shoulders and sat upright in his chair.

"Are we ready, Eliazar?" Whitestone pressed. "Even with Painter's death . . . are we ready?"

Vengeance visited the Israeli's eyes. "Eleven days . . . midnight of the twenty-seventh. The teams are already in place and surveillance of the targets is constant. It's the nineteenth day of Ramadan, the day they mourn the martyrdom of Imam Ali. Nobody works. The country comes to a stop. The targets will be hit, and eliminated in less than an hour."

"And you can trust the men . . . trust their silence?"

"Don't worry, Jon. These men are handpicked, each with a powerful, personal reason to hate the Iranians. To a man, they consider this action an honor. They will never reveal the truth. My concern is, are you ready on your end? We will cripple them, but you will destroy them."

We're doing the right thing. Whitestone whispered that to himself over and over. "We're ready. Within an hour, their economy will cease to exist."

Jerusalem

It was one sheet of copy paper, but in Levi Sharp's hand it felt like he was trying to lift Israel's highest peak.

"Those are all the names my staff and I can think of who had knowledge of the incursion into Jordan," said Colonel David Posner. "Twenty-four people . . . at least, twenty-four who are still alive."

The director of Shin Bet read the names on the sheet.

"Twenty-*five*," he said, not moving his eyes from the paper. "You haven't included the prime minister."

"I— I . . ." Posner stammered.

"It's okay," said Sharp, lifting his gaze to the younger man. In bearing, dress, personality, and presence, David Posner, acting director of Mossad for less than twenty-four hours, had a regal bearing. His sandy hair was swept up off his forehead in a mass of contained waves, his skin was smooth, his nose long— Caesarean—holding court between angular cheekbones and full lips. Posner looked like the scion of a patrician family, the young, pampered son of ridiculous wealth, his flawless face erased twenty years from his actual age. Sharp, though, knew what the façade masked.

The newly promoted colonel was pushing fifty. He rose through the ranks of Mossad with the well-earned reputation of tackling the toughest assignments his government could conceive. Posner survived two years in the terror-laced chaos of Mogadishu. While there, he thwarted three terror plots aimed specifically at Israel, personally assassinating two senior Al Qaeda operatives who mistakenly thought they were safely hidden beneath the Somalian anarchy. Two tours in Chechnya, tracking Muslim terrorists . . . eighteen months embedded in the Syrian president's residence as a French sous chef . . . commander of a lightning-strike commando unit that extracted threatened agents from Iran to Yemen.

Under the effete exterior lay a hardened partisan, a deadly foe to the enemies of Zion. And, Sharp knew, a fervent loyalist to authority, a relentless stalker of their traitor.

"We need to include everyone who had knowledge," said Sharp. "But you and I both know where we will find the traitor."

Posner nodded his head. "In the shadows. Someone with a secret." He reached into the breast pocket of his tan, starched, uniform shirt. "That's why I compiled this list myself." He handed the paper to Sharp. "Four names."

A current shimmered through Sharp. He didn't know if it was admiration for Posner's trained instinct, or apprehension for the fate of one of these four with whom they had all worked so closely.

"A week—more or less," said Posner, "and I will come back to you with one name."

Sharp nodded his head.

"Or one body."

New York City

"I don't care what you think, Sammy, what I know is that this adventure is over for us. And don't give me those big bug eyes and deep sighs. You already know Annie and Deirdre are going to stomp to death any idea of us getting involved in the scroll again."

Rizzo was frustrated. Not so much with the fact that his short legs were marching double-time to keep up with Joe Rodriguez's long strides. He was accustomed to that. No, this frustration was spawned by a gnawing fear that his great adventure was over. A ragged, livid scar on his right bicep still throbbed where he had been wounded, their lives were constantly at risk, and people died. Yet, Sammy had to admit to himself that he had never felt so alive, so vital, as when he had been swept up with Tom and Joe and Doc in the Temple adventure. On this quest, he was an equal. It was a position he was loathe to surrender.

Rizzo pushed his thick glasses back up to the bridge of his hooked nose. "Yeah, but why did Sam Reynolds want to talk to Tom? And why has Tom asked us all to get together again? And why does he want to meet in the library?"

"And why meet in the Reading Room?" Rodriguez asked. "What's wrong with my office?"

"What's wrong with your office is that it's your office and not my office. I'm getting tired of being stuck in that subterranean hole-in-the-wall. I think a man of my stature should command a more stately abode."

"A man of your stature should be in a Hobbit house . . . little round door, with fur on your feet."

"There you go again, belittling me. You got something against little people, dragon breath?"

"No, I just have something against you: your mouth."

"Watch it, slim jim, or I'll hit you with a hate crimes suit."

The cadence of their footfalls echoing up from the marble floor, Rodriguez and Rizzo strode through the ornately decorated McGraw Rotunda on the second floor of the Humanities and Social Sciences Library. On their right was the Edna Barnes Salomon Room—a large, open gallery that held only one book, the Gutenberg Bible, safely in the womb of a climate-controlled, bulletproof, clear Lexan case. But they turned left into the large antechamber of the fabulous Rose Reading Room.

This first room, the Blass Catalog Room, was nearly one hundred feet long and nearly as wide, stocked along the entire left side with flat computer screens, portals to the treasures of the Rose Reading Room, sitting on well-worn wooden tables, a phalanx of curved-back chairs stretching down one side of each table.

To the right of the central aisle were the gatekeepers, the librarians in their large, half-walled wooden booth of a guardhouse who would review every request slip, making sure the catalog code was copied precisely, before the seeker could advance to the next desk where the slip would be stamped with the time, a numbered code scrawled on the top, and the two parts of the form separated— one page to the requester and the other dispatched down a vacuum tube to a retrieval team in the underground stacks.

Rodriguez gave a brief wave to the heavyset librarian behind the wall, a man who sneered back in return.

"I don't think Jack likes your uniform," said Rodriguez

Sammy looked down at his clothes. He was wearing cut-offs that were partially hidden by a Ryan Howard official XXL Phillies game-day shirt. "He must be a Mets fan."

Sammy stopped in the middle of the floor and turned to the bespectacled, frowning librarian. "Hey, Jack, you're a Mets fan, right?" he said loudly, batting his eyelashes as he turned to his audience. "Say, the Mets, do they still play baseball?"

Jack the gatekeeper fumbled out a protest, but Sammy, a wicked smile emerging from his heart, was already moving off toward the Reading Room.

———∽∿∾———

Tom sat off in the far corner of the Rose Reading Room at one of the long, oak refectory tables that filled the cavernous space. The Reading Room was nearly two city blocks in length and nearly thirty yards wide, but what gave the space its unique open feel were the huge, arched windows stretching down each side of the room and the fifty-two-foot-high ceilings adorned with expansive murals of blue sky and vibrant clouds. Doc and Brandon McDonough were already sitting across from Tom. Rodriguez moved to Bohannon's side and pulled up a chair as Sammy stood on the far side. A thin, flat, black book, about twelve inches on each side, rested on the table in front of Bohannon.

"Sorry I had to ask you all to come here, but I wanted to show you something and this is the only place I could do it. Even Sammy wouldn't be able to get this book out of this room."

The book's cover was blank—no title, no author. Bohannon slipped his fingers under the stiff, thick cover and brought up his left hand to steady the cover as he gingerly opened the book. "This book is called *The Tabernacle in the Wilderness*. It was published over two hundred years ago. Obviously, this copy wasn't treated very carefully."

Inside the covers were a few, large pages, heavily darkened at the edges, that were as brittle as thin ice and ragged from years of misuse. None of the pages were attached to the cover, the book's binding a victim of time.

"This is what Sam Reynolds wanted to talk about," said Bohannon, opening the book to a color drawing of a large, rectangular structure surrounded by what appeared to be four walls of thick curtains.

The silence that greeted Bohannon's introduction had nothing to do with library rules.

"The Tent of Meeting?" asked Doc. "Forgive me, Tom, but I just don't understand this at all."

Bohannon turned another page, uncovering another drawing of the Tent of Meeting from a different perspective as he looked up at his four companions. "The Israelis are preparing to rebuild the platform on the Temple Mount. Alex Krupp has offered his men, equipment, and expertise to help."

"That's a good thing, right?" said Joe.

"It would be," said Bohannon, "except that the Israelis are not going to allow the Arabs or the Waqf to return to the Mount when it's rebuilt."

"Holy Jerusalem, the Jews are looking for the Tent!" exclaimed Rizzo. "They're gonna rebuild the Mount, put up the Tent instead of a Temple, and stick it to the Muslims, right?"

"That would be suicide," whispered Johnson. "The Arab world would erupt."

"Exactly," agreed Bohannon. "Which is why the president contacted us."

"President Whitestone thinks we may have an answer to the location of the Tent of Meeting?" Johnson asked.

"No," Bohannon corrected. "He thinks Abiathar may have provided an answer, either in the scroll or on the mezuzah. He's come to the same conclusion we did. If Abiathar took the time to build a temple, maybe he took the time to put a back-up plan in place."

Bohannon turned over another page and revealed a drawing much more detailed. The dimensions of the Tent were huge. Before the others arrived, Bohannon worked up the math in his head. He figured the Tent of Meeting probably weighed over ten tons. It took three clans of Levites and six wagons to move it from place to place.

Joe Rodriguez reached out a hand and placed it on Bohannon's right arm. "Tom . . . I've seen things . . . and done things . . . in the last few months that a year ago I would have sworn were impossible. So, it's a little more difficult for me to say to you, now . . . I mean . . . nobody's seen the Tent of Meeting for, what, three thousand years? I know it's a crazy idea . . . but—" Rodriguez looked at the assembled gathering—"Sammy and I think we may have an idea where to start. We—"

"Just one minute," interrupted McDonough. "As me sainted mother would say, 'tis difficult to choose between two blind goats. But my colleague and I have a few thoughts of our own on Abiathar and his intentions. See, it's our belief—"

"Hang on, Doc," said Rizzo. "As *my* sainted mother would say, 'Joe's got the floor, and we've got something important—'"

"Calm down, will you," said Bohannon. "We're already attracting too much attention." He turned to Rodriguez. "Joe, is your office available tomorrow?"

"Sure . . . always."

"Alright," said Bohannon. "Tomorrow afternoon—one o'clock. Bring your ideas, but leave your attitudes at home. If we're going to work on this again, let's work on it together. Maybe we do have a couple of places to start. Where to start is not the problem. What happens if somebody else finds the Tent, that's a problem."

〰〰

Standing on the steps of St. Francis of Assisi Church in Washington Heights, Joe Rodriguez felt like a hypocrite. He wasn't here under his own volition. The steely-eyed redhead to his right was the reason he was walking up these steps, into the domain of the dreaded Monsignor McGarrity.

"Are you sure . . ."

"Don't ask me one more time, Joe."

Deirdre Rodriguez had a firm grip on Joe's right hand. Joe knew she would not let go until she got an answer . . . got this issue resolved once and for all. He was surprised that his wife didn't drag him to meet with her pastor. Instead, she insisted Joe accompany her to his old, family parish church to meet with the man who ruled St. Frannie's like a small fiefdom. It was late Saturday afternoon and the monsignor would be in his usual place of power—hearing confessions and providing absolution.

The church bells ringing the Angelus, Monsignor McGarrity exited the confessional and crossed the large church to the center aisle. He didn't get far.

"Excuse me, Monsignor," said Deirdre, her voice echoing more loudly than she expected in the cathedral-like expanse of St. Francis's massive stone sanctuary.

Monsignor McGarrity was an old, stoop-shouldered, white-haired priest, in a plain, black suit. He was a big man, not fat, but massive. It took a moment for him to change the direction of his bulk. But when he did, Deirdre caught the full power of the monsignor's famous, scowling countenance. Lesser mortals withered and fled under that stare, but Deirdre matched the monsignor's stare dagger-for-dagger.

Joe loved her so much when she was in the midst of battle—particularly with someone else. He really believed it was Deirdre's fire that welded their marriage together all these years.

"Monsignor . . . you know Joe," Deirdre announced. "And I need you to talk some sense into his thick, obstinate head. He won't listen to me so, here"—she released Joe's hand in the monsignor's direction—"you do something with him."

The priest looked at one, then the other. "Is it divorce?"

"Hah!" blurted Deirdre. "He should have it so easy. You won't believe this one."

Deirdre spun on her heel. "Joseph . . . tell him the story. Let's see what he's got to say."

Twenty minutes later, the three of them now sitting in pews, Joe finished his retelling of the Jerusalem adventure.

"So . . . Joe, how can you be thinking of leaving your family once more and getting mixed up again in this dangerous business?" asked the monsignor. "You need to stay home and take care—"

"Stay home? Are you kidding?" Deirdre moved closer to the monsignor, who moved farther away. "If I wanted him to stay home I didn't have to come here. He's the one who wants to stay home," she said, hooking a thumb over her shoulder. "He says he's worried about us, wants to take care of us."

Deirdre turned her head and shot a lethal glance in Joe's direction before turning back to the monsignor, who still looked at Deirdre as if she were speaking in Latvian. "Do you think I need somebody taking care of me?"

McGarrity's eyes blinked . . . his head moved hesitantly from side to side . . . and he looked like he wanted to escape. "Well, I—"

"Right," Deirdre said triumphantly. "I told him if he didn't do this, he would never forgive himself. Worse, he would never forgive me. And the last thing I need, Father, is Joe spending the rest of his life regretting this decision." She stuck out her hand. "Thank you, Monsignor. You've been a great help."

McGarrity's brain was still in freeze-frame when Deirdre swiveled on her hip to come face-to-face with Joe. She lifted her hands . . . and gently held both sides of his face.

"Joe," she said, her voice a lover's caress, "you are the most honorable, fearless man I've ever known. You would give your life for us without a thought. I know that. But I know this is something you want to do, that you *should* do, and that some misguided sense of responsibility doesn't have the right to keep you from doing."

The fingers of her right hand slid down his cheek bone and stopped at his lips.

"Go and be the hero I know you are." Deirdre kissed him, long and hard.

And Joe loved her so much . . . this Celtic warrior queen that God blessed him with every day.

18

SUNDAY, AUGUST 16

New York City

The next day, an ugly, gray, humid New York summer afternoon, Bohannon brought the team back together again in the comfort of Joe Rodriguez's office in the dark and deserted Humanities and Social Sciences Library. The five men—with Brandon McDonough on board as an adopted member of the club—benefited from the efficient climate-control system that kept the rooms, halls, stacks, and offices of the library cool and dry every day of the year. Five bodies made even Rodriguez's generous office space feel cramped and tended to obscure the richness of the oak paneling. But Bohannon could tell that his friends were anxious to share what they had discovered.

So was he. But Joe took the lead.

"Well, I think we've discovered something that will give us a place to start looking," said Rodriguez. "Or, more accurately, *who* to start searching for."

"The answer to our problem," Sammy Rizzo jumped in with a flourish, "is Jeremiah!"

"The prophet?" asked Doc.

"No . . . Jeremiah Johnson, the mountain man," snapped Rizzo. "What Jeremiah do you think could have anything to do with the Tent of Meeting? Aunt Jeremiah's pancakes?"

Embarrassed, Richard Johnson tried to skewer Rizzo with his most withering stare.

"Stuff it, Doc baby. I'm the one who came up with the solution." Sammy jumped off his stool and sauntered in Johnson's direction, his thumbs tucked under the red suspenders that held up his taxi-yellow Bermudas. Like a diminutive general about to address his officers, Rizzo snapped an about-face and pinioned Tom, Joe, and Brandon with his big brown eyes, magnified to the tenth by Coke-bottle lenses.

"Think back to the scroll's message. There was one line in Abiathar's letter that didn't really fit with the rest of the message. It came almost at the end of the letter. He said, "Look to the prophets for your direction." We didn't pay any attention to it then, because it really didn't have anything to do with our search for the Temple. But . . . now . . . now there is a reason to pay attention."

Sammy stepped closer to Bohannon, who was balanced on the edge of the leather loveseat, and put his hand on Tom's knee. "You're going to like this one," he said, nodding his head, a wicked smile creasing his face. "Joe and I went surfing through the library's database, looking for 'prophet' and 'Tent of Meeting.' We got a mess of hits right away. The first was a Bible reference in the book of Maccabees."

Bohannon saw his own face reflected back from the thick lenses on Rizzo's glasses. "Maccabees? That's not in my Bible."

"It used to be in a lot of Bibles, but not anymore," Rizzo offered. "Maccabees is one of a bunch of books included in the early versions of Scripture that were later tossed out of the game by the Council of Trent, which decided they weren't really inspired. They became known as the Apocrypha. For a long time, both Catholic and Protestant Bibles included the apocryphal books in a separate section, apart from the Old and New Testaments. But, starting a couple hundred years ago, many Bibles excluded the Apocrypha—Maccabees, Tobit, Judith, Esdras—altogether. But there's a reference in the book of Maccabees that isn't found anywhere else. You got it, Joe?"

Rodriguez handed each man a printout. "This is in chapter two of Second Maccabees," he said. "This translation is from what's called the Good News version . . . written in more contemporary language.

"We know from the records that Jeremiah the prophet instructed the people who were being taken into exile to hide some of the fire from the altar, as we have just mentioned. We also know that he taught them God's Law and warned them not to be deceived by the ornamented gold and silver idols which they would see in the land of their exile. And then he urged them never to abandon the Law.

"These same records also tell us that Jeremiah, acting under divine guidance, commanded the Tent of the Lord's Presence and the Covenant Box to follow him to the mountain where Moses had looked down on the land which God had promised our people. When Jeremiah got to the mountain, he found a huge cave and there he hid the Tent of the Lord's Presence, the Covenant Box, and the altar of incense. Then he sealed up the entrance."

"So, you see," said Rizzo, "look to the prophets for your direction!" He took a step into the center of the room, puffed up his chest, his thumbs stretching his suspender straps away from his body. As punctuation, he let the suspenders fly. "Ouch! Ewwww . . . that smarts. Okay . . . the Bible says Jeremiah took the tent and buried it on Moses' mountain, right? Well, after that, Jeremiah and a bunch of his Jerusalem buddies got outta Dodge before the Babylonians could come back and take them into exile. Wher-r-r-e?" Rizzo gave them his best crazed Jack Nicholson smile. "In Egypt! So, there's our answer, right?"

"Well, actually," said Brandon McDonough, "these verses are talking about Mount Nebo, in Jordan. Mount Nebo is the mountain Moses stood atop to look over the Jordan River and into the Promised Land. God didn't permit Moses to enter the Promised Land because of his disobedience. So, tradition and the Bible tell us, Moses died and was buried on Mount Nebo. And that's where Maccabees tells us Jeremiah buried the Tent and the Ark of the Covenant."

"It's been at least twenty-five hundred years," Bohannon said, shaking his head. "If the location of the Tent and the Ark are so clearly indicated, why hasn't anyone found it?"

"Several possibilities come to mind," said Doc Johnson, stretching his long body. "Perhaps it has been found . . . destroyed . . . lost. Or, decayed beyond recognition. Perhaps it was never hidden there in the first place. Perhaps the text itself gives us an answer. If we are to believe what is written in the Bible, then God will not allow the Tent and the Ark to be discovered until he gathers his people together and the dazzling light of his presence comes in the clouds—language very much of the prophesied second coming of the Christ. I don't believe the world has yet seen this dazzling light of God's return."

Johnson got up and approached the whiteboard Rodriguez pulled into the room with them. "So, if we're looking for clues to the location of the Tent of Meeting, we first need to consider Tripoli, in Lebanon," he said, writing the name at the top left of the board. "That's where Abiathar fled when the Crusaders sacked Jerusalem. And there must be a reason he traveled to Tripoli. It's twice as far from Jerusalem as Tyre, where he and his community first fled when the Seljuk Turks invaded. Why did he go that far? What's in Tripoli? More important, if Abiathar did have a back-up plan, did he leave us any clues in Tripoli?"

Johnson drew a vertical line from the top of the board to the bottom.

"Now, we have a second possibility . . . the Maccabees verse that identifies Mount Nebo as the place where Jeremiah concealed the Tent of Meeting and the Ark of the Covenant." Johnson wrote Mount Nebo at the top of the second column.

"Holy Spielberg!" sputtered Rizzo, pointing at the board. "The Ark of the Covenant! Hey, this has movie rights written all over it. Listen." He swung his arm and pointed his pudgy finger at Bohannon. "I got dibs on playing Indiana Jones, okay?" Rizzo jumped up and stood on top of the chair that once held his body. "I always wanted a whip. Hiiiyaaaa!"

Rizzo had a valid point.

"Wait a minute," said Bohannon. "Do we really want to admit to ourselves that we're chasing the Ark of the Covenant? Much as I hate to admit it, Sammy is right. This is the stuff of high-decibel, Saturday matinee adventure movies. The Ark has been pursued for nearly three thousand years."

"And it hasn't been found," said Rodriguez.

"Yeah . . . but—"

"But there are other possibilities as well," Doc Johnson interrupted. "One of which Brandon suggested a few days ago as we examined the exterior of the mezuzah, one that I've been following up over the last two days. And, while I haven't found any connection to Jeremiah, there may be a connection to some other acquaintances of ours."

"Who's that?" asked Rizzo.

Doc stared down the slope of his aquiline nose at Rizzo. "Simply the Prophet's Guard, that's all," said Doc. "Simply those blood-thirsty beasts with that wretched amulet around their necks . . . the ones who killed Winthrop and who would likely kill us if they could get their hands on us. That's all. I think I may have found a connection between the mezuzah and the Prophet's Guard."

⸺∿⸺

As Doc spread the black velvet cloth over an empty portion of Joe Rodriguez's desk, he was surprised—stunned, actually. There it was. Small, but undeniably present. Lurking in the suburbs of his consciousness, tucked into an alley around the corner of his heart. A flicker of excitement. The tickle of anticipation. A drip of adrenaline. The thrill of the search was emerging once again, encapsulating his grief, shading his guilt.

Dr. Richard Johnson knew it was unlikely he would ever forgive himself for the death of Winthrop Larsen. In his mind, he was just as responsible as the men with the Coptic cross amulet with the lightning bolt slashing through on the diagonal—the ones who rigged Winthrop's van with the bomb.

Sure, he was attacked. So was Tom . . . and his daughter. They were all in danger during that insane week in, and under, Jerusalem. But Winthrop . . . Winthrop was innocent. Special. Gifted. He never should have . . .

Doc placed Abiathar's mezuzah on top of the black velvet cloth, chasing away the devil of his thoughts. He pulled two large, powerful magnifying glasses out of his bag and set them alongside the bronze cylinder. He looked at the palms of his hands . . . they were moist with perspiration. His throat was dry. He felt like a first-year professor again, suffering the ever-present anxiety attacks before stepping behind the lectern. *I'm a fraud*, Doc would tell himself in those days. *What do I know? What do I have to tell these students that is worth anything?*

He rubbed his hands against his well-pressed khaki slacks. *Do you really want to do this? Do you really want to get involved again . . . take these risks again?* The pounding of his heart was so strong he felt as if his eyeballs were thumping along with the beat.

Johnson took a deep breath, trying to breathe away his anxiety. Then he stepped out.

"At Brandon's suggestion, I studied the etching on the outside of the mezuzah, looking for a clue or a pattern. We know that Abiathar and Meborak developed a code, using the extinct Demotic language, for conducting their most important and secret communications.

"Therefore," said Doc, looking around the desk, "I believed it also a fair assumption that if there was any message or clue or direction on the mezuzah, it would likely also be in some form of code, and probably in Demotic.

"First, we have to start with the base understanding that Abiathar and

Meborak were residents of the eleventh century. Unfortunately, Mr. Rizzo, that is about seventeen hundred years after Jeremiah and the other exiles fled from Jerusalem to Egypt. So, the history of Jeremiah the prophet was certainly well known by both of these leaders in the Jewish community. I think it's also a fair assumption that both Abiathar and Meborak were aware of the story in Maccabees—written about 125 BC—that Jeremiah buried the Tent of Meeting and the Ark of the Covenant on Mount Nebo.

"Remember the stone stellae we found in the Hall of the Sanhedrin? It was Meborak laying out the code for Abiathar's use. Now, it's possible that the code may have come down to Meborak from Jeremiah, but, for our purposes, it really doesn't matter where it began. The question in my mind was whether I should be looking for Demotic symbols on the outside of the mezuzah."

Doc grabbed the knurled end of the shaft that passed through the middle of the mezuzah and gave it a twirl. Without the scroll inside, the shaft spun easily.

"Well," Tom broke in, "did you find any?"

A knowing, satisfied smile spread across Johnson's face. "No," he said, tapping the side of the cylinder, "but I have discovered something equally interesting."

Doc reached into his bag again and pulled out a rolled up piece of art paper, slightly longer than the mezuzah itself. As he spread out the sheet, he anchored the corners with items from Joe's desk. On the white paper was a rubbing . . . a picture of the etchings on the surface of the mezuzah made by tightly wrapping the paper around the outside of the cylinder, securing it, and then rubbing against the paper with a piece of carbon.

Doc pointed at the image on the paper. "It wasn't until I looked at everything on a flat surface that I understood."

Doc pulled a sharpened Ticonderoga #2 from the pocket of his blue, button-down oxford shirt, leaned on the desk, and began to trace the course of his journey of discovery.

"You can see the predominant design—branches and leaves that curve and swirl all around the outside of the cylinder. Looks like it's meant to depict vines, perhaps grape vines." Doc moved his pencil point. "Then there are these obvious animal shapes that are rather large, a lion on one side and a lamb on the opposite. Then . . . can you see there . . . flanking the animal shapes are two arcs of letters, one on each side."

Johnson glanced up at the faces surrounding the desk. "Do they look familiar?"

"It's *aleph* and *resh*," said Rodriguez, "that's Abiathar's signature. He put his hallmark on the scroll. And he put his signature on the mezuzah, as well. That's our guy."

"But that doesn't get us anywhere," said Bohannon. "That's no surprise."

"No, it isn't," Doc agreed. "But *this* was."

Johnson picked up the mezuzah and handed it to Bohannon. "Examine the mezuzah closely and tell me what you find."

Bohannon took the brass cylinder in both hands, hefted it. He picked up one of the magnifying glasses and launched into a vigorous examination of the cylinder's surface. Around once . . . twice. The second time, he stopped, put down the magnifying glass, and rubbed his fingers against the etched ridges.

Doc wasn't sure if Bohannon had figured it out until he saw Tom close his eyes and take both his thumbs and rub them along the surface of the cylinder. Like a blind man reading Braille, Bohannon rubbed his thumbs back and forth over the etched surface. His eyes still closed, he addressed Doc Johnson.

"Some of these markings"—Bohannon's thumbs still worked the surface—"these *tau* symbols, the palm trees, they're different. The edges are different. They feel different." He opened his eyes. "Now that I know, they even *look* different." Bohannon handed the mezuzah to Rodriguez, reaching over Rizzo's upraised arms.

"Hey, watch it," Rizzo deadpanned. "You guys are discriminating against a minority here." Rizzo turned back to Johnson. "So, what does it mean?"

"I'll tell you what it means. But it cost me a great deal of pride to find out."

One Week Earlier

Philadelphia, PA

The circular expanse of the Chinese Rotunda surrounded Johnson as he and McDonough crossed the dark tile floor toward the Egyptian wing of the University of Pennsylvania Museum. Trailing in the formidable wake of Joshua Silver, being in his presence again, Johnson's fragile ego fed a growing anger.

"I'm sorry to disappoint you, but I don't think your boy Abiathar is responsible for the markings on the outside of this mezuzah," said Silver as he led them from his office. "At least not all of them."

Dr. Silver, curator-in-charge of the Egyptian collection at the University of

Pennsylvania museum, ducked to his right and entered an arched stone landing, stone stairs leading down to his left. Before he could blink, Johnson lost sight of his long-standing nemesis.

Johnson grabbed McDonough by the arm, halting him in the curve of the arch. "You see," Johnson said, "I told you this would be a waste of time. Silver doesn't care about anything except his own rising star—which should crash under the weight of all his grandstanding, publicity-hogging personal posturing. Let alone his faulty thinking."

"Aye . . . you had me shakin' there, love." McDonough patted the hand on his arm. "Just because Silver unearthed the royal tomb of Senwosret III before you got to the Valley of the Kings is no reason to demean the work of the museum. The university has done extraordinary work in Egypt for more than a century. And Dr. Silver has helped this museum remain one of the finest archaeology museums in the world, you know that. Set aside your ego for a moment, Richard. Joshua is a good man, and a good scientist. And he thinks he may be able to help."

"Are you two coming?" Silver's voice echoed off the curving stone walls of the stairway.

McDonough removed his arm from Johnson's grasp and scrambled down the circular stone steps.

Silver was waiting at the bottom in a dimly lit room filled with display cases. "From what you told me in your email, and what I could see on the attachment of the mezuzah rubbing, I really think your hypothesis is faulty," he said, further fueling Johnson's ire. "What was the primary passion of Abiathar's life? To rebuild the Temple? No! It was to restore the ritual sacrifices of Israel. Without sacrifice, without what the Jews believed was the manifest presence of God, the Temple is just another building."

Johnson shook his head dismissively as Silver turned and walked away between the cases. "Quite original thinking, Joshua," Johnson mumbled. "Always the obvious and easiest answer—sound-bite archaeology."

Josh Silver was twenty years younger and one hundred pounds heavier than Johnson. So, when his antagonist stopped, spun on his heel, and took a step toward him, Johnson's breath caught in his throat and he struggled to hold his ground.

"Richard, ya gotta let it go."

Both broad-shouldered and thick at the waist, with a bushy reddish-brown beard and wild shock of hair, at six-six Josh Silver had the bulk and mangy hide of an angered brown bear.

"I didn't jump the gun at Abydos. We were all waiting for you and your team to arrive before we started digging. Then that fool backed a truck into the side of the mound and we found ourselves staring down an entry shaft. What would you have done? Wait around and hope nobody went for a late night stroll and corrupted the site? C'mon, you would have done the same thing we did—run down that shaft to see what lay at the other end. So, give me a break, will ya?"

Just as quickly, Silver was off again, pounding down the aisle between partially unwrapped mummies who now lived under airtight glass canopies.

"Gets a bit complicated, doesn't it, now?" quipped McDonough as he followed the museum's curator.

Plotting his revenge while looking for an exit, Johnson trailed his colleagues.

Silver rested against a desk at the end of the aisle, folded his arms over his significant chest, and allowed a smile to widen the only gap between his whiskers. The smile infuriated Johnson more than the man himself.

"Can I see the mezuzah . . . please?"

Johnson reached into the padded leather case that hung over his left shoulder, withdrew the wrapped mezuzah, and handed it to Silver.

The bearlike scientist rested the bronze cylinder on the desk with the gentleness of a nurse with a newborn, unwrapping it and setting it on a thick cloth. He picked up a magnifying glass. With a deft touch, Silver rotated the mezuzah slowly, searching every inch of its surface.

"You've already identified the aleph and resh figures that arc up the sides of the cylinder," Silver said as he traced his fingers over the different markings, "the signature of this Abiathar. But the symbols under these two animals—the lion and the lamb—have stumped you, correct?"

"Well, Joshua, not entirely," McDonough interrupted. "We looked at those lines of symbols on the structures under the animals—they look like ornamental or decorative lines. But when you look more closely, there are recurring sets of symbols. One we know—the Hebrew letters *kaf, shin*, and *mem*—the letters for *mishkan*, meaning the residence, or dwelling place. It's the Hebrew word that was used to mean the Tent of Meeting. Then there are four arches, then kaf, shin, mem repeated again."

"What about the rest?" asked Silver.

"We don't know," McDonough admitted. "Some tau symbols, the budding staff, a scorpion. We know the symbols. We just don't know how—or if—they go together. That's why we're here."

Now the cleft in Silver's bushy whiskers stretched from ear to ear.

"Very well, Dr. Silver. The theatrics are not necessary. What is it that you wish to tell us?"

The curator pulled himself upright and his self-righteous smile disappeared beneath his whiskers.

"Of what family was Abiathar . . . what priestly family?" Silver asked.

"He was an Aaronite," said Johnson, "a descendant of the high priest Zadok and thus a member of the family line that faithfully carried out the duties of the sanctuary . . . the only priests allowed into the sanctuary of the Temple, the Holy of Holies."

"And you're looking for his plan B? What he would have done if the Temple he built was lost or destroyed, right?"

"Yes, yes, yes!"

"Okay. There are six sets of symbols creating these ornamental lines on the mezuzah. The first set is the aleph and resh, Abiathar's signature. The *mishkan* is the second set, alternating with the four arches, which is the third set. But look here . . . follow me on this. The fourth set, these tau symbols—three together in repeating order—is called the Triple Tau. It is a very old symbol—predates Abiathar by a millennium—and one that has been misused and maligned throughout history. As you both know, the tau is the last letter of the Hebrew alphabet. But this Triple Tau design—with the upright *T* standing on the two *T*s lying on their sides, like an *H* shape—has been part of the Hebrew Kabbala ever since Moses helped the Hebrews escape from Egypt. Supposedly, it was decoded from the Talmudic declaration of God—"I Am that I Am." Among other things, the symbol means Templum Hierosolyma—the Temple of Jerusalem."

The Temple? Johnson's petulance began to ebb.

"It has other meanings, too. The Triple Tau has also been translated to mean a key to a treasure . . . or . . . a place where a precious thing is concealed . . . or . . . the precious thing itself."

Johnson's heart felt like the strumming of a twelve-string guitar, his animosity for Silver vanishing with each word from his mouth.

"Sadly, this symbol has been hijacked and corrupted from its original meaning." Silver turned to his two guests, leaving the mezuzah on the desk. "Back in the sixteenth or seventeenth century, when Free Masonry got its start, the Masons adopted the Triple Tau, enclosed in a triangle and surrounded by a circle, as a sacred symbol of progression. Then"—Silver shook his head—"the Ku Klux Klan took the symbol of the Triple Tau and used it as the central symbol on the Klan's flag."

"Aye, that's mad," said McDonough. "From the divine to the profane. Such a sad report."

"Yeah . . . but what interests us is its original meaning—the Temple in Jerusalem," said Silver, "particularly in light of this other set of symbols separating it. If Abiathar, a priest of the Hebrews, was behind these etchings and he was sending it to his peer in Egypt, then this third set . . . the four arches . . . most likely represents wilderness. The four arches are hieroglyphic symbols—four tens—meaning the number forty. To a Hebrew priest, forty means wilderness. Israel was tested for forty years in the wilderness. Jonah preached judgment to Nineveh—spiritually a wilderness—for forty years. If you consider that the Triple Tau can not only represent the Temple, but could also mean a place where a precious thing is concealed, then I think there is a high level of probability that this series of symbols on the outside of this mezuzah . . . the Triple Tau and the four arches . . . is attempting to communicate that the Temple is in the wilderness."

"No . . . it must be the Tent," said Johnson, jumping into the conversation in spite of his bruised ego. "Abiathar knew where the Temple he built was hidden, under the Temple Mount. He must have been giving Meborak a second message, that the Tent is in the wilderness. But where? Joshua, do the other symbols help us?"

Silver shook his mangy head, picked up the mezuzah, and held it out in front of him. "That's what I was saying before. I thought I saw something on that rubbing and I just confirmed it when I examined the mezuzah. I don't believe all of these symbols are from your boy Abiathar.

"Look, between the sets of Triple Taus is the fifth symbol set—a budding staff and a scorpion. The budding staff is the symbol of the Aaronic priesthood, right? The scorpion—well, I've got to admit I simply don't know. Could be anything, but those symbols go with the first four sets. But, what is most interesting is *this*. Here . . . rub your finger over this line of symbols—the sixth set, a single tau and a palm tree, repeated three times."

Silver held the mezuzah out to Johnson as if it were a peace offering, sweeping the last of Doc's reluctance into the past. Johnson closed his eyes and ran his fingers over the etched surface. When he reached the single tau, his breathing skipped a beat. "It's different," he whispered, almost to himself. "The symbols . . . they feel different. There's a different edge to them."

"That's because they were made by different tools . . . at different times," said Silver. He picked up the magnifying glass. "Look, you can see the rougher edges on the single tau and the palm symbol. I felt it right away when you handed it to me. All the other etchings on the mezuzah were done with a smaller tool. Everything was polished to smooth edges. Except the sixth series, the single tau and palm tree images. They were added later."

With a quick step to Johnson's side, McDonough put his hand on Doc's shoulder. "Ah, that's it, then, isn't it," he said. "Fantastic!"

Johnson stepped back, the mezuzah still resting gently in his hands.

"It was lost," he said as he looked from McDonough to Silver. "The mezuzah and scroll probably never made it to Meborak. Somewhere in transit it was lost, and it remained lost for seven hundred fifty years until it popped into Charles Spurgeon's hands in Alexandria in the late nineteenth century. You're saying that whoever was hiding the mezuzah, wherever it was, added the single tau and the palm?"

Silver stepped over to Johnson with a big grin on his face and wrapped his right arm around Doc's shoulders. "Now it's payback time, Richard." Johnson stiffened. "I know where it was . . . and I know what those symbols mean."

Before a word could escape from Johnson's stunned lips, Josh Silver half-carried him to a case in the middle of the corridor while speaking over his shoulder to McDonough. "The tau represents many things, Brandon, but the tau and the palm tree together reminded me of something. For centuries, and in many places still today, the tau is called Saint Anthony's cross. Here . . . look."

Silver released Johnson from his grasp, made room for McDonough, and the three men gazed into a large, dimly illuminated glass case. It was a desert exhibit, a cave entrance constructed against the left wall, artifacts scattered on a sandy floor and—dominating the center of the exhibit—a large, three-dimensional picture of an emaciated, brown-robed man with a scraggily, white beard reaching down to his waist.

"This is Saint Anthony the Great," said Silver. "An Egyptian, a Coptic Christian, known as the father of monasticism . . ."

"A Coptic?" blurted Johnson, his eyes opening wide as he pored over the three-dimensional image.

Silver gave Johnson a quizzical look before continuing. "Yeah . . . a Coptic Christian. They were the majority in Egypt at the time. Saint Anthony was the first ascetic monk to go into the wilderness and live most of his life as a hermit, living first in a cave, then locked into the ruins of a Roman fort. When he died, in 356 Common Era, a monastery was built above his burial site. It's still there at the base of the al-Qalzam Mountains in Egypt, surrounding the huge al-Quiddis oasis. And it's still a monastery, the longest occupied monastery in the world.

"The tau became known as Saint Anthony's cross later in the tenth century and was worn as an emblem on the tunics of the Hospital Brothers of Saint Anthony. There was an illness called Saint Anthony's fire—a condition caused by eating rye or barley contaminated with a fungus. The disease caused convulsions and gangrene—eventually eating away its victims. It got its name because several monks of the Order of Saint Anthony were successful in treating the ailment."

"Joshua . . . what does all this have to do with the mezuzah?" Johnson said, trying to suppress his impatience.

"Look over at the right wall. See that drawing? It's a copy of a Coptic icon depicting Saint Anthony in the desert with several other images around him. On the left he's meeting with Saint Paul. On the right are several classic Egyptian symbols . . . the flying trident, the three fans, and the flanking lions. But look at the symbol above the lions . . . the markings that are inside that cartouche."

Johnson looked at the drawing, then down at the mezuzah in his hands. "They're the same," he said. "It's the same symbol, the tau and the palm tree."

Josh Silver turned away from Johnson to face the other two scientists.

"Richard, I don't know where the Tent of Meeting may be hidden, or if it even exists. There are other symbols on the mezuzah—vines, flowers, a lion, a lamb—I have no idea what they mean or if they are even connected. There's nothing obvious, and nothing in my experience, that would connect those other symbols to what we've already found.

"But one thing I do know. Wherever that mezuzah ended up, it spent time at the Monastery of St. Anthony. That cartouche, with those symbols," he pointed over his shoulder, "is carved into the stone over the doorway to the monastery's library. If you're looking for the Tent . . . the Temple hidden in the wilderness . . . I think you have to start looking in Egypt."

THE PRESENT

New York City

His story completed, Johnson stretched again, pulling out Rodriguez's chair from behind the desk and planting himself in its ergonomic cocoon. He leaned forward in the chair and rested his elbows against the desk.

"I'll tell you what I think. As much as I hate to admit it, I think Dr. Silver was right. Abiathar etched—or had someone etch—the outside of the mezuzah with everything except these three pairs of symbols, the single tau and the palm tree. I think he was telling us—anyone who looked—that he knew where the Tent was hidden. That's why he etched the word *mishkan* inside that structure under the lion. The home for the Lion of Judah. The home for his God. But somebody else etched in the single tau and the palm tree."

Johnson pointed across the desk. "Brandon, to bring you up to speed, it appears the mezuzah, and the scroll that was inside it, were kept in a locked room in the Bibliotheca Historique de L'Egypte in Suez from sometime in the eleventh century until sometime in the nineteenth century. At first, the room was the private domain of a small group of men—Coptic Christians of Egypt—who called themselves the Temple Guard. Then, about two hundred years ago, there was some violent overthrow. A new group—Muslims this time—calling themselves the Prophet's Guard, wrested control of the room and the scroll from the Coptics. Not long afterward, the mezuzah and scroll disappeared from the locked room . . . called the Scroll Room . . . and, for a time, the Prophet's Guard appeared to vanish."

Johnson slid from the chair, moved behind the desk to a large map of the Middle East that Rodriguez had pinned to corkboard. With his finger on Suez, Doc turned toward Bohannon. "Tom, do you know where Taphanes, the city that Jeremiah and the exiles escaped to, is located? Here"—he inched his finger up—"along the Suez River, just north of Suez. And, right here, just south of Suez, at the foot of Al-Qalzam mountain range, is St. Anthony's Monastery." Doc rested his hand on the map. His hand and fingers more than covered all the land from Taphanes in the north to the monastery in the south. "Pretty close together, right?"

Johnson bowed his head and ran the fingers of both hands through the long, silver curls that flowed like rapids around the nape of his neck and over his shirt collar. When he turned to face the room, Tom saw weary resignation in his eyes.

"Gentlemen, if the president of the United States truly wants us to find the Tent of Meeting . . . if such a thing even exists . . . then I think we have to consider a certain confluence of evidence. Jeremiah is the last person reported in possession of the Tent. Jeremiah escaped to Egypt with Jewish exiles who were fleeing Nebuchadnezzar's army. Abiathar's mezuzah was sent to Egypt with a message—a message that appears to have failed to reach his coconspirator, Meborak. The mezuzah we found has what appears to be a newer set of markings including the symbol of the tau, the symbol of Saint Anthony's cross. St. Anthony's Monastery is close to Suez—the home of the Prophet's Guard—where our mezuzah and scroll were either hidden or protected for over seven hundred years in the Bibliotheca de L'Egypt. Correct me if I'm wrong, Brandon, but my experience tells me that if I'm looking for a clue to the location of the Tent of Meeting, perhaps a good place to search would be the Monastery of St. Anthony."

∾∿∿∾

"So, is that it, then?" blustered McDonough. "Tripoli, Mount Nebo, and a monastery in the middle of the desert? Just hold onto your britches. If we're talking about Jeremiah being a catalyst in this search for the Tent of Meeting, then I believe there is an entirely different path we may need to follow in looking for clues to the Tent's ultimate destination."

Brandon McDonough's round, jovial face and Irish brogue were as warm as the glowing bed of a peat fire. Under his academic tweeds there was little evidence of the Belfast boy from Bogside who survived bombings along the Shankill Road and who fought his way out of "the Troubles"—the religious guerrilla war spawned by four centuries of English occupation of the Irish nation.

His smile was as big as the tales he told, but there was a steely resolve under the good-natured veneer—the determination of a man who refused to accept "you never can" as a determinate of his future. McDonough was a formidable apologist. And he wasn't prepared to give any ground.

"In Jeremiah's day, after Nebuchadnezzar crushed Judah, destroyed Jerusalem and the Temple, a group of rebels—or patriots, depending on who's telling the tale—scooped up Jeremiah and his scribe, Baruch, in their fleeing band. Their number also included Zedekiah's daughters, including the princess Tamar, or Tephi, and her handmaidens . . . clearly an attempt at securing and continuing the royal line of Judah. And this whole motley crew headed to Egypt and the promised protection of the Egyptian Pharaoh, Hophra.

"The exiles from Judah settled in the city of Taphanes, but Jeremiah prophesied that God's wrath—in the form of Nebuchadnezzar's armies—would find the Jews in Egypt. In other words, it was time to leave.

"From biblical history, that's the last we hear of Jeremiah," said McDonough. "But not from recorded history. There are many historians who claim ancient writings prove Jeremiah not only left Egypt, but that he also sailed—along with Baruch, the princess Tephi, and her servants—first to Gibraltar and then to the most beautiful place on earth."

"So Jeremiah ended up in California?" asked Rizzo.

"Ah, not exactly California," said McDonough. "No, Jeremiah sailed to Ireland. And Zedekiah's daughter, Tephi, married the king of Ireland."

"And I'm the queen of the fairies," snapped Rizzo. "Have you been hitting the sauce? Next you're going to tell us that Jeremiah ended up sharing an apartment with Saint Patrick and Santa Claus and a couple of leprechauns with a pot of gold."

McDonough crossed the room to the whiteboard and, taking a marking pen from Rodriguez, added a fourth column and labeled it Ireland.

"This is no fairy tale, Samuel," he said, turning back to the room. "It's the stuff of legend and lore, most certainly. But there is enough legend, and enough support to those legends, that we need to take this possibility seriously. Look," McDonough said, swinging his right arm to include them all, "you really don't have much hope of finding the Tent of Meeting, no matter what you do. But, if you are seriously going to consider the first three as possibilities, then you've also got to at least consider this possibility . . . particularly when you look at all the evidence linking Ireland, Egypt, and Israel."

In spite of himself, Bohannon was intrigued by McDonough's story. "What kind of evidence?" he asked. "We might as well listen."

McDonough scanned the faces of his audience, nodded his head, and perched himself on the corner of Joe Rodriguez's desk.

"According to ancient lore, many believe the lost tribe of Dan—one of the twelve tribes of Israel—also settled on the Emerald Isle. *The Psalter of Cashel*, an ancient book of Irish history, states that the Tuatha de Danaan ruled in Ireland for about two centuries, and they were also said to have possessed a grail-like vessel.

"The kings of Ireland were called Ardagh. That's a Hebrew word—*Ard*, meaning commander and *Dath* meaning laws or customs . . . the commander of the laws. And, up until the time of Saint Patrick, the law of Ireland was identified as the Law of Moses."

Silence hovered in Rodriguez's office, wrestling with the lingering aroma of stale coffee. No one challenged McDonough's theory, perhaps because they didn't know him well enough to skewer him. It was Doc Johnson who pounced first.

"Now, Brandon, you're talking about an incredible leap here. Do you really think there's a connection between Jeremiah, Abiathar, and the Irish? The Tuatha De Danaan, they invaded Ireland, what, seven hundred years before Christ?"

"More."

"So, there's at least fifteen centuries, an ocean, and a continent between the Tuatha Da Danaan and Abiathar," said Doc. "Jeremiah in Ireland . . . seems to me you are desperately grasping at straws. Do you really think we should be putting our faith in myths and legends?"

"Aye, you are most certainly correct," said McDonough, with a twitch in his eyebrows and a twinkle in his eye. "Exceptin' that it may not be so much myth and legend, after all."

"How can you be so sure?"

"Sure, now, I wouldn't want to be takin' you on a fairy hunt," said McDonough, "and I would chalk it up to a wee tendency to exaggerate, for which the Irish are famous, except for three very fascinating facts."

McDonough looked around the room at the expectant faces and allowed the pause to lengthen into silence.

"Jeepers creepers, Saint Patrick," snapped Rizzo. "Spill it, will ya?"

McDonough rubbed the side of his nose and a chuckle tumbled from the corners of his lips. "Richard, I know you have some experience with the Elephantine Papyri, is that not so?"

"Yes . . . yes," Johnson grumbled. "What of it?"

"Well, I've taken a trip to Brooklyn," said McDonough.

Johnson sat bolt upright in his chair as a self-righteous smile spread from Brandon McDonough's toes to his teeth. "Wilbour's treasure?" Johnson whispered.

"Aye . . . yes, Richard." McDonough leaned back against the desk, taking them all in. "Charles Edwin Wilbour was a very unique individual—a linguist, a reporter, and a lawyer, he was tarnished through some scandal involving Tammany Hall and Boss Tweed. In 1871 he went into self-exile in Paris and studied to become the first trained American Egyptologist.

"But Wilbour is best remembered for a remarkable purchase he made in 1893 on one of his many trips up the Nile. During a stop at Aswan, he bought a group of papyrus documents that were dug up on the Nile island of Elephantine by the locals. Wilbour died three years later. The Paris hotel where he lived packed all his belongings into a trunk and stuck the trunk in its attic, where it remained for the next twenty years. When Wilbour's possessions were finally returned to his family in 1916 they were donated to the Brooklyn Museum where it was discovered that his purchase was the first of three discoveries of what has come to be known as the Elephantine Papyri. These documents, written in Aramaic I might add, record much of the history of a Jewish community which lived in Egypt, even built their own, small temple, from the fifth century before Christ."

Crossing the room with a measured gait, McDonough placed a hand on Richard Johnson's shoulder—a peace offering—as he took the long way around to the whiteboard. "I went to the Brooklyn Museum this morning, enlisted the assistance of the principal librarian of the Wilbour Library of Egyptology, and studied these papyrus documents. One of them was different . . . appeared much older. The librarian said it dated to the early sixth century BCE, one hundred fifty years earlier than the other papyri, about the time of Jeremiah's exile. It was a legal document of a man purchasing property . . . in Persia.

"The librarian showed me a notation that was applied to the papyri at a later date by Azariah, an official of the temple at Elephantine. Azariah recorded on this papyrus document that this man left Egypt with his scribe, Baruch, and the daughter of King Zedekiah, and left the document in Azariah's safekeeping. Even though the papyrus is written in Aramaic, it concluded with this—"

McDonough turned to the whiteboard and drew an extended, vertical oval. Inside the oval he began drawing symbols. Without turning around he pointed to the symbols. "The first section has three lines—hieroglyphics, Aramaic, and

Demotic. In the middle is a pictograph—a budding shepherd's staff. The final sign is the massive rock—Gibraltar—with the hieroglyphic sign for travel."

He swiveled his head and set his eyes directly on Doc Johnson. "It's a signature," McDonough said. "The first three lines mean the same thing. Using the Aramaic you can decipher the Demotic—Prophet of God. The budding staff is the symbol of the Aaronic priesthood.

"I believe this papyrus records that the prophet Jeremiah purchased some property in Persia, deposited the deed with a secure Jewish population in Egypt, left the country, and sailed to the island of Gibraltar. And this cartouche," he said, pointing to the entire large oval with Jeremiah's name, "is Jeremiah's signature, validating the document."

"Okay, so you get the J-man to Gibraltar," said Rizzo, "but you haven't convinced me on the Irish Eyes thing yet. How can we ever know where Jeremiah's scrawny carcass ended up?"

"Aye, most certainly, that's the other two points. The first is the *Fadden More Psalter*. Five years ago, a man harvesting peat near Bir, in County Tipperary, found a twelve-hundred-year-old manuscript, a leather-bound book of Psalms. After four years of study, Ireland's National Museum recently revealed that it had discovered fragments of Egyptian papyrus inside the leather cover and that the leather binding probably came from Egypt. The museum described the finding as 'the first tangible connection between early Irish Christianity and the Middle Eastern Coptic church.'"

"Well, hit me with a hurling stick," said Rizzo.

"And the second point," said McDonough, a leprechaun's glint in his eye, "is that Jeremiah is buried in Ireland."

Four voices were raised in various levels of disbelief, but McDonough raised his hand, put flint in his voice, and sliced them to silence. "Jeremiah's tomb rests in County Meath, in Loughcrew, near Oldcastle. On large stones inside the tomb are carved hieroglyphics that many believe prove this is the tomb of Jeremiah, who came to Ireland from Egypt. And who's to say that some of those markings might not lead us to the whereabouts of a certain Tent, eh? Don't you think, Dr. Johnson, these markings might be worth a look?"

19

WINTER, 589 BC

Jerusalem

Baruch cursed himself for wanting to kill the king. But the thought warmed his blood. A sharp knife, quickly, through his lung and into his heart.

But it wouldn't be enough to save them.

Not now.

He ran through the Market District, the scroll tucked tightly under his arm, concealed under his cloak, his gulping breaths frosting the evening air. Baruch entered the city through the Water Gate and was now climbing the Ophel toward the Temple and the palace. It was late, so the Street of the Bakers was empty and quiet, except for the sound of his sandals slapping on the stones as he plunged forward with his news, his dread, and the book.

Nephussim, the scribe, initially refused to surrender the scroll. But Baruch was very persuasive. There was no time for debate.

Baruch skirted the outside of the temple court, a shadow darting under the porticoes. He slowed to a trot as he turned the corner of the palace wall and desperately tried to slow the deep gulps of frozen air he was pulling into his lungs. Geshur was at the gate.

"Someone chasing you, Baruch?"

Geshur leaned heavily on his spear, his shield absently propped against the portal of the gate. *Soon, he will not be so careless.* "I . . . I"—Baruch reached for breath—"thought there was someone . . . in the darkness . . ." The scroll suddenly felt like a boulder under his cloak.

"Your master is sleeping."

"More misery for me, then." Baruch raised a limp hand in farewell. He crossed the courtyard of the guard, the sweat on his brow stinging in the cold. The sour aroma of unwashed bodies and human waste assaulted him as he approached the guardhouse. Baruch passed the open door to the duty room, where oil lamps still burned brightly, and approached a small, wooden door bathed in shadow.

He hesitated at the threshold, then inched open the door as if it were made of water waiting to spill at the slightest quiver. Brittle in the cold, the leather hinges snapped in the silence.

A stirring in the dark heralded the rebuke. "Why have you come to disturb my sleep?" The rasping rattle of his voice had deepened in this place. "Have an urgent purpose, or leave as you came."

Closing the door behind him, Baruch leaned against the wood.

"The king is throwing his lot with Hophra."

"Egyptian swine," rasped the voice in the darkness. "And Hamutal has a fool for a pup. He has decreed a death sentence for all of us. You are certain?"

"Zedekiah will not pay tribute this year. His messenger left tonight. I was in the stables." Baruch waited, but no answer came.

He crossed the dirt floor, found the oil lamp, and took it to the hearth. He dug out an ember, ignited a rush, and lit the wick. Baruch placed the oil lamp back on the solitary table and turned to face his master.

Jeremiah looked all of his seventy years. His tunic hung from his bony shoulders as he creaked into a sitting position. Head hanging limp, stringy white hair falling over his face, Jeremiah coaxed one leg, then the other, off the bed and placed his feet on the floor.

Baruch had worried about his master's health for many months. Perhaps not in prison, but confined nonetheless in the courtyard of the guards, Jeremiah was withering under this sentence. The once flaming spirit was dimmer each day.

A whisper rose from Jeremiah's chest. "Nebuchadnezzar will crush this city under his heel. He will leave nothing standing this time."

Then, a miracle.

Before his eyes, Baruch watched a transformation in the aged priest and prophet, burdened and bruised by so many years of opposition, his conscience rubbed raw by the unfettered idolatry of his people. Baruch saw life put on Jeremiah's bones like a new cloak. His spine straightened. He pushed his hair and his shoulders back into place. The fire in his eyes, long banked embers, glowed brightly once more.

"Zedekiah is a dead man," said Jeremiah, sitting on the edge of his bed. "The Babylonians will come soon. It is time for us to move, my son."

Jeremiah turned his face to Baruch. His skin looked like the dry wadis in the desert, deeply gouged and pulled tight over his sharp chin and beaked nose. But a new resolve pulsed just under the surface.

"Call together the Korahites . . . and the house of Hilkiah," he said. "We must begin to build the carts and platforms. Have the priests come to me. We can no longer hide the dwelling place of the Lord in this city. It is no longer safe. Soon, Jerusalem will be only ashes and dust."

Jeremiah lifted his right hand and pointed at Baruch—a hand suddenly strong and steady. "And the scroll, Baruch. We need to change the scroll. Somehow you must convince . . ."

Baruch reached under his cloak with his right hand, withdrew the scroll from the pit of his left arm, and held out the bronze cylinder to his master. "Yes, master . . . I already have."

He handed the mezuzah to Jeremiah. "Make the changes now," said the old man. "Rewrite the scroll. Should anything happen to me, you know the plan. Tell the scribes the dwelling place of the Lord rests with Moses."

SUMMER, 586 BC

So many bodies littered the streets, Baruch couldn't run. Even if he had the strength.

Fireballs fell from the sky. The entire Second District was ablaze. Siege engines pounded on the walls at the northern end of Jerusalem, the city's most vulnerable side, the place where invaders always attacked. Nebuchadnezzar's two-and-a-half year siege would end tonight.

There was no water in Jerusalem for so long, that there were no tears to accompany the wailing of the wasted bodies that stumbled along the street. Famine was so pervasive, many of the poor souls trapped in the city were reduced to eating their own waste. Some fed on their children.

Baruch struggled on, sick in body and spirit. As he reached the courtyard of the guard, he could hear the tumult of hand-to-hand combat near the Fish Gate. The Babylonians had finally broken through.

There was no guard at the gate. The courtyard was quiet and empty, except for the old man sitting on the steps to the palace.

"Zedekiah has deserted the city." Baruch's voice echoed as he crossed the courtyard. "He and his royal guard fled through the gate near the king's garden. They are trying for the Arabah."

Baruch sat down heavily beside Jeremiah.

"Zedekiah's fate is sealed. Ours is not," said Jeremiah. "We may be subject to the whims of this Chaldean butcher, but we remain in the hands of the Lord. And remember, my son, we have fulfilled the will of the Lord. We have spoken the word of God to these idolaters in the house of Judah . . . you have written down those words . . . and we have ensured the safety of the Lord's dwelling place."

Jeremiah had a distant, troubled look on his face. Baruch thought his master was in pain. "My father, are you . . ."

"Did you replace the scroll?"

"Yes, master."

"Then it is safe. Only you and I, and the line of Aaron, know the truth."

The sounds of battle, and the screams of those being slain, were coming closer. Burning flesh scented the fetid air. Baruch lamented his fear. Jeremiah's hand, light as the wing of a dove, rested on Baruch's shoulder. "Be still, my son. Remember, 'Hear, O Israel: the Lord our God, the Lord is one.'"

"Do you really think the Shema will protect us against the swords of Babylon?"

Baruch felt the old man's hand on his hair. His heart fluttered, his breath caught in his throat, and his chin quivered as he turned to the man he had served for so many years.

"We recite the Shema Yisrael morning and evening," said Jeremiah, his words barely carrying above the clamor closing on the streets around the palace. "It is the most important part of our prayers . . . our last words. There is nothing after the Shema, nothing except faith." A peaceful smile cracked the creases of Jeremiah's face, a surpassing peace. "Have faith, my son."

A clattering came from the area around the gate, wresting Baruch's attention from his master's face. He turned to his right. Striding across the courtyard was a tall, muscular, bearded man, bronze armor covering his chest, silver helmet on his head . . . blood dripping from his drawn sword.

20

Sunday, August 16 (Continued)

New York City

Joe Rodriguez stood in front of the portable whiteboard, now covered with notes and questions arranged in four general columns. Looking at the board, a combustible mixture of fear and exhilaration raced through Rodriguez's body, rippling nervously over his spine. He had built a notable career as an expert in electronic library science, emerging from an educationally ambitious Puerto Rican family in the Washington Heights section of Manhattan to a position of responsibility and authority in the New York City library system. Not only did Rodriguez oversee the material and operations of the Periodicals Room in the Humanities and Social Sciences Library on Bryant Park, but he had also built an international reputation as a visionary with his two books on the cyber information revolution sweeping through the world's greatest libraries.

But scrape away all the sheen and Joe Rodriguez was still only a librarian. In the library, his boundless energy and New York attitude often felt confined. An athlete in his youth, still lean and muscular with long arms, his intense brown eyes and relentless gait shimmered with restrained power. He was an inmate of the marble floors and richly ornamented rooms of New York City's most famous library—an uneasy inmate now that adventure once again collided with his quiet, measured life.

Rodriguez looked at the symbols on the whiteboard and his spirit heard hypnotic songs of mystery, discovery . . . and danger . . . like a drug, once experienced, now luring him into temptation.

He took a breath and shook his head, then turned to the world map covering a large corkboard on the far wall of his office. He picked four pushpins from his desk drawer and stepped in front of the map.

"Tripoli, in Lebanon—Abiathar's destination after the fall of Jerusalem to the Crusaders."

He pushed in a second pin. "Mount Nebo, in Jordan—according to the Bible, the place where the prophet Jeremiah hid the Tent of Meeting and the Ark of the Covenant in a cave."

Rodriguez traced a meridian south. "The Monastery of St. Anthony, the oldest inhabited monastery in the world, in the eastern desert of the Sahara, deep in the Red Sea wilderness."

"And, lastly." Rodriguez traced his finger northeast over the map, and settled on a small island, where he inserted his last pushpin. "County Meath in Ireland . . . according to the good Dr. McDonough, the legendary tomb of Jeremiah."

Joe turned back toward the others sitting in his office, sweeping his left arm in the direction of the four pins on the map. "Quite an assortment of locations, or possibilities," he said.

"Well, there is another," said McDonough. "If one of you gentlemen happen to return to Jerusalem, below the hill of Golgotha, outside the walls of the Old City, is Jeremiah's Grotto. Tradition—legend?—holds that this is where the prophet Jeremiah was held prisoner by King Zedekiah and where he wrote the book of Lamentations. Having been underfoot of tourist traffic for hundreds of years, I doubt the Tent could be hidden in Jeremiah's Grotto. But perhaps a clue?"

A smile crept onto Joe Rodriguez's face and the crinkly lines at the corners of his mouth charted the rapid beating of his heart. "So . . . now what?"

"I don't know about you, but I need a break," said Rizzo, hopping off his chair and heading to the door. "How about we start with lunch?"

~~~~~

Doc Johnson balanced the remnants of a roast beef on rye as if it were a fragile shard of Egyptian pottery. "Gentlemen, please, before we wander any further down these wispy threads of conjuring . . . I know and understand the thrill, the adrenaline rush, of the hunt for hidden treasures. Yes, I feel its tug myself. But, can one of you tell me why we should even entertain the possibility of rejoining the arena of international conflict?"

The peppery sweet aroma of hot pastrami floated in the air of Joe's office, barely masking the brackish scent of growing anxiety.

Bohannon wiped his fingers on a well-used napkin. "Well, Doc, I told you—"

"Yes, I know. The president thinks we might find some clue to the location of the Tent. The president has the full force of the military, the FBI, the CIA, and God knows how many clandestine strike forces, at the snap of his fingers. Why can't the most powerful government on earth inspect these four locations? Why should we risk our lives again?"

Tom was losing his patience with Doc. "Why?" he said. "First, because Whitestone asked—the president of the United States, remember? Second, he got the Israelis to back off and allow Kallie back into the country. And, third, we're in the same predicament now that we were in two months ago . . . the guys with the amulets know who we are, where we are, and what we've got. And they want it back. And they want *us* erased from the equation. It's simple, Doc. We're in this whether we like it or not.

"I know *I* don't like it. If it were my choice, I wouldn't consider getting involved. But, Doc, I think my family and I are safer if we cooperate with the most powerful man on earth, than if we tell him to shove off, we don't care about the fate of the world. So, I'm going to help—even though I'm not crazy about it. What you do is up to you."

21

MONDAY, AUGUST 17

Greenwich, CT

Conflicted and confused, Bohannon pulled into the parking lot at Harvest Time Church looking for counsel . . . guidance . . . answers. Looking for help.

Harvest Time Assembly of God Church straddled the border between New York and Connecticut, more on the Greenwich side. It was a thirty-minute drive from Riverdale in the Bronx, but a drive the Bohannons gladly made each Sunday and twice a month on Friday for a soaking in praise and worship. Googled by Annie when they were searching for a church, the first day they walked into Harvest Time both Tom and Annie knew they were home.

Pastor Glenn Harvison waved Tom into his office, shook his hand, and hugged him at the same time. "Hi, Tom. It's good to see you. C'mon, sit down."

Harvison was ten years younger than Bohannon, about the same height, but carrying a couple dozen extra pounds around his midsection. His face full, but welcoming. Only his eyes were concerned.

"You know I love to see you," said Pastor Glenn, settling behind his desk, "but you usually don't show up here on a Monday afternoon. What's up?"

It wasn't only the soft, wingback chair that gave Tom comfort. He felt safe . . . confident that he was in the right place. "I don't know what to do."

Pastor Harvison smiled. "You would be surprised at how many conversations in this office start off with that same statement. But, first . . . let's pray."

Bohannon closed his eyes, bowed his head, and allowed Pastor Harvison's prayer to wash through him, settle his heart, and bring peace to his mind.

"Now, tell me, how can I help?"

"You know what I've been involved in."

"Yes . . . a miracle."

"Well, the whole thing is cooking up again. There's a situation that is developing in Israel, in Jerusalem, that appears to be connected to our search for the Temple. President Whitestone asked me—well, me and the other guys—to look for more clues on the scroll and mezuzah. We found some, and now it looks like we may be pulled back into this—maybe it's never stopped. It looks like the Prophet's Guard is still after the scroll and mezuzah. Like they're still after us."

Bohannon took a breath. Pastor Glenn didn't try to fill the silence.

"I don't want this, Pastor. I'm scared. My family is scared. Annie is frustrated, angry, worn out with worry. I don't know what to do." He shook his head and looked out the window at the woods behind the church. "The first time, I felt called. Like God selected us. Now, I don't know. Part of me wants to help. Part of me feels like I'm being selfish and arrogant. Why do I need to be involved? Why do they need me? Why can't somebody else take care of this?"

He turned his face and looked at his pastor. "And part of me . . . I have to confess . . . part of me is excited. I've never been so afraid, or felt so alive, as I did breaking the code, searching for that Temple." Bohannon felt the catch in his throat, the moisture in his eyes. "God help me, Pastor, part of me wants to go back."

Glenn Harvison moved forward, placed his elbows on the top of his desk, rested his chin on his thumbs, and leaned his face into his steepled fingers.

"Tom . . . what do you have to be thankful for?"

"I'm sorry?"

"What do you have to be thankful for?"

Bohannon's confusion grew to a new level. "My wife . . . our marriage . . . our children," he said. "I'm thankful for my job, this church, my salvation. A lot."

Pastor Harvison tipped his head to the right. "And how many of those blessings came from God?"

"All of them."

"And how many of those things that you're grateful for belong to God? How many of them are in his hands?"

"All of them."

"And how many of those blessings are you worried about?"

Bohannon's gaze focused on his pastor. "All of them."

"Does that make any sense?" asked Harvison.

Bohannon shook his head, clarity entering his heart. "No, none of it."

Pastor Harvison leaned back in his chair. "Tom, you know that God has a sovereign will and a permissive will. He gave man the capacity to choose. We all have the ability to make choices that impact and influence our lives. That is God's permissive will. But there is also God's sovereign will. The almighty creator of all things . . . he has a plan. A plan that he ordained before the beginning of time. A plan that can never change. All things . . . *all* things . . . are under God's control. And that includes each of our lives.

"A believing Christian, who earnestly and honestly seeks to know and understand the fullness of God's will for his life—and do that will—is under the ruling power of God's sovereign will. Tom, God's sovereign will for your life will never be compromised by his permissive will for others. His sovereign will for your life cannot and will not ever change. Nothing . . . *nothing* . . . can ever change God's sovereign will for you, for me, or for this world. It is sealed.

"So, circumstances may influence your life, but they can never change your destiny."

Now it was Bohannon's turn to sit and wait in the silence.

"I don't have any doubt that God's hands are at work in what he clearly has called you into," Pastor Harvison said. "Only God knows why. *Why* isn't a question God often answers. Maybe adventure originally captured you, but prayer—God's answered prayer—led you to that Temple. And prayer will lead you to the right decisions now. But . . . Tom . . . this is your destiny. It's clear. God's power is at work here, at work in your life, at work in this quest you've been handed. If this is God's sovereign will for your life, you need to be prepared, because God's sovereign will for your life cannot ever be changed."

Bohannon didn't feel any better. But he now knew better.

"Tom, I suggest you go home and pray with your wife. Pray for God's direction. So that you will both have peace. Because I'm pretty certain what answer you will receive. And, Tom"—Pastor Harvison stood behind his desk and extended his hand toward Tom—"may God go with you."

New York City

"I've been to Tripoli," Johnson said, dodging the late afternoon bicycle traffic and hordes of tourists as he and Joe Rodriguez navigated Fifth Avenue on the east flank of Central Park, headed to the Metropolitan Museum of Art. "The

British Museum sent a team of us there to review the Crusader castle, Krak de Chevaliers, when it was first being considered as a UNESCO world heritage site. The castle was the base of operations for the military order of the Knights Hospitaller."

"So, why would Abiathar escape to Tripoli?" Joe asked. "The first time his family and the Jews were forced to abandon Jerusalem they went to Tyre. Why go a lot farther this time, all the way to Tripoli, if the Crusaders were already there?"

Johnson was having a tough time keeping up with Rodriguez's long, loping stride. He seized on a fortuitous red light at 86th Street to liberate a nearby park bench.

"Doc?" Rodriguez turned around at the street corner, a puzzled look on his face.

"Joseph, please. A moment of respite for an old man?" Johnson patted the empty bench beside him. The late afternoon sun escaped the clutches of Manhattan's skyscrapers, those long fingers that snatched the light from so many New Yorkers, and its heady warmth bored through the gaps in the leafy limbs of the Central Park forest. Johnson's aging bones sucked in the warmth.

Rodriguez retreated and sat on the abused green slats.

Doc's heart was warmed whenever he spent time alone with this surprising librarian. It was more than the young man's quick mind, a fine asset. There was a . . . what . . . a gentleness . . . a sweetness about Joe Rodriguez that even Washington Heights couldn't dilute. In many ways, Joe reminded Doc of Winthrop Larsen. Perhaps there was some transference of affection, some self-preservation in shifting his allegiance from the painful memory of Winthrop's violent death. But Doc often found himself smiling when he saw Rodriguez, the smile ignited by what Johnson could only imagine was akin to a father's pride. He would have been grateful for a son like Joe.

"I think," he said, turning slightly to look at Rodriguez instead of the teeming throngs sluicing along the sidewalks of Fifth Avenue, "there were two reasons Abiathar traveled the extra distance to Tripoli. First, Tripoli was still free. The Crusaders laid siege to most of the coastal cities of Palestine, and captured most of them, including Tyre, on their march to Jerusalem. But they bypassed Tripoli. It would have been too difficult to subdue, so they skipped it and continued on toward Jerusalem, the ultimate prize.

"It was only after Jerusalem fell into their hands that the Crusaders turned their attention to the unfinished business of Tripoli." Johnson closed his eyes and allowed the intense afternoon sun to wash through his eyelids. He stretched his neck back and forth and flexed his shoulders. It was like a cosmic massage. He kept his eyes closed, luxuriating. "The Europeans dispatched their most accomplished warrior, Raymond of Saint-Gilles, Count of Toulouse, to crush the Muslim defenders of Tripoli. He surrounded the city and laid siege, but it took ten years, and Saint-Gilles was long dead, before Tripoli finally fell in 1109. True to their reputation, the Crusaders totally destroyed the old city, massacred the inhabitants, and built a new city over the Muslim town."

Doc lifted his head, turning his face to perfectly capture a shard of sunlight slashing through the leaves. It was decadent.

"So . . . Doc . . . what was the second reason?" There was a thin edge of exasperation in Joe's voice.

"Oh, yes. Forgive me, Joseph. I feel like I'm being hugged by the universe." Doc's body gave a little shiver, and he turned his attention back to Rodriguez.

"At the time Abiathar escaped Jerusalem, Tripoli lacked Crusaders," said Johnson, now fully engaged. "But it possessed one of the greatest libraries of the ancient world—the *Dar al-Ilm* the Muslims called it, the house of knowledge—and, in Abiathar's time, the Dar al-Ilm held three million manuscripts in its halls. But the Crusaders brought the same savage butchery to Tripoli that they unleashed against Jerusalem, destroying the city and burning its significant Muslim buildings, including the Dar al-Ilm."

Johnson's train of thought was broken by the image of three million ancient documents going up in smoke, victims of ignorance and bloodlust.

"Doc . . . are you okay?"

"Yes . . . yes, Joe." Johnson ran his fingers through his hair.

"Okay, so why did Abiathar need a library?"

"To be honest, I'm not positive. When you consider Tripoli as a destination, there are few reasons why Abiathar would take on such a long journey from Jerusalem. Tripoli was the major silk producer outside of China. It had flourishing citrus groves spread across the broad plain from the Abu Samra escarpment on the east to the seacoast. And it was an important port city for landlocked Damascus. Its fortress dominated the traffic on the coastal road."

"Okay, Doc, but we know Abiathar was probably not interested in silk, lemons, or fish."

"Correct, Joseph. Which essentially leaves us the library." Johnson clasped his hands behind his head and leaned back against the park bench. "And, if my friend Dr. McDonough is correct about Abiathar putting in place a Plan B, perhaps the Dar al-Ilm held the information he needed to implement that plan. Or"—he cast a glance in Joe's direction—"perhaps there was something that Abiathar wanted to deposit in the Dar al-Ilm for safekeeping, eh? And where better to hide a document than in a library with three million other documents?"

Feeling as if his energy tank had been refilled, Johnson sprang to his feet.

"I'm not sure, Joseph. From Kallie's earlier research we know Abiathar traveled to Tripoli for his second exile. And he must have had a pressing reason to do so. Well, let's get a move on. We're not going to get anything accomplished sitting around the park all day. We've got work to do, my boy." Johnson turned on his heel and quick-stepped across 86th Street in defiance of the red, blinking hand that suggested time was short. He would need a lead, just to keep up with the long-legged Mr. Rodriguez.

Amman, Jordan

Abu Gherazim, foreign minister of the Palestinian Authority, looked down from the podium in the Jordanian parliament hall. King Khalil was a man of his word. He must have asked, threatened, and cajoled . . . and pulled in a number of favors. The hall was nearly full, the diplomatic corps had turned out en masse, but also the Jordanian senior officials. Staff from every Islamic embassy along with a goodly number of Jordanian political, economic, and religious leaders. The press gallery was overflowing with reporters from around the world.

But would they listen? The ones who most needed to hear the truth . . . would they listen? Those faces turned toward him were delivering a mixed response. Gherazim stepped to the microphone. After the required greetings, Gherazim eschewed a preamble and got right to the point.

"Across the face of the world, Muslims of goodwill proclaim Islam as a way of peace, a religion of acceptance, an extension or completion of other prophets revered by Jew and Christian, including Abraham, Moses, and Jesus. Muslims are devout citizens—Americans, French, English, Indian. Men and women who are loyal to their country while still being faithful to their religion.

"In a peaceful Islam, coexistence is not a dichotomy," said Gherazim. There was urgency to his voice, but also a confident assurance that appeared to calm much of the assembly's anxiety. "Sadly, for the true followers of Islam, our faith—the words and spirit of our prophet, Muhammed, the revelation of the truth of Allah—has been abducted and held captive by a minority of extremists. These disciples of violence represent the smallest segment of Islam but, because of their addiction to the heresy of terror, they receive almost all of the attention and define our faith to the world—a critical misunderstanding.

"The Christian Bible contains a great deal of violence—violent warfare, violent family confrontations in the Old Testament. And the violent words of Jesus himself: 'Do you think I came to bring peace on earth? No, I tell you, but division . . . They will be divided, father against son and son against father . . . If anyone comes to me and does not hate his father and mother, his wife and children, his brothers and sisters . . . he cannot be my disciple.' The book of Revelation tells of Jesus coming back to destroy the world and three-quarters of its inhabitants."

Gherazim looked across the room at the now bewildered faces turned in his direction.

"Why, then, is Christianity considered, in the main, a religion of peace? A religion of love?" he asked. "Because its believers are no longer driven by a desire to violently destroy all who fail to embrace their faith—as they were a thousand years ago—but by a confident expression of their doctrine, 'the meek shall inherit the earth.'

"I ask you, my brothers, what should be the confident expression of Islam? What is the desire of our God, Allah, the most high? What is the message of our prophet, Muhammed? Words of peace?

"'And those who believe and do good are made to enter gardens, beneath which rivers flow, to abide in them by their Lord's permission; their greeting therein is, Peace.'

"'And spend in the way of Allah and cast not yourselves to perdition with your own hands, and do good; surely Allah loves the doers of good.'

"Or," said Gherazim, "is the message of our Prophet these words of warfare and violence: 'And kill them wherever you find them, and drive them out from whence they drove you out, and persecution is severer than slaughter, and do not fight with them at the Sacred Mosque until they fight with you in it, but if they do fight you, then slay them; such is the recompense of the unbelievers.

"'And Nuh said: My Lord! leave not upon the land any dweller from among the unbelievers.

"'Surely we have prepared for the unbelievers chains and shackles and a burning fire.'

"In whatever way you count your calendar, the modern world moves forward while many of the voices of Islam are determined to keep our religion a captive of the Dark Ages, in the womb of a hatred first conceived ten centuries ago. How can the modern world accept a religion that stones young women to death, cuts off the hands of thieves, and sentences children to a life of ignorance and bigotry? Even worse . . . that straps explosives to the bodies of our children and sends them to their death in the name of God?

"Brothers—" Gherazim leaned against the podium—"I beseech you. Please, let us take up the call of Allah to love and do good works. Let us pick up the Islamic standard—not just peaceful coexistence, but willing acceptance of all other faiths. Let us make the choice to step boldly into a future in which Islam embraces peace and reforms itself from within, purging itself of a misguided doctrine that corrupts the true faith of every Muslim. Let us not only renounce terror, let us also reform our doctrine and remove all traces of the dark age of jihad and the fanaticism it foments."

He took a deep breath to quiet his nerves and gauge his reception. His pulse thumped like the drums of war. The parliamentary hall remained silent.

"Brothers, next week I will convene here in Amman a colloquy of Muslim clerics, men—like me—who believe the moment is here, is critical, for us to firmly establish peace-loving, inclusive Islam in the twenty-first century. I pray that Allah will lead you to join us."

As Gherazim stepped away from the podium, applause spattered the hall like the first heavy drops of a summer squall, but it failed to build and faded to an awkward silence.

"Heretic!" someone shouted from the back.

"May Allah curse your children," rumbled another.

It would be a long road.

New York City

It hung in the air between them, this overstuffed brown manila envelope with the gilded seal of the U.S. State Department at the top left corner. Reynolds held it out, but Tom was reluctant to touch it, as if it carried a virus that would take his life. Reynolds had made the trip to Riverdale to deliver the package, and the president's briefing.

"The war has been joined on one side for a long time, Tom," said Reynolds, dropping his arm to his side. "We've just not been willing to admit it. Now, we have tangible, visible evidence of boots-on-the-ground warfare. Muslim boots against Muslim governments, yes, but the rebellions of the Arab Spring—in Tunisia, Yemen, Bahrain, Egypt, Syria—are not rebellions *against* Islam. They are *for* Islam, mostly against governments that had the audacity, the courage, to build relationships and alliances with the West. Make no mistake. These rebellions in the Middle East and Northern Africa are not rebellions in the true sense of the word. They are coups. Overthrows of legitimate governments by a hidden, nefarious military power. A growing military power that has one clearly stated goal—the destruction of all modern Western governments and cultures and the imposition of Islamic rule throughout the world. We once feared world dominance by Communism, by its nuclear weapons. What will we face, what will we fear, when radical Islam controls nuclear weapons?

Bohannon grimaced. "Sounds like we need a miracle."

"It's coming down to survival—whether our way of life will survive. In ten years, what will our world look like? Shoot—right now, we don't know what our world is going to look like ten days from now. Everything changed with Osama bin Laden's death. Tomorrow, everything could change again."

Reynolds held out the large manila envelope one more time. "This is no time for soul-searching, Tom. There is a new leader in the East and he is calling for a Holy War that could destroy the world as we know it. We don't even know who he is. But we've got to stop him."

1937

Kazimain, Iraq

Thick, red-black blood pulsed from his neck and mixed with the ocher grit of dust and sand.

Beyond the surprise that his disciple could be treacherous and murderous, and the embarrassment that his nephews would see him lying dead in the street, Ayatollah Haydar al-Sadr was frightened. Not of death. Death comes to all. And, even though he was only forty-six, death came for him now.

No, the ayatollah was frightened for his two nephews. True, they were sons of Shi'a imams, descendants who could trace their lineage directly back to Muhammad. But they were not ready. Their young minds were still grasping to understand truth. Sayeed seemed to understand. But Moussa . . . ah, Moussa was another matter.

So sad to die before Moussa had understanding.

Haydar al-Sadr turned his face to the merciless, burning Iraqi sun—and felt no heat. Only sticky goo as it spread around his face.

——

Moussa al-Sadr looked down at the pool of blood surrounding his uncle's kaf-fiyeh, fouling his beard, staining his black kaftan. Then he looked once more in the direction of the fleeing assassin.

Moussa fixed his eyes on the murderer's back, now slipping into the shadows of their Islamist school building. With the recklessness of a ten-year-old—his skirts raised—he ran to the far side of the school. He pulled a small dagger from his waistband, extended his turban-covered head around the corner, and scanned the area.

There was no one in sight.

——

Nine-year-old Sayeed sank to his knees, soaking his kaftan in his uncle's blood. His thin, short arms reached out and cradled his uncle's head.

Haydar's eyes searched for the sun, then turned to Sayeed. "God is good, my nephew. His word is true. God loves all men. Remember that. Will you . . . will you, Sayeed? Will you remember?"

——

Moussa al-Sadr edged along the back wall of the school, the dagger hanging at his side. At the next corner he heard deep, rasping breaths. He looked around the edge.

The assassin stood with his back flat against the mud wall of the school. His eyes were wide in surprise. His neck was opened wide in a false grin, springs of blood pouring from the deep slice that curved from ear to ear. Only the muscular left arm of Jafar, the ayatollah's faithful servant, held the assassin fast against the wall.

⌁∿∿⌁

Sayeed took his hand and brushed the coarse sand from the side of his uncle's face. Blood smeared from his fingers, the smear blotched and spotted where Sayeed's tears found his uncle's face. "Yes, my uncle. I will never forget. I will never forget you. I will never forget God's goodness."

Haydar's eyelids fluttered, then opened wide. A halting gasp, a shiver in his shoulders. And his spirit left a now limp, lifeless body.

Sayeed pulled his uncle closer, hugging the man to his chest. His weeping was silent.

⌁∿∿⌁

The assassin's eyes still blinked with life, but that life was pumping quickly out through his neck. Moussa stepped forward, focused on the man's eyes. He edged around Jafar and stood in front of the assassin until the man looked down into his young face. Then he reached up and plunged his dagger into the man's heart. The dying man's final gasp faded into a soft gurgle. Moussa slowly drew the dagger out halfway, then pulled the two-edged blade sharply to his left, slicing open the man's chest. "Now you die, infidel pig."

Moussa's robe was glued to his back, the perspiration dripping from his armpits. But not from the heat. He had killed his first man. His body felt as icy as snow in the Zagros Mountains. The sweet smell of fresh blood, mingled with the escaping gas of death, made his head swim. The man's eyes rolled to the back of his head.

"God is good, uncle," Moussa whispered, as a prayer. "God is very good."

THE PRESENT

New York City

As Reynolds pushed the envelope into his hands, Bohannon realized protests were futile. He was going.

"You're flying into Lebanon as tourists with a purpose. Pretty close to the truth . . . two librarians researching the history of the Dar al-Ilm," said Reynolds. "Fly into Beirut, then take a train to Tripoli. The tickets and directions are all inside. There's also an academic journal in there with an article about the Dar al-Ilm, authored by Joseph Rodriguez of the New York Library System. And employee badges and business cards for both of you from the Bryant Park library. You've got visitor's visas, which are good for the next thirty days, and a pair of well-worn passports—in your own names—that reflect stopovers in cities with great libraries."

Standing on his front porch, Bohannon felt as if he were having an out-of-body experience. "Is all this necessary?"

"Precautions," said Reynolds, "but necessary precautions now that Hezbollah has taken control of the Lebanese government. You'll be fine. The current political situation throws a note of uncertainty into our planning, but you'll be fine. Nobody is expecting you to show up in Tripoli."

"The others?"

"No problem," said Reynolds. "McDonough is simply going home. Dr. Johnson and Mr. Rizzo are simply themselves—an archaeologist returning to Egypt once again and his collaborator. Even with Rizzo's penchant for drawing attention to himself, they won't cause even a blip on the Egyptian radar. We got them a flight directly to Suez, so they won't be going anywhere near Cairo. And the Israelis have greased the doors for Annie and Kallie. I think they want to see Kallie come and go as quickly as possible, so there will be no glitches on their end.

"Don't worry." Reynolds reached out and tapped the envelope still hanging at the edge of Bohannon's fingers. "Everything's in there you'll need. They sent you your watch?"

"Yeah."

"Okay, good. And the instructions?"

"Yes!"

Reynolds sank into a rocking chair.

"All right. There's one other thing I've got to tell you."

An alarm went off in Bohannon's spirit and he focused closely, anxious about Reynolds's next words.

"If . . . and I say 'if' confident you're not going to need an 'if' . . . if something goes wrong, if you feel in any way that you are compromised, or in danger, then I want the two of you to leave Tripoli immediately. On the spot—got me? Don't go back to your hotel. Leave everything behind if necessary. Take a taxi to a bus stop, get on a bus heading south, and get in touch with me.

"Take the bus to the border crossing town of Adaisseh. It's a pretty small town. Come to the crossing gate at 9:11 a.m.—you can remember that. Go into the travel shop that sits across the road from the border gate—it sells every-thing, exchanges money for travelers. Lay two one-hundred-dollar bills on the counter and ask the clerk if he can exchange them into euros. He will take you out the back of the building and through an empty warehouse. He'll show you a door. Go out the door, cross an open square and through the portal on the other side—and you are in Israel.

"He will keep the hundreds," said Reynolds. "If he asks for your name, leave and come back in an hour. If he asks for your address, come back in two hours. If he asks for your name and address, leave and don't go back. Get ahold of me. If you can't reach me . . . well, keep trying. Or then you'll be on your own."

The envelope hit the porch with a thud.

———∞∿∿———

Somewhere nearby, a fire engine responded to an alarm, its claxon resonating into the night.

Midnight was approaching and Bohannon sat on the loveseat, looking sight-lessly out the window, searching for wisdom, waiting for a breeze.

"Are you coming to bed?"

He turned his head. Annie had her light summer robe pulled around her. Bohannon was sweating in the heat and humidity coming through the open windows. But Annie liked it cold in their bedroom and she was still shivering from the air-conditioned iciness. She sat next to him and inched closer, seeking his warmth. He put his arm around her shoulders. Her skin was always so soft, so smooth, like cashmere.

They were leaving tomorrow—all of them—going their different ways.

"I know this sounds hypocritical," Tom whispered, "but I don't want you to go."

"You're darn right it's hypocritical," Annie bristled. "You and Joe are going to Lebanon, right? Doc and Sammy are leaving for Egypt, right? Even McDonough has a task to fulfill when he gets back to Ireland, right? Right?"

Bohannon's emotions were on overload. "But it's such a risk."

"Of course it's a risk . . . everything is a risk." Annie squirmed in his arms, but her words softened. "Unless we went and lived on the moon, I don't know if this . . . this . . . danger . . . is ever going to pass us by."

Pulling away, Annie turned to face Tom. She took his hands in hers. As she spoke, her thumbs caressed the tops of his hands.

"Tom, I'm proud of you for going to see Pastor Harvison today. It gave me a lot of comfort and confidence when you told me about your conversation and we prayed for guidance." She lifted her hand and stroked his cheek. "I think Pastor's right. We're involved in this because God intends for us to be involved. But I also understand that, after all of that, you can still worry."

A mountain of long-past regret settled on Bohannon's chest and he felt as if his ribs would be crushed, his heart smothered. He struggled to draw a breath. "But, last time, so much went wrong. So many died. If this is God's sovereign will, how could so much bad come from it?"

Her hand stopped on his cheek and she stalled his worries by the look in her eyes.

"Just because it's ordained, I know, doesn't guarantee that we'll be safe," said Annie. "Any of us could be hurt. Staying at home, tomorrow we could be dead or alive. We don't have any control over that. But obedience is a choice we can make."

"I don't know. I just don't know."

"You don't know *what* . . . if you can trust God?" There was a trace of unbelief in Annie's question.

"Honestly . . . I don't know," Bohannon admitted. "I want to trust God. I mean . . . I do trust him. But . . . well . . . maybe I just don't trust myself."

Once again he felt "not good enough." Once again he felt defeated. Once again he felt alone.

She stroked the hair at his temple, the headstrong locks falling over his ear.

"Remember God's words: I will never leave you nor forsake you. Remember Joshua: Be strong and courageous. Do not be afraid. Remember our prayers and God's answers—that's what I'm trying to do," said Annie. "I believe God is at work here, that he's ordained this time for our lives. It's not about me doing a photo shoot—not anymore. And I know Kallie doesn't need me there. She's a strong woman, a warrior when you get away from the outside and look on the inside. I wish I could be more like her.

"But it'll be okay. We'll be waiting for you at Kallie's apartment when you get back from Lebanon and we'll all be back here before you know it."

Her voice was a whisper, her lips brushing the side of his face. "And, Tom . . . God will never leave you, the kids will never leave you. And I'll never leave you."

Tom Bohannon sat in the dark long after Annie returned to bed, trying, once again, to believe those words.

PART TWO

SANCTUARY
OF GOD

22

TUESDAY, AUGUST 18

Tripoli, Lebanon

He had barely lifted the phone to his ear before the caller started talking.

"They are on their way. Are you prepared?"

"Everything is in place."

"Do not fail me."

He knew that failure was not an option that he would live to tell about. "They will come, but they will not leave."

"See that they don't."

The caller hung up.

Jerusalem

The cell phone was in his hand, waiting, when it rang.

"They are on their way. Are you prepared?"

"Yes."

"Do you understand your instructions?"

"Yes. We will succeed. You will have what you need."

"What I need is them . . . alive. Do not fail."

A smile of anticipation creased his face. "We do not fail."

"See that you don't."

The cell phone went silent in his hand.

Suez, Egypt

One of the large men who guarded his safety handed him the ringing cell phone.

"They are on their way. Are you prepared?"

"I will be waiting for them, personally."

"That is a risk. Is it necessary?"

"My friend, I have been waiting for this moment a long time." His left hand toyed with the amulet beneath his robe. "We cannot miss this opportunity. My days are numbered. I must make sure all goes as planned. I dare not leave it to anyone else."

"Go with care. And may Allah go with you."

"And with you, my brother."

He closed his eyes and held the amulet tighter.

London, England

"He is on his way. Are you prepared?"

"When will he arrive?"

"Are you prepared?"

For a moment, offense rose in his heart. But the voice on the cell phone was his master. He bent his head. "Yes . . . yes, do not concern yourself. I leave in an hour. I will be there, waiting."

"You understand what I seek?"

"Not the man, certainly. If it is there, I will get what you seek."

"Call me . . . immediately."

His jaw clenched, he squeezed the phone. And vowed not to fail.

Jerusalem

Levi Sharp leaned against the black stretch limo and waited for the older men to catch up. Surrounded by a diamond-shaped cordon of security officers, Baruk and Orhlon walked slowly along the path through the shading pine trees of the Hertzel Memorial Garden following the short, very private memorial for Lukas Painter. To Sharp's assessment, both men had aged, and carried more of a burden, after the last three days. He waved off the driver and held the door for the two most powerful men in Israel.

Baruk and Orhlon disappeared into the dark confines of the limo and Sharp was right behind. He sat on the jump seat, facing his two bosses. Baruk had his eyes closed, his breathing heavy hearted. Orhlon faced out the window, but there was no evidence of recognition in his eyes.

"What's next," asked Sharp.

"I'm sorry?" Baruk's eyes didn't open. "What do you mean?"

Orhlon didn't stir.

"What's next," Sharp repeated. "Mount Nebo didn't work . . . We're probably not gettting back there. Where do we take our search now?"

Sharp was encouraged as Baruk straightened and returned his gaze. Orhlon's attention shifted to the conversation in the car. But neither spoke.

"I have some ideas," Sharp offered. He didn't want to lose the initiative, or waste any time. "First, let's have the Israel Museum call together a group of Talmudic scholars, under some kind of pretense, and have them scour the historic documents for evidence of the Tent's fate—who had it last, where it was, perhaps other clues.

"Second, Mr. Prime Minister, do we have any private funds we can tap?"

Baruk nodded. "Yes, more than enough."

"Good. Let's get Alexander Krupp to hire some private helicopters and equip them with ground-penetrating radar equipment. I can arrange for some permits from the Jordanian government, say they're doing an emergency survey for the Jordanian Geo-Thermal Institute. We'll have the helicopters survey all of the area of Jordan around Mount Nebo, but concentrating on the mountain itself. Let's see what we find."

His mind flashed back six days.

"I'm sorry," said Sharp, feeling once again the gnawing regret that haunted him, "I should have thought of that before—"

"Have Krupp buy the helicopters and paint them with his colors and logo," Orhlon interjected.

Sharp nodded, then continued. "Third, I've got some men, retired Shin Bet, who are private contractors. They're ready to move at my word. Allow me to send a group of them to Lebanon, to Tripoli, to see what they can find out about that priest's trip there in exile.

"And last, for now, we've been informed that the Americans—Bohannon and his team—all left the United States earlier today, with the State Department's assistance. They weren't all headed to the same destination, but you can bet some of them are coming in our direction along with the two women. The

Americans must have discovered something else about that scroll. Mossad has agents in the U.S. trying to find out more about the destinations and what got Bohannon moving again. I want to call in a dozen of my best agents—more if necessary—pay them off the books and have them blanket the unconventional routes into Israel and also keep an eye on the women. Whatever Bohannon and his team are looking for, we want to be there when they find it."

Baruk moved forward on the seat, closing the distance between himself and Sharp. "Thank you, Levi. This is no time for regrets. Put all those things into action.

"And find those Americans.

"Maybe it's a good thing we let the women come back after all."

23

WEDNESDAY, AUGUST 19

Tripoli, Lebanon

"The streets of Tripoli were purposely designed like this," Rodriguez shouted as his shoulder once again was thrown against Bohannon's side. "Narrow and winding to inhibit the progress of any invader."

Their taxi driver executed a sudden, darting left turn, throwing Rodriguez against the car's door. The taxi narrowly missed a vegetable cart and frightened two elderly women who were picking their way through the traffic hurtling in all directions through the intersection.

"The plan seems to be working," Bohannon shouted back.

"It worked for the Mamelukes, too," said Joe. "A lot of these streets and alleys are dead ends. The bazaars were all laid out in different directions, each ending at a crossroads. Passageways were tight and twisting. Anything to confuse an invader. Then they built homes and shops, raised above the streets and alleys, which allowed the citizens to defend themselves by throwing stones or hot oil from the windows and roofs. These people were tough to beat. Kind of like folks from Brooklyn."

The windstorm created by the taxi's headlong dash through the streets carried the scent of grilling meat, replaced almost immediately by the nauseating, sickly sweetness of rotting produce. From all sides their ears were assaulted by the incessant cacophony of car horns, street hawkers, bleating goats, and the normal morning tumult of Tripoli's Old Town market.

Dark brown masonry walls rushed by on both sides, tight to the street. There were few windows in the walls—except for narrow firing slits that dominated the walls at each intersection—the preferred Lebanese home opening to a central courtyard.

The taxi burst out of Old Town onto al-Masaref Street, bore right onto relatively modern El Mina Road, raced past the shopping district, and rocketed around the El Mina circle.

Rodriguez was thrown forward by a sudden stop, thudding into the back of the front seat. "I hope you have insurance," he shouted to Bohannon.

"Oh, yes, good sir," replied the cab driver, smiling broadly as he looked over his shoulder at Rodriguez. "Much insurance. Enough to pay all funeral expenses."

Rodriguez opened his mouth to respond, but thought better of it as the driver accelerated again and swung his head and the taxi to the left. The shouts of a startled truck driver were jumbled in the turbulence of their wake.

"Will you please pay attention to—"

The taxi screeched to a halt in front of the Nada Center on Rahbat Street in the Nejmeh District, jumbling Rodriguez, Bohannon, exhaust fumes, and relief into a ball in the center of the cab's rear seat.

"Delivery achieved, good sir," chimed the driver, reaching his right hand over the back of the seat. "Fifteen thousand pounds." He smiled angelically. "Or, ten dollars, American."

Cheap. Rodriguez handed over the American greenback. *I'd pay him ten times that amount just to be out of this cab in one piece.*

The Nada Center tower, south of the Port of Tripoli and the Old Train Station, commanded a breathtaking view over the rooftops of the Old City, but Rodriguez didn't bring Bohannon to Tripoli to sightsee. They came to meet Tariq Barkawi.

"If there is anyone in Tripoli who can give us information on the Dar al-Ilm it's Barkawi," said Rodriguez, leading the way through the main door. "He's president of the Tripoli city council's Historical Committee and a member of every important architectural, historic, and renovation group in the city. In Tripoli, he's the king of historical preservation."

And I hope he has some direction for us.

They got off the elevator on the seventh floor. Rodriguez rechecked the directions he'd been given at the hotel, turned to his left, and knocked on the door of a nondescript office, with no identifying markers, at the southeast corner of the building.

"Come in, Mr. Rodriguez," an inflected English answered the knock. "It's open."

Barkawi had changed little since Rodriguez saw him last. An Omar Sharif look-alike, Barkawi was blessed with thick, jet-black hair, and a mustache to match, and the lean, but short, body of a long-distance runner. Barkawi's eyes were also black, and they were shrouded within deeply set, cave-like openings that were kept in shadow by the jutting overhang of his heavy eyebrows. He dressed like a Wall Street banker and spoke with the whisper of a librarian.

They were fifteen minutes into the required pleasantries, the wariness Rodriguez remembered from their first meeting at a convention replaced by an unexpected eagerness and warmth, when Barkawi finally asked how he could help.

"We have a simple request," said Rodriguez, glancing at Bohannon. "We would like you to tell us what you know of the Dar al-Ilm, the great library that was destroyed by the Crusader invaders."

Barkawi's desk was strategically situated at an angle, spanning the corner of his office, with vast windows filling the walls on both sides, giving Rodriguez and Bohannon a dazzling panorama of Tripoli's old quarter—dozens of minarets reaching to the sky, some thin and elegant, others square and sturdy, along with the solid, squat brown walls of the city's ancient citadel in the distant haze.

Leaning back into his chair, seeming to meld into the skyscape, Barkawi turned his shadowed eyes to Rodriguez. A thin smile pushed at the corners of his mouth.

"Tell you what I know of the Dar al-Ilm?" Barkawi's whispered question carried the slightest edge. "Well, Mr. Rodriguez, that could take a minute . . . or it could consume the entire day. May I ask, please, why you seek information about the Dar al-Ilm? Your answer may help me formulate a more informed answer. When you contacted me you said you were researching the history of Jewish refugees in Tripoli during the Crusaders' siege and needed help in uncovering historical records from that time. Is that your purpose?"

Joe and his brother-in-law had discussed, and argued about, this moment during most of their trip from New York City. Tom urged caution, arguing they should limit to a minimum any information they shared, with anybody. Rodriguez believed that being circumspect would only lead to dead ends and wasted time.

"My brother-in-law and I believe that a book, or a document, of some interest to us, may have been deposited in the Dar al-Ilm after the fall of Jerusalem. We know some writers at the time claimed the Dar al-Ilm contained nearly three million books, scrolls, and parchments. And we know it was completely destroyed, along with nearly all of Tripoli, when the Crusaders finally breached the city's walls in 1109. So we also know that our search has a limited chance of success. But we believe if anyone might have information or insight into the great library, it would be you."

The shadowed caves under Barkawi's brows continued to point at Rodriguez, unsettling his calm veneer. "And, for this, you came all the way from New York to Tripoli? Not a phone call? Not an email? You both flew nearly halfway around the world to ask me that question? This book," Barkawi said, leaning into his desk, "must be quite important."

"Well, I wouldn't call it important," Joe hedged. "It—"

"—must have something to do with the recent unpleasantness in Jerusalem," Barkawi interrupted. "Something about a temple, hidden from the Crusaders, I think."

"Look, Mr. Barkawi," Bohannon butted in. "We don't need—"

Joe reached out with his right arm and put a hand on his brother-in-law's elbow.

"Yes, we do, Tom." He tightened his grip on Bohannon's elbow as he turned his attention back to Barkawi's smiling face. "There was a man, a Jewish priest, named Abiathar. He, and his father before him, were the men behind the construction of the hidden Temple in Jerusalem, the one we discovered."

"Now destroyed," Barkawi whispered.

"Yes, now destroyed," Rodriguez replied, "along with everything else that was in, or on, the Temple Mount. There is nothing left."

"Still, you are here."

"Yes . . . and we need your help." This was the moment of truth. "Just prior to the fall of Jerusalem to the Crusaders, Abiathar left the city and traveled north. Once before, when the Seljuk Turks invaded Jerusalem, Abiathar and his community of Jews fled to Tyre. But, this time, Abiathar traveled to Tripoli . . . a long distance . . . to escape the Crusaders. Why would he travel twice as far, add another two hundred kilometers to what was already dangerous travel, to come to Tripoli? What did Tripoli have that Tyre did not?"

Barkawi inclined his head toward Rodriguez and nodded in agreement. "The famous Dar al-Ilm . . . the House of Knowledge?"

"Yes . . . a library," said Rodriguez. "One of the greatest libraries of the ancient world. And what would Abiathar bring to a library but a book. Or, he came here to look at a book, to do some research, to follow a trail."

The light was behind Barkawi. Joe wished he could see the man's eyes, judge Barkawi's level of interest.

"So . . ." Barkawi spread his hands wide, "what is this book that is so important?"

Immediately Rodriguez felt a weight dragging down his spirits as well as his shoulders.

"We don't know," he admitted, feeling foolish and vulnerable, "but we believe Abiathar had some information that was very important: information that he wanted to preserve, to protect. Perhaps information about the hidden Temple that he wanted to ensure was not lost. Perhaps other messages."

"Other messages?"

Across the desk, Barkawi rubbed the mustache on his upper lip with the index finger of his right hand, a large gold and ruby ring glinting in the sunlight. Interest and suspicion flashed across his face. Rodriguez felt like a smuggler at customs, guilty but not yet discovered. He shot a quick glance at Bohannon, wondering if their smoke-screen story would have the plausibility they desired. He leaned in toward Barkawi's desk, closing the distance between himself and the Lebanese academic.

"Remember, I told you that Abiathar's father was the one who began the con-struction of the hidden Temple? There were certain articles the Jews would need ready, prepared in advance, in order to complete a ritual sacrifice. We believe Abiathar's father may have assembled some of those articles and intended to keep them hidden until the secret Temple was completed. We believe a clue to the location of those articles may be in the book Abiathar brought to the Dar al-Ilm." He paused . . . waiting.

"Hah!" Barkawi exclaimed, slapping his thigh. "You are treasure hunters. Why didn't you say so from the beginning?" He got out of his chair and came around the desk, stopping before Rodriguez and punching him playfully in the shoulder. "You had me worried for a moment. I thought your real purpose may have been to actually find an old book. So," he smiled, lowering his voice, "I'm in for a third."

Bohannon jumped out of his chair. "What?" His face turned red and he took a measured step toward Barkawi. "Who do you think you—"

"Fifteen percent," Rodriguez interjected. "We have other partners. This is not a negotiation. That's as far as we can go."

"Done."

"Okay," said Rodriguez. "Tell us what you know."

Barkawi eased himself up from the edge of the desk he was leaning against. "You are correct, the Dar al-Ilm was one of the greatest libraries of the ancient world," he said. "It contained the accumulated wisdom of the Levant—scientists, philosophers, astronomers, doctors—yes, over three million manuscripts. Outside of Alexandria, perhaps the greatest collection of wisdom in the ancient world.

"The Europeans were butchers and brigands," Barkawi lamented. "They reveled in the annihilation of Islamic culture almost as much as they rejoiced over the death of every Muslim martyr. But Tripoli was a stronghold that did not break easily. It took ten years of siege to finally breach the walls and take the city. During that time, many of the city's treasures were smuggled out of Tripoli to safekeeping. There is a library in the city of Baakleen, on the southwestern slope of the Shouf Mountains, on the route to Damascus. The library was established a decade before the Crusaders arrived and it was small enough to be overlooked by the ravenous Europeans."

Barkawi crossed his office and stood in front of a large map of Lebanon. "It's still there today," he said, pointing to a spot in the mountains southeast of Beirut. "It's the national library of Lebanon. It's possible your mysterious book may be waiting on the shelves of the Baakleen Library."

Rodriguez shot a look at Tom, then turned again to Barkawi. "How would we get there?"

In spite of his well-cut suit and air of importance, Barkawi reminded Rodriguez of a fast-talker on the streets of Washington Heights. Perhaps it was the smirk with the hint of malevolence. Perhaps it was the attitude of one who thinks he knows more than you and is about to use that knowledge to your disadvantage. Joe knew he was being scammed.

"Oh, I don't think 'we' will be going anywhere," said Barkawi. "Because there is a second possibility that is just as likely as the Baakleen." He twisted at the waist to look back at the map, his thumb tapping at a point in the desert, northeast of Lebanon. "Your book could also be here, at the Krak de Chevaliers, the greatest Crusader castle of the time. Before the Dar al-Ilm was obliterated, Bertrand, son of Raymond St. Gilles, commander of the Crusaders, ransacked the great library and carried away many of its treasures to the Crusader fortress. A library remains there to this day. Your book may also be gathering dust in this great castle."

Joe looked at the point on the map that Barkawi was tapping and shook his head. "But . . . that's in Syria."

"Yes, I know," said Barkawi. "And the two of you were just in Israel recently, weren't you?" A greasy smile smeared across his face. "Did you know that no one with an Israeli visa on their passport, or with plans to travel to Israel, is allowed entrance into Syria? And the Baakleen is closed, except to academics . . . by appointment. It so happens that one of my cousins is in charge of making appointments at the Baakleen . . . and my uncle is secretary of visas and passports for the immigration department in Syria . . ."

Joe felt the hook. He knew what was coming.

"Perhaps my assistance will be worth more than fifteen percent after all," said Barkawi.

—∿∿∿—

Barkawi stood motionless at the large window, looking down into Rahbat Street as the taxi containing Rodriguez and Bohannon pulled into the uncontrolled mayhem of Tripoli traffic. The veneer of welcome disappeared as soon as they departed his office.

He pulled the acrid, Turkish cigarette from his full lips and flung it at the window toward the image of the taxi's retreating taillights. His eyes were burning, black pits. He moved with measured malice, a jungle cat smelling blood. Ignoring the smoldering butt and the ash stain on the window, he turned back to his desk and opened a small drawer on the right side. From the drawer he pulled a mobile telephone.

"*Salaam*, Defender of the Faith," he said, reverence scenting his words. "They are on their way . . . the tall one to Baakleen, the leader to Krak de Chevaliers. Yes, I arranged it all myself. The tall one will be under the knives of your black-clad messengers. And the leader—if he finds anything—it will soon be in our hands."

Barkawi listened to the voice on the other end of the line as he pulled something else from the desk drawer . . . an amulet—a Coptic cross with a lightning bolt slashing across on the diagonal. "Yes, Holy One, we will not fail."

⟜⟋⟋⟋⟋⟋⟍

"The Baakleen Library is a wild-goose chase," said Rodriguez.

They were standing in a corner of the Tripoli bus station, attempting to avoid the maelstrom of bodies, odors, and raucous noises that swirled across the geometrically colored mosaic floor. "I've heard of that library. There was an ancient Baakleen Library, as Barkawi said, but it was destroyed by an earthquake centuries ago. The current Baakleen is the Lebanese national library. It's housed in a former prison. But it wasn't opened as a library until 1987. It's not a bad library, but there's no chance that any ancient documents from a thousand years ago are housed in the Baakleen. It's just not possible. That's not the Baakleen's purpose."

A gnawing sense of discomfort roiled in Joe's stomach. Bohannon was trying to decipher the bus schedule from Tripoli to Syria. Joe put a hand on his arm.

"Tom . . . why would Barkawi point us to Baakleen?" he asked. Bohannon looked up.

"What?"

"Barkawi is as trustworthy as a picket-fence canoe."

"What?"

Rodriguez squeezed Bohannon's arm in frustrated urgency.

"Look, the guy would know the Baakleen. He knows what's in there. And he knows sending one of us there is a waste of our time."

The perplexity on Bohannon's face vanished. "So why would he do it?"

"I don't know. But I think we have to assume we're in enemy territory here," said Joe. "Maybe he has allegiances to people who don't want us to succeed."

"The Guard?"

Rodriguez shrugged.

"Maybe we should just get out of here," said Bohannon.

Leaning against the wall of the bus station, Joe said, "Only one problem with that. He was right about the Krak. If the Crusaders plundered the Dar al-Ilm before destroying it, if Abiathar planted anything there—and it still exists—the most likely place to look would be that fortress. That was the Crusader stronghold, their storehouse for anything valuable." Shutting out the riot of noise around them, Joe focused on his brother-in-law. "I think we need to go to the Krak."

"But . . . if the Baakleen was a bum steer . . ."

"Then somebody could be waiting for us at either location. Going to that castle is a risk . . . if Barkawi is setting us up."

"And," said Bohannon, "Barkawi is as trustworthy as—what did you say, a picket-fence canoe? You're weird, Joe. Okay, doesn't matter. We've got to try. Look, we also need to check out Jeremiah's Grotto in Jerusalem, right? So I'll go to the fortress and you get to Jerusalem."

"I don't like that idea." Joe's dread spiked. "The last thing we should do is split up."

"You're right," said Bohannon. "It's probably not a good idea. But time's running out on us already. We need to move fast."

Joe felt waves of anxiety wash over his body. He pushed off the wall and got right in front of Tom's face. "Wait a minute, Tom. I promised you I would walk with you through this . . . what? . . . assignment? . . . and I'm not going anywhere without you. And you shouldn't be going anywhere without me. Who's going to watch your back if I'm not there? No . . . I don't like the way this is going. We have to stay together."

Tom's hand found Joe's shoulder and gave it a squeeze. "We haven't found anything yet and the clock keeps ticking. We have too much ground to cover and not enough time to get it done. You know it doesn't make a lot of sense for both of us to go to the castle. I'll be okay. You get to Jerusalem." Tom moved closer to his brother-in-law and Joe felt the strength of his resolve. "And keep your eyes open."

County Meath, Ireland

It was the four tractors stacked on top of one another, sitting by the side of the road outside the village of Rathbeggan, that yanked Brandon McDonough's attention from daydreams about the secret of the mezuzah to the traffic on N3. *Better keep your mind and eyes on the road.* It had been a long flight.

Brilliant days like this one were rare in Ireland. A scorching blue sky hung over the green landscape, punctuating each color with an exclamation point as McDonough drove from the Dublin airport to Cairn T at Loughcrew. It was the kind of day that made you want to walk barefoot across the patchwork fields of green, feeling the moistness of the ground and the cool caress from each blade of grass.

But there would be no stops this day. Not to marvel at the four tractors stacked to the sky, nor to take a detour to visit the hill of Tara—one of the seats of power of ancient Ireland—nor to investigate the medieval tower that soared into the blue sky from the winding, history-laden streets of Kells.

Brandon McDonough was on a mission and neither the glorious weather nor his native curiosity could deter him. There was a legend waiting for him and he would not be late for his appointment with history.

On the flight from New York, McDonough reviewed the websites claiming that Cairn T—a five-thousand-year-old passage tomb commanding a hilltop in the County Meath countryside—was the burial place of the prophet Jeremiah. Five hundred years older than the pyramids of Egypt, one thousand years older than Stonehenge, Cairn T was one of three passage tombs located on this hill just outside the village of Loughcrew. And it was the most mysterious.

Not uncommon in Ireland, passage tombs were large mounds of stone and earth, typically erected on the highest hill in a region, containing a long central passage that opened into a cross-shaped burial chamber, off of which were three smaller chambers. The most famous of the ancient Irish passage tombs was Newgrange, a massive, megalithic mound about fifteen kilometers to the east of Loughcrew, a place of legend and fancy.

Compared to Newgrange, Cairn T in Loughcrew was a historical backwater. Where Newgrange had a visitors' center, guided tours, and strict rules and supervision, the cairns at Loughcrew were generally ignored and abandoned by both tourists and locals. In fact, in order for McDonough to gain access to Cairn T, all he needed was to arrive at the rustic coffee shop of the nineteenth-century Loughcrew Gardens, surrender his driver's license as security for the key to the tombs, and let himself in. No guards, no admission fee—no eyes to follow his search.

One of the websites he studied while on the plane claimed it could prove that Cairn T was the final resting place of the prophet Jeremiah. The cairn was also referred to as the tomb of the Ollamh Fodhla in Irish history, a title that in both Hebrew and Irish means possessor or revealer of hidden knowledge. The website's author took the Neolithic carvings on several of the stones inside the cairn—particularly those on what he identified as the "journey stone" and the tablet-shaped "end stone" which caught the first rays of the sun on the solstice—and used those images to spin the tale of Jeremiah's journey from Egypt to Gibraltar and on to Ireland. It was an ingenious interpretation, one that could be filled with fancy or fact. It was McDonough's mission to find out which. And, if true, to see if Cairn T contained any clue that would connect it to the story of Jeremiah and the Tent of Meeting.

A mission unlikely to bear fruit. But for a man who spent most of his life buried in a book or wandering the lonely storage caverns of the British Museum, a mission of flesh and blood, of urgency and expectation. And not a mission of detours.

Driving toward the junction at Oldcastle, McDonough was once again visited by a sense of dread. It happened first on his flight from New York. On the airplane, McDonough couldn't shake the feeling that eyes were always on him. He chalked it up to residual anxiety brought on by close proximity to Richard Johnson and his colleagues, who appeared to be the targets of a ruthless band of killers. Hearing of their near-death experiences would scare the starch out of any man.

For the hundredth time in the last hour McDonough looked in his rearview mirror. *Is that the same blue car, or is it a different one?* McDonough's glance in the rearview mirror moved from the nondescript blue car to the hazel eyes staring back at him. *Fool of a man. Fanciful dreams. Come back to reality, you old coot.*

McDonough pulled into the gravel driveway of the Loughcrew Gardens Coffee Shop, parked under the large red maple tree, and crossed the lot into the cedar-sided building adorned with posters trumpeting the Loughcrew Garden Opera's upcoming presentation of *La Traviata* and the Loughcrew Adventure Course (Prior Booking Essential!). He was immediately seduced by the sultry smell of fresh baking and reminded that he overlooked breakfast.

Fortified by strong tea and a still-warm scone, with the key for the cairn in his pocket, McDonough drove back to the carpark for Cairn T and began the quarter-mile, uphill trek to the mound's entrance. The walk, and the view, were spectacular. Yellow-blooming Irish gorse bushes lined the walk and dotted the slopes of the hill, leading to a panoramic view of the distant Boyne River Valley. He skirted the stone remnants of two ancient ring forts and approached the gated entrance for Cairn T.

It didn't look like much from the outside. Where Newgrange was nearly one hundred yards in diameter and neatly kept, the cairns on the hills of Loughcrew were a rugged and less-pampered bunch. Much smaller, about forty feet in diameter, Cairn T sat at the pinnacle of the hill. Its circumference was created by an interlocking stack of flat-topped, pewter-gray stones. No mortar held them together but they had withstood the wind and rain at the top of this Irish hill for more than five thousand years. About four feet up from the base of the cairn, the circle of stones began the formation of a dome that climaxed at a rounded top about fifteen feet off the ground. Whether purposely, or by the hand of nature, the dome was covered with a grass-covered layer of earth and clay.

A brisk wind whipped across the plains of Meath, pushing cotton balls of cumulus across the brilliant blue sky, etching spotlights of shade on the valley floor.

McDonough's reverent Catholic upbringing, the resting place of long-latent shame, called out in chants of condemnation. He was about to violate a sacred place. Though there was no one within sight, he felt as if he were under the eyes of the law. Whether with anxiety or the climb, his heart rate was accelerated. Cold perspiration chilled his skin and dampened his shirt. "'Tis better to be a coward for a minute than dead the rest of your life," he said to the wind. *This gives me the creeps.*

He hesitated for a long moment, then unlocked the creaky iron gate, turned on the battery-powered torch he received with the key, and ducked his head to enter the low-ceilinged passageway into the tomb.

The passageway was tight, cold, and smelled as if small animals lived and died here. It was flanked by standing stones festooned with Neolithic carvings. McDonough ducked under a low, stone lintel at the end of the passage and entered the cross-shaped burial chamber.

The burial chamber was a smaller version of the outside of Cairn T—round walls of stacked stone about thirty feet across, and a steep-sided, vaulted ceiling about eight feet high at its apex. McDonough had to stoop at the waist to move about its rim. The wide beam of light not only illuminated the chamber and the richly ornamented stones that occupied its edges—and those that flanked the openings to two smaller chambers at right angles to the entry—but also increased his adrenaline flow as the light fell on the low opening to a larger crypt, opposite the entry passage.

McDonough peeked into the crypt. His torch illuminated hieroglyphic sun symbols and spirals around the entrance and on the back wall of the crypt, but what captured his attention was an empty sarcophagus tucked snugly into the right side, as if fit for the space.

A large stone rose from the floor at the portal to the crypt and a low lintel forced McDonough to place the torch on the floor inside the crypt so he could squeeze through. The light was blocked as his body filled the opening. The circular burial chamber behind him collapsed into darkness and rushed in on McDonough, who stumbled, and fell inside onto the floor of the crypt.

As he picked up the torch, its light flashed across the low ceiling and McDonough halted its arc in amazement. There, a few feet above his head, was something he had never seen in his entire career.

The symbols were similar to those in the outer chamber, but these looked untouched by the harsh Irish climate. The edges of the stone carvings were clearly defined, not eroded by time. More remarkable was the ocher-colored paint that still vividly adorned each of the carvings. Five thousand years, and these carvings appeared as if they were completed a month ago.

McDonough studied the symbols closely. There was a six-petaled flower design inside a circle and the common sun symbol in a circle, identical to those elsewhere in the cairn. But others were unique, and stunning.

On the left was a nine-bar rainbow arching across the sky, painted in sweeping bands of ocher alternating with the gray stone. Above the rainbow, a strange, helix-like circle curving in on itself with a long, curving tail that forked about halfway down its length. A comet? To the right-center, what could only be considered a ten-legged insect with two tentacles extending from the base of its head. And, in the center, a flat-topped symbol with raised arms that looked like a bench . . . or an altar.

McDonough took a deep breath, ran his eyes once more over the carvings so close to his face, then turned the light on the sarcophagus. It was empty, its lid missing. There was no adornment or carving on any of the sides that he could see.

Wondering what had become of the sarcophagus's cover, McDonough moved the beam of light through the crypt opening and back into the burial chamber. On the far side of the chamber, he noticed for the first time that one of the illustrated stones was different from the others. This one was as long as a man's body. It lay on the floor, flat on the bottom and rounded on the top . . . the capstone of the sarcophagus.

The capstone called to him. McDonough could feel his years as he squeezed through the tight crypt opening once more. He crossed to the far side of the chamber, stooped like an old man by the low ceiling, and washed his light over the stone.

The markings on this stone were different from the others . . . long, sweeping lines and curves running along its sides. His breath caught in his throat.

On top of the capstone were two carvings—one a cartouche enclosing the budding staff, the symbol of the Aaronic priesthood, and three lines of script—hieroglyphics, Aramaic, and Demotic . . . Prophet of God.

McDonough could feel tingling in the ends of his fingers. He knelt to the floor in the bowels of this ancient burial chamber and reached out a hand, tracing the weathered edges of the second carving. A cool breath of stale air trickled down his spine.

McDonough knew what the carving was . . . the four symbols were very familiar. But he was clueless as to why they were here, on top of this sarcophagus in an Irish burial ground. *Is this your resting place, my elusive friend?*

McDonough nearly had a heart attack when the iron gate at the entrance of the passage tomb slammed shut.

And footsteps advanced down the passageway.

Dayr al Qiddis Oasis, Egypt

In two hours, Richard Johnson and Sammy Rizzo traveled a little more than thirty miles from Ras Zafarana on the Red Sea coast along a ruler-straight desert track that laughingly called itself a road. Thirty miles, and they were in another world. Far from the white sand resorts along the Red Sea, this was the vast Wadi Araba in the eastern Egyptian desert, a lifeless, flat moonscape stretching off into the haze, shimmering heat waves obscuring the mud brown mountains that brooded in the distance. Nothing lived here. Nothing grew here. Except sand and rocks . . . and heat.

And this fragile little Fiat he was driving into this wasted terrain threatened, with each cough and sputter, to leave them stranded in a dry and desolate no-man's land.

"Hey, Lawrence of Arabia," Sammy said from the passenger seat, "this lush landscape makes me kind of miss Manhattan, you know. Like a food vendor on every corner . . . if they had corners. Are you sure there's life out here?"

Doc's head throbbed with a pain that mirrored the ache in his hands as he gripped the steering wheel with a growing desperation. In spite of years of archaeological digs in the most severe deserts of the world, his tolerance for penetrating heat had disappeared long ago. But it wasn't only the heat that stirred up his anxiety. He worried that somewhere he had made a mistake. That they might be on the wrong road. That they might be driving south into a wasteland that would swallow them up and hide their bones forever.

So, when Doc saw the two towers rising ahead of him along the ribbon of road, he pointed into the bug-splattered windshield. "O ye of little faith."

As the southern Gaiala Plateau, an escarpment of bare rock that pushed five thousand feet into the blue sky, closed on their left, the shape of St. Anthony's Monastery rose from the floor of the desert. Two fifty-foot towers crowned with golden crosses flanked the portal that swallowed the desert road. The towers were the same champagne color as the fortress walls that stretched out to either side of the entry—a champagne that was dry, bleached, and gritty.

"Hallelujah," screeched Sammy. "I hope they have a Starbucks."

"Visigoth," mumbled Doc.

St. Anthony's Monastery, founded in the fourth century, encircled the oasis Dayr al Qiddis. So Doc wasn't surprised to see palm trees poking up from behind the high walls. But he was shocked by their numbers. As he drove the car through the gate, the vastness of the monastery community struck him. Its buildings and streets stretched into the distance.

"Not the cave in the rock I was expecting," said Rizzo, bounding out of the car.

—⌁∿⌁—

Every monk in the community looked the same to Richard Johnson: small men, their long black robes scraping the ground. The only things visible from under their embroidered, black hoods were long white beards, hooked noses, and veiled, faraway eyes. Why would he expect different from the monastery's superior? But Brother Walid, taller and thinner than Johnson, moved with an air of aristocracy that would be comfortable in any European palace or American boardroom. The long beard was there, speckled with gray, but so was a twinkle of expectation.

"Dr. Johnson, it's a pleasure to welcome you to St. Anthony's," said the superior, his American New England accent as clear as the bell to afternoon prayer. "I've read some of your monographs on the dig at Khoum. Very impressive. I'd like to discuss the cult of the Ibis with you if we have the time."

Doc's eyes blinked in disbelief. "What? I'm sorry, I . . ."

"Oh, forgive me," Brother Walid said, extending his hand. "It's so seldom I get to talk about anything other than the status of our crops, the lack of initiates, or the schedule for overnight prayer. In my previous life my name was Lionel Gaul. I was an archaeology student at Stanford when I came to Egypt for a dig in the eastern mountains and stumbled upon this monastery. That was thirty-six years ago. I've left these walls only once, for my mother's funeral. But we do receive mail. And old dreams are loath to die."

The superior turned away and looked down at Sammy Rizzo. "And this must be Mr. Rizzo?"

Sammy pushed the brim of his safari hat away from his eyes and tilted his head to the sun to grab a look at the monk. "No, I'm Bear Grylls and I'm here for the *Man vs. Wild* show. Where's the alligator pit?"

"What?"

"Never mind, padre," Sammy said, offering his hand to the monk. "Say, how can I get my hands on one of those cool embroidered bonnets?"

Brother Walid edged back a bit and turned his head to the side, as a scowl creased his forehead. Then he turned back to Johnson. "So, my dear doctor, welcome to our monastery. I hope you will be comfortable during your stay. I'm sorry that we can only offer you some rather rugged cells that were occupied by monks when our ranks were larger. But, I must admit, what I am most curious about is why you are here. What can we poor monks do for you?"

"Well, I have a story to tell you, and a favor to ask."

Stepping forward, Brother Walid took Johnson by the arm. "Wonderful. Sounds like a mystery. Come," he said, turning Johnson around and nodding his head toward Rizzo. "Let's get out of this pitiless sun."

⌁⌁⌁⌁⌁

Palm trees rose high above, shading the men from the sun. Brother Walid sat on one bench, his back resting against a tree trunk. "Wow . . . that is an amazing story," he said to Doc, seated on another bench across the white pebbled path. "Certainly much more remarkable than mine. But you want to get to the library. Let's head over there while I tell you more about the monastery.

"St. Anthony lived here as a hermit. Up there, in a cave on the side of the mountain." Brother Walid pointed to a platform high up the side of the escarpment, a long, winding staircase leading to it from the wadi floor. "It wasn't until after he died that his disciples began to build this monastery. This was an excellent location. There were three springs of fresh water then. Even though there is only one now, flowing out of the side of the mountain, it's more than enough to give us all the water we need for our community, our vegetable gardens, our orchards, our groves of olives and palms."

The superior led them through a series of tight, twisting lanes, dodging in and out of the late afternoon sun. "The remoteness of the monastery's location preserved it from Arab and Muslim influence, and it developed into a flourishing center of spiritual and cultural life, particularly between the twelfth and fifteenth centuries when the monastery became a haven of scholarship, art, and translation. But in 1483 it was attacked by marauding bedouins . . . the buildings destroyed, the monks killed or expelled, and the library ravaged. The attackers used the books and parchments they looted from the library to fuel their cooking fires. So much was lost.

"That's when they rebuilt the wall—forty feet high and six feet thick—and, at that time, there was no gate. The only way to gain entry was over there"—he pointed—"in that building against the wall. There's a hand-cranked hoist in there. Anything that needed entry to the monastery—people, food, whatever—was lifted up by the hoist. The monastery now covers fifteen acres in which are seven churches and chapels, the various offices and workshops, the communal facilities, and the low two-story buildings containing the monks' cells. And this . . ." Father Walid stopped suddenly and waved at an ornately carved wooden door. "The library, which you've come to see. My presence is required in the kitchen, but, go in, the door is open and you'll find an old man in there who has been a faithful volunteer to our library for years. If you need to find anything, he is the man to help you. But, Dr. Johnson," he said, casting a glance at Rizzo and his Jay-Z sunglasses, 50 Cent tee shirt, and baggy jeans, "I will rely on your reputation and experience to protect and preserve any documents or books you investigate."

Brother Walid turned and walked away, down a light-dappled alley. Johnson didn't see him leave. He was looking at the space above the wooden door to the library. The space where a cartouche—encapsulating the budding shepherd's staff and the scorpion—was carved into the cream-colored stone.

～～〰〰～

Dark and quiet, dust particles dancing in the few shafts of sunlight that interrupted the shadows, the monastery's library was stunning—both in its size and in the quality of its contents.

A long center aisle stretched the length of the room, about one hundred yards. On the right a series of rough-hewn refectory tables fronted packed bookcases along the wall, also the length of the room and reaching to the ten-foot ceiling. On the left was an irregular series of map stands, scribe tables, and another room-length series of bookcases.

Doc wandered down the side aisle, next to the bookcases, and marveled at some of the richness he observed. Clearly . . . the monks of St. Anthony's Monastery toiled at more than their irrigated garden. Doc eased a leather-bound volume from one of the shelves. Rendered by hand onto vellum sheets with an artist's grace was a copy of Saint Augustine's legendary *Confessions*, written in Latin on the left-hand page and in Greek on the right. Doc turned over the sumptuously decorated pages to the end of the book. Inside the back cover was the scribe's signature and the date—Father Gregorious, MCCXCIII.

"Hey, Doc . . . give me a boost, will ya?" Rizzo was behind Johnson, on the far side of the room, scanning the bookcases against the far wall. As he turned to see what Rizzo was calling for, Johnson came face-to-face with a vision of the desert, clothed like a man. Startled, Doc stepped back. And bumped into the bookcase.

"A beautiful book," the desert man spoke. He seemed as ancient as the sands, his skin dried into brittle, leathery cracks by the sun. He wore a plain kaftan. Only his eyes—one yellow, one brown—crackled with an intense fire that stunned Johnson to silence. "Is it what you desire . . . or do you seek another?"

The old man bent from the waist and inclined his head, the closest he could come to a ceremonial bow. "*Salaam alaikum.*" He touched his fingers to his brow, then to his chest. "Perhaps I can be of some assistance?"

As Johnson regained his composure, a response on his lips, Rizzo bounded into the space between the two men.

"Hey, Omar, you know your way around here, right? Well, I'm looking for Lawrence of Arabia, and I can't find him anywhere."

A shadow passed over the old man's face—or covered Doc's eyes. Johnson's skin felt like the inside of an oyster—hot and slimy. In a fraction of a second, the shadow was gone and the old man was smiling down at Sammy Rizzo. But Doc knew something evil had passed.

"Yes, I can help you find your way. But, first, I must assist the good doctor in his important quest." The old man turned to Johnson and spread his arms wide. "Tell me . . . what is it you seek?"

⁓⁓⁓

Rizzo slept on top of one of the refectory tables, the dozen or so books he'd collected from the library in stacks at his feet—one opened, resting on his chest. What little light invaded the small windows high in the walls had disappeared along with Doc Johnson's stamina and patience. Led by the old man, Johnson endured a dizzying and frustrating search through the ancient records spanning the monastery library. A search without any indication that they were closer to information about the mezuzah's elusive history.

"I regret, as your friend noticed, that the monks here have apparently employed no system for the collection," the old man said. "It is only through years offering my services here that I began to find things I was looking for. Perhaps, again, if I knew more of what you are seeking . . . that would help. I do not know where to take you next. You are interested in the monastery's history in the early part of the reign of Saladin the Great, what you call the twelfth century. I have shown you what I know. Without more information . . ."

He lifted his arm and waved it toward the length of the library, as if saying, *Take a guess.* Johnson would leave here empty-handed unless he revealed more information to his guide. Father Walid, in a short visit to inquire after their progress, treated the old, nameless man with respect. Doc wasn't sure. But he had no other option, besides wandering aimlessly and picking books at random. Doc took the chance.

"We are in possession of a mezuzah—a brass scroll holder—and the scroll it carried. The scroll is a separate story. It is information, history, about the mezuzah that we seek. The outside of the mezuzah is etched with designs. Upon examination, the etchings and the designs were applied to the outside of the mezuzah at different times by different tools. We know that the mezuzah spent several hundred years in a library in the town of Suez. And one of those sets of symbols contains the mark of Saint Anthony's cross along with a budding shepherd's staff and a scorpion—the two symbols carved above the entry door to this library. So, we believe it is very likely that the mezuzah and its scroll spent some of its history in this library."

Doc weighed and measured his words. He hadn't given too much away, not yet.

"And why do you pursue the history of this mezuzah? There are many scroll holders here, many quite old, many more mezuzahs in the lands of the Zionists. What is it about this mezuzah that has brought you to this desolate corner of the world? It must be very important. If I knew, perhaps it would help uncover its history here."

Two thoughts held Doc's mouth in check. This man was very smart—under the well-worn trappings of a desert nomad simmered a quick, calculating mind—and he was a wise old Muslim, living in the shadow of St. Anthony's Monastery. A wise Muslim man who probably knew a great deal more than he was revealing. Johnson relished a chess game, a contest of intellect, but not tonight. Each thrust and parry with the old man increased his wariness. Still— he needed to give something if he hoped to find any reference to Abiathar's scroll and the mezuzah that carried it into this wasteland.

"The scroll we found contained a message, in an ancient code, that led to the discovery of . . . well . . . a Jewish temple hidden under the Temple Mount in Jerusalem."

"Al-Haram al-Sharif," the old man countered. "Yes, I have heard of this discovery. And the destruction it caused."

Doc bristled. "I believe an earthquake caused the destruction."

Bowing slightly from the waist, the old man nodded. "Yes . . . but all is destroyed, is that not true?"

Running a hand through his hair, Johnson stalled for time, trying to reign in his rampaging emotions and come up with an appropriate response.

"This mezuzah," said the old man, breaking the silence, "came from Jerusalem at the time of the European invasion?"

"Yes."

"Then I know where we may look."

The old man turned quickly and moved away, down the main aisle and toward the wall on the left. The lower shelves of two bookcases were protected by leaded glass doors. He went to the doors, pulled them open, and—after a momentary search—drew out two leather-bound books. One was large, its leather well oiled, a metal hasp holding the sides together. The cover of the smaller one was dry and cracked and appeared to be seldom used. As the old man turned with the prize in his hands, a cool breeze rushed in from the suddenly open library door.

"Are you still here?" bellowed a monk as round as he was tall. "Out! It's time to lock up . . . well past time."

"Lock who up? I'm innocent, I haven't done anything," said Rizzo, rolling over and dangling his legs from the side of the table as he rubbed his knuckles in his eyes.

The old man held the book out in front of him. "Forgive our imposition, Brother. But I was just about to show this book to our guests."

"Take it with you," said the round monk with a wave of his hand. "He can return it tomorrow. Father Walid trusts him. But out. It's time to close. Midnight Praise is at four-thirty and the bells for first liturgy ring at six. Morning arrives quite early in the desert."

Johnson gathered his notes into a battered leather briefcase. The old man had his arms wrapped around the two books in a respectful embrace. As they passed Rizzo, Sammy hopped onto the seat of a chair, then to the floor, falling in beside Johnson.

"Is it time for breakfast?"

24

Thursday, August 20

Dayr al Qiddis Oasis, Egypt

With the notes from the previous afternoon's research in his left hand, Doc once again scanned the thick, cracked pages of the illuminated manuscript on his room's table.

"So was it this Temple Guard who first brought the mezuzah to the monastery?"

His body ached. The last time he slept was in the airport hotel in Suez. He didn't want to count the hours. Throughout the night, Johnson toiled over the larger of the two ancient books—a rambling collection of observances and essays recording various events at the monastery—coaxing clues, fighting for information from its aged secrets while the old man offered slices of the monastery's history, as if he were unfolding his knowledge, chapter by chapter. Rizzo had long since abandoned their efforts in his need for sleep. But Doc was compelled to continue, to seek the truth of the mezuzah's history, to search for the clues he hoped were left behind. Sunrise could not be far off, but the old man in the opposite chair showed no sign of weariness. In fact, his mismatched eyes still burned with an intensity that continued to unnerve Johnson and communicated a thinly veiled animosity. As the old man lowered his chin and leaned closer to the table, his stare pierced Johnson's academic veneer.

"You have some knowledge, but much ignorance," said the old man, his words like a gloved slap to the cheek—a challenge to the duel.

Johnson laughed in spite of his weariness and unease. "I am certainly grateful for your assistance this afternoon and tonight, but I don't believe you know me well enough to call me ignorant."

The two candles on the hand-hewn table sputtered and flickered, offering no heat and only minimal light inside the small, spartan monk's cell. From the corners, shadows crept closer to the table.

"Western intellectuals . . . do your universities teach arrogance along with ignorance?"

Johnson placed his right hand on the table and closed the distance between himself and the old man. "Perhaps you mistake confidence for arrogance, but either way, I did not accept your invitation to investigate this book, to have you share some of the history of this monastery, in order to be insulted."

The old man did not look away, did not waver. But he slightly inclined his head toward Doc, momentarily diffusing the tension that simmered above the table. "Forgive me, good doctor," he said with slippery sincerity. "There was no offense intended."

Yellow and brown, the old man's eyes glowed with a fierce, consuming magnetism, at odds with his bent, frail body. "Perhaps I may still assist you? There is still much that you do not know—but should." Those eyes, a fanatic's eyes, disarmed Richard Johnson.

Hungrier for the story than he was unnerved by the Arab's attitude and intensity, Johnson nodded his head in the old man's direction. "Perhaps much that you should have told me this afternoon, I think. Please . . . enlighten me."

"More than nine hundred years ago, some pilgrims came to this monastery. They were part of the great European invasion—*Crusaders,* you call them— those who captured Jerusalem and slaughtered its people. These men were also part of a lay order, the Brotherhood of Saint Anthony. But it is not the pilgrims, or their pilgrimage, that is important to you. Rather, it is what they brought with them—a scroll holder . . . with a message."

"I knew it!"

"Yes, my good doctor, the same mezuzah and scroll which came into your possession."

A coil of dread began to wrap itself around Johnson's heart, like a boa constrictor determined to squeeze the life out of his spirit. "How did you know that?"

"There is much that I know about you, Dr. Johnson . . . and I know much of what you seek to know."

Another thrust. This one Johnson declined to parry.

"The mezuzah, and scroll it contained, was a great mystery to the Coptic monks who occupied this monastery. They knew it was composed in the ancient Egyptian language of Demotic. But none of them could determine what the message meant. For two hundred years its meaning eluded them. Then a man came and joined the monks of the monastery. A man who loved books, and puzzles. A Coptic . . . and a cryptographer. It took this man five years, poring over the scroll while the other brothers tended the flocks and gardens, before he broke the code and revealed the message."

Johnson was startled. "You know . . . they knew?"

"You are not the only one to solve this puzzle. The monks of St. Anthony's Monastery knew for seven hundred years that there was a Jewish temple hidden under the sacred mount in Jerusalem."

"But . . . why not reveal the secret?"

"Ah, what were they to do? The Umayyad caliphs controlled the land—Egypt, Judea, and Jerusalem. The blessed Haram al-Sharif, the Dome of the Rock, and the Al-Aqsa Mosque were erected six hundred years earlier by the caliph Abd al-Malik. And Jerusalem was over five hundred kilometers distant, through deadly deserts rippling not only with heat, but with ruthless bedouin bandits. Even if these men were released to leave the monastery, it would be a two-month journey. So, instead, they hid the mezuzah and its scroll in a small crypt carved into the foundation of the library building.

"Ultimately, the few brother monks who knew of the mezuzah formed a group of guardians; the Temple Guardians they called themselves. They swore on their faith in the cross of the Nazarene to protect the scroll, its mezuzah, and its message—to keep it a secret until the right moment, the right time to reveal the existence of this hidden temple."

A chill slipped into the room like a thief, stealing the heat. Johnson shivered and crossed his arms in front of his chest for warmth.

"Over the course of time, this monastery has often been attacked by nomadic bands of raiders. Even after the massive walls were erected, this isolated outpost of Christian heresy remained an inviting target for hungry or greedy bandits. So the monks of the Temple Guardians evolved into a military sect of warrior monks, determined in their defense of the scroll, men who pledged their first allegiance to what became known as the Temple Guard, rather than to the Monastery of St. Anthony. For a time, they succeeded. And the mezuzah remained safe, and secret."

Johnson's distrust of the man's motives increased at the same pace as his interest in the man's story. *Why is he sharing so much with me?* Distrust prevailed when another man, dressed in the same kaffiyeh and kaftan as the old man, slipped silently through the door and took up a sentry's post in the shadows of the cell.

"Excuse me! And who are you?" Johnson asked the dark, silent shape.

"Forgive me," purred the old man, the disdain of the powerful dripping from his words. "My servant. He is concerned about my health and welfare at this late hour."

It's my health and welfare that concerns me.

"May I continue?" said the old man, gathering up the folds of his kaftan as he shifted his ancient bones in the chair opposite Johnson. "It is very hard to keep a secret for hundreds of years, passing it down from generation to generation, particularly in a closed community such as this. Eventually, knowledge of the mezuzah and the scroll—most importantly, of its message—came to a man of the desert. A man, I am proud to say, whose bloodline still runs in mine after countless generations.

"No wall could deter that man and his Muslim brothers from rescuing the scroll. Its message was a threat to the Haram al-Sharif. Our holy shrines to the prophet Muhammad were at risk if knowledge of the hidden temple was ever revealed to the world. So these sons of Allah also vowed themselves to a warrior brotherhood—servants of the defiled cross."

The old man reached inside the neck of his kaftan and withdrew a Coptic cross with a lightning bolt slashing through on the diagonal.

"Defiantly, they called themselves the Prophet's Guard. With the aid of a faithful brother on the inside, this small army breached the walls and put every warrior monk under the blade during a frenzied battle. There was a little gold, and an abundance of stored food. But what they took back into the desert was the monastery's greatest prize."

Johnson's mind scrambled to put aside its growing apprehension and make order of the new facts with the parts of the story he and the others had uncovered.

"But," said Johnson, "I thought the Temple Guard brought the mezuzah to the Bibliotheca de Historique in Suez?"

Out in the night a camel bleated into the lonely dark.

"You are mistaken because you possess only partial understanding," said the old man. "In this hidden corner of the desert, many generations have killed and pillaged in pursuit of the scroll. Nearly two hundred years ago, it was stolen once more by a reincarnation of the Temple Guard who took the mezuzah to the French for safekeeping, where it was held in great secrecy, where they thought it was safe. But," he laid something in the folds of his robe and spread his hands, "there are very few secrets that can survive over hundreds of years. Ultimately, my brothers regained possession of the scroll and put it in a place where they believed no one would ever look—in a bookstore along the back alleys of Alexandria. Where a fool allowed it once again to slip from our grasp."

Johnson ran his mind through the rest of the story—how Charles Spurgeon purchased the mezuzah and its printed silk cover while wandering the streets of Alexandria; how the Prophet's Guard followed its trail to London; how Spurgeon dispatched the hunted mezuzah to his friend Louis Klopsch at the Bowery Mission in New York City. But an overriding question kept interrupting Johnson's thoughts.

"But why do you still care? What difference does it make to you, to the Prophet's Guard, who has the scroll? Not only has the message been deciphered, but the Temple has been found, and destroyed. What good is the scroll to you? Why . . . why are you here?"

The old man's smile held no warmth, only the promise of violence, a predator playing with his prey. "You do not understand because you possess only partial understanding," he said again. "It is not only the scroll we seek. In that you are correct. But there is a greater treasure, a treasure of which you have not dreamed."

━━∿〜━

Rizzo was on the floor before the sound of the bells registered in his mind. And the floor was probably softer than the bed from which he'd fallen. The world was black and it was several startled moments before he remembered where he was. A monastery in the Egyptian desert in the dead silence of deep night.

He climbed back up into the Egyptian excuse for a bed. Fingering the threadbare blanket, he pushed against the slab of a mattress, and decided he'd endured enough. Early or not, he would go across the corridor. Doc must be awake. Those bells could wake the dead.

Rizzo lit the candle in the holder on the room's small table and wrapped the blanket around his shoulders against the desert cold. It trailed behind him like a king's robe as he pushed open the door and crossed the hall. Candle holder in one hand, the blanket clutched in the other, Rizzo stood at the wooden door to Doc Johnson's cell, befuddled for a moment by the voices he heard from inside. Clearly, Doc had one of the monks in there, regaling him with stories of the monastery's history.

Rizzo pulled the blanket more tightly around his shoulders and headed off down the corridor. He wasn't going to get any more sleep. Time to do some exploring. Maybe he could find that bucket that lifted people over the walls.

⸺⌁⌁⸺

"What treasure?" Johnson tried to stoke his curiosity, but dread dulled his enthusiasm for understanding. "We saw the symbols etched on the surface of the mezuzah," Johnson protested. "That's what brought us here. But there was no hint of treasure."

"Fool. You look only on the surface. I thought you were a scientist."

Johnson winced at the rebuke, but his eyes remained on the old man's face while his fear was fueled by the unmoving shape in the shadows. There was no chance of escape. He was trapped.

"You seek a tent. A childish quest. You pursue something long destroyed by the decay of time." The old man picked up the smaller book and opened it where a marker was placed.

"We seek to regain the key to a greater treasure. A key that is hidden, even from you and your associates. A key that will determine the future of humanity. It will lead us to the final Caliphate—the rule of Islam over the breadth of this earth. It will herald the death of everything that is revered by the godless in this modern world. The key—the hand of God—that will bring all of you to your knees."

Johnson's pulse beat a brisk tattoo through his temples. His chest squeezed against his lungs. *Oh, God.* "This is madness."

"Madness? I will show you now what you should not know. Then you will tell me if our dream is madness. Here . . . learn."

As Johnson listened, the old man shared a story of this ultimate secret. Working his way through the text of the book, and its many notations in the margins, the old man revealed an impossibility that now made so much sense; a dime-novel tale that now presented a monumental threat to millions. And

Johnson accepted with finality that he would never leave this room alive. *I have helped make history, and I thank God for that. I only wish I could have seen . . .*

The old man finished speaking. Johnson's thoughts cleared as he saw the old man rise from his seat, reach into the folds of his kaftan, and withdraw his hand.

Convinced as he was of his inevitable fate, Johnson's heart still twisted in his chest as he looked into the old man's outstretched hand. "Oh, my God," he whispered.

———

Rizzo found the stairs leading to the top of the wall, but when he reached the flat rampart he forgot about hitching a ride in the bucket. He saw the faintest contrast define the arch of the horizon to the east. Above his head, ten million stars shone just for his eyes. This was the rim of the world, and Sammy was balanced on the edge of eternity. How long he sat there, only the stars would know. He was getting colder when . . . he felt the movement more than saw it. When he looked along the length of wall to his left, there was nothing—an empty rampart with a small, round turret about one hundred yards away. Something stirred in the shadows of the turret. Unbidden, vivid memories flashed across Rizzo's mind. Doc nearly pushed onto the subway tracks in New York City; Winthrop Larsen's body blown all over 35th Street; Bohannon's daughter nearly kidnapped from Fordham.

In the dead silence of the desert, the total darkness broken only by starlight, Rizzo could imagine anything. But he wasn't imagining this—a large man leapt out of the blackness inside the turret and started running toward him.

Rizzo jumped to his feet and, leaving the blanket in his wake, ran for the stairs to his right.

He might be small, but he was fast. He burst onto the top of the stairwell, grabbed the metal leg of the railing, and swung his body down the stairs. At the bottom of the stairs he hesitated, listened.

A faint footfall to his right.

Clinging to the shadows, Rizzo sprinted left along the monastery's wall and darted behind the corner of a building that jutted out close to the wall's inner surface. He ran headlong down a narrow alley and ran through the next intersecting alley, chased by the sound of footfalls behind him.

The monk's dormitory was still one building away when he heard the running feet stop, but Rizzo didn't slacken his pace. He sprinted to the arched portal of white stucco, pulled hard against the heavy, wooden door, and threw the bolt when he got the door closed again.

Rizzo crouched behind the closed door, hands on his knees, as he gulped air into his pleading lungs. He had to warn Doc.

Racing down the corridor, he stopped in front of Johnson's cell, debating whether to knock, and then noticed the door was ajar. He pushed against it, and the ancient hinges screeched in protest. Doc was still in his bed, buried under his blanket.

"Yo, Doc." Rizzo crossed the floor with urgency. "C'mon, get up. I think we've got unwelcome visitors here. C'mon, get up."

One of the candles, low and guttering, remained lit. Rizzo pulled it across the small table, away from a small, leather-bound book, and turned to the bed. He reached out his hand, touched Johnson's shoulder, and gingerly gave him a shake. "Get up—"

It was the blood on the top hem of the blanket that stopped him. *Cut himself shaving?* Rizzo shook Doc again and the blanket pulled away. He stumbled backward, tripped over the blanket, fell against the table, and knocked the candle onto the floor. The candle's flame sputtered against the stone floor, but Doc's waxy, white face . . . blank, staring eyes . . . and bloody, punctured neck told a tale that needed no illumination.

Rizzo felt his stomach turn, a brackish bile rising in his throat. Rapid, shallow breathing; pain in his chest; doubt, fear, alarm torching his emotions.

A trio of large, scaly scorpions crawled across Doc's face and neck like sentries guarding their prey. But they no longer hunted for food.

⌁⌁⌁

Sammy sat on the floor. The weight pressing on him felt so heavy he might never get up. Emptiness engulfed him. He felt as if he were sitting on the deck of the *Titanic*, watching its bow slip under the waves. The adventure movie ended. Reality, finality, Doc's lifeless body, numbed both his heart and his bones. Sammy needed to convince himself to breathe.

He sensed movement by the door. No noise, but they were there.

There was no running this time. Rizzo set his jaw and tightened his muscles.

A hand reached for his arm, gently, urging him to get up.

"Come . . . please."

Rizzo's gaze didn't leave Johnson's contorted death mask. He no longer felt fear. But rage erupted like magma on a mission.

His left hand closed around the pewter candlestick lying beside him on the floor and he swung it across his body with all the force he could leverage.

"You, bas—" A strong, calloused hand caught his wrist.

Sammy pushed off the floor, throwing himself at the man to his right. A second hand grabbed his shoulder and forced him back to the floor.

"I'll— you—," Rizzo sputtered, flailing blindly against the force that held him in place.

"Mr. Rizzo. Please, we must leave, now."

It struck him that the man kneeling at his side spoke to him as a servant trying to rouse his master. Courteous killers?

Sammy's hands latched onto the cloth of the shirt on the man's arms, heroically wrestling to free himself. But, now, the fire left his mind and his eyes cleared. Next to him was kneeling a vision from an old B movie. A red checked kaffiyeh, held in place by two black ropes, framed the face, its ends trailing onto the leather vest the man wore over a white muslin shirt. Well-worn, blousy blue pants were tucked into calf-high leather boots, kept in place by a wide, red sash that now trailed on the floor. If it wasn't for the gleaming rifle slung over one shoulder, the bandolier of cartridges strapped across his chest, or the vicious-looking short scimitar tucked into the sash, Rizzo would have been arrested mostly by the man's face. A black mustache exploded under his prodigious nose and dropped off each side of his mouth to frame his chin. His eyes were black, but filled with the fire of life and a gladness of spirit. A ragged, screaming pink scar ran from his left cheek, across the eyebrow of his left eye, above his nose, and sliced across his brow until it disappeared beneath the kaffiyeh.

"Who? . . . What? . . ."

"The Prophet's Guard killed your friend. We didn't get here quickly enough, though we came as soon as we heard you arrived. But we must leave. You are not safe here."

A second man, dressed identically, was standing just inside the door. He crossed the room in two steps, swept the scorpions from Doc Johnson's chest with the back of his hand, and ground each one to oblivion with the sole of his boot.

Rizzo's eyes were blinking as fast as his mind was turning. Whoever they were, they weren't the enemy. "Who are you? Why should I trust you?"

The man reached under his thin muslin shirt, pulled out a chain, and showed Sammy what hung from it—a Coptic cross. "But no lightning bolt," the man said, searching Sammy's eyes.

"I will ask for your faith. My name is Hassan. That is my cousin. We—our families for generations before us—are members of the Temple Guard who once guarded the mezuzah and the message of the priest, Abiathar. But the others, those who seek to destroy us and destroy you—those with the lightning bolt desecrating the cross—have not completed their work this night. Come . . . we must leave."

The man stood to his feet and held out his right hand. Sammy searched the face. He could discern no trace of treachery, no sign of deceit. It was a risk. But staying here was also a risk. He took another, final look at Doc's waxy, white face, grabbed Hassan's hand, and pulled himself to his feet.

"Let's go. Let's get out of here. Wait. Where are we going?"

"To the answer."

Hassan swept up the book and motioned to his cousin, who sidled up to the door, listened, stole a glance around the corner, nodded his head, and was out the door and to the right like a bullet.

"Follow him. Quickly. Silently."

Three doors down the corridor, the first man stood at the threshold, his face turned to the length of the hallway, his left hand waving behind his back, directing Rizzo through the open door. His two guardians followed, closed the door, and moved immediately to the open window. Hassan led the way, feet first, through the window, dropping to the ground outside without a sound. Rizzo followed, getting a boost through the window, and Hassan grabbed him at the hips as he cleared the ledge. The other man slipped out the window like a moon shadow. They turned away from the brightening sky and all three fled into the retreating darkness.

Jebel Kalakh, Syria

Bruised from the hard, wooden seats, covered with the ocher stone dust of the desert that billowed through nonexistent windows for the six-hour trip through the Homs valley, Tom Bohannon thanked God that he finally escaped from the ancient green bus that now belched and bumped its way down the steep slope.

Rodriguez had gotten the better of the deal.

Bohannon was caked with desert grit, withered by the sun, and still had a six-hour bus trip back to Tripoli to endure.

He removed the handkerchief he had desperately wrapped over his nose and mouth to minimize the damage to his lungs during the interminable trip. He pulled a plastic bottle of water from his backpack, soaked the handkerchief, and rubbed at the dust coating his face and neck as if it were a carcinogen eating away at his skin.

It was only then, wiping the grit from his eyes, that Tom looked at the walls towering above him.

The mountain of gray stone stretched to the azure sky that spread from horizon to horizon, dwarfing the vistas that loomed in all directions.

Krak de Chevaliers—"the perfect castle" according to Lawrence of Arabia— guarded the heavily traveled trade route between Antioch and Beirut . . . from the Syrian interior to the Mediterranean Sea. The limestone fortress, first constructed in 1031 for the emir of Aleppo and later the impregnable keystone of Crusader power, rested atop a steeply sloped hill, twenty-three hundred feet above the floor of the Buqai'ah Valley, with a sheer drop on three sides. Overrun by local villagers for hundreds of years, the castle was rescued by the French Department of Antiquities in 1934, restored over the decades, and declared a World Heritage Site by UNESCO in 2006. And it was huge.

Bohannon pulled out the English guidebook he purchased in Tripoli, studied the map on the inside flyleaf, and followed the rest of the weary and dusty tourists across a stone bridge and through the large, arched gate in the sixteen-foot-thick wall. Robed children ran after the knot of tourists ahead of him and Bohannon could hear their plaintive offers to provide "first-class" guide services.

"Perhaps I could assist you, sir?"

Bohannon jumped at the sound of a voice by his shoulder. He looked to his left and found a young man with hungry eyes looking him over.

"Please forgive my boldness," the young man said, bowing slightly at the waist. "But there is no other way for me to offer my services as a guide."

He was shorter than Bohannon, but not by much, and wore a crisp, white kaftan that failed to hide the bulked-up muscles of a body builder. Under his white kaffiyeh, his black eyes were bottomless. His smile was bright, but far too vibrant, as if he had painted it on this morning.

"I am Zaka Alaoui, a student at the university in Homs. This is one way

I help to pay for my studies. My knowledge of the castle is extensive and my English is without compare. Perhaps you would allow me to guide you? The castle's passageways are labyrinthine and one is easily confused."

Alaoui tried earnestly to appear at ease, deferential, a servant for hire. Bohannon took a step backward, out of the young man's sphere of contact. Then he held up the guidebook and shook his head.

"Thank you, but I don't believe I'll need a guide."

The young man's painted-on smile turned down at the edges and his eyes hardened, sending a shiver up Bohannon's spine in spite of the beating sun.

"Very well," Alaoui said, backing away and bowing slightly, touching his fingers to his forehead. "May Allah go with you."

Alaoui's final words may have been a farewell, but, to Bohannon, the look on his face was more like a warning. Unsettled, but determined, Bohannon pulled out his map of the Krak, quickly got his bearings, and began his search for the castle's library. Walking through the courtyard between the outer and inner walls of the castle, Bohannon was amazed at the wonder of this Crusader fortress. The outer, or curtain, wall was about twenty feet tall with a crenellated battlement running along its crest. It was fortified by thirteen towers spaced at the corners and along the sides of the wall. While formidable, the outer wall was dwarfed by the monumental size of the Krak de Chevaliers' inner keep.

Across a narrow, separating moat, now filled in places with stagnant water, the inner walls of the castle rose eight stories tall and sloped away from the one-hundred-foot-thick base at an eighty-degree angle, making assault on the walls nearly impossible. Huge, half-round towers jutted from the inner wall halfway up its angled sides. If the Knights Hospitaller were forced to abandon the outer wall's defenses, the higher inner walls would afford the castle's defenders a perfect perch for raining death on invaders. And if an attacking army ever breached the massive inner wall, the interior of the castle was a maddening warren of narrow, zigzagging, vaulted passageways that could be sealed by dropping iron gates from the ceiling.

Checking his map, Bohannon measured his progress past the small Gothic chapel and entered a low, dark, narrow passageway with a severe upward grade. He emerged into the light on an overgrown platform that connected to another covered passageway and led to a spiral staircase that wound up into the central of the three powerful towers.

Bohannon bypassed the tower's stairs and came out into the inner court of the keep. Turning left, he entered an elegant portico with seven rib-vaulted bays and followed the sun-dappled walkway to the Great Hall. Standing in the doorway, he checked his map once more. According to the guidebook, the Hospitallers library lay beyond the Great Hall, up another steep, narrow passageway. And, if the guidebook was correct, the French not only rescued the citadel and its priceless frescoes from the ravages of the local villagers, but also unearthed a library hidden by the Crusaders seven hundred years earlier. It was the library that lured Bohannon to Krak de Chevaliers.

As he turned to step through the door, Bohannon caught sight of a flash of white to his right. Zaka Alaoui stood motionless at the end of the porticoed walkway, no longer a painted smile on his face.

Egyptian Desert, West of St. Anthony's Monastery

Rizzo was belted into the rear seat of the Jeep, vacantly staring at a tawny, treeless landscape he didn't really see. The image in his mind was lying on a bed, back among those ochre buildings with the domes and narrow windows with arched tops. Neither of his rescuers uttered a word during the long drive into the morning. He didn't care.

The Jeep lurched and pounded over a dusty, stone-covered hillock, slamming Sammy's sore butt against the rock-hard seat and pulling his thoughts back to the present. Heckle and Jeckle were in the front seats, the scarves covering their heads whipping in the wind. Rizzo followed their gaze as they both looked to the west.

Like a beige cliff rising from the ground, billowing up and over itself, an enormous cloud of sand and dust rolled across the flat desert floor, covering everything it passed in a swirling fog.

The Jeep jumped forward, its engine whining a complaint. The old bucket of bolts raced across the desert floor, the cloud closing fast.

"Hold on!"

The abrupt voice jolted Rizzo's attention back to the driver. He couldn't see over the dashboard or out the windshield so he wasn't prepared as his shoulders were pinned against the seat back and his head snapped backward as the Jeep collided with something, and lost its connection with the ground. Rizzo could feel the change in the weight, the displacement of the vehicle. It was floating.

Until it crashed heavily against its groaning springs, launching Rizzo against the restraint of the seat belt.

"Yo, Pancho Villa, where'd you learn to—" Before Rizzo could finish his sentence, the Jeep plunged into a dark cavern, the throbbing protest of its engine echoing off the cavern's walls, competing in decibels with the screaming sandstorm that howled just outside the cave's entrance.

Jebel Kalakh, Syria

What was once a great library was a dusty ruin. The rows of empty shelves attested to years of looting and unchecked weather.

"At one time—one point of history—was not this library a marvel?" said the curator to Bohannon. "So much knowledge in such a remote place. But was that not the same cause of its own destruction? Was there no one here to guard or care for the books?"

A small man, his robes sweeping the worn, stone floor, the curator wore a small, white, circular cap on top of his round, almond-colored head. The hat was as exposed to the elements as the Krak, and looked much less secure. He waved with the back of his hand to the small assemblage of books, scrolls, and pamphlets that occupied a lonely corner of the great library. Lonely . . . but well protected. "Only these survived."

The documents were enclosed in a two-sided Plexiglas cube, the front and right sides of which formed a square in the corner of the room; a third piece of Plexiglas served as a cover, twenty feet off the floor and ten feet short of the arched, stone ceiling.

"A few only remain," rasped the curator, "but are you pleased with what survived?"

Standing outside the climate-controlled enclosure, Bohannon scanned the shelves, looking for anything that might look familiar. "How were these saved?"

"Aaahhhh"—the curator sounded like he was gagging on his last breath—"how did they survive?" He pointed to the square stones on the floor. "Was it under here? Hidden, a stone vault? How many false tunnels protected them? Lost to time, but are these not treasures?"

Bohannon looked at the collection mere feet away and put his hand on the Plexiglas.

"I may help you?"

He didn't turn. "I'm looking for a document—probably not a book—that came here from the Dar al-Ilm in Tripoli."

"From the House of Knowledge?"

Bohannon nodded his head, his eyes still scanning the shelves. "It may be a scroll or a scroll holder. I don't know exactly. But I think if I could get close to those books in the case, if it's there, I should be able to identify it."

"Inside?"

Bohannon turned to the curator. The small man's eyes were bulging. A look of horror covered his face.

"That is the only way for me to know."

"No . . . no . . . none can enter," said the curator, shaking his head. "How do you know it is here? How would you know it?"

Good question. Bohannon wondered that himself. *Divine inspiration?*

"Do you know Phoenician?" Bohannon asked.

The curator stepped back and regarded Bohannon with a new level of interest. "You do?"

"Enough to know what I'm looking for," said Bohannon. "It's probably a brass mezuzah, etched on the outside. Somewhere, there are probably the letters aleph and resh on its face."

The curator's head spun around so quickly, checking the length and breadth of the Great Hall, that he almost lost his hat.

"What do you know? Why are you here? What do you want?"

Bohannon took a step closer to the curator. "I want to get inside and look through that collection. Then, I'll tell you everything you want to know."

Settling his hat squarely on the top of his head, the curator stepped to the large, double doors that created an air lock. He pulled a key as long as a dagger from the folds of his robe, opened a huge, ancient padlock, and slid the first door along a sealed runner. Both men stepped into the air-lock. Bohannon was about to remark on the dated security when the curator placed his palm on a small LCD pad and leaned close to a lens that scanned his retina.

The second door swung open. The smell of old, dry leather—like the smell of his grandfather's attic—lured them in.

With his robe dragging behind him, the curator crossed through the enclosed space and stopped in front of a bookcase with drawers in its two bottom sections.

He creaked open the top drawer, its wooden surface polished by a thousand hands, reached inside, and pulled out an etched, brass mezuzah. It was larger than the mezuzah that had launched their journey—probably twice as large, about four inches in radius and about eighteen inches long. Even though this was what he was looking for, Bohannon was still startled to see it right before his face, held out in the hands of the curator.

"This is what you seek, perhaps?"

Bohannon stepped forward as the curator turned the brass cylinder over in his hands. "The aleph and resh you seek?"

There it was, Abiathar's hallmark, the Phoenician letters aleph and resh surrounded by a circle. Bohannon took another step and lifted his hands to receive the tube from the curator. "Yes."

But the little man pulled the mezuzah away, and held it back toward his body, out of Bohannon's reach. "Is it the mezuzah, or what it protects, that you seek?"

Bohannon looked at the curator with the baffled fury of a spurned lover. "What?"

The curator took a small step backward. "What do you seek? This, the holder? Or what was inside?"

"I . . . well . . . I don't know," Bohannon stammered, anxiety and frustration bubbling up to the surface of his emotions. "Both, I guess. What difference does it make?"

A sigh escaped from the curator's chest . . . an edgy rattle of a sigh.

He held the mezuzah away from him and grasped the metal bar that spanned about three-quarters of its length—a three-sided square piece of etched bronze fitted tightly to the outer surface of the mezuzah. The curator looked at Tom with the compassion of a coroner as he pulled the scroll holder's handle away from the mezuzah's surface.

"A great deal of difference, don't you think?"

The handle separated from the mezuzah, but there was nothing there—no scroll attached to the handle—nothing to unroll. "Gone . . . a very long time ago, I believe."

Bohannon looked at the empty space between the mezuzah and its handle—and that was how he felt. Empty. All this way—what was he doing?

〰〰〰

Hunger gnawed at Bohannon's stomach as furiously as frustration gnawed at his emotions. He walked along the ramparts of the Krak de Chevaliers in a trance. After a frustrating and unrewarding hour examining the nondescript decorations on the surface of the larger mezuzah, he emerged from the library in a state of mental fog and in an area of the castle that he didn't recognize. The labyrinthine twists had brought him to an unknown corner in a dead-end tunnel, except for a stone stairway that led up, into the light. He climbed the solitary staircase and found himself on the far, southeast corner of the castle's walls, on the opposite end of the fortress from the main gate.

He looked along the line of stone ramparts to the north. In the distance was the Tower of the King's Daughter and the tourist-filled restaurant that beckoned to Bohannon's growling stomach.

His mind wandered over the past and present as he walked along the empty castle rampart, the parapet wall to his right. The Buqai'ah Valley stretched out far below. The late afternoon sunshine filtered through distant billows of dust and sand. What to do next? Exhaustion hung on his bones. He was more than tired. He was worn out and discouraged to his core. The adrenaline accompanying the president's plea, the excitement of the chase he'd felt on the flight to Tripoli, the miracle of a second brass mezuzah—all were now displaced by a feeling that he was merely a captive of his own foolish, self-serving pride.

Really . . . why am I here in the middle of the Syrian desert? I'm just a normal guy. What am I doing?

Across the valley to the east, the Alawite Mountains radiated a golden glow. From this height—more than two thousand feet above the valley floor—he could see forever across the flat desert plain. Bohannon was lost in his thoughts, in his doubts.

"I sincerely hope your considerable efforts have been rewarded."

Startled, Bohannon stumbled against the parapet wall.

Standing behind him, a short way back along the rampart, was the student from the gate.

"Forgive me for interrupting you," said Zaka Alaoui, that painted-on smile failing to bring any softness to his hardened features. "I noticed you walking along the wall. I only wanted to ask if your visit was satisfactory. Perhaps there is something I could help you with after all?"

His demeanor was deferential, but his eyes betrayed a man of many motives. Bohannon didn't like this guy, or the vibes he was generating. He eased away.

Simply speaking to this smarmy young man soiled his soul. "I found what I came to see."

"Ah . . . so the curator of the library helped you find . . . what was it you said you sought?"

"I didn't say. Look . . . I've got to go. I need to get something to eat before I can think about getting back on that bus."

Alaoui moved closer, forcing Bohannon's back against the wall. "Did he show you something?" Now the smile was gone. "A scroll, perhaps? A book? A mezuzah etched with symbols?"

Pushing out his left arm to move the young man out of his way, Bohannon stepped to his right, along the parapet wall, making for the sanctuary of the restaurant in the Tower of the King's Daughter. Before he could take two steps, the young man clamped his right hand on Bohannon's left wrist and twisted, pulling Bohannon's arm back and pushing his wrist up, just under Tom's shoulder blades. Tom now felt the power of the muscles he'd noticed earlier. And pain, as the young man nearly lifted him off his feet, pressing his wrist higher while pushing him face-first toward the wall.

Bohannon drove the pain from his mind for a moment, and filled his lungs with enough air to launch a call for help. But Alaoui's left hand came up and wrapped itself around Bohannon's throat, pressing down on his windpipe.

Alaoui had short, powerful arms that drove the bigger man forward. Tom's stomach slammed into stone, knocking out of him whatever air was left. Legs scrambling for purchase, choking from lack of oxygen, his left shoulder straining against its socket, he was clearly conscious of only one thing. The man's strong arms were lifting him, inch-by-inch, onto the top of the parapet wall.

The higher he was pushed, the more Tom could see the sheer drop from the castle's wall, and the cliffs below it, tumbling into the valley. His head was spinning—whether from lack of oxygen or vertigo it didn't really matter. The fear that drove the flailing of his arms and legs rapidly turned to panic. He scraped his knees against the parapet, his free right hand grasping at the air, looking for . . . anything. Bohannon's waist was now above the top of the wall.

"What did he show you?" Alaoui hissed. "What did he tell you? What did he give you?"

The thought came suddenly, through the blackening fog. *He can't get me over. His arms are too short.* Bohannon closed his eyes. He fought desperately now to visualize his position in relation to the body of the man behind him.

With all his remaining strength he grabbed the outside edge of the parapet wall with his right hand and pushed his body out, over the parapet even further. As he did, Alaoui lost his grip on Bohannon's throat and a fresh intake of air cleared his mind. As the pressure on his left arm eased, Bohannon used the leverage of the wall as a fulcrum, and kicked both of his legs like the pistons on a huge, diesel engine, driving his boots into Alaoui's chest, throwing him backward with a violent thrust.

Bohannon heard scrambling behind him and a short yelp, but his concentration was now solely focused on regaining his balance. Propelled forward by his desperate kick against Alaoui's chest, Tom's head, chest, and hips now tipped over the two-thousand-foot drop into the valley below. He could feel in his stomach and see in his mind his body plummeting to its death in the Syrian desert.

He dug his thighs into the top edge of the parapet wall, ignored the stabbing pain in his left shoulder, and grabbed the top of the wall with all the strength left in his arms and hands. His left palm pressed against the inside corner of the parapet, worn smooth through the ages. He tried to hook his legs, his feet, against the inside edge of the wall, his right hand scraping against the face of the fortress, frantic for some traction.

A seam . . . his right hand found a seam between two of the stacked stones, an edge against which he could wedge his hand. He shoved his fingers and part of his palm into the gap between the stones—but the shift in his weight tipped the scales. Bohannon's body began to roll into space.

His heart jumped . . . his entire body tensed . . . his shoulder dipped into the void. He was going over. "Oh . . . God . . ." He could see Annie's face. "Ohh . . ."

Bohannon screamed—whether from fear or hope, he would never know—as two strong hands grasped his ankles. With the weight pushing down on his legs, Bohannon's body lifted out of the abyss. He pushed his hand against the seam in the stones, felt his shoulders rise above the parapet, the balance of his weight shifting to the inside of the wall. Then he thought of the young man, Alaoui, and he tensed once more, ready to fight for his life again. But . . . why?

"Are you safe?"

It was the dry, scraping voice of the curator.

Bohannon's body slipped over the corner of the parapet wall, again abrading his thighs against the unforgiving stone. As his feet hit the rampart, his knees buckled, and his stomach began vomiting out his fear. Bohannon collapsed onto the stone walkway. His eyes closed, his heart racing, the bile in his stomach burning his throat, sobs of relief fought with the impulse to retch, rocking his shoulders, as tears slipped down his cheeks.

"Why was that young man following you?" whispered the curator. "With such hatred in his face? A thief perhaps? An assassin?"

He put his hand on Bohannon's shoulder.

"I watched, and then followed. I was below when he attacked. Perhaps his hatred was its own executioner? Come . . . you must leave. Do you want to be held for questioning by the police, I don't think?"

Bohannon's body was lathered in a full sweat. He felt like he was ready to pass out. He didn't have the strength to lift his head, let alone move. With knuckles, knees, and thighs all scraped and bleeding, Tom tried to lift his body. The curator crouched by his side.

Three feet away, the rampart's inner edge gave way to a thirty-foot drop into an upper square of the castle. A thick, rough, sisal hemp rope was strung along the inner edge of the rampart, passing through iron stanchions at regular intervals. It was a warning.

Two ragged-edged pieces of white linen cloth hung limply from the coarse surface of the rope. There were two scrape marks leading over the edge of the stone rampart, just below the torn pieces of kaftan snared by the yellow rope.

Jerusalem

Joe Rordiguez left the Old City by the New Gate and turned toward the honking chaos and exhaust poison of Suleiman Road, which skirts the city on the northeast. As he passed the *C*-shaped stairs down to the Damascus Gate, a tour bus squeezed by on his left, skirting the earthquake damage that still pockmarked the road. A seemingly endless human tide streamed through the Damascus Gate and were greeted by the competing shouts of street hawkers who lined both sides of the stairs.

A hundred yards down the hill he came upon the doorway to Solomon's Quarries, a huge cave at least two football fields long that sloped to the south, toward the Temple Mount. Discovered in 1852 and considered to be the source for the stone used to build the temple area, little is known about the cavern except that several huge, half-hewn blocks of limestone litter the floor and the walls show clear evidence of quarrying. But Rodriguez wasn't interested in the quarry.

Across Suleiman Road, at the end of a short alley and cut out of the rock, he could see the dark indentation of an entrance that ran under the far hill, a cavern known as Jeremiah's Grotto—the place where Jeremiah was imprisoned by King Zedekiah and where, according to legend, the prophet wrote the book of Lamentations.

From the shadowed doorway to Solomon's Quarries Rodriguez appeared to be scanning a Jerusalem tourist guide. In spite of the long bus ride from Tripoli, that drained the energy from his body, Joe kept close watch on the gate at the far end of the alley. The sun was hard to the west, casting long shadows across the street, but heat still pounded off the asphalt, sucking the moisture out of his skin and driving most tourists to the air-conditioned indoors. Pedestrians were primarily locals, most in kaftans of many colors, who threaded their way through crates of fruits and vegetables. Joe considered each one a suspicious threat. No one approached the grotto.

Joe's self-preservation clicked in enough that he looked up and down the street for a careening vehicle. There was no wheeled threat, so he crossed Suleiman Road and entered into the cool darkness of the grotto's entrance.

To the left of the entrance, protected from the sun in deep shadow, a man—his yarmulke-covered head resting on his arms atop a battered wooden desk—slept loudly, his snores echoing down the cavern.

Joe stopped for a moment and debated. It wasn't a question of ducking the ten-shekel admission. He felt his investigation might go more smoothly—alone. Eyes adjusting to the dim light, Joe felt like a kid stealing candy as he skulked deeper into the grotto.

The space was larger than it appeared from the outside. It was a wide, square cavern with a high ceiling and several ancient, wooden doors exiting to the north of the main cave. The air was stale, heavy, and smelled of chalk dust. Joe pulled a compact flashlight from his pocket and swept its intense beam across the wall surfaces. Scrubbed graffiti, vandalism from across the ages, scarred much of the grotto's surface. But the north wall, with the doors, was cordoned off by a low stone wall above which hung a thick rope tied to metal rings secured to the sidewalls.

Joe sat on the low wall, swung his long legs to the other side, slipped under the rope, stood to his feet, and began to study the north wall.

"We are trying to keep the north wall clean . . . no graffiti."

Joe's heart pounded at the sound of the voice behind him. But the voice held no enmity, only invitation. "This sorry excuse for a barrier is there to protect it from . . . oy . . . I told them it would not work."

He turned to find the man who had been sleeping behind the desk, a smile waiting for him.

"Is there something I can help you with?" the man inquired. "Perhaps I can show you some of the rare carvings on the wall that has caught your interest? Oy . . . I sound like I'm still selling leather jackets on Orchard Street."

Rodriguez started. "The Lower East Side?"

The man's eyes lit up the dim cavern. "Ahhh . . . and you?"

"Washington Heights."

"Well, then, Washington Heights, what can I show you?"

Joe relaxed. He had found an ally. "Was this really—"

"Just a moment," said the man, holding out his hand. "Ten shekels, then we begin your education."

"Okay," said Rodriguez, dropping a handful of coins into the man's right palm. "How do you know for sure that this is—"

The man's left hand came up, palm out. "Patience, my New York friend. Patience. For ten shekels, I throw in my sales pitch, for free. It's a bargain." He pointed. "Sit."

Rodriguez was now a prisoner of someone else's timetable. He sat again on the low wall and stretched his long legs.

"Thank you," the man said, reaching forward for Joe's hand. "Ronald Fineman, formerly of Queens, New York City, retired owner of Leather World on Orchard Street." Ronald Fineman's thinning hair was swept straight back from a prominent brow. His head nodded punctuation to every word he spoke and the goatee on the end of his chin bobbed like a teacher's pointer. "You've heard of it?"

"Sorry, no. I'm Joseph Rodriguez, raised in the Bronx and now living in Washington Heights. Curator of the Periodicals Room at the Humanities and Social Science Library on Bryant Park. It's a pleasure."

"Ah . . . the one with the lions," Fineman said of the iconic pair of crouching lions that flanked the main entrance to the ornate, Beaux-Arts Library on Fifth Avenue. "A beautiful building. I've been there to see the Gutenberg Bible. And the Jewish division"—Fineman's dark eyes sparked with an inner joy and flanked a thin, pointy nose—"that is right next to the Periodicals Room . . . the one with all the beautiful murals of the old newspaper buildings in Manhattan, correct?"

"That's right . . . the DeWitt Wallace Periodicals Room. It was named for the founder of *Reader's Digest* magazine, who used it to find articles he then condensed in the magazine. That is my domain."

Fineman nodded his head, his goatee bobbing as if to a musical beat. "So, Joe the librarian, what can I sell you today?"

Joe looked around the large cavern then back at his host. "Well, Mr. Fineman—"

"*Rabbi* Fineman . . . I've had a change of occupation. That's what brought me to Jerusalem."

"Okay, rabbi, I'd like to know more about why this place is called Jeremiah's Grotto. I mean, does it really have anything to do with the prophet Jeremiah?"

"Ah," purred Fineman, "the speech." He sat on the wall next to Rodriguez, put his hand on Joe's arm, and captured him with the earnestness of his eyes. "There are many stories and legends about this cave. Some say it was a tomb. Some say it was only a prison. Others, who reject the older site within the city and believe the hill above us is Calvary, the site of Jesus' crucifixion, believe this place was a stable, a place where pilgrims to the site kept their donkeys. And some say Jeremiah wrote the book of Lamentations in this cave while he was in prison.

"There are also legends about this place in the book of Islam," said Fineman, shrugging his shoulders. "There is a tradition that when Nebuchadnezzar was a poor, afflicted lad his future greatness and the misfortune of this battle-scarred city were foretold by the prophet Jeremiah. Flattered by the prophecy of greatness, Nebuchadnezzar extended an amnesty to Jeremiah . . . a safe-conduct that would protect him and keep him unharmed from the future Babylonian invasion. Jeremiah pleaded with Nebuchadnezzar that Jerusalem be spared, but the Assyrian emperor was in no mood to be lenient toward Zedekiah, the king of Israel who led a rebellion against Nebuchadnezzar's rule. Jeremiah, however, did receive a promise from Allah, the god of Islam, that he would witness the restoration of the city.

"But the Assyrian siege was so devastating, Jerusalem and its inhabitants suffered so severely—many starving people cannibalizing their own children—the situation was so appalling to Jeremiah that he lost hope and doubted God. So Allah, the god of Islam, brought a sleep onto Jeremiah that lasted for one hundred years. When Jeremiah awoke, the skeleton of his donkey also awoke, put on skin and flesh, and began to bray. At the calling of the donkey, both Jeremiah and the donkey were admitted to Paradise."

Fineman lifted his hands and twisted them back and forth while shaking his head. "An interesting fable, perhaps, but there are lots of stories and fables about this place."

"So," asked Rodriguez, "what's the truth?"

Fineman's body audibly creaked as he pushed himself to his feet. "Come over here. Let me show you something that might interest you." The old man walked into the shadows at the southeast corner of the grotto. Joe followed him over to a shallow alcove. "In this grotto, this alcove is the closest you can get to the site of the old Jewish Temple. Here . . . throw your light onto this wall."

Rodriguez pulled out the flashlight and followed Fineman's finger to a group of symbols etched in the stone. "This one on the top," said Fineman, "this is Jeremiah's signature in Hebrew."

Joe ran his fingers over the markings. Next to Jeremiah's signature was a symbol that looked like an angel's wing next to a door. Below those a set of symbols Joe was becoming quite familiar with, a budding shepherd's staff and a scorpion. And below those, a pair of Phoenician letters with which Rodriguez was intimately acquainted. "Abiathar's signature!"

"How do you know this?"

"Oh . . . something I read once," said Rodriguez. "Ah . . . this one, the angel and the door, what does that one mean?"

Fineman also reached out his hand toward the markings. "The house of God, the Temple or, perhaps, the Tent of Meeting. The place where God lived."

He turned to face Rodriguez again. "But . . . tell me, Joe from New York, how do you know Abiathar's signature? You may have read something about him recently . . . his name has been in the news. But not his signature. Only a few select people on this earth would know the significance of the aleph and the resh."

Rodriguez felt the old man's eyes on him. He tried to regain his composure, but exhilaration and panic were racing through his body like an August thunderstorm. "I've seen those symbols before."

Fineman reached out his right hand and placed it on Rodriguez's arm.

"You were one of those who found the Temple, yes?"

"Yes," said Rodriguez, nodding his head. He held the man's gaze and read a litany of unasked questions revealed in his face. Fineman squeezed his arm and smiled, but kept silent. "And I'll bet that the staff, scorpion, and Abiathar's mark were added to the wall after Jeremiah's signature."

"Where did you see this mark before?" Fineman asked, gesturing toward the staff and scorpion carved into the wall.

"The sign of the scorpion and the budding staff were etched into the surface of the mezuzah that Abiathar sent to Egypt," said Joe. "The same two symbols are carved into the lintel over the door leading to the library in St. Anthony's Monastery in the Egyptian desert."

Fineman nodded in thought. "So now you are chasing clues from the mezuzah itself?"

"I'm not sure what we're doing, yet," said Rodriguez. "We're just trying to make some sense of things we've found."

Rodriguez turned his back to the wall, leaned up against it, and tried to read the expression on Fineman's face. But the elderly rabbi was anxiously waiting for more.

"The scorpion mark and the budding staff were added to the surface of the mezuzah some time after the original designs were etched into it. The markings were different . . . made by a different hand, a different tool, like these." He gestured over his shoulder. "We believe the scorpion image, and some other images, were added in Egypt where the mezuzah was hidden, probably in the monastery.

"And we've found another mark with Jeremiah's signature," Rodriguez added. "There was a group of papyrus documents found in Egypt in the nineteenth century, the Elephantine Papyri. One of them, an older document that was passed down from father to son for three generations, is a record of Jeremiah acquiring ownership rights to land in Persia, of all places. At the bottom of the document is a cartouche that contains the hieroglyph for sounding out Jeremiah's name and—like this—the shepherd's staff, along with a symbol for the island of Gibraltar. But no scorpion.

"What do you think, Rabbi Fineman? What does it mean?"

Fineman looked out of the side of his eye as if assessing Rodriguez for the first time.

"Did you know, my friend from New York, that there is a book in the Christian scriptures that claims Jeremiah took the Tent of Meeting and the Ark of the Covenant and buried them on Mount Nebo?"

"The book of Maccabees," said Rodriguez, "says that the Tent was buried on the same mountain where Moses was buried."

Ronald Fineman rubbed the yarmulke over the top of his head as his eyes searched the shadows. "I think your knowledge of these symbols means you are on another quest, are you not?" Fineman asked. He turned his body to face Rodriguez. "You seek something that has been lost to antiquity. The House of God, if I am not mistaken. Your friend, Abiathar, sent you on a quest for a Temple, eh? Now, if my hunch is correct, you are following Abiathar's clues on a quest for a Tent, eh?"

Joe nodded his head.

"Well, I may know where you should look."

———⁓〰⁓———

"There are only two possibilities."

Colonel David Posner and Levi Sharp paused in front of the graves of Golda Meir and Yitzhak Rabin in the Mt. Herzl Memorial Park in the western part of Jerusalem, near the Knesset. The path through the Garden of Heroes was shaded by rows of native pine and cypress trees and ranks of cedars of Lebanon that guarded its flanks. Sharp wore dark sunglasses against the afternoon glare. Still Posner could feel the power of the director's stare radiating from behind the lenses. If not for the discipline of his military training, or the rage that blotted out all his other emotions, Posner would have been sick to his stomach at the report he had to give.

"Major Mordechai and I have spent the last four days reviewing every name, every history," he said. "Mordechai has posed as a reporter, writing a feature story about each of the original twelve, and interviewed old friends and family members, looking for flaws, breaks in the narrative. We focused most of our time on the four I showed you and pored over every detail of the past two weeks. We searched for some change in routine, some time that could not be accounted for, some motive that might drive one of them to betray us."

Sharp gently pressed his hand against Posner's left elbow. "We should keep walking."

Posner felt foolish, taking precautions against being spied on in the middle of Jerusalem. But he knew the two names on the piece of paper in his pocket— powerful and resourceful men. Ridiculous as it seemed on the surface, he and Sharp must take every precaution. This was dangerous territory.

"Go on."

"There were only two who separated from the others," said Posner. "And that only because of something we found in each of their past lives. Something very personal. Something that could turn a man's heart and soul from one path to another."

They rounded the corner of the path and walked alongside the reflecting pool. Posner withdrew the slip of paper from his pocket.

─────

"Come over here." Rabbi Fineman returned to the low wall and sat. Rodriguez joined him as the old man reached a finger toward the floor and began scratching in the dust. "This priest, Abiathar, did leave you another message." Fineman drew a straight, vertical line in the dust and added two irregular circles at either end. "This is the Jordan River," he said, pointing to the line. "Here is the Sea of Galilee in the north, the Dead Sea in the south." He made a mark on the eastern side of the Jordan.

"Here is Mount Nebo, on the far side of the Jordan River, opposite Jericho." He swept an oval to the west—"the Mediterranean"—pierced the south with the shape of a dagger—"the Red Sea"—then drew a triangle to the east and a square to the west of the Red Sea—"the Negev desert here and Egypt there. We know Jeremiah traveled to Egypt with the exiles."

Fineman turned quickly toward Rodriguez, then back to his dust drawing. In the middle of the Negev, Fineman scratched out a familiar symbol—the scorpion.

"These carvings on the wall in the alcove are directions," said Fineman. "Mount Nebo is the starting point. This," he said, stabbing his finger into the midst of the scorpion, "was one of the destinations."

"The scorpion means desert?" asked Rodriguez. "The Negev?"

Fineman shook his head back and forth. "No, but it is a place. The Ascent of Akkrabim."

"The what?"

Fineman chuckled. "The Ascent of Akkrabim, Mr. Rodriguez. *Akkrabim* means scorpion and there is a place in the Negev called Scorpion Pass . . . the steepest road in the entire country of Israel. It's an ancient trade route through some of the most barren, God-forsaken land in the world. It winds nearly straight up from the basin of the Dead Sea, the Wadi of Arabah, through the mountains of the Negev, and into the lusher interior of Israel. And, along the

Ascent of Akkrabim, my friend, are hundreds of caves eroded out of the brown stone by the ages. Its climate is very similar to, and its location close to, the Essene caves which held and preserved the Dead Sea Scrolls."

Joe felt his heart racing. *This was it.* He was sure of it. *Only . . . which cave?*

"Someone has been leaving you clues, Mr. Rodriguez. I'm not sure who took the Tent of Meeting to Scorpion Pass. Either Jeremiah on his way to Egypt, or Abiathar before he fled to Tripoli. But both Jeremiah and Abiathar are pointing you toward Scorpion Pass."

Rodriguez looked once more at the crude drawing in the dust, shook his head and launched himself to his feet. "Okay . . . well . . . thank you, Rabbi. Really . . . thank you. But I've got to get going. It looks like a long journey and I don't have a lot of time." Rodriguez stuck out his hand.

"Not so fast, Joe from Washington Heights." Ronald Fineman rose to his feet, the bones in his knees cracking. "There is more you need to know."

Forty minutes later, Fineman escorted Rodriguez back to the grotto's entrance. He moved closer and Rodriguez was startled when the old man reached out his right hand and placed it with care against the left side of his neck, between Joe's ear and his shoulder. Fineman closed his eyes. "May the Lord bless you and keep you," the words whispered through the cavern, "may the Lord make his countenance shine upon you and be gracious to you, may the Lord turn his face toward you and give you peace."

Fineman's dark eyes opened and searched the depths of Rodriguez. "Go with God, my son. Go with God."

25

Friday, August 21

Kallie Nolan looked over at the clock on the table next to the sofa. Green numerals mocked her open eyes—4:44. This was no time to be awake.

But Kallie's mind had been racing when she lay down on the sofa hours earlier. Tomorrow she presented her dissertation to the review board after two days of nonstop prep. And tonight, at dinner, Annie Bohannon had shared her faith. Kallie was still trying to get her head around Annie's words, which stirred her soul and ruined her sleep. Could there be any truth in Annie's faith?

With her roommates—and their furniture—long gone, it was a battle to convince Annie to accept Kallie's bed while they stayed in the apartment. But after a couple of sweltering days wandering around Jerusalem's refugee camps with her cameras, Annie was grateful and, so far, Kallie also had slept like a rock. Until tonight.

She rolled off the sofa and padded softly to the kitchen. Some of the orange-pineapple juice was left. Cool on her throat, the memory of the tropics rising in the sweet smell of pineapple, she walked over to the east-facing windows, her favorite in the apartment. She leaned against the window frame and pulled aside the white lace curtains, the ones her mother sent from the farm in Idaho. Off in the east, the walls of Jerusalem were bathed in a soft, golden glow, lit from below, shimmering at their ramparts. Minarets spiked the sky. Shadowed domes protected their treasures.

Her heart began to ache . . . again. *I love this place.* Tears formed at the corners of her eyes. She missed her roommates, dispersed by Israeli security when they locked down her apartment. She missed her work, leading tourists through the ancient history of Jerusalem. And she missed her studies—even the tedious days in the sun, gingerly brushing away the dust of centuries. Most of all, she grieved over the thought of leaving this city whose living spirit beat in time with her heart. Jerusalem was alive. And the flow of its life washed through her soul. Leaving would kill something inside her.

Even though her gaze was fixed on the distant walls, movement at the corner of her eye caused Kallie to glance down, to her left, into the bushes and shadows that bordered the parking lot off the Bar-Lev Road. Something had moved in the early morning black.

Then she saw it. A man in a black hood moved to the corner of the building. He waited, peeking around the corner, while three more black-clad, hooded men silently lined up behind him.

Kallie gripped the glass tightly in her right hand, the acidic juice turning bitter in her stomach. She knew who they were. And who they were after.

Icy fingers of fear gripped her spine, belied by her exterior calm. Kallie set the glass of juice on the windowsill. She pivoted on her toes and, pleading with her feet to fall softly on the floor, raced through the apartment and burst into her bedroom. Before her body settled on the edge of the bed, her right hand covered Annie's mouth and she was whispering through the bandana holding Annie's hair in place.

"They're here . . . men with hoods . . . coming through the shadows." Her whispers sounded like shouts to her own ears. Annie's eruption into wakefulness sent shockwaves through the bed. When she saw recognition in Annie's eyes, Kallie removed her hand. "We've got to get out of here. There's a shelter in the basement—rocket shelter. We can lock the door from the inside."

Annie slipped out of the bed, pulling the blue, cotton nightshirt tightly around her. Kallie stopped at the bedroom door. Listened. She pulled in a deep breath, crossed to the front door, looked over her shoulder at Annie, and, with calculated care, slipped open the deadbolt. Kallie pressed her ear to the opening around the doorjamb. Silence. Annie was at her side. *Follow me*, Kallie mouthed.

Holding her breath, she inched the door open. The hallway of the apartment building was dimly lit by two wall fixtures flanking either side of the elevator. Kallie hesitated in the doorway. Her apartment was on the fourth floor, in the southeast corner. The elevator was to her right, in the middle of the hallway. Fire stairs occupied the corners of the building, at the ends of the hallway.

If they know where I live, they'll know my apartment. They won't take the elevator.

"They'll come up this side," she whispered over her shoulder. "We need to get down the hallway, to the other fire stair."

Kallie slipped out the door, feeling Annie at her back, easing the apartment door shut behind her. They ran to the right, down the hallway, hugging the wall. Kallie's heart stalled as they approached the elevator and heard its motor running. She was about to break into a sprint when Annie grabbed her shoulder and brought her to a skidding halt.

Spinning on her heel, pleading on her lips, Kallie was stunned to see Annie pull the bandana off her head, wrap it around her right fist, and reach up to smash the bulb in one of the light fixtures. "Go," Annie urged.

Dusky half-light engulfed them as they turned once more toward the fire stairs. Annie crushed the bulb in the second fixture as they ran down the now-darkened corridor. Kallie reached the fire door just as the hallway erupted. A shaft of light behind them split the dark and, at almost the same moment, they heard the crack of splitting wood.

Without pause, crouched down near the floor, Kallie grabbed the knob and pushed open the heavy fire door. "Now, while they're distracted." On hands and knees, Annie scrambled through the narrow opening and held the door ajar for Kallie.

Crouched on the landing of the stairs, Kallie's heart slapped against her ribs and her gulping breath hissed through her teeth. Rocking on her haunches, she forced herself to wait, and listen. Silence filled the stairwell. Five flights to the basement. Kallie took a peek through the railing. No movement. Gingerly she padded down the stairs. *Get to the basement. Swing away the wooden shelves hiding the entrance to the shelter. Safety.*

Third floor. Kallie gripped the stair railing with both hands, pressing them in front of her as she pushed farther down the steps, trying to mix speed with stealth. Annie gave a clipped yip as she stumbled into Kallie's back.

Forcing herself to stop between the third and second floor landings, a chill rippled over her skin. Her shirt was soaked with perspiration; her light fleece pants clung to her legs.

Above them, a muffled voice.

Kallie released the railing, planted her left hand against the concrete wall, and bounced down the steps two at a time. Now there was no stopping. Her eyes were riveted on the stairs beneath her feet, her ears straining above her, her hand rubbed raw by the rough concrete. They raced past the ground floor, descending into the growing gloom to the basement. More voices.

Annie's hand was on Kallie's shoulder, her fingers pressing into her flesh, pleading for speed.

They thudded onto the basement landing and Kallie threw her body against the door, spinning aside as Annie barreled through the opening.

Glancing upward, Kallie followed Annie through the door, hope beginning to kindle in her heart.

Hands, like iron clamps, grabbed her arms and held them fast. A scream started, and was snuffed out by a wadded cloth in her mouth. Something heavy shrouded her head. The iron hands slammed her body onto the cold floor. Wide, thick tape ripped around her wrists and ankles. She bucked, desperate for traction. Then a blow to her jaw, and the world went black.

⚡⚡⚡

Joe Rodriguez climbed into the battered, army-green Land Rover as the sky pinked over Jerusalem. Back in Washington Heights they would call this place Rent-a-Wreck. Here, at the intersection of Salah ad Din Road and the Derech Shechem, across the road from three major hotels, David's Vintage Autos reflected the city's fundamental struggle between modern metropolis and ancient archaeological site. But it was open early, the still sleepy attendant asked few questions about a last-minute rental, and the engine and drive train, under the Land Rover's battered shell, felt solid and sounded strong.

The night before, Rodriguez walked from Jeremiah's Grotto, through the A Sa'ira Cemetery, along the Salah ad Din Road, clinging to the shadows and bypassing all of the large, tourist hotels. He wanted to be as invisible as possible. He found a small, nondescript bed-and-breakfast around the corner from the district court building, but was out the door before the coffee was warm.

Rucksack on the rear seat, his first stop was the back-street garage where Sam Reynolds had arranged for some extra supplies and special equipment to be waiting for Rodriguez. He put on a tan, cotton hat, with a wide, circular brim, and pulled it down tight, just over his eyes. He put on sunglasses even though the streets were still dusky and shadowed, and scrunched his tall frame deep into the Land Rover's unforgiving front seat.

No one, other than Bohannon, should even know Rodriguez was in Jerusalem. But he wasn't taking any chances. The Israelis and the Muslims both wanted what he was hunting. Only he knew where to look.

Rodriguez revved the engine to warm it, buckled up, and headed out onto Highway 60, south, into the desert.

Adaisseh, Lebanon

Small was a generous description for this town. Without the border crossing into Israel, Adaisseh would be a forgotten dot on the map. Bohannon rested his backpack on the dusty floor of the cramped, cinder-block bus station and scanned a map of the town that was pinned to the wall beside the door. The border crossing was only two streets away. He glanced out the door. Heat ripples shimmered above the asphalt street. An hour to kill, Bohannon crossed the street to a tiny café. Two small tables, shaded by a large awning, sat in front of the café's window. He ordered tea and closed his eyes.

A barking dog startled Bohannon awake. His tea, untouched, sat on the table, the playground of several large, black flies. Bohannon rubbed his eyes, stretched his neck—then thought of his watch. Nine twenty-five. "Awwww . . . shoot!"

Bohannon jumped to his feet, pulled the wallet from his back pocket, and dropped his last Lebanese thousand-pound note—about sixty-six cents—onto the table and took off at a fast walk toward the crossing.

The travel shop, occupying the corner of a squat, one-story building across from the border crossing, wasn't hard to find. As Bohannon crossed the street, he glanced at the border to his right. And a chill ran up his spine.

Large, thirty-foot-high guard towers flanked the entrance to the crossing at both ends. A razor-wire-topped fence stretched away from the entry into the distance, twenty feet high. A sand-bag labyrinth snaked from the road to the first gate, guarded front and back by heavily armed, helmeted soldiers who looked anything but welcoming. Leading away from the Lebanese entrance was a fence-lined run of concrete, ten feet wide and about a football field in length. Weeds sprouted through cracks at the edges of the concrete. At the other end of the crossing was an even more fortified Israeli outpost, barrels of machine guns poking from turrets in a reinforced concrete bunker.

Between the two armed camps and the two sets of fences stretching off into the distance, was a no-man's land, a killing zone through which all travelers were forced to pass—carrying their luggage—before being scrutinized and interrogated by Lebanese or Israeli soldiers.

The border crossing was empty. But not the entrance.

In addition to the Lebanese soldiers, three men loitered in the shade of the sandbag wall. All three were looking directly at Bohannon, with no attempt at subterfuge, and now started to move in his direction.

Hoping not to look suspicious to the Lebanese border guards, Bohannon picked up his pace, ducked into the cooler shade of the travel shop and let his eyes adjust. At the back of the shop was a glass case on top of which sat an ancient cash register. Beside the cash register stood an ebony-colored man, about six-two, well muscled, wearing a loose, white cotton shirt and a look of animosity that matched the threatening aura of the crossing itself. Bohannon glanced at his watch. Nine thirty-five. He was late.

With a look over his shoulder, he crossed the weathered tile floor, pulled out his wallet, peeled away the two hundred-dollar bills from behind the wallet flap, and, looking into the ebony man's eyes, laid the two bills on top of the glass cabinet.

Suddenly unsure of himself, realizing the risk he was about to take, afraid to say the wrong thing and blow the password, Bohannon stood mute, staring at the man. "Aaahh . . . can I get . . . I mean . . . aaahh . . . I want to get—I mean convert—these dollars into euros." The man behind the counter had thick, red lips, a wide nose, and dark eyes that seemed to drill through Bohannon's skull.

The man's eyes broke away from Bohannon's face, looked over his shoulder toward the door of the shop.

"You're late," he said, his eyes never leaving the door.

"Yes, I know," Bohannon stammered, "but I fell asleep at the café while I was waiting and I—"

A black hand grabbed Bohannon's wrist. A vision of years in a Lebanese prison flashed through his mind.

"Settle down." The voice was melodic, tinted with the traces of many accents. "I've been keeping watch for you. So have those guys across the street. Your buddy came through yesterday. He's fine. And don't worry. I'll get you out of here and across the border."

Relief swept through Bohannon, washing away the strength of his legs. His knees buckled. The hand held him steady.

"Easy." The eyes once more swept toward the door. "Go over there and look at those tee shirts at the back of the shop." The black man gave a flick of his head to the left. "Look at every shirt. When you're done, make an about-face and walk through the door at the back of the shop. I'll meet you there."

Before Bohannon could move, the black man's hand squeezed his wrist and picked his hand up from the counter. The man's other hand swept up the two hundreds. "Overhead."

Thirty-one . . . thirty-two . . . thirty-three . . . Bohannon found himself counting the brightly colored shirts hanging from the round, metal rack. . . . *thirty-four . . . thirty-five . . . did I see that one before?* He shook his head, forced himself not to look at the front door, and self-consciously marched through the back door and into a narrow, darkened alley. Bohannon pressed against the back wall of the building, trying to remain in what little shadow there was. *What if he doesn't come? What do I do next?* He looked down the darkened alley to his right, the second floor of the buildings on either side extending over the street. *Should I run?*

"Quickly . . . they think you're in the outhouse on the other side of the building."

Without pause, the black man crossed the narrow alley and entered a large building, Bohannon on his heels—until he was blinded by the dark inside the warehouse.

"This way."

Bohannon followed the voice as his eyes adjusted. Ten steps and the man stopped at a closed door.

"On the other side is an open square, but it's not visible from the street. On the opposite side of the square is a portal with a door. Go through the door. Don't stop for anything until you're through that door. If someone calls out while you're crossing the square, just keep going. Keep your eyes on the door and your head down. I'll take care of the rest."

"But . . . who are you . . . those men?"

The big, black man smiled. "I've been here a long time. They think I'm one of them. So, no sweat. And you can just think of me as Uncle Sam."

Bohannon returned the smile. "Thanks, uncle. Take care of yourself."

"Go. Don't stop."

And Bohannon was out the door.

Jerusalem

Flashing blue lights reflected off the leaves of the trees surrounding the parking lot, turning them a deathly pale gray, as the taxi turned off the Bar-Lev Road into the lot surrounding the six-story apartment building. Half asleep in the back seat—drained by the heat, the emotional turmoil of his near-death experience in Syria, and the clandestine route required to return to Jerusalem—Tom Bohannon took little notice of the police presence at the far corner of the building.

When the taxi drew to a halt, Bohannon threw his backpack over one shoulder and was happy to find he had enough Israeli shekels in his wallet to pay the driver. Feeling the weight of the last few days, he shuffled to the apartment entrance, punched in the code for Kallie Nolan's apartment, pushed through the solid glass security door, and waited for the elevator. *I wonder if Joe's here. If he's heard anything from Doc or McDonough.*

Thoughts sludged through Bohannon's brain, slowed to a crawl by his numbing fatigue. He stepped out of the elevator into a darkened hallway, but stopped short. Policemen were gathered at the far end of the hall and one was kneeling at the doorway of an apartment, brushing powder against a splintered door frame.

Kallie's?

The backpack fell to the carpet and Bohannon reached out for the wall to steady his legs. The same dread that triggered his instinct to run down the hallway clamped his feet to the floor. He took a staggering step forward and stumbled down the hall as a soldier stepped out of the shattered doorway and advanced toward him. A shout strangled in his throat.

"Mr. Bohannon?" asked the soldier.

Tom tore his eyes away from the door, hanging drunkenly from one hinge, and forced his gaze to the face of the soldier standing in front of him. The man raised his right hand and grasped Bohannon's bicep. The muscles in Tom's legs threatened to stop working.

"There's no one here . . . but there's no blood," said the soldier, his grip growing firmer on Bohannon's arm. "There was a forced entry last night . . . early this morning, perhaps. But we think your wife and Ms. Nolan got out of the apartment."

A hundred thoughts, a thousand emotions clamored to be recognized. But Bohannon simply shook his head, trying to focus. The soldier turned Bohannon around and began moving him back toward the elevator.

"I'm Major Levin, of Shin Bet," said the soldier. "I have many questions for you, but they'll wait. Here." The soldier pointed a flashlight to a light fixture on the wall of the hallway. "You see the bulb is broken?"

Bohannon looked at the fixture, the shattered bulb still screwed into its base, and failed to comprehend. His mind wanted to stand in the doorway to Kallie's apartment, as if by looking he could find Annie sitting there, or coming out of the kitchen. Why was he looking at this fixture?

"The other fixture on the other side of the elevator is the same as this one . . . the light bulbs shattered in place," said Major Levin. The soldier looked expectantly at Bohannon. "Somebody did this purposely. Possibly the same people who broke into the apartment, but we don't think so. We believe the attackers, whoever they were, came in through the far stairwell." He pointed over his shoulder. "It's closer to Miss Nolan's apartment. We believe this was done by someone who was trying to escape . . . your wife and Miss Nolan."

"They got away?"

Major Levin turned Bohannon around again and steered him toward Kallie's apartment. "We don't know," he said. "We know your wife and Miss Nolan aren't here. Our men are checking each apartment in the building, but we don't expect to find them here. And we haven't heard anything from them or . . . well . . . we haven't received any demands, either."

The police in the hallway parted and Bohannon stood in the doorway with Major Levin at his shoulder. The apartment looked pristine. Everything was in its place. Nothing was destroyed, except for the door. Bohannon felt fury rising from that primal place bequeathed to man by ancient hunters. He turned on Major Levin.

"What *do* you know, Major?" The implied threat in Bohannon's voice would have cowed a lesser man.

Levin took a short, menacing step in Bohannon's direction. "I know that you and your friends were involved in at least five homicides the last time you were in Jerusalem and broke enough laws that I could throw you in jail for ten years. And I know enough that would make it very difficult for your friends in Washington to get you free."

The beating of a war drum echoed between Bohannon's temples and his temper rose like the River Liffey at high tide when Levin reached into the pocket of his trousers, pulled out an object, and allowed it to dangle in front of Bohannon's eyes.

"Do *you* know what this is?"

Hanging at the end of a leather thong, gently swinging in front of Bohannon's face, was a Coptic cross, a lightning bolt slashing through it on the diagonal.

The Negev, Israel

Rodriguez pulled to the side of Highway 25, east of the town of Dimona, just short of Rotem Junction. His back hurt, his knees ached, and there were still miles to go—perhaps the most risky part of his journey. But he needed to stretch his body, unwind from the tight confines of the Land Rover.

Even when he stopped in Dimona for gas, Joe didn't get out of the vehicle. He asked the attendant to check the water level in the radiator, his hat pulled down, sunglasses snug against his face. Compared to the desert road from Jerusalem to Be'er Sheva, there was too much traffic in Dimona. Shopping malls flanked the highway. He wasn't about to take a chance.

But here, in the tawny desolation of the Negev, not a tree in sight, the highway an empty asphalt ribbon stretching away into the shimmering distance, Joe felt a little more secure. He pulled a bottle of water from the cooler on the floor of the passenger side, lifted his map from the seat, and spread it across the Rover's hood.

Somewhere out there, Ronald Fineman warned him, were two large military installations. One was the Negev Nuclear Research Center, with its nuclear waste dump, which was flanked by Highway 25 and Route 206. But the other was a super-secret military airfield, hidden in the vastness of the pale brown desert, tucked behind one of the massive, barren hills of rock and sand. Roving military patrols traversed this Judean wasteland, both on-road and off, in unpredictable, random cycles. His American passport and amateur archaeologist equipment should get him through any on-road inspection. The real danger was later, when he pulled off the road and began searching through the desert.

Rodriguez traced the route with his forefinger . . . south on 206, deeper into the unforgiving desert, then east on 227, around the big horseshoe loop that skirted the geological park, then to the top of the Akkrabim.

Rodriguez turned to the west, looking over his left shoulder. Summer blessed him with long days in the Israeli desert, but the sun was well past its apex. His destination was the steepest road in Israel, a wild, coiled, switchbacking, often single-lane, heart-thumper that dropped into the Desert of Zin. He needed

daylight, not just for navigating the Ascent of Akkrabim, but also for finding
. . . what? A cave? What cave? And where was it?

Daylight. Joe needed daylight.

He quickly folded the map, threw it on the front seat, and climbed into the
Land Rover. This was going to take a miracle.

Ten thousand feet overhead, a drone flew long, slow loops above the
Rotem Junction. Not only had the drone's cameras captured a clear picture of
Rodriguez's face, but it also followed the tracing of his finger along 206 and 227,
captured the word *Akkrabim* from the map—and even recorded what brand of
water he was drinking.

Jerusalem

"Oh . . . we checked the answering machine on the telephone," Major Levin said,
pointing to a small table in the corner of Kallie's living room. "There's a message
for you, from a Dr. McDonough in Ireland. He left a call-back number."

Bohannon glanced at the small machine under the telephone. *Thank God Joe
hasn't called.*

"Mr. Bohannon . . ." Tom looked up as Major Levin stood. "If your wife
is half as resourceful as you were under the Temple Mount, she'll be fine.
Regardless, the full force of the Jerusalem police and the Shin Bet are searching
for her and Miss Nolan. We'll find them. Believe me. And we'll find the men
who are responsible. But . . ."

Tom knew what was coming.

". . . no more heroics, all right? Leave this work to us. We will contact you
here as soon as we have any information. Just stay out of it, Mr. Bohannon.
Don't get in our way. You could put your wife, and Miss Nolan, in even greater
danger."

Standing in the middle of Kallie's living room, Major Avram Levin looked
like a bird of prey—long arms straight to his sides, intense eyes flanking a beak
of a nose. *He's only trying to help.*

"Major, I don't need your lecture." Bohannon was surprised at the steely
resolve that reverberated from his voice and filled every cell in his body. "I need
you to find my wife. The Prophet's Guard has tried to kill me twice, killed one
of my friends, tried to abduct my daughter in New York City. These men are
relentless and determined. They don't want my wife. They want the mezuzah

and the scroll that was inside it. But they will do anything—absolutely any-thing—to regain control of that scroll. You need to find them and you need to find them soon. I'm not the guy you have to worry about." Bohannon's under-hand flip threw the amulet across the room to Levin. "Those are the guys you have to worry about."

꧁꧂

"My God, that's awful."

Brandon McDonough's brogue rumbled along the phone lines from Ireland. But Bohannon was only half listening. His mind and heart were already searching the streets of Jerusalem.

"The Israelis are very resourceful, Thomas. And ruthless when they want something badly enough. We must have faith."

Faith? Are you kidding?

"I don't know what faith is going to do, Brandon, but I know what I'm going to do," said Bohannon as he absently wrapped the phone cord around his hand. "As soon as Joe shows up, the two of us are going to start our own search. I'm not going to sit around here rubbing my hands together, I'll tell you that."

"Mr. Rodriguez is not with you?"

"No . . . and I don't know where he is." Bohannon's mind suddenly shifted gears. "He came back to Jerusalem before I did, to check out Jeremiah's Grotto. We were supposed to come here, stay put until the others showed up. Wait for your call and a call from Doc. See if we could put together enough pieces to know where to look for the Tent. I don't know where he is."

There was a long pause on the other end of the line.

"What is it, Brandon?"

"Well . . . two things." McDonough's voice became low, conspiratorial. "Thomas, first . . . I found it. Jeremiah's Tomb—it's really there. And I found something else. I think I know why the Guard is still pursuing you. It's not because they want something back; it's not about the scroll and mezuzah. It's because of something else—something they won't allow you to find, can't allow you to find."

"That's great, Brandon," Bohannon broke in. "Exciting. But we can talk about your discoveries later." He started looking around the room for his back-pack. "I've got to get moving."

"Wait, please wait, Thomas. There's the other thing . . . it's important."

Bohannon stopped and turned his attention to McDonough's voice. "What?"

"Well, if I must confess, I scared the bejesus out of meself at Cairn T," said McDonough. "I was in the tomb—Jeremiah's crypt after all—when I heard the gate slam shut, footsteps coming down the passage. I would surely have expired at that very moment if Mrs. Pekenham hadn't called out my name. Seems I had lost track of the day and it was well past closing time at the Gardens' coffee shop. And she charged me a ten euro fine to get my driver's license back."

Tom ran his hand through his hair. "Look, that is all very interesting—"

"That it 'tis, but you misunderstand me," said McDonough. "I was ashamed of meself, thought I was spooked, fearful of the fairies. Are you with me there, love? I felt like a fool. So, when Dr. Johnson didn't call, I gave it no mind."

Oh, God! "What . . . what are you saying?"

"Richard intended to communicate with me this morning," said McDonough. "He was to call on his satellite phone from the monastery and we would compare notes if we had discovered anything."

Bohannon felt a stab as his fear multiplied. This was no coincidence. There were no coincidences where the Prophet's Guard was involved. He was attacked at Krak de Chevaliers . . . Annie and Kallie probably abducted . . . Joe missing . . . Doc and Sammy out of touch.

"I was nearly killed when I went to the Krak de Chevaliers," said Bohannon. His voice came out flat. "They were waiting for me . . . one of them, anyway . . . tried to throw me off the top of the castle's wall. It was only grace that sav— Brandon, where are you?"

"I'm at the university. I have a class to teach at half-three."

"Stay there. Stay near other people, security officers if you have them." Bohannon's voice accelerated. "The Prophet's Guard is way ahead of us. They were here—I know they've abducted Kallie and Annie. They tried to kill me in Syria. And I'm scared, Brandon . . . I'm scared for Joe, for the rest of you. Listen, keep trying to reach Doc and Sammy. Let me know if you hear from them . . . leave a message here."

Bohannon took a breath and was surprised by a searing pain in his left hand. He looked down and saw the telephone cord, wrapped like a tourniquet around his blue-tinged fingers.

"Thomas, lad . . . what are you going to do?"

Fear and fury wrestled for control of Bohannon's soul. Suddenly his thoughts cleared. And he began to plan revenge.

"I'm going to get a weapon. Somewhere, somehow, I'm going to get some kind of weapon . . ."

"Lad . . . lad . . . you pick up a gun, sooner or later someone gets a bullet. So is that it, then?"

"Brandon, I don't have time to debate moral dilemmas," said Bohannon. "I've got to find Joe. But then I'm going to find these animals and I'm going to wipe them from the face of the earth."

Normally, Tom Bohannon would have begun praying for God's help. But not today. If God was in Jerusalem, he was a long way off.

Tel Aviv, Israel

Prime Minister Eliazar Baruk sat in the basement of his Tel Aviv residence. It was Shabbat and the prime minister was home. Not to rest. Not to worship. But to conspire.

Only his wife knew about the true purpose of the bunker-like room hidden behind the metal shelves filled with canned goods. The room was small, packed primarily with the latest in secure, satellite communication gear—transmissions encrypted and hidden, embedded, within the daily communication traffic between America's Federal Aviation Administration and Israel's Civil Aviation Authority. Baruk sat in a padded black office chair, mindlessly swinging back and forth on the chair's swivel, as he communicated with Jonathan Whitestone.

"How good is your security, Eliazar?"

Baruk bristled at the question.

"Tighter than yours, most likely. On this end, you are talking to one of only three people who have full knowledge of what we plan and what we intend to accomplish. None of the troops on the ground are active military. They are part of an elite paramilitary force that doesn't exist. It has no records, no office, no business. To ensure the safety of their homes and families, some for the joy of personal revenge, they will go anywhere and do anything and never be heard from. The four team leaders know only the details of their part of the mission."

"Can four teams inflict that much damage in such a short time," asked Whitestone, "to their oil wells, their storage, their pipeline?"

"The destruction will be devastating," Baruk affirmed. "The teams will use magnesium-charged, replicating explosives. The charges are set for different times, a sequential series of explosions. The magnesium ignites white-hot, is dispersed through the flaming oil, and each explosion is an extension of . . . builds on . . . the one that went before. Their beloved oil industry will burn with the heat of a thousand suns."

"Your military is very good at black ops; you've proven that in the past. Are you as confident about your plan for Fordow and the Iranian treasury?"

"You and I both know there's no way we can get to the enrichment labs at Fordow, or to the vault in the treasury, from the outside," said Baruk. "This plan is our only real option. It's taken years to prepare, but now we have the assets to strike Fordow and their gold reserve from the inside. There's a risk, but it's a risk we must take. You know that, Jonathan."

"And you're certain the radiation will be contained within the treasury vault? This action will enrage most of the world's leaders enough without civilians becoming contaminated with radiation sickness."

Baruk shook his head. Whitestone was a good man. He could trust him. But, on some things, he wasn't very knowledgeable.

"Jon, you think of a nuclear device and you see mushroom clouds and massive fallout," said Baruk. "There will be no explosion—at least not a detonation anyone outside the vault would register. This device is small, compact . . . think of an insect fogger. You set it, leave the house, and the fog permeates everything and kills all the bugs. This is pretty much the same idea. Within minutes, the entire gold reserve of Iran will be radioactive, useless, worthless. And it will stay that way for a thousand years."

And both of these things will make me rich beyond counting.

26

SATURDAY, AUGUST 22

Balata Camp, Nablus, West Bank

"The two women are secure, Holy One. They will be taken to the tower at the proper time. Their leader is at the apartment, but Shin Bet just left and there may be surveillance."

"And the tall one?"

"We don't know. We lost him when he came back to Jerusalem. He was in the Old City and then he vanished."

Moussa al-Sadr sat behind the rough-hewn table, his prayer beads spread before him. Three nonstop days had taken their toll. The old wounds in his body throbbed. But it was his heart that troubled him. How long would this weakened vessel beat?

"He must be found." Al-Sadr's voice barely stirred the dust in the sunbeam spilling through the open window. "We can't afford to lose two of them."

"Two?"

"The old one is dead, but the little one escaped from under our hands in Egypt. Our enemies, we believe. Vanished into the night. The old man was in a rage. They did not possess any knowledge of the secret—it has eluded them. And the treasure we seek continues to evade us."

Youssef, commander of the Al-Aqsa Martyrs' Brigade, stepped from the shadows, the shard of sun dancing on his muscled bicep. "But, we have the women."

Al-Sadr picked up his prayer beads, rubbing them lovingly between thumb and forefinger. "Yes . . . and it is their time to be of some use. Send the message.

And get the cameras ready. We will achieve both of our goals—force the Jew to relinquish the holy Haram and finally recover the vessel of our hope—or we will insult the Great Satan once more and grind its pride in the dust . . . with the blood of these infidel whores. Go."

Jerusalem

The tennis courts flanking University Boulevard were empty at midday, the soaking heat and relentless sun driving everyone indoors except mad dogs and Englishmen, and Tom Bohannon. On foot, Bohannon passed the courts, crossed Aharon Katsir Road and entered the grounds of Jerusalem's Regency Hotel.

A line of taxicabs was staged to the north of the hotel. Whether he had learned it from Sherlock Holmes or James Bond, Bohannon couldn't remember, but he went to the third taxi in line and got in. If you were being followed, the third taxi would never be manned by surveillance. Bohannon gave the driver an address, asked him to turn up the AC, and, despite the flurry of honking from taxi one and taxi two, started his rescue mission.

The driver maneuvered onto Katsir, through the roundabout, past St. Joseph's Hospital, and turned left on Route 60, Bar-Lev Road, heading south, farther into Jerusalem. Bohannon knew it would take some time to reach his final destination, but neither the sweltering summer heat nor the feverish imaginings of his mind would allow him to rest. Fifteen minutes later the taxi turned onto Yafo Road, heading northwest, and turned left, pulling up in front of the Jerusalem Regional Police Headquarters. Bohannon asked the driver to wait. His plan had only begun.

A pale blue sedan pulled into the parking area, drove past the police building, and parked at the very end of the lot.

Inside the police station, the duty sergeant recorded Bohannon's version of the break-in but refused to disturb any of the detectives. "This is a Shin Bet matter," the sergeant said one more time. "Any cooperation between Shin Bet and the police will take place at a much higher level than mine or the detectives. You have done what you can do, Mr. Bohannon. Go home . . . back to this apartment, if that's where you're staying. Don't worry. We'll find your wife and her friend. Don't worry about that. I'm sure you will be hearing something from Major Levin before we do."

As Bohannon left the police headquarters, he looked to his right. The pale blue sedan was still parked in the far corner. He could walk to Jeremiah's Grotto from here, but it was too early. He got in the taxi, only once looking over his shoulder.

"Back to the Regency Hotel."

⌁⌁⌁

As instructed, the taxi pulled up to the Regency via the wide, circular drive and stopped in front of the main entrance. Bohannon paid the driver and got out on the hotel side. Reflected in the hotel's plate-glass façade Tom could see the pale blue sedan coming to a halt on the far side of the circle. With manufactured calm, he walked straight into the lobby.

Inside, he continued purposefully through the lobby and down the wide hallway in front of the Grand Ballroom. He turned right into a corridor of overpriced retail shops and restaurants, never breaking stride until he pushed through a set of glass doors, back out into the heat and sunshine. The cab was there, waiting.

"Thanks."

"Man," said the driver—young, dark-haired, olive-skinned, whether Jew or Arab who could tell—"for fifty dollars I'll meet you anywhere. What next?"

"Crowne Plaza Hotel. And if you can get me there quickly, there's an extra fifty in it for you."

"You got it," said the driver. "Quick is my middle name."

The taxi pulled away from the rear of the hotel.

"This must be one hot date you have lined up, going through all this trouble," said the driver. "I hope the lady is worth it."

"Yeah," said Bohannon, sobering, turning from the chase to the task, "she's very worth it."

No car followed them as they retraced their steps through Jerusalem.

⌁⌁⌁

Following a halfhearted meal in one of the Crowne Plaza's restaurants—where only Annie's picture and his fear kept him company—and a time-wasting stroll through the Israel Museum, another taxi delivered Bohannon to the front of the Garden Tomb, just north of the Old City's Damascus Gate. He waited for the taxi to pull away and then walked south, away from the Garden's entrance. A narrow walkway appeared on the left, ensconced by white walls, green vines running across their tops, eight feet off the ground. Bohannon ducked into the walkway and was soon out of sight of the street.

Bohannon stood just inside the end of the walkway and looked across an alley running north from the Suleiman Road. Checking his watch, he waited the five minutes. At 5:30, a tall man wearing a blue and white striped robe, came out of the darkened doorway on the opposite side of the alley, withdrew a sliding, plastic panel from a sign to the right of the door and changed "Open" to "Closed" as he slid the panel back in place.

The man was visibly startled when Bohannon moved quietly to his side.

"Forgive me," Bohannon said. "But I must speak with you."

"But, we're closed," said the man, sweeping his hand in the direction of the sign.

"I know. I've been waiting for you to close."

The man took a small step backward.

"I'm looking for my friend," said Bohannon. "I know he came here. That was probably Thursday morning. I haven't seen him since and I'm getting worried. This is the last place I know . . . the last place he went."

The man smiled broadly. "Are you Washington Heights, too?"

It took a moment for the question to register.

"No . . . the Bronx."

"Well, come, come Mr. Bronx," said the man, gesturing Bohannon through the door to Jeremiah's Grotto, "we have much to discuss."

Bohannon put his hand on the man's shoulder. "I'm sorry. I don't mean to be rude. But I don't have time for a discussion. I need to find my friend. It's very important . . . serious."

The man ran his eyes over Bohannon's face like a mapmaker memorizing a coastline, then placed his hand on top of Bohannon's. "You are their leader."

Tom shook his head. "No . . ."

"I have set Joe on the trail to Abiathar's secret," said the man, wrapping his fingers around Bohannon's hand. "Now, I am not so sure I did the right thing. But, for you, I have something else. Please, come in. Your timing is excellent. I . . . my friend and I . . . won't take much of your time. Please."

Bohannon's feet were itching to move, to find Joe, to do something to help find Annie. But the man's words unexpectedly touched his heart. "I'll give you ten minutes. But I want to know where you sent Joe."

"I will only take five." He took Bohannon's hand off his shoulder, and shook it gently. "I am Ronald Fineman, formerly of Queens, New York City, and retired owner of Leather World on Orchard Street. You have heard of it?"

When Bohannon said no, Fineman shrugged and walked through the door. Bohannon quickly followed. Though his mind was telling him he should be more cautious, after the events of the past two days, he felt a strange peace about Ronald Fineman of Queens.

"I want to tell you something God has been pressing on my heart ever since your friend walked out this door," Fineman said.

"Listen . . . Mr. Fineman, I—"

"*Rabbi* Fineman. I've had a change of occupation. That's what brought me to Jerusalem."

"I see. . . . So a Jewish rabbi leading tours of Jeremiah's Grotto on the Sabbath. How does that work?"

"Well, I'm not a typical rabbi," said Fineman, leading Bohannon through the interior of the grotto. "I lead what is called a Messianic Jewish synagogue—Jews who believe that Jesus was, in fact, the Messiah. That Jesus fulfilled all of the prophecy of the Talmud and came to save mankind from its sins. So that gives me a unique perspective on what is called the Old Testament. It also allows me to work here on a Saturday. I am no longer under the requirements of Jewish law. And my friend who is here is a Muslim . . . a good Muslim. He hasn't converted to Judaism or Christianity, and I doubt if he ever will."

Fineman turned into a small office and brought Bohannon closer to a small man in a white kaffiyeh and kaftan. "My Bronx friend, Tom Bohannon, this is my Muslim friend, Abu Gherazim, foreign minister of the Palestinian Authority. He and I met at a fund-raiser for the Palestinian Authority . . . I know, an odd place for a Jewish rabbi. But he and I both believe in reaching across the barriers to peace. Which brings us here, tonight, with you." Fineman gestured to three wooden chairs around the small table just to the left of the grotto's entrance.

"Mr. Bohannon, if you permit, I will get right to the point," said Fineman, sitting in the chair opposite Tom's. "I'm sure you wondered why the Temple you discovered was destroyed. It appeared as if your efforts were ordained, as if God himself were guiding your steps. Why then would God allow the Temple, now discovered, to be crushed, pulverized?"

Bohannon winced at the question he had asked himself so many times, without any answer.

"Forgive me, you have lost much," said Fineman, rubbing the top of the rough wooden table. "But there is a reason I ask the question. My friend and I have a theory. Today, many Jews are praying for a place to make sacrifice. And the Arabs are trying to hold onto a place they consider sacred. And they both want the same place . . . the root of all Middle East violence."

Gherazim opened his hands, palm up, on the tabletop. "What if," he said, "Jesus of Nazareth was the Messiah?" His voice was as unimposing as his appearance. "There is one thing at the core of Christianity that is a trip stone for both Judaism and Islam: Did Christ die and rise from the dead? More than two thousand years have passed and no one has ever been able to disprove what Christianity claims, and history records, of those fateful few days. What if it were true?"

Bohannon was confused. And he was already feeling restless. Here was a leader of the Muslim community positing the divinity of Jesus? It didn't make sense.

"In light of the recent destruction of both the Temple and the Dome of the Rock by a very localized earthquake, there is a question that should be asked— a question that makes perfect sense," offered Gherazim, apparently reading the question on Bohannon's face. "Perhaps God does not want a Temple today."

The white-robed Arab gestured to the thin rabbi.

"Christian theology holds that each man who accepts Jesus as his Lord and Savior becomes a temple of God's Spirit," said Fineman. "When Christ died, it was reported that the veil in the Temple . . . the curtain that hid the Most Holy Place, God's earthly dwelling place . . . was torn from the bottom to the top, opening a way into God's presence.

"The Jews are intent on building God a dwelling place when he doesn't need one anymore. God doesn't need a temple of stone to make his home. He already has a temple of life—skin, blood, and bone; mind, heart, and spirit. A living and breathing temple, millions of them. Each of those people is a place of worship and a place of sacrifice. They are God's sacred place."

Bohannon shook his head. "But what has all that to do with us?"

"Because you search for that which Jeremiah hid . . . the Tent of Meeting," said Fineman. "I can only surmise that the Israeli government wants the Tent, perhaps our government also. Perhaps others. But the real question is, what does God want?

"I believe that God will never be limited to just one place ever again. Through those who accept the name and sacrifice of Christ, God is now doing the work of salvation and sacrifice through them, through his human temples. But men keep trying to build something God no longer wants or needs. Some men want God to be in his place. And to keep him there, safely locked up, back in the past. I believe . . . and my Muslim friend has come to accept the possibility . . . that God will keep destroying the inanimate temples of men because now they are false. He no longer lives there nor will he ever allow his Spirit to be confined there.

"God has set a new course—a deeper, more personal intimacy with those who themselves are temples that will never be destroyed. That is where God's peace now reigns."

"There is only one problem." Gherazim's muted words drifted into the shadows. "The ruler of this world doesn't want peace. The evil one wants to destroy all peace. So he sets us against ourselves, fighting about a place for temples that are no longer needed. God doesn't want to be worshiped in a place, or as a prophet, but by a people.

"Many Muslims are mistaken because, by worshiping a prophet, they think that they are exempt from personal responsibility for their actions. Religious Jews believe they remain the Chosen People—they have a special, exclusive right to God—and thus they are exempt from personal responsibility. And some Christians hide behind 'election' to consider themselves exempt from personal responsibility.

"That is not faith. All of us, all men, have a personal responsibility to God. Not to a place; not to a prophet; not to a theology. Not to any false temple."

Fineman leaned in, closer to Bohannon.

"We believe the time has come when God is willing to accept only one temple, the temple he has created of man, not the temple man creates for him. And he will destroy every temple man erects to wall him in. The destruction has begun. Time grows shorter each day."

Bohannon now knew what was coming.

"Don't help them, Mr. Bohannon," said Fineman, his words heavy with regret. "I never should have helped Joe. I didn't think . . . I didn't ask. And I was disobedient." Fineman slowly shook his head back and forth.

"You've seen what happened, Tom. This race to find the Tent of Meeting will only end in more destruction, more deaths. This search is doomed, my friend. Please," Fineman reached out and touched his arm. "Don't put your hand to it."

Tom felt like Solomon, faced with the two women who claimed the same baby. Where was the right choice? What was the right thing to do?

"You don't understand." Bohannon slapped the top of the table and pushed off his chair. "I don't want to find it. I don't want anyone to find it, not anymore. Me . . . I want to destroy it."

Fineman looked as if someone had stolen his most cherished beliefs. "What?"

"Look, my wife has been abducted by some Muslim murderers who have been determined to stop us from the beginning. No tent, I don't care how old it is or how important it might be, has any value to me if my wife is harmed. And—" he pointed a warning finger in Fineman's direction—"if the Israelis find the Tent they will erect it on top of the Temple Mount. And that will light the fuse for a Middle East conflagration. You just don't understand . . . Someone's got to try to stop this madness. And who else is there?"

27

Sunday, August 23

The Negev, Israel

Every muscle called out in protest. And his knees signaled a miserable, aching day ahead.

Joe Rodriguez peeled himself from the cracked leather back seat of the Land Rover. The thermal blanket he had gathered up from the garage in Jerusalem kept him warm. But it did nothing to relieve the consequences of the contortions he'd gotten into during the interminable night of fitful sleep. Stretching, his neck creaked.

Outside the Land Rover, light was beginning to play along the tops of the earth-brown, sandstone buttes, carved into undulating curves, sanded smooth by the incessant sirocco winds off the desert. But down in the narrow defile, tucked under an outcropping of stone, darkness still surrounded Rodriguez and his battered ride. Fortunate to have found this hiding place in the fast fading light of a desert evening, Joe was relieved to be off the road and out of sight. It gave him a semblance of security. But not enough to bless him with real sleep. Which may have eluded him anyway.

What to do now?

He was here, in the upper reaches of the Ascent of Akkrabim, the snakelike slither of Scorpion Pass falling away into the Dead Sea valley far below. He had come this far. What was next? Rodriguez pulled out one of the two things he prayed would give him hope.

Joe pushed open the rear door of the Land Rover, activating the dome light. On his lap he spread out the document that Fineman created before Joe left

Jeremiah's Grotto. Fineman kept up a running explanation as he scribbled, calculated, and measured over the face of a long, unrolled length of poster paper.

⸺◠◠◠◠◠⸺

"You could spend the rest of your life searching the hundreds of caves that per-
forate Scorpion Pass," Fineman instructed Joe. "And you could lose your life in
any one of them. The sandstone of the Akkrabim escarpment has been pounded
by violent torrents of exploding thunderstorms and eroded by centuries of desert
wind. The erosion has occurred outside, on the cliff faces, but also inside, in the
labyrinthine corridors that weave through the depths of the canyon walls. Not
only is it easy to get lost—fatally lost—" Fineman shot a look over his shoulder,
"but it's also easy to get drowned."

"Fatally drowned?"

"Yes, mister wise guy Washington Heights, fatally drowned."

Fineman went back to his work. Joe could see it was another rough map of
the land south of Jerusalem—Dead Sea to the east, the Mediterranean to the
west.

"Imagine being deep in the sloping switchbacks of these caves when a sudden
storm erupts above the pass, unleashing a torrential flood that those cliffs can't
possibly absorb. What happens then? Where does all that water go?"

"The Bronx?"

Fineman reached for a long, straight, flat piece of wood he had pulled out
of his office. He placed it on the poster paper and drew a long, straight line on
the left side of the paper, a ragged curve of coastline farther to the left. Then he
measured three marks, and drew another long line to the east. Fineman stood
up and looked down at his handiwork. "Wise guy," he muttered. "I should just
let you go out there in the desert and wander around until your fingernails grow
as long as your arm."

"Okay . . . okay, I need your help," said Joe, noting the twinkle in the old
man's eyes. "Are you going to tell me what your finger painting is all about?"

With a sweep of his hand, Fineman stepped back from the table. "It's about
where you should look. What else would it be? Here, look . . . I can get you this
close."

Joe looked down at the paper on his lap and tried not to forget any of the
rabbi's instructions. He pulled a compass from his jacket pocket, opened it, and

placed it on the paper, resting on his knee. Then he traced the lines Fineman had drawn across the face of the paper.

"You must remember the time in which Abiathar lived," Fineman told him back in the grotto. Then he moved his hand along the left side of his page. "The Crusaders controlled the coastline, the major cities along the coast, and all the coastal flatlands that ran up into the hills of Palestine. To get to Scorpion Pass, Abiathar would not normally have traveled in that direction. But it's good that we can now rule it out entirely. If, in fact, he was moving the Ark of the Covenant, and the Tent of Meeting, he would have avoided the Crusaders like the plague. So, he didn't go by the coast—or anywhere near the coast."

Fineman then pointed at three dots on the right side of the design, through which another of the straight lines was drawn.

"But, he could not have moved through the desert, either. See these dots? There was a line of Muslim fortresses in the desert guarding the trade route between Egypt and Damascus. While the powerless Fatimids controlled Jerusalem and presented little real opposition to the Crusader invasion, a massive Arab army was raised in the east, hundreds of thousands of soldiers under the command of the great general, Sal-ad-Din. Despite its size, the Arab army was not strong enough to challenge the armored knights and powerful war horses of the Crusaders. But they were powerful enough to garrison a string of fortresses, protect the vital land routes, and provide a formidable deterrent to any further European expansion. Sal-ad-Din, who was a brilliant tactician, decided to wait, watch, and outlast these infidel invaders."

Joe put a hand on Fineman's shoulder, drawing the old man's attention from what was now clearly a map on the table. "You seem to know an awful lot about this."

"Rabbi school," said Fineman, whose face took on an offended scowl. "And I was a history geek in school. You think you have a corner on the curiosity market?"

Without waiting for a reply, Fineman turned back to the map.

"So, Abiathar could not go along the coast and he could not venture into the desert and try to go by the caravan routes." Fineman traced the path of the two long lines as they traveled south. "From Jerusalem," Fineman said, "these are the boundaries of Abiathar's safe travel. On the east"—he pointed at an elongated oval—"the Dead Sea. Can't go that way, either." Then his finger traced an imaginary line, from north to south, to the east of the Dead Sea. "And this is the great Dead Sea defile, over one hundred miles of cliffs and canyons . . . roadless waste. Abiathar was not going to transport heavily laden wagonloads over this kind of terrain."

Fineman pointed to a thick, curving line and waited for Rodriguez.

"So Abiathar had to come into Scorpion Pass from the west, from the heights," Rodriguez offered. "That's the only route left open to him. And that helps how? No, wait . . . I know . . . if he's pushing and pulling six wagons loaded down with the Tent, if he's carrying the Ark, he does not want to go down Scorpion Pass. He's going to be looking for a place to hide not long after he gets into the pass."

"Exactly," said the rabbi, his chin whiskers bobbing up and down in agreement. "Which brings us to the second thing that will help you in your search."

Fineman picked up a piece of carbon from the table and, placing it on its edge, traced a wide, light gray path along the line of Scorpion Pass. The pastel path of the carbon started down along the original line from the north, then soon diverted away from the line of the pass and wove a separate course to the desert floor below. Then he turned to Rodriguez.

"Israel's history is filled with many things, my friend. One of them is earthquakes."

Joe flinched at the memory.

"Yes . . . you know about the earthquakes here." Fineman turned back to the map and his pastel path. "Along here is the Dead Sea Fault, about a seven hundred mile long fault line that is the deepest known break in the earth's crust. It is part of the Great Rift Valley that runs for three thousand miles between Syria and Mozambique. Up here, from Haifa to the Jordan River, runs another active fault. In this area, earthquakes are very common. The big ones hit about every four hundred years."

"Like ours?"

"Your earthquake?" Fineman's voice held the incredulous tone of one startled by effrontery. "Your earthquake was a burp. In 1546, Jerusalem was hit with the third strongest earthquake in its history, a quake that destroyed the Dome of the Rock and pulverized the soaring dome on the Church of the Holy Sepulcher. A quake that mangled the earth up and down the Dead Sea Fault."

This time Joe didn't know where this conversation was leading.

Fineman tapped the swath of carbon on his map. "That earthquake was so strong it moved the cleft that is the Ascent of Akkrabim."

Joe looked at the map in his lap. Fineman's history lesson had made his quest fairly simple. More than two thirds of the Ascent of Akkrabim that wound its way below him would have been inaccessible to Abiathar one thousand years ago. It didn't exist.

If Joe had any hope of locating the hiding place of the Tent of Meeting, it was in this relatively short stretch from its Roman crest to a spot Fineman calculated, a few hundred yards below his current location. His search was narrowed considerably.

Then there was the toy Sam Reynolds provided.

Ma'ale Adumim, West Bank

Nearly half an hour remained before the imams would sing the invitation to prayer from the hundreds of minarets sprouting from the sun-bleached buildings of the West Bank. Black shadows were deep on the silent streets. Three of them moved with the stealth of those whose purpose is lethal.

The shadows were long-limbed and dressed in tight-fitting, black assault uniforms and hoods. Only their eyes were uncovered. They moved with swift, silent precision, executing an alternating dance across each open space, disappearing into the next refuge of black shadow.

At the corner of an empty market square they paused for a moment, then ducked inside an open archway and stopped in the shadow beside an open courtyard. The shortest of the three pointed to a building on the right flank of the courtyard and the three moved with haste to a closed door. The short one forced the lock and they vanished into the building.

〜〜〜〜

Sayeed al-Sadr—the man most of the world knew as Abu Gherazim, foreign minister of the Palestinian Authority—sat beside a small, round table, his neglected coffee long grown cold, and pondered his future. However short.

The Jordanian king risked his own safety by inviting Abu Gherazim to speak in Amman. The speech was well received by some, but an hour later an avalanche of abuse and incessant threats poured forth from the Muslim community with the force of a savage thunderstorm.

It was a risk, calling for a reformation of Islam, a repudiation of the doctrine of jihad and martyrdom. But it was time. Someone needed to take the risk, to speak the truth first. Abu Gherazim did not regret his words. He only wondered how many chances he would have to repeat them, how long he would retain his position as foreign minister. Dissent was not encouraged within the Muslim community. Heresy was a capital offense.

He glanced across the rooftops of what he hoped, someday, would be part of a true Palestinian homeland. As the sky turned from black to gray, he wondered if there would be enough time.

⸻

The three shadows raced effortlessly up the stairwell at the corner of the building, paused for a heartbeat to ensure the hallway was unoccupied, and moved on padded feet to a closed door just off the stairwell.

⸻

I should sleep . . . perhaps a few moments of rest before prayer.

Abu Gherazim rose from his chair, glanced at the cold coffee, and carried the burden of his thoughts to the sleeping pallet in the corner. He felt a movement in the air behind him. He lifted his head as if listening to the air. The dagger pierced his carotid before pain could awaken, then sliced open his throat.

I thought, hoped, I would have a little more time.

The man who was once Sayeed al-Sadr felt the life flowing out of his neck and thought of his uncle, laying in the dusty street of Kaisiman so many years ago, his blood soaking the sand. He remembered his brother, Moussa, architect of hatred and father of Hezbollah—so long gone from his life. Memory faded as each pulse pumped life from his body.

I'm coming, Uncle. Allah have mercy on us.

Jerusalem

"I was wondering when you would get to me," Major Avram Levin said bluntly, "so I wasn't surprised by your summons."

"Why is that?" asked Colonel David Posner.

It was mid-morning and the two men sat in a nondescript office in a forgettable concrete block building on the Kiryat HaYovel, overlooking the southeastern sprawl of Jerusalem. The sign on the exterior of the building identified it as the headquarters of the Council on Israeli Agriculture. Within its windowless walls, Mossad ran one of the most sophisticated and effective intelligence-gathering organizations in the world.

On the left was the obligatory wall mirror, a fixture of interrogation rooms, behind which—no surprise—was the listening and observation post that no doubt held other Mossad agents and the equipment to record this conversation, as well as to read all of Levin's vital signs transferred from the specially built chair containing dozens of biometric sensors. Levin was a pro. He knew there was no hiding in this room.

"Because of my mother . . . because she was a Palestinian . . . because she died in a terrorist bus explosion." Levin had rehearsed those words many times before, to others who had questioned his background, his loyalty. But never in such a precarious situation.

"Yes, we know about your mother," said Posner. "It's in your file. You were very forthcoming in dealing with a sensitive issue like that. But my question today is not about your mother."

Levin measured Posner. Their paths had crossed a few times, momentarily. All Levin could recall was reputation and hearsay, all of which said Posner, despite his movie-star looks, was ruthless in his pursuit of any who threatened Israel's peace and security. Which was fine for those who bore the same patriot's DNA and devotion to country. Levin knew that was what Posner intended to find out.

"Only a few of us knew the details of the incursion into Jordan," said Levin. "A highly skilled unit was waiting for Lukas Painter and his men. Someone, in a very small circle, is a traitor and sent those men to their execution." Levin looked directly into Posner's eyes with a challenge. "And you are investigating whether that traitor is me."

More than silence, what hung in the air above the table, between the two men, was an unseen but easily felt contest—a collision of wills, watching and looking for advantage, probing for weakness, searching for truth. Posner moved a file folder in front of him, his eyes never leaving Levin's.

"We believe those who killed Painter and his team were Syrian-trained, an elite Hezbollah unit that operates out of Dar'a, on the Jordanian border. You know Dar'a, don't you?"

Levin's throat constricted. He had not expected this.

"Your wife was born and raised in Dar'a, was she not? Before becoming an Israeli citizen? And that . . ."

Posner pointed to a photograph in the file, a young man with a full, black mustache, dark eyes, smiling. He was wearing military camouflage. On his head was a red beret, cocked to the side with the insouciance of youth, a green scimitar moon crossed with a dagger stitched to the left side. In his hands, an AK-47, Hezbollah's preferred assault weapon. Levin's mind was spinning furiously.

". . . that soldier is her brother? Yes?"

Levin lifted his gaze from the picture to face the accusation in Posner's words and attitude. Levin waited for what he feared was coming.

"This is Captain Hamid. We have good reason to believe he was the leader of the unit that ambushed Painter's patrol."

Levin groaned inside. He waited for more.

"Dar'a is thirty kilometers from Mount Nebo. A thirty-minute drive for a military vehicle. I'm told that your Mossad counterpart informed you of the incursion ninety minutes before Painter and his men gathered at the base of the mountain."

Perspiration was dripping from Levin's underarms. The palms of his hands were wet.

"So . . . Captain . . . please tell me where you were for those ninety minutes. And, also"—Posner took a piece of paper from the breast pocket of his uniform, unfolded it, and pushed it toward Levin—"please explain the telephone call you made to Dar'a about twenty minutes later."

The Negev, Israel

Rodriguez spent the morning moving quickly along cliffs and through ravines, checking caves for any sign or evidence. But hope for a quick discovery dimmed as the sun, and the temperature, rose higher. Returning to the Land Rover, Joe put the map aside and hefted the large, metal box that rested on the seat beside him. It wasn't that heavy, but Joe knew he would need the shoulder straps and harness to carry it. With this thing strapped to his chest, climbing up and down the pass in the heat of the desert, scrambling over sandstone ridges and exploring caves, would beat up his aching body even more.

But it was too valuable, too essential, to leave behind.

The box was about twenty-inches in height and width and a foot thick. On its top surface was an LCD screen, elevated toward the carrier and hooded to protect the screen from glare. On the right and left flanks, near the front, were two large black knobs, almost half the depth of the box, with serrated edges on the circumference of the knobs. Developed by NASA, the device was a high-powered version of ground-penetrating radar. Whereas normal GPR used radar pulses in the microwave band of radio frequencies to locate things underground, NASA added new technology that allowed this machine to also discern subtle changes in carbon emissions. It was designed to be used by astronauts on the moon. Sam Reynolds got the obligatory red tape cut away to free the device from the clutches of NASA. Then he shipped it to a FedEx office in Jerusalem, where it was waiting when Joe arrived.

Some techie had convinced Sam Reynolds that this little device could differentiate between the carbon footprints of two mismatched items—such as the difference between a two-thousand-year-old assortment of animal hides and acacia wood poles and nearly anything else that might be near it. Before leaving the States, the box had been calibrated to respond to carbon footprints that were two thousand to twenty-five hundred years old.

Joe wasn't convinced. But he was told to point the box at the opening of a cave, twist and turn the knobs, and see if the sensor images from the radar antennae converged on each other and started to blink. If they did, he was back in the cave exploring business. Which was not too cool, considering the events of his last venture in spelunking.

Heat ricocheted off the canyon's western walls as he returned to his search. Wind from the desert below carried the scent of passing camels and blooming hawthorn. It was time to get moving. One hundred yards south of the current road were the ruins of a Roman fortress, which those invaders erected to protect the crest of the Ascent which had been in use for one thousand years before they conquered Judea. The current road had been cut by the Israeli Corps of Engineers in 1957. But Rodriguez would not be searching that road. It was the faint remnant of the track the Romans paved in the first century that would occupy the rest of his day. He gathered up his provisions and water, slung the backpack high on his shoulders, and secured the magic box to his chest. He felt weird. Probably looked weird. But he was on a mission. And, because of Rabbi Fineman, Joe felt a lot closer to discerning the truth.

Jerusalem

A scratching noise from the door woke Tom Bohannon from a fitful sleep. The clock on the wall read one-twenty. Night or day? The last thing he remembered was returning to Kallie's apartment. After leaving Jeremiah's Grotto, Tom knew he couldn't follow Joe. Joe was on his own. Tom would never leave Jerusalem . . . not until Annie was found. He wandered the streets of Jerusalem and the Old City until well after midnight, when nearly every business was shuttered, carrying Annie's picture with him, stopping at outdoor cafes or small, out-of-the-way hotels, anywhere someone may have seen something. He thought about getting a room in the city, but he had told McDonough to call the apartment with any news.

Shin Bet probably put the apartment under surveillance. He was walking straight back into their hands. But he needed a break. He needed to think.

When he got back to the apartment he sat his weary body on the sofa, trying to determine his next step. That was the last thing he remembered until now, stretched out on the sofa, his back aching, his mouth dry, and his sleep-deprived mind swimming.

Before he could respond, or even move from where he lay on the sofa, the front door swung open and there stood Sammy Rizzo, keys in hand, balancing on top of an overturned trash can. And he looked as beaten down as Bohannon felt.

"Why do they always put these locks so high?" Rizzo steadied himself with a hand on the doorjamb, hopped off the trash can, and walked across the room toward Bohannon. His eyes, magnified under the thick lenses of his glasses, were red-rimmed and bloodshot; he needed a shave; and his clothes—a light, white shirt and baggy blue pants, with a red sash and thigh-high leather boots—were unusual, even for Rizzo. Sammy reached the sofa and leaned heavily on one arm as if he had no other source of support. His eyes were on the floor.

"Doc's dead."

Oooohhhh, God! The weight on Bohannon's chest got heavier.

"Annie and Kallie are gone."

Rizzo's face twisted in agony.

"I think they've got them."

Twenty minutes later, Bohannon and Rizzo still sat side by side, each in their own cocoon of silence. Memories haunted the room like broken promises.

Bohannon broached the silence.

"What about Doc's body?" *What about Doc's soul?*

Rizzo leaned over at the waist and covered his head with his hands. "I don't know. Those guys from the Temple Guard were not going back. They threw me into the back of a Jeep and drove into the desert with no lights. I didn't care. Something told me they were helping me out but I didn't care. I kept thinking of Doc, what he must have—"

"We can't go there, Sam." Bohannon reached out with his right arm and wrapped it around Rizzo's shoulders, pulling the little man closer. "We can't afford it. We can't afford to get paralyzed by our emotions. There are too many of them, too many to deal with. We go down that road, our emotions will suck every drop of life out of our bodies. We've got to focus on what we can do . . . whatever we need to do to find Annie and Kallie. I know they're still alive. And they're counting on us. The dead will wait for us to grieve."

Rizzo ran his thick fingers through his thicker hair, rubbed the back of his neck, and looked up at Bohannon.

"We can't leave him there."

"No . . . we can't. It's not too early . . . I'll call Sam Reynolds, tell him what happened. He'll help. The State Department will get somebody down to that monastery to get Doc's body back. Don't worry"—he gave Rizzo a hug—"we'll take care of Doc."

Bohannon went to his backpack and pulled out the wristwatch satellite phone that was to keep him in contact with Reynolds. He pushed the default key. After two beeps and it was picked up at the other end.

"Tom?"

"We've got trouble. Doc Johnson is dead. We need your help to get his body, and get it back to the States." Bohannon pulled in a deep breath. "But that's not the worst part . . ."

⸎

After completing his call with Reynolds, Bohannon went to the kitchen for a glass of water. When he returned, Rizzo was sitting on the edge of the sofa, staring at the floor. Tom pulled up a straight-backed chair and sat in front of Rizzo.

"I've got an incredible story to tell you," Sammy said, raising his head. "But first, what do you believe happened to Doc? I mean . . . well, where do you think he is?" Rizzo looked into Bohannon's face with a pleading cry in his eyes. "You know what I mean? Where is he?"

Now it was Bohannon's turn to rub his head, trying to dislodge the cobwebs and arrange all the discordant thoughts.

"I . . . I'm not . . . I believe God created us, created everything," he said. "He made us, and he wants us . . . wants to have a relationship with each of us. And I believe God doesn't give up on any of his creation. I'm hanging onto that belief for Annie and Kallie, But I believe it's possible for some of God's creation to give up on him. I want to believe that God didn't give up on Doc. What I don't know is whether Doc gave up on God. Doc was asking all the right questions . . . Is God real? Can man really know God? . . . I just don't know if he got any answers." Tom turned away from Sammy and fixed his gaze on the floor. "Or, if he did, what he did about them.

"I prayed for Doc. Prayed for him to make a wise choice. I don't know. Never will in this life. And that is what I'll grieve, Sam. I'll miss Doc . . . I—" Tom's voice was snared in the net of his loss. "But it doesn't do any good for me to pray for Doc now. Doc's life, his chance to choose, is gone.

"And, to be honest, it hasn't done a whole lot of good for me to pray for anything. My hope is running pretty dry. But I have to . . . I have to hope for Annie. For Kallie. We can't give up. We can't get buried in our grief or our fear. We can't. We've got to—"

There was a sharp knock on the door—unlatched, it swept open on its own—and four Israeli soldiers, Uzis at the ready, entered the room. A sergeant stepped to the front.

"You two are in military custody. You are to come with us. Now. If you don't, we'll put hand and leg irons on you and carry you out. You have made some people very angry. Let's go."

Tel Aviv, Israel

"So, Jon . . . have you decided how you will justify freezing all of Iran's assets in the United States? Your part is less dangerous, but much more public, than mine."

Baruk searched the televised image of Whitestone for any indication of weakness or wavering. President Whitestone appeared to relax comfortably in his seat. This night, Whitestone was the calm one.

"Mr. Prime Minister!" the president exclaimed with mock astonishment, "I am sure you will be as alarmed and appalled as I to discover that the Iranian government has been financially supporting domestic terrorists right here on our own soil." Whitestone edged toward the camera. He was good. "We had our concerns and fears before. But, now . . . the FBI and the National Security Administration just completed a massive investigation that uncovered forged bank records, dummy corporations, and direct payments from Iranian government accounts to known terrorist cells here in the United States. So . . . we have no other choice but to quarantine—I love that word, much more ominous than 'freeze'—quarantine all Iranian assets in the U.S. until we have a full and accurate picture of how pervasive this terror funding has been."

"And I'm sure you have the proof."

Whitestone's smile could have stripped the paint off a wall.

"Enough to keep Iran's assets locked up for a decade." The president pointed his finger at the camera. "They will never recover from this. Kiss your nuclear program goodbye, Essaghir. It's back to the desert for you."

"Seven days, then," said Baruk. He looked into the screen. "I will call you the night before . . . same time. Sleep well, Jonathan."

Jerusalem

When he walked into the High Altitude Reconnaissance Control Center just before the late afternoon shift change, Major Levin could actually taste the fear and frustration of the men in the high-tech security post. The acrid bite of high-anxiety sweat filled not only his nose, but also coated the edges of his tongue. It tasted like salt. His presence would not lessen the tension.

Their drone lost contact with Rodriguez in the growing twilight the night before, the most difficult time for high altitude cameras, which get distracted by shifting shadows and shapes of nightfall. The military controller was slow in switching to infrared. And Rodriguez disappeared.

Still smarting from his interrogation, Levin, the veteran surveillance officer—the legendary Hawk, who missed nothing and caught every prey—walked up to the duty officer, who was slaving over two screens—one visual and one radar. Levin put his hand on the lieutenant's shoulder.

"Hello, Daniel. How is your family?" Levin placed another hand on the officer's other shoulder and, like a close relative—a brother—massaged the knot of muscles at the base of the lieutenant's neck. "Your eldest, is he still in university?"

The lieutenant tried to turn, but Levin's strong hands held him in place. "We haven't seen the American for hours. I'm sorry, Major. We know he's down there somewhere, but we lost him. We've got patrols on the ground, driving up and down the pass, and we've got two in the sky. But I can't tell you where he is or what he's doing. I'm sorry."

Levin continued to work the stress out of the lieutenant's shoulders.

"I know, from personal experience, how elusive these men are. Sometimes I think they're under some divine guidance," said Levin. "I've lost them myself . . . more than once." The lieutenant stopped working the screens and looked over his shoulder at the Hawk. "Yes, it's true. But, don't worry, Daniel. You will find him. I'm confident you and your men will find him. He will emerge eventually. Our men are in place, prepared to move."

Levin patted the lieutenant firmly on the shoulder, then spoke to the other members of the reconnaissance team. "You will find him, men. He's not a ghost. He can't remain hidden forever. Just stay vigilant."

As Levin turned to leave, he patted the lieutenant on the shoulder once more. "Give your wife my regards. And tell her I think her matzoh soup is the best I've ever tasted."

The Hawk left the HARC Center. He couldn't see the faces of his men. But he could taste resolve and determination clearing the air.

Riyadh, Saudi Arabia

"This war is not against our brothers," said King Abbudin. "It never has been, except for those Shi'a heretics who have blackened the name of Allah all these years."

Even here in the palace, the desert night brought a chill. He waved his hand and one of his servants—deaf to keep conversations secret—came forward, picked up a small silver pot, and filled the two, tiny cups with the syrupy-sweet black coffee that looked so much like the oil that kept them all in power. The servant bowed over the cups, handed one to King Abbudin and the second to Baqir al-Musawi, president of Syria, who sat across from the king in a small, carved wooden chair.

"The West rejoices when we fight ourselves," said al-Musawi. "We blow ourselves up in the streets of Baghdad, or Homs, or Aleppo and the West sleeps in peace."

King Abbudin raised the cup to his lips, but stopped. "This is no time for fratricide. Not now. This is the time for jihad."

The king placed his cup on the ornately carved table that separated the chairs and leaned closer to the Syrian president.

"And this Shi'a dog expects to build his own empire on the ruins of Syria, on the other Islamic governments he's destroyed? This al-Sadr will be sent back to the dead where he's been hiding for the last thirty years."

"Al-Sadr has many allies," al-Musawi said over his coffee cup.

"The friend of my enemies is my enemy," said Abbudin. "Al-Sadr believes the Brotherhood is overthrowing these traitors so that he may usurp power for himself. He will soon regret his misguided arrogance. You, Baqir, will regain control of Hezbollah once you finally crush those rebellious puppets of al-Sadr; you will eliminate Nazrullah, and Hezbollah will answer to Syria once again. Our brother Qaddafi did not have your will—nor your array of weapons. You will survive and resume our punishment of Israel. The Brotherhood has solidified its power in the new Egyptian government and manipulated the election to control the new parliament.

"We are ready, Baqir. Not words of jihad, not threats, but power. World dominance—the Caliphate once again. Not by invasion and bloodshed." Abbudin toyed with the small cup sitting on the ceramic tile top of the table, then poured some of its syrupy contents onto the tiles, running his finger through the thick, black liquid. "Not by force, Baqir. By oil, through the greed and excess of the West. The world is already in our hands. Now we close our fist around it."

King Abbudin felt a rush through his eighty-four-year-old bones. It gave him the hope of life, of victory over the cancer that was rotting his body. He lifted his hand and pointed toward the far door. It was immediately pulled open and Crown Prince Faisal entered the room, his glorious robes flowing behind him, his royal presence outmatched only by the fervor of his stride. Abbudin knew he had little hope for his own life. His days were numbered.

But Faisal. Faisal was his hope . . . the hope of the family Saud. The future of his family, his dynasty, rested in this young man's passion and loyalty.

Abbudin had reason for his feud with Imam al-Sadr—more than the Sunni hatred for the apostate Shi'a. More even than his desire to avenge himself for all of al-Sadr's insults, particularly for the scorn and derision al-Sadr felt so comfortable spewing in front of the Brotherhood. Yes . . . this was personal. But there was an even more powerful spring to Abbudin's hatred.

The kingdom of the family Saud was one of the poorest on the face of the earth. Unemployment ranged between twelve and twenty-five percent, depending on whose figures you believed, and of the six million people employed in the country of thirty million, nearly five million were foreigners. Fewer than one percent of Saudi men had a job of any kind. School was for the rich, and the rich were only members of the royal family and those critical to maintaining their power and control. Abbudin knew, without a doubt, that if al-Sadr's plans bore fruit, that harvest of rebellion would mean the destruction of his family, the overthrow of his government, and the loss of the two hundred sixty billion barrels of liquid gold that rested beneath Saudi sand. Al-Sadr would ensure that the Arab Spring of revolution would come to his peninsula. His family would be exiled, or worse, unless al-Sadr's plans could be thwarted and the rising tide of revolution turned to his advantage.

And Faisal would do the turning.

The crown prince stood in front of his father, powerful, proud, determined.

"Give me your hands."

Faisal stepped closer and held out his hands, palms up, lowering them to his seated father. Abbudin placed his hands on top of those of his eldest son. He looked into the eyes of his hope.

"Save your family, Faisal," he said, his words carrying the solemnity of a coronation. "Save your heritage, your inheritance, the future of your children. Save us."

Jerusalem

"Where are you taking us?"

Bohannon shifted uncomfortably in the back seat of the Humvee. It was black, instead of the mandatory army olive drab, with heavily smoked black windows on all sides. Perhaps the two soldiers in front could see clearly. Tom knew they were moving, but that was all.

"Where are you taking us?"

No response.

Rizzo was in the second Humvee with two other soldiers. Tom figured they would be split up, even if Rizzo hadn't tried to escape as they exited the elevator to leave Kallie's building. Rizzo kicked one of the soldiers in the soft tissue behind his knee and, as the soldier's body buckled, pushed him into a second soldier in the back of the elevator car. Sammy barely had time to yell "Run for it!" before the sergeant whipped his burly arm around Sammy's neck and lifted him—gurgling and swinging—off the floor. So Tom had Sammy to thank for the manacles around his wrists and ankles. But the little guy had guts.

"Has there been any word about my wife?"

"I told you to keep quiet."

"Yeah, you did. Has there been any word about my wife?"

The sergeant turned slightly in the passenger's seat and looked at Bohannon with both warning and compassion. "I told you to be quiet. We're not going to answer any of your questions." The sergeant's voice lowered. "And, no, there has been no word."

Tom wasn't sure if he was relieved, or more fearful, or both. He tried to keep his mind from traveling to those images that haunted his sleep. But they were there, lurking in the shadows of his dread, waiting for an opportunity to rock his world once again.

Balata Camp, Nablus, West Bank

"Yes?"

Moussa al-Sadr glowed with the knowledge of how fully the Israeli leader had been betrayed. "You have a choice, dog of Zion."

"Who is . . . how did you get this number?" asked Eliazar Baruk.

"How is not your concern. Your concern is what the American president will do when the American women are executed."

"We don't negotiate with scum like you." Baruk's voice was defiant. Al-Sadr smiled. This moment was a glimpse of Paradise.

"You have forty-eight hours to withdraw from al-Haram al-Sharif. Remove all of your soldiers, all of your police. Return the Haram to the Waqf."

"Or?"

"Ah," purred al-Sadr. "Allah be praised. If you do not withdraw, the world will watch—on television, on the Internet—as we open the throats of the American women. Their blood will spill and your shame shall spread, Jew. Then we will slice off their heads, for all the world to see, and leave their bodies twitching before the cameras. Will you allow the death of these women? Are you willing to incur the wrath of the world? Forty-eight hours. I rejoice in your suffering."

28

MONDAY, AUGUST 24

The Negev, Israel

Rising on his elbows, Rodriguez looked past the mouth of the cave. It was as dark outside as it was inside. He couldn't see his watch. It didn't matter.

I only needed to get out of the heat.

Joe found refuge from the blistering sun sometime in the late afternoon. He remembered that. The cliffs along the old Roman road were honeycombed with openings and he spent the afternoon checking dozens of caves with his carbon finder and trying to remain in the shade of the overhangs as he moved from one to the next. But the heat had finally overwhelmed him. He felt disoriented. A bad sign. So he took refuge, just for a few minutes. He remembered putting the magic box on the floor of the cave, propping his backpack against the wall, taking a long drink of water. The sun was throwing long shadows in the desert then. Now, it was completely gone.

Too many days without sleep. Too much stress. The body can't go forever. The mind can't function without rest. But none of that mattered now. Joe didn't know how much time he had. Others must be looking for him. The Israelis were pretty sharp. And they were certainly looking for the Tent. No, not much time.

Rodriguez ran his fingers through his nappy, gray-flecked hair and scratched his head. He may have slept, but he didn't feel energized. In fact, he sat on the floor of the cave and began to despair. He couldn't find anything in the day-light, how could he ever hope to find anything at night? He'd probably fall off some cliff edge and kill himself. Or get lost in this God-forsaken wasteland and die of thirst. God-forsaken. That's how Rodriguez felt.

This must be what Tom's been feeling. All alone, forsaken, hopeless. *Man, this stinks.*

Groping to his right, he found the magnetized halogen flashlight, stood it on its base, and turned on the light. Checked his watch. Just after midnight.

Rodriguez reached into his backpack and pulled out a bottle of water, drank half, and poured the rest over his head, rubbing the sweet moisture into his face.

What would Tom do . . . where would he put his faith?

Rodriguez had grown up in a Roman Catholic family, first generation immigrants from Puerto Rico. His mother was in church more than the priests. His father worked three jobs—daytime in the Hunts Point market, nights in a corner bodega not far from their apartment, and, often, driving his cousin's taxicab on weekends. So he didn't get to church much. But Joe was an altar boy, serving at Mass at least three times a week.

Once out of school, though, Joe quit going to church until he married Deirdre, and then only sporadically—either to keep peace in their home, or for the baptism of their eldest son. He was fine without God-stuff. Until Jerusalem. Until he was crawling around in the bowels of the Temple Mount, rubbing up against some of the most sacred dirt in the world. Something was . . . well . . . something was there. Something lived there. And it wasn't flesh and blood. It was spirit. Even Doc felt it.

Joe couldn't deny that his thoughts about God had changed during that time. He just hadn't been able to sort out what those feelings were. But those same feelings were now sending off alarms in his heart. He was on holy ground.

Underground again, this time in the middle of the Negev, scrambling through a honeycomb of subterranean passageways, searching once more for an ancient artifact that could change the course of modern history. It all felt the same—except this time he was alone. And he didn't have a clue where to look. But at least no one was chasing him.

He picked up the flashlight and turned its beam toward the back of the cavern. Thirty feet ahead, the halogen lamp's beam bathed the yellow walls in a wash of blue light. It was time to move. He wasn't going to find anything sitting here. Rodriguez pulled himself to his feet, gathered up his backpack, the GPR detector, and headed in the direction of the light.

Shortly, Rodriguez came to a fork in the tunnel passage. He pulled the fluorescent yellow dots from his pocket. This is one trick that sure helped. As Doc had done in the caverns under the Temple Mount, Joe stuck three small, fluorescent circles near the floor, just inside the tunnel he was entering. Then he turned, crossed the junction point, and put three circles on the opposite wall and moved to his left and put two yellow circles at floor level just inside the tunnel he was exiting. If he came to another point where he needed to make a choice, Rodriguez would put four circles at the beginning of the tunnel he was entering. That way, he could follow the yellow circles and find his way out, or realize he had doubled back on himself.

From his pocket he fished out a shekel and flipped the coin in the air. *Right or left?* Heads. *Okay, right.* Joe swept the beam of his flashlight down the length of the right-hand tunnel, then up along the right wall, across the ceiling and . . .

The blue beam wavered . . . swinging in arcs back and forth in response to Joe's shaking hand. Above his head, at the apex of the tunnel's curved ceiling and just inside the portal, the beam of light reflected back and fell on Joe with a soft, golden glow. Within the light gleamed four sets of familiar symbols—*aleph* and *resh*; *kaf, shin, mem*; the four arches; and the Triple Tau. They looked as if they were inlaid with gold. And they spoke to him of an old friend.

In spite of the passing of ages, the golden-toned paint nestled inside carved grooves held a richness of color that threw light back into Joe's face. He stretched to run his fingers over the surface of the carvings, over the pitted, but intact, paint and—not for the first time—felt as if he were being beckoned onward by a force outside his understanding, but not outside his experience. As there had been under the Temple Mount, there was a palpable spirit in this cave, a living presence . . . a feeling that he wasn't alone, and he wasn't here by chance.

Joe glanced down at the top of the carbon detector. Alternating with each turn of Joe's body, the display on the screen bounced back and forth. He turned to face the shaft with the symbols . . . and the radar cursors collided in the middle of the screen and pulsed with the strength of a healthy heart.

Drawing in a deep breath, he surprised himself with a short prayer, something that rose unbidden from his years in Catholic school. He aimed the beam of light down the shaft, and followed the calling in his heart.

12:56 a.m., Jerusalem

"Levin checked out," Colonel Posner said. "The brother-in-law dropped out of sight ten years ago and no one in the family has seen him since. They had suspicions, but no evidence he was involved with Hezbollah."

"The phone call?" asked Orhlon. The general filled the space behind his desk, spilling over the sides of his chair.

Colonel Posner poured himself another cup of coffee from the eternal pot that sat on a sideboard in Orhlon's office in the Defense Ministry's command center.

"Levin ordered a computer for his son. The phone number is registered to ITech Technology—which could mean anything. It took awhile to track down the owner . . . he's a one-man show. An American, if you can believe it, named Daniel Cantwell. He has his main office in Jericho, but a shipping facility in Dar'a. We had one of ours pay him a visit. All the paperwork was there. He still had the phone message on his recorder. And Levin has the computer and the receipt."

"How did he handle it all?"

"The interrogation?" Posner shrugged one shoulder. "He told me he would have taken the same steps if he was in my position. He's a pro—although he lit up the board when we showed him the photo and the phone records. But who wouldn't? There is always that initial panic until reason establishes control." He set his cup on the corner of General Orhlon's desk.

"Now what?" the general prompted.

Posner placed a photograph on Orhlon's desk. "If I'm not mistaken, there's only one left. I'm planning to see him tomorrow." Posner pushed his bottom lip back against his lips, contorting his porcelain features, and shook his head. "Maybe my list—my hunch—was wrong. I should know by tomorrow night."

"Hard to believe, that's for sure," said Orhlon. "But we can't move until we are absolutely certain . . . and not until we've briefed the prime minister. Understood?"

"Yes sir," said Posner, standing. "But he won't go anywhere without a team of eyes on him at all times."

1:08 a.m.

Leonidas listened to the voice-mail message, replaced the telephone handset in the cradle, and looked at the clock on the wall of his office. They were too close.

It was time to move . . . now. Tomorrow would be too late. Tomorrow he could be in military custody.

1:32 a.m.

"Major Levin . . . we've picked up something on our radio wave scanner."

Lieutenant Stern pointed at a split screen on the right edge of a bank of screens that surrounded his desk. Levin closed the space with the speed of a diving hawk. "What is it?"

"Honestly, I don't know," admitted Stern. "See this reading? It's being recorded by our drone. There's some sort of electronic signal being generated, but it's not radio, it's not satellite phone . . . it's not showing the characteristic range of any kind of communication we normally register."

Levin leaned over Stern's right shoulder. "It's not bounce-back. Too steady for bounce-back."

"No sir, there's something down there emitting a signal. Faint—it's very localized. Its travel loop is very short. But it's there. And . . . sir . . ."

"I know . . . it's moving," said Levin. "Can you locate it?"

Stern ran his cursor over the screen and clicked on a crosshairs icon. The signal analysis screen faded and a map replaced it: a high-altitude, infrared view of the Negev. Stern clicked his mouse again and the screen zoomed in at diz-zying speed.

The image on Stern's screen stopped moving . . . hovered a moment over a barren plateau that fell away into a deep defile to the east. The crosshairs shifted, as if smelling for a scent, then pushed the view southward and zeroed in on a series of cliff faces and ravines. The crosshairs on the screen kept descending, slower now, seeking. Then they stopped, settled finally on a cleft of shadow and light so stark in its contrast that everything in the cleft, lying below the surface, was blacker than the far side of the moon.

"Scorpion Pass?" asked Levin.

"No, sir . . . not exactly. One hundred and thirty-seven meters south of Scorpion Pass. Whatever is emitting that signal is several hundred meters below the sightline of our drone."

"Underground."

"Yes, sir."

Major Levin picked up the telephone to his left and hit the top, red button.

"This is Levin," he said to the Central Command dispatch officer. "We've got him. Send everyone to thirty degrees; fifty-five minutes north . . . thirty-five degrees; seven minutes east. He's underground. There's got to be a cave down there. All right, a lot of caves. Get our men in there and find him. Now—"

Levin stopped in midsentence as the dispatch officer's voice was replaced by the commanding baritone of General Orhlon. "Yes, sir—good evening. Yes, sir, I believe we have located the American. He's down in the caves, south of Scorpion Pass. Yes, sir, we'll find him."

Levin listened again, his face contorting into a grimace. "Due respect, sir, but I'd rather stay at it with the men here until Rodriguez is apprehended. He—The Mount? Yes, sir, I know they will . . . but . . . yes, sir. I'm on my way."

He eased the handset into the cradle, afraid that if he slammed it as hard as he wanted to his men might think he was insubordinate. Levin pried his fingers from the handset.

"General Orhlon has ordered me to the Temple Mount," Levin said to the wall. "Rumors of Hezbollah infiltrators getting into the city. He wants the Mount secured." He glanced down at Lieutenant Stern. "Don't lose him. Stay on that signal."

2:47 a.m., The Negev

Steadying the carbon detector and the halogen flashlight secured by its magnet to the side of the metal box, Rodriguez picked his way along the uneven, rubble-strewn floor of the cavern like a man walking across spring ice. He didn't want to fall and damage the sensor. The tunnel carved a sweeping turn to the right, curving back around on itself as it dropped deeper under the surface. At the end of a nearly complete arc, Rodriguez entered a small, circular space where the ceiling of the cavern lifted, and two tunnels branched off. He pulled the flashlight away from the box and swept its beam across the inside ceiling of each tunnel. There were no symbols, no clue to lead him. Joe looked down at the display on the carbon sensor. It was blank. He twisted the dials, tapped the screen, and shook the box in his hands. The display remained blank—black—as if all power was lost. Useless.

As Rodriguez looked at the opening of each shaft, he felt a growing unease and an escalating urgency to finish this search and get back above ground. A sense of, what? Danger? Fear? Or reverence, as if he were sneaking into church and God was watching him. He looked at the sensor—switched it off, then back on again. Nothing. Joe put his flashlight on the floor and slipped the carbon sensor from his shoulders, lowering it with a reluctance that mirrored the turmoil in his spirit.

Not going to get any closer standing here.

He reached into his pocket, pulled out the same shekel, and flipped it. *Tails.* Joe peered into the darkness of the left shaft, took a deep breath, reached down for his flashlight, and took one halting step, then another.

Israeli patrols in heavily armed Jeeps entered the desert wadi at both ends— three from the south; three from the north—units peeling off at the entrances to several caves.

"Lieutenant, can you get us any closer?" His headset linked to the High Altitude Reconnaissance Center, the patrol leader motioned his vehicles to a halt. "There are too many caves here."

"He's one hundred meters south of you," Stern replied. "That was our last signal, just a few minutes ago."

"But which way is in?" The patrol leader flipped the switch that illuminated the spotlights welded to the roll bar of the Jeep. The sandstone cliffs turned gray, the cave mouths a mocking black. He looked up and down the dry defile, as far as he could see in the beams of light. "I can see six . . . eight . . . ten cave openings from right here."

"I don't know how to tell you to go," said Stern's voice. "I can only tell you where we believe he is. How you get there? I'm afraid that's up to you."

The patrol leader knew he didn't have the luxury of time. "One man to a hole . . . constant contact . . . engage your GPS beacons." The men in the first Jeep were already on the ground, running, before the leader's last words left his mouth.

He was back in the small, circular chamber. The tunnel to his left just led him to a dead end.

So much for flipping a coin. As he turned to look down the shaft to his right, his eyes fell upon the ground-penetrating radar, left abandoned on the chamber's floor. *Why not?* He stooped over the stainless steel box and flipped the power switch—just to know that he had tried. The display lit up, the cursors hard and true to the right tunnel.

"Hallelujah!"

⟨⟨⟨~∧∧~⟩⟩⟩

"We've got him!" Lieutenant Stern dialed in the crosshairs and overlaid the patrol leader's GPS coordinates. "Micah, lay down a track of the previous transmissions."

Stern toggled a switch to his left. "We have contact," he told the patrol leader. "He's almost directly below you, but he didn't enter near your location. He entered . . . Micah?" The soldier to his right passed Stern a topographical map with coordinates written on it and a large X over a cut in the cleft.

"Fifty-four meters to your south . . . western wall. His path, as far as we have it, switched back twice and had several turns. Recall the rest of your men and I'll guide you through the best I can. But he's there . . . right below you."

⟨⟨⟨~∧∧~⟩⟩⟩

Once again the metal box hung from his shoulders, against his chest. But he didn't need to touch the dials. He was dead on. And he was getting very close.

The lower the shaft dropped, the heavier the air became . . . a whisper of weight, a constraint against his skin. His lungs struggled for breath and, with each step, his legs got heavier, the effort to move more demanding. He was being pulled forward and held back at the same time. But he kept moving—downward.

The shaft ahead of him took another hard turn to the right. And the magic box went to sleep once more.

Something was around that corner.

⟨⟨⟨~∧∧~⟩⟩⟩

"You're breaking up on me," said the patrol leader. "We're in a small chamber. There are two shafts. Which one do we take? The one on the right, or the one on the left? Stern?"

Rodriguez set the box on the floor and edged up to the corner. There was no one there. He felt like a kid at the Saturday matinee, waiting for a slasher to jump out of a closet in some awful B movie that would give him nightmares for a week.

I've got to get out of this line of work.

The beam of the flashlight bounced to the beat of his shaking hands. He stepped out, into the corridor, and looked down its length.

"Stern?" His whispered question hung in the stale air.

The patrol leader pushed on the radio's earpiece with his right hand, as if that would improve the reception, and the flashlight in his left hand fell to his side. That's when he saw the four fluorescent yellow dots at the bottom of the left tunnel. Pointing rapidly at his team and the shaft in succession, he sent his patrol down the tunnel on the left.

Fifty feet in front of Rodriguez, the cavern shaft came to an abrupt end—not the end of the tunnel, but a wall. A man-made end. The wall filled the tunnel completely, huge limestone blocks at its base, smaller ones reaching to the ceiling, mortar filling in every ridge and groove up to the curving roof. But in the middle, near the base, was a low door—or, what looked like a door—a heavy wooden lintel, with stones now sealing the opening shut. Joe stepped up to the wall, extended his hand, and massaged the stones. *You've been here, haven't you?*

The patrol leader held up his left hand—the two men in front were stopped at a corner, the tunnel snaking a hard turn to the right. He stopped his team in its tracks, slipped past the men on point, and pressed his back against the tunnel wall, just short of the corner. The beams of their lights, the noise of their running boots, gave them away. So there was little need for silence. If there was anyone with evil intent around the corner . . . He motioned one of his men to the opposite wall of the tunnel, dropped into a crouch, and darted his head out from cover as the soldier opposite pointed a bright beam of light down the tunnel.

Off in the distance, the curving shaft came to an abrupt end . . . a dead end.

⸺⸺⸺

Joe sat cross-legged in the dust of the cavern's floor, his hand on the solid stone filling the doorway, his imagination on the other side of the stone. Somebody has been here . . . the wall is protecting something. Could it be the Tent? Could it be more? Only one way to find out. He retrieved a pickax from his backpack, raised it over his head, and drove the pointed end deep into the ancient mortar between the blocks of stone.

⸺⸺⸺

The clang of metal against rock—a rhythmic claxon—echoed up from the depths of the cave. The patrol leader heard it before he emerged from the left tunnel. He and his men curled through the small chamber and poured into the right shaft—two-by-two, leap-frogging down its length.

⸺⸺⸺

It was easier going than he expected. The mortar was intact, but degraded over the ages so that it was soft under his pick and pulled away from the stone like corn bread—falling in crumbs at his feet. Four of the stones already lay on the floor next to him; only two more and he could squeeze through the hole. But curiosity trumped expediency—Joe picked up his flashlight. He had to see what was inside.

As his light played over the space on the other side of the wall, Rodriguez figured it was about ten yards deep. But it was so wide that he couldn't see the sides. That didn't matter. In front of him was a wooden platform, about half the depth of the space, up against the back wall, extending to the sides beyond the point that Joe's light illuminated. At the rear of the platform were several mounds covered in what appeared to be animal skins of some kind. The mounds also extended into the darkness on both sides. The mounds were each about four feet high and six feet wide and rounded on top. In front of the mounds, stacked neatly, were dozens of thick, stout, long wooden poles. And running along the front of the platform were smaller rectangular objects, also wrapped in some kind of animal hide. The covering on one of the smaller objects had fallen away. As Rodriguez played his light over the surface, its carved legs glistened and reflected a deep, golden glow.

"Holy cow!"

Holding his breath, his pulse thudding against the walls of his arteries, Joe pushed his arm and his head through the small opening, throwing the light down the length of the left side of the enclosure. More mounds and poles extended into the far reaches—the space much larger than he first imagined—and ended in the distance, where he saw a huge, wooden cask. Bonded by straps—leather or metal, he couldn't tell from this distance—holding down a massive, arched, wooden lid.

At the sight of it, Joe jumped. His head hit the top of the stone opening, he bit his tongue, and swallowed the expletive that wanted to burst from his mouth. Pulling his head out of the hole in the wall, he tested the extent of damage to his tongue with his free hand, turned around to find his pickax—and found himself looking down the barrels of too many guns in the hands of too many stone-faced Israeli soldiers.

The patrol leader approached Joe, eased him to the side of the tunnel, approached the hole in the door and shone his light into the opening. After a few, quiet moments, he turned around to face his men.

"Take him back to the surface and hold him there. No . . . wait . . . restrain him. He's not getting away from us. Then get on the radio to General Orhlon. Tell him we have the American. And—well—just tell him we found it. Then send in the engineers."

4:23 a.m., Tel Aviv

"Remind me never to play poker with you," said Orhlon.

Baruk's long, thin body was buried in the corner of a lush, chocolate-brown leather sofa tucked between the bookcases in his home library, a top secret Mossad report by his side. His shoes were off, his jacket draped over the back of a chair, his silk tie neatly folded on his desk. Baruk pulled his eyeglasses down the length of his nose and transferred the phone to his right hand. "You have money to lose?"

"Not on my salary," said Orhlon.

"They found the Tent?"

"Actually, the American . . . the tall one, Rodriguez, found it. Using some NASA-developed gizmo. It was sealed up behind a wall, deep in a cave along the Ascent of Akkrabim."

"The what?"

"Scorpion Pass, down in the Negev. Elie . . . he actually found it. And it appears as if it's still intact."

Baruk finally stirred. He swung his legs off the sofa, resting his right arm along the top of the sofa's back. "Three thousand years old, and it was just sitting there? I never really believed it was possible. Now . . . well . . ." The prime minister took a long, deep breath. "Now is the difficult part, eh? How long before we can get it to the Temple Mount?"

The silence from the phone confirmed the difficulty of Orhlon's task.

"Yes, sir . . . the difficult part," he said. "It'll probably take most of a day just to get the pieces here. We have to get a whole fleet of Krupp's heavy haulers from Shimona down into a very rough area that is off the main road through Scorpion Pass. That will take hours in itself. We're airlifting in a corps of rabbis, scientists, and archaeologists along with some engineers. They've got to figure out what we've got, figure out a way to get it loaded onto the trucks without destroying it—if that's possible—and then get it back here to Jerusalem. Twelve . . . eighteen hours at a minimum. Could be more like twenty-four, who knows?"

Baruk calculated the angles and the options, weighing the possibilities in his head.

"Make it happen," said the prime minister. "And lock down the Mount."

4:29 a.m., Jerusalem

Major Levin walked across the flat expanse of the new Temple Mount platform and even the concrete smelled fresh. The platform, what had been completed so far by the crews from Krupp Industries, was flat and empty, except for the few trees on the northeast corner that survived the quake. That end of the platform rested on bedrock and some of it survived the destruction. The greatest damage was the gaping maw on the western side that swallowed the Dome of the Rock and the entire southern half of the thirty-five-acre Temple Mount platform, taking with it the Al-Aqsa Mosque. Miraculously, the Western Wall itself remained standing.

Walking to the south, Levin once again checked the hand-cranked pulleys and coils of rope that stood on the precipice. Krupp's engineers were concerned about the amount of weight the platform could support until it was completely finished, fastened to and supported by the massive Herodian walls that mostly evaded the ravages of the earthquake. So they eschewed modern steel scaffolds or any heavy machinery and reverted to more historical means of lifting material into place to repair the cracks that did exist in the walls. But it wasn't the platform's sturdiness that concerned Levin this night. It was the two sets of reports he was receiving on his radio.

One series of messages kept him updated on the progress of getting the Tent of Meeting prepared for transport. The second series were updated intelligence reports which hinted—strongly—of a pending attack by a disparate group of Islamic militants. Both scenarios were difficult to believe.

On the one hand, his men in the field had tracked the tall American into the desert, trapped him in a cave along the Ascent of Akkrabim, and now had in their possession what they believed were the actual pieces of the Tabernacle of Jehovah that the Israelites carried through the desert for forty years before entering the Promised Land. Levin didn't know if what his men had under guard was, in fact, the Tent of Meeting. It would take a team of rabbis, scientists, and archaeologists to ultimately determine what had been found. Some had been airlifted to Scorpion Pass to oversee the transfer. Others were on their way to him. It didn't really matter to Levin what was in the trucks. His job was to work with the army, secure the Mount, and have it available for the convoy when it arrived.

"Worried about the Tent?" asked Major Abner Katz of the Israeli Defense Force, Israel's standing army of two-hundred-fifty thousand soldiers. "I'm not. It's going to be at least twelve hours before they get here, probably more. That gives us plenty of time to prepare and be ready. And whatever they have in the trucks is what it is. What rocks me is what just came over my radio."

Major Katz looked as if his head had been bleached. A man of normal dimensions was topped by a swept-back thicket of white-blond hair, reprised from his eyebrows to the pointed beard on his chin. His skin was pale, as though he never saw the sun. High cheekbones gave him a craggy edge.

Katz joined Levin, who was looking out over the lights of the Old City.

"What is it now?" asked Levin.

"I have a good man—IDF—who was embedded with the Northern Islamic Front for years. He just transmitted a blast . . . which means he's on the run . . . that the Front's entire apparatus has gone dark. No communications, no meetings. And he doesn't know why. He's been on the inside for a long time, trusted, part of the inner circle. But nobody in the Front told him what was going on."

"Not a good sign," said Levin.

"Especially for him. He's trying to get back, but . . ."

"But it confirms everything else we've been hearing. Rumors and conjectures, sure, but those rumors are adding up." Levin turned away from the view and started walking south where members of Katz's outfit were stringing razor wire along the platform's perimeter. "Shin Bet got information this morning from a normally reliable source that the Martyrs' Brigade has been activating its members for days and that many of them were on the move. Now we hear that Hezbollah infiltrated the border with some of its most fierce and experienced soldiers—and has been doing so for weeks."

"I just didn't believe it, Abe. Our border with Lebanon is solid, well guarded, heavily policed. The border crossings are some of the toughest we have, outside of Gaza. Hezbollah getting a large number of soldiers into Israel without us knowing about it? I wouldn't have thought it possible. But, now, with all these reports? This is no coincidence. The Tent of Meeting is coming here. And, I'll bet, so is a strong force of Islamic fighters."

"The Temple Mount is always a target, Avram."

"Perhaps you're right . . . but now I feel the crosshairs on our backs."

Katz was regular army, a man accustomed to being in command. Here, on the Mount, it was Levin who was in charge, even though the IDF troops outnumbered those of Shin Bet. But the Hawk was neither foolish nor proud. There was no operation manual for this situation—securing the Temple Mount for the arrival of the Tabernacle.

Levin stopped near a series of openings, entry points for the stairs coming up from the Huldah Gates and the Western Wall. Beyond the stair shafts the platform was a ragged tangle of iron rebar and unfinished concrete—bare and open, both above and below. Tough to defend.

"I want you to take tactical command. I've already told my men and run it up the chain of command. I don't have any battlefield experience. And we're going to need that experience." Levin had known Abner Katz since cadet school. This was a man he could trust and depend on. "I don't know how they found out; this secret was pretty tightly held. But the Muslims are coming and they're coming after the Tent. General Orhlon has reinforcements on the way. But, for now, it's up to you and me."

4:35 a.m.

Leonidas had several cell phones lined up in front of him. Each one had only one purpose. Each one had only one phone number programmed in its memory.

He looked at the clock on the wall opposite his desk. In less than an hour he would be independently wealthy. In less than an hour it would be over. He would be gone. The legacy he would leave behind would be chaos.

⸺⸺⸺

"Hello, my friend."

"Friend? I doubt that," said Moussa al-Sadr, surprised that Leonidas would be calling at this hour, and fearful that his fighters had been discovered. "A friend remains in contact. A friend returns calls. You have been quite obvious by your absence, Leonidas. Perhaps you have discovered other friends?"

"I have no feelings. Your sarcasm is wasted on me, my friend."

Al-Sadr stepped away from the map on top of the table—the map outlining the maze of tunnels under the Temple Mount, a map drawn from the memory of those who chased the Americans prior to the earthquake. He was in no mood to joust with this heathen informer.

"Why have you called?"

The raspy breathing in the receiver transformed into a gurgling chuckle. "Why? Why do I ever call you? I have information. Valuable information."

Al-Sadr waited to hear more, but only rasps came through the earpiece. "What is it?"

"Ah . . . first, the price," said Leonidas. "Information has become much more valuable—so many seeking reliable intelligence about the Mount, the Israelis, . . . their search. Supply and demand, yes?"

"What do you want?" al-Sadr snapped. "Tell me. I have little time for negotiations."

"Yes, I'm sure you are busy in that little house in the Balata camp," said

Leonidas. "Particularly tonight, eh, my friend? Yes, well, since you have not the time to negotiate, the price has doubled."

Al-Sadr squeezed the phone as if it were Leonidas's neck. *Someday . . . when I have you under my knife.* "Tell me what you know."

"The Israelis have the Tent of Meeting. Shin Bet followed the tall American. Somehow, he was led to one of the many caves dotting the cliffs over Scorpion Pass. That the Tent was hidden in that cave is . . . well . . . miraculous. So, Shin Bet has the Tent. They are debating how to handle it, how to move it. But once it's loaded on trucks the convoy will be on its way to Jerusalem disguised as building materials for the reconstruction of the Temple Mount. I leave it to your imagination what they intend to do with the Tent once they reach the Temple Mount."

Al-Sadr circled the walls of the small room while he listened. As he passed the table, he looked at the Hezbollah brigade commanders who were now huddled over the map. Their objective was now more important, and more difficult.

"Thank you . . . my friend." Al-Sadr nearly choked on the words. "Again, you have done us a service."

"My pleasure, since you're the one paying."

⌇⌇⌇⌇⌇

Major Avram Levin's cell phone vibrated in his pocket and the Hawk immediately tensed. Only his wife had this number and she never called him during an operation. Something was wrong.

Levin looked at the vibrating phone in his hand. There was no incoming phone number. "Yes?"

"Good evening, Major. Congratulations on your promotion."

The voice on the phone sounded as if coarse sandpaper had shredded its vocal cords. "Who are you?"

"Don't bother asking questions," the disembodied voice gurgled. "There's no time for that. I have something you need to act on immediately. There is a new leader of the Muslim Brotherhood who has come out of Hezbollah. He is very powerful and he is planning to launch an attack on the Temple Mount as soon as—"

"Give me some proof or I hang up now," Levin snapped.

"Your men call you *the Hawk*. Your wife, who is partial to pink sweaters, is the only person with this number. Israeli soldiers are, at this moment, preparing the biblical Tent of Meeting for transport to Jerusalem. And you had better listen to me or many Israeli soldiers will die."

Levin shuddered. "Tell me."

"First, Hezbollah has been infiltrating fighters into Jerusalem for days. There is a large force massed and ready to attack. They are only awaiting the order."

"I know that. Our intelligence is far better than yours."

"Is it? . . . I know where the American women are."

———∽∿∼———

Out in the harbor of Tel Aviv, swinging at anchor, the Liberian freighter *Les Bon Amis* rolled heavily in the growing wind.

"The launch . . . it waits for you at the far end of the wharf, *n'est pa?*" Captain Longines said into the cellular phone. The man's skin was as black as his heart. A Somali pirate who, over the years, parlayed abduction and ransom into a mostly legitimate coastal freighter, Captain Longines maintained order on his ship through his powerful stature and ruthless vengeance. A man of many motives, he was neither to be trusted nor trifled with.

Leonidas had little choice. He needed an escape route. One that could not be traced. What better way to disappear than on a ship that also needed to disappear. It was Leonidas who—without Captain Longines's knowledge—arranged for the illegal cargo of munitions and missiles to be loaded onto *Les Bon Amis*. And it was Leonidas who could be sure the Captain had no hidden connection to Mossad or the police.

"Has my luggage arrived . . . my computer?" Leonidas wiped the palm of one hand on his wilted pants, but it didn't stop the sweat. Much of his plan now hung in the balance. He needed the dollars, the gold, and the diamonds, hidden inside his computer console, to guarantee the many stages of his long, circuitous escape route. If Captain Longines hesitated, it probably meant his hidden treasure was no longer hidden.

"Ah, *oui*, all is at the ready," said the Captain, no hitch in his voice. "You come, we go. But . . . any delay, it may endanger your plans, eh? This weather, she has changed her mind. And it will, soon, become *tres* nasty. Come soon. Or, maybe, we no go."

"Just be ready."

Sixty seconds later, Leonidas threw the third phone into a small, ceramic stove that kept him warm on winter nights, but now turned all his records and personal files to ash.

⌐∿∽∾∿⌐

Leonidas swung his chair around to face the computer screen. The Swiss bank's Web site was already loaded. He typed in his user name, his password, and the three additional identification requirements that were necessary to access the bank's most secure server. Leonidas then keyed in an untraceable number on the satellite phone that rested on his desk.

"Guten abend."

"Good evening," said Leonidas. "Six-four-roger-kilo-nine-three-three-zed."

"Was ist Ihr schlechtester Albtraum?"

"My worst nightmare? Not getting revenge."

"Geben Sie bitte Ihren Ermächtigungscode, jetzt ein."

Leonidas keyed in the long, multilayered authorization code.

"How may we be of assistance?"

"Is the transfer prepared?"

"Of course."

"Implement the transfer."

Leonidas tapped his foot against the leg of the table.

"It is complete."

He opened the other windows on his browser. Kigali. Johannesburg. Penang Island. Auckland. Adelaide. And, finally, the bulk of it, Papeete. All the banks had wired coded messages of delivery. His path was prepared. Now, his final transaction.

The one that counted. He made his fourth call.

"Good evening, Leonidas. I've been awaiting your call." A voice as slippery as an oil slick came across the phone. "Are our plans in motion?"

"Is my money in the bank?"

"Yes, of course. Check your account online if you insist. I'll wait."

Leonidas punched in the last few keystrokes and his numbered account in the Cayman Islands came up on the screen—the one that received all of the "deposits" and then was immediately swept clean. It was all there. So many zeros!

He took no time with pleasantries.

"Al-Sadr is poised to launch his attack on the Temple Mount, but now he will wait until the Israeli soldiers and priests get the Tent erected. Shin Bet knows of the attack and where the women are being held."

"Good. What else?"

"Baruk is home. He will soon receive information about al-Sadr's planned attack. When he does, he and his bodyguards will consider leaving his home and trying to get to Central Command. The cars will be prepared, but they will delay. That is your opportunity. Al-Sadr and his bodyguards are in a house near Nablus, in the Balata refugee camp. I sent the GPS coordinates to you attached to an email. He will be there for the duration of the attack on the Temple Mount. It is his command post. You have time."

There was a long silence on the other end of the line. Leonidas stole a quick look at his watch.

"Well done," said the voice. "You have fulfilled all of your promises. And I will fulfill mine. You will be fully compensated for all of your service to us. Goodbye, Leonidas. Go with Allah."

Leonidas closed the cell phone, looked at it for a moment, then threw it into the stove. He got up from his desk, reached out, and picked up a framed picture that he meditated on every night. The photo was of a relatively young man, standing, posed, with his arm around a woman, two young boys by their sides. The man wore the uniform of the IDF—Israeli Defense Forces. On the lapels of his shirt, the bars of a lieutenant. On the breast pocket of his shirt, the winged sword with crossed lightning bolts—the insignia of Israel's Special Forces. On his face, the smile of the innocent—a face that looked so much like his own, so many years ago, long before he learned to satiate his pain with food. His twin brother—twin in birth, in soul, mind, and spirit.

"Tonight, we have won, my brother. Tonight, we have repaid everything. Life for life. In an abundance. Your sons will never want for anything. Your wife will not be left destitute. And your life, squandered in such a useless manner, has been avenged. Rest, my brother. Rest in peace."

Leonidas straightened his shoulders, started to turn, and then stopped. Perhaps he could make just one more call. He reached into his pants pocket and pulled out his personal BlackBerry. It wouldn't matter now. Everything was in motion just as he planned. Except this call . . . the one he hadn't planned. But the thought was so sweet.

He dialed the number.

⋙∼∿∼⋘

"Good evening, my friend."

"I have no more need of your services," the voice said in reply.

"Yes, that is correct," Leonidas said through the voice distorter. "You are out of business. Shin Bet knows of your plans. All of your plans. The Tent will be in place before you can act. And they will be coming for the women."

Leonidas relished the slight intake of breath on the receiving end, and the final words he so long desired to say to Imam Moussa al-Sadr. "Burn in hell, you madman."

⋙∼∿∼⋘

Leonidas carried the framed picture to a small bag by the door, inserted it into a padded pocket inside the bag, pulled closed the zipper, and left his office, his home, his legacy.

"Can I help you, sir?" said the guard by the gate.

"No, sergeant, thank you. I'm just going for a short walk. It's a bit windy, but a beautiful night."

"Yes sir . . . good night, Mr. Shomsky."

29

MONDAY, AUGUST 24 (CONTINUED)

5:08 a.m., Balata Camp, Nablus, West Bank

"How many are in place?"

"Three hundred . . . one hundred under the Haram, the rest in the two houses at the other end of the tunnel," said Youssef. "They will be through the tunnel within minutes of the assault. There are another five hundred within a kilometer of the Haram. They will have to fight their way through."

"Is that enough? Will we succeed?"

"Yes, Holy One, it is enough for what we hope to accomplish. But why don't we strike now? Before the Israelis bring more troops . . . before the Tent arrives?"

Al-Sadr placed his hand on the commander's massive arm, a gesture of endearment that was lost neither on Youssef nor on his master. Only al-Sadr knew the gesture was simply for effect. "Be patient. We want the Zionists to erect their sacrilege—it gives us just cause in the eyes of the world, and it rallies our brothers. It will stir the heart of Islam to outrage. The great mosque, the beautiful Dome, lying in ruins and these usurper Jews bury them beneath concrete and then try to steal the Haram from Islam? They have no right! This is insult . . . sacrilege. So, let them commit their abomination. Then we will attack with the ferocity of the wronged. We will destroy this sham of a temple and reclaim the Haram."

"But, can we hold it?"

The old man walked over to a small window that looked out over the Balata camp. In the distance the barking of dogs mixed with the smell of charcoal cooking fires to fill the early morning air. "There is no need to hold it," he whispered. "We only need to gain possession of the Haram, destroy the infidel's tent, and claim it as the rightful domain of the Jordanian Waqf. When the Israelis counterattack, which they will—and they will succeed—we have legitimacy in the eyes of the world. And they look like the brutal oppressors they are. The future of Jerusalem, of al-Haram al-Sharif, will soon be out of Israel's hands. The world court, world opinion will decide, will force Israel to make concessions for peace. The holy mountain will be restored to Islam. The Dome, the Al-Aqsa Mosque, will rise once more . . . and the Brotherhood will be united under one banner."

Al-Sadr turned from the window to look at Youssef. The ambient light from the Balata camp filled the window, creating a shimmering, almost angelic glow behind the old man.

"The Brotherhood continues to sow seeds of revolution. Jordan will be next—that puppet king will lose both his throne and his head," said al-Sadr, his voice rising like the tidal wave of chaos that was spreading over the Middle East. His right arm rose, punctuating every pledge. "And our Syrian president should not feel comfortable tonight. He, too, will soon feel the wrath of the unleashed unwashed. Syria, too, will drop into the waiting hands of the Brotherhood. And then the Jew will be surrounded with enemies once again—no more of this blasphemous peace with the Jews."

He took a step forward. "But my eyes, Youssef, are on the Saud . . . the fat, the arrogant Saud . . . how great will be their fall."

9:35 p.m. Eastern Daylight Time, Washington, DC

Jonathan Whitestone sat in the quiet and the dark of the Rose Garden, the velvety soft aroma soothing his nerves. Too much was happening, too quickly. The risk of taking a misstep was high, and a misstep could be cataclysmic.

Bill Cartwright entered the garden and walked down the path toward the president. The look on his face telegraphed his message.

"More bad news, Bill?"

"Yes, Mr. President," said the CIA director. "The Israelis are in possession of the Tent of Meeting. It appears that Joe Rodriguez uncovered some clues to its location. He found it in some place called Scorpion Pass, down by the southern end of the Dead Sea. Rodriguez didn't have it long. Shin Bet had him covered like a blanket, and they closed in immediately. The Tent will soon be on its way to Jerusalem and the Israelis have locked down the city. My contact said Baruk has given the order that the Tent be assembled immediately . . . tonight . . . so the Jews can reestablish ritual sacrifice on the Mount and declare sovereignty over the entire Mount platform."

Whitestone felt the bottom fall out of his stomach. "That would be a disaster. How good is your contact?"

"High up . . . on the inside of the Israeli government."

The president rose and started back toward the White House, then turned to face Cartwright. "Bill, do we still have a black ops team in place in Israel?"

"Yes, Mr. President. They can be on the move with a phone call. I've had them on standby since yesterday."

"Good." Whitestone took a step toward the CIA director. "Put them in play." Whitestone took a deep breath to try to calm his thumping heart. This was the biggest gamble of his presidency. "Bill, we have to do everything in our power to ensure that Tent does not remain in Israeli hands . . . or fall into the hands of the Muslims. Tell the team to take whatever steps they can to secure it or destroy it, before it can be assembled. Make it look like an accident."

Cartwright's eyes searched the president's face. "Jon, I don't know if we can get it done. And, if we do, Baruk . . . the Israelis . . . will go ballistic if they find out we were behind the destruction of the Tent."

Whitestone put his hand on his old friend's shoulder. "Don't I know it. This could be a political and diplomatic nightmare." He sighed, and shook his head, trying to escape the weight that pressed down on his neck. "But anything is better than World War Three. Get the team moving. And let's pray we're making the right decision."

5:22 a.m., Tel Aviv

Black against black, the *Zodiac* was invisible even though it was being thrown around by three-foot waves. The wind continued to build. The bursts were so violent, so low, the wind sucked water from the surface of the sea and drove the spray before it like a sandstorm in the desert. The waves rolled higher, but the *Zodiac*'s powerful, silent, electric engine pushed the bouncing inflatable intractably onward toward the freighter. Three black-clad, black-masked men watched the harbor launch pull away from the ship, its passenger climbing the gangway like a drunken sailor, and guided the *Zodiac* to the far side of the ship.

While attention was fixed on the ship's sole, arriving passenger, the men in the *Zodiac* used magnetic moorings connected to long ropes to attach the inflatable to the freighter amidships, where the gunwale was low to the water. They hooked an assembled ladder to the side of the ship, then scrambled up, over, and into the shadows before the next big wave could roll the top rail out of reach.

No one was on this side of the ship. One stayed in the shadows beneath an overhang to guard the boat. The other two moved forward, opened a door, and disappeared from sight.

———〰〰———

Captain Longines was not entirely pleased with the half-now, half-later nature of the transaction, but Shomsky knew that the half Longines had already banked would keep this tug running for a year—without any supplemental income. Now secure in his cabin, Shomsky was certain the fortune that awaited Captain Longines would keep him safe throughout their voyage.

"You may desire to secure your belongings . . . that computer," said the captain, pointing to Shomsky's bags. "The sea, she is very angry tonight. We shall all be punished for our sins, monsieur. I think, none of us will escape her fury, eh?"

A chill gripped Shomsky's heart at the captain's choice of words but, as the door closed behind him, Shomsky dismissed Longines's prophetic warning as the fanciful fears of an ignorant and superstitious thug. He was safe on this ship, finally safe after so many years of planning and executing his revenge. Lukas Painter was the commander who sentenced his twin, his only brother, to death in the sands of Libya. His country never acknowledged the loss or the sacrifice. Israel never admitted its complicity in his death—that one of his own soldiers, friendly fire, ripped apart Lieutenant Shomsky's chest with a burst of automatic fire and then left him to die. It was as if Hillel Shomsky, 33rd Brigade, Red Raiders, never existed. He was never mourned. Never honored. Never buried. It had taken Chaim ten years to track down the members of the patrol, to finally extract the truth.

Now, at last, he was avenged. Painter had already paid. Now Israel would pay. And Shomsky was free.

There was a knock on the door. The captain with another warning?

Shomsky opened the door to his small room. He saw nothing. He peered out into the hallway. A hand clamped closed over his mouth and a forearm pressed into the back of his neck, cutting off his breath. He was lifted off his feet, pushed back into the room as a second figure, covered in black head-to-foot, entered and closed the door. Shomsky was quickly trussed and gagged, only his eyes able to move. The two looked about the room. One pointed to the computer console.

One of the black-clad men picked up the computer, the other picked up Shomsky's considerable body and tilted it over his shoulder. They moved, without sound or hurry, into the short hallway, then aft. Shomsky couldn't speak, or move, but his mind was screaming for help.

The crew was busy getting the freighter under way. They came to a halt. Shomsky was lowered, turned around, and pushed through an open door.

The men turned right and slipped through the shadows of the overhang. Near the end they stopped and lowered Shomsky to the deck. Without a wasted motion, they pulled him to a seated position. One pressed the computer console into his chest while another secured it to his body with the same immovable rope that bound his hands and feet.

Chaim Shomsky looked at the computer in his lap. Fitting. He thought of all the money that would rot and go unclaimed in those banks, of the diamonds that would now be lost in the silt of Tel Aviv harbor. Then he thought of Painter, executed on the slopes of Mount Nebo. He thought of what must be, or would be, occurring on the Temple Mount at any moment. He thought of his brother. Fitting. It was all fitting. Even this.

The two men picked him up, shoulders and ankles, and carried him to the side of the freighter. The ship was in a long, rolling arc, this side just past its apex and now falling back toward the blackness of the Mediterranean. Just as the gunwales kissed the top of the waves, the two men slipped Shomsky noise-lessly into the churning sea. He began to sink immediately, the money, gold, and diamonds adding to the speed of his descent.

I'm coming.

7:17 a.m., The Negev

Belching diesel engines and the heavy grinding of low-geared trucks snapped Rodriguez out of an uncomfortable, fitful sleep. He was strapped into the front seat of an Israeli Defense Force off-road vehicle, an X-harness holding his body in place while his hands and feet were bound with metal shackles. He couldn't locate an inch of his body that didn't hurt.

Down through the cleft of the wadi, kicking up choking plumes of gritty sand, weaved an endless line of heavy transport trucks, some filled with soldiers, some filled with tools, some empty, awaiting their precious cargo. And the precious cargo was not Joe Rodriguez. He might get to ride along—to jail—but these trucks were reserved for the Tabernacle . . . the Tent That Moves. And it would be moving once again.

Rodriguez tried to find a comfortable position, but it was impossible. This was going to be a long day.

7:53 a.m., Jerusalem

Rizzo looked at the impossible-to-identify mound of steaming stuff on the flimsy paper plate, and then looked up at the jailer. "Hey, Abraham . . . where's my blueberry pancakes, eh?"

The Israeli soldier on the other side of the bars reminded Rizzo of the ferret he once owned as a kid, a hand-me-down pet from his cousin Shaun who had a dozen of the furry rats running around his home. Long of nose, weak of eyes, jerky in his movements, all the soldier was missing was the brown fur. Rizzo was already planning how he was going to staple a fur coat to the soldier's back if he ever got the chance.

"Eat it or don't eat it," said the ferret. "It makes no difference to me." He put down on the floor, near the bars, two paper cups filled with water. "But you might be here a long time."

Shut up, you jerk.

Rizzo turned to the cell on his right. After exhausting himself with screaming for a phone call, for the American ambassador, for his freedom—and pounding on the bars until his fists began to bleed—Bohannon had dropped into a fitful, moaning half-sleep that kept Rizzo up all night with concern. For the last few hours, Tom hadn't moved a muscle.

Now, at the words of the ferret jailer, Bohannon was up again, poised on the edge of his bunk for another assault on the thick steel bars. Rizzo acted to circumvent Bohannon's attack.

"Hey, Tom. Glad to see you're awake. You're just in time for this great breakfast. It's some kind of hybrid—something between oatmeal and goat meal, I think. But it's hot and there's a lot of it. You should eat. We're going to need our strength when we get out of here."

It worked. Bohannon took his eyes off the bars and turned his head to look at Rizzo.

"I was just talking to Ferret Face. He said we'll probably get sprung in a little while. So just sit—"

"I was awake," said Bohannon. His voice had all the life of a mortuary. "I heard what he said. We're not going anywhere."

Bohannon lifted himself off the bunk and walked over to his steaming mound of mystery cereal. He picked up the plate in both hands and walked to the bars beside the cell door. Turning up the sides, he passed the plate through the bars and held it on the far side, his arms extending through the openings between the bars. Rizzo watched as Tom shifted the plate to his right hand, crooked his arm back against the bars and catapulted the plate and its contents into a splatter on the far, cinder-block wall.

"Let me out!" Bohannon screamed, his voice raspy from overuse. "I want my rights! I want to talk to the American embassy! Let me out of here!"

Without thinking, Rizzo took the plate in his hands and lifted it to throw at the wall. The mound of mystery cereal slipped off the paper plate; wilted his billowy, blue pants with a splosh; slid down his leg; and gathered into a pool on, in, and around his borrowed, child-sized leather boots. Rizzo looked down at the slop all over his leg and launched himself at the iron bars.

"Let me out!" Rizzo screamed in harmony with Bohannon. "Let me out of here you furry—"

"Let us out!" screamed Bohannon.

Both men beat their balled fists against the unforgiving iron bars.

5:30 p.m., The Negev

The first truck sounded like it was trying to give birth. Its engine roared and its gears ground and screeched, its massive tires spinning divots into the soft, gritty pumice of the Negev.

Maybe we're not going anywhere after all.

Rodriguez watched as the truck's tires gained traction, and the heavily laden hauler began the long journey to Jerusalem.

Major Avram Levin approached Rodriguez as he and his babysitters were the last to emerge from the troop-carrier.

"Good evening, Mr. Rodriguez . . . Major Levin." He saluted as he spoke. "I've seen you many times, mostly through the lens of a surveillance camera. I've looked forward to this meeting, but I've got more pressing matters at the moment."

Levin's eyes were pulled toward the unloading trucks.

"What . . . did we inconvenience you the last time we were here?"

Levin turned back to Rodriguez. Another American with an attitude. "Do you know how many laws you've broken on this trip to Israel alone? Not to mention the mayhem that accompanied your previous visit. Our city is still trying to recover. So don't give me any trouble, Mr. Rodriguez, or I'll throw you into the same jail with Bohannon and Rizzo."

"You arrested them? What are they in jail for?"

"For interfering with a police investigation . . . for immigration violations . . . for just getting in the way, as you are doing now. I don't have time for a debate, Mr. Rodriguez."

Levin looked across the Temple Mount at the caravan that continued to arrive atop the restored platform—a line of more than two dozen, heavy-duty, canvas-covered construction trucks with the orange "K" on a field of pale blue that symbolized Krupp Industries. It was not unlike many other deliveries of construction materials made to the Mount over the past months, though few deliveries had demanded six armored personnel carriers and two troop-carrier trucks as escort. The soldiers in the trucks and APCs jumped from their vehicles and joined those already on the ground, some forming a human wall around the flatbeds, others stepping up to help unload.

Levin glanced up at the truck behind Rodriguez and turned to the soldiers at Rodriguez's side.

"Put him up on the hood," he said, nodding toward the truck. "He's the one who found it . . . he's earned the right to see it erected."

Levin returned his gaze to Rodriguez. "I have many questions for you, Mr. Rodriguez. I hope you will afford me the time to ask them in a more relaxed environment later. For the time being, enjoy the view. Thanks to your own efforts, you'll be watching history as it's made—and the future as it's changed."

Levin nodded his head and turned to the guards. "Keep him shackled. He's disappeared too many times already."

30

Tuesday, August 25

12:06 a.m., Jerusalem

The engineers and soldiers moved with cautious precision. Beside them, several at each truck, stood the priests, guiding, directing each of their movements. The deliberations and instructions started hours earlier. Major Levin had been part of the initial discussions, but the teaching sessions continued nonstop from the moment Shin Bet first secured the Tent. Now Levin watched in awe as Krupp's engineers and ranks of Israeli soldiers unloaded the trucks.

First came some very heavy bundles, still wrapped in coarse, bulky coverings that looked like hairy animal skins. Dozens of soldiers, struggling under the weight of the bundles, moved past Levin.

"This is incredible, isn't it?"

Major Katz came up to Levin's side. "Look at the poles," he said. "They may be weathered, but they look as solid as the timbers holding up my porch."

"Look at the time," responded Levin. "This is taking too long. We're totally exposed out here. This was a crazy idea and we're just sitting here waiting to get hit."

Katz gave Levin a little poke in his ribs. "Avram . . . nothing is moving within a kilometer of the Temple Mount. This part of the city is totally locked down. We're going to get this done. We're going to be part of history."

More bundles kept emerging from the trucks, all under the watchful eyes of the priests.

"When the priests started measuring out the dimensions and marking the concrete," said Katz, "I thought they were mistaken. I thought, *This was a tent, you know? A tent!* This thing will be massive."

Levin turned to watch as a group of twenty soldiers unwrapped their packages—golden stands, tarnished by time, but gleaming nonetheless—and placed them on the markings left by the priests.

"Yes, it's large. And yes, it will change history," said Levin. "Now . . . tell me one more time, how well are we defended?"

Levin and Katz began yet another circuit of the Temple Mount platform.

"We have five hundred men on station at this point; another five hundred on standby at the Mevaseret Tsiyon base. The majority of our force is distributed below us, restricting all access. All streets and roads in the area are closed, blocked by barriers manned with armed soldiers. There are no pedestrians. The Western Wall and the Western Wall tunnel are closed and guarded. We are just about to raise the security screen, blocking visual observation of the platform from most of Jerusalem. No one is going to get near the Temple Mount tonight, Avram."

Levin was grateful for, but not convinced by, the major's confidence.

"In addition, we have four, fully manned machine gun batteries up here, one on each corner. Each battery contains a dozen riflemen."

"Grenades?"

Katz threw back his head and barked a laugh. "Are you kidding? Not unless you want to get me fired. I was instructed, in no uncertain terms, there were to be no explosives . . . nothing incendiary of any kind. That's all I need, to go down in history as the commander who erected, and burned down, the Tent of Meeting, all in one night. No . . . no, Avram . . . no explosives. Honestly, I'm even concerned about the sparks coming off my guns, if we have to use them. That's one reason why all the batteries' muzzles are turned away from where the Tent will be erected. I don't want any mistakes."

"All right," said Levin. He looked to the black void at the southern end. That was the point where the Kidron and Hinnom valleys fell away from Mount Zion. Where the Temple Mount was at its highest point off the ground. It was also the only section of the platform that Krupp's engineers had yet to finish. It was a gaping maw and its open presence kept gnawing away at Levin's peace. He felt as if burglaries were occurring in the neighborhood around his home and he couldn't remember if he locked his door.

"Look, Abe . . . I know I gave you command. But can you do me a favor?" said Levin. "Send a squad to secure the southern edge, okay? That big, empty space down there just bothers me."

~~~

Deep in the caverns beneath Levin's feet, Muslim fighters began to edge their way closer to the surface. They moved beyond the tunnel that the Martyrs' Brigade dug into the Mount during the tumultuous weeks since the earthquake and through some of the caverns that were untouched by the selective destruction that moved the earth under Jerusalem.

Hassan, commander of these fighters, thanked Allah there was a way through the damage. Had all the karstic caverns collapsed, the Temple Mount would simply be a mound of rubble, never to be rebuilt. But many of the Herodian arches remained intact. His teams had conducted scouting missions before this night, probing and marking a route to the surface.

Now, hundreds of trained fighters twisted through the tunnels in a long, serpentine, single-file line, their singular destination a confrontation—a battle—for control of al-Haram al-Sharif.

12:58 a.m., Balata Camp, Nablus, West Bank

Moussa al-Sadr looked at the small clock. "We must make sure the Tent is completed before we take action. Call the house where the second group is waiting. Send a messenger—wait, absolutely wait, until I tell them to attack. Not before."

Al-Sadr pulled a cell phone from the pocket of his robe and hit the speed dial.

"Mr. Prime Minister"—he relished the words—"your time is up. You have no intention of vacating the Haram, so there is no reason for us to wait. Watch your television. It will be an unforgettable broadcast."

1:17 a.m., Jerusalem

Levin orbited the edges of the Temple Mount platform, checking on positions, talking to soldiers, looking into the night. Trying to make himself feel a level of comfort that was alien to him. But, if he kept moving, at least he was covering ground. At least he was doing something.

His orbit swung past the parked convoy. Joe Rodriguez was seated on the hood of the truck where Levin left him, his back resting against the windshield, a wide-brimmed hat pulled down over his eyes.

"Comfortable, Mr. Rodriguez?"

With shackled hands, Rodriguez pushed the hat away from his eyes.

"I hope this show is worth the price of admission," said the American. "It's been an awfully long wait, you know? And there are other things I'd like to be doing."

Levin swiveled slightly to his right. "Don't you appreciate history, Mr. Rodriguez?" he said, looking up at the American. "This is a momentous occasion."

"Right. It's been four hours and they still haven't gotten peg A into slot B. Wake me up when something interesting happens." Rodriguez started to pull the hat back down over his eyes, but stopped and returned his gaze to Major Levin. "Since this is such a historic moment, why don't you bring my two pals out here to watch it with me? Tom is more responsible for this moment than any of us. Besides, I'm bored and I could use Sammy around to help pass the time. We could swap prisoner stories."

Despite the American's appalling manners, Levin found something likeable about him. As he walked away from the trucks, toward the growing frenzy of activity around the pile of material slowly taking shape atop the Temple Mount, Levin clicked the field radio attached to the epaulet on his left shoulder. "Is Fischoff's squad still at the detention center? Good. Tell him to grab the two Americans and bring them along on his way back. No, we're not letting them loose. Not on your life. I think Mr. Rodriguez would enjoy the company."

⸻⁓⁓⁓⸻

"Major?" Levin's radio came to life with the voice of Mossad's deputy director.

"Yes?"

"Mordechai here. We just caught a break. One of our informants relayed information about the two kidnapped American women. They're being held at the Citadel. Could be in a sub-basement cell off the Alley of Secrets or at the pinnacle of David's Tower."

"They're still alive? That's good news," said Levin. "What are we going to do?"

"Something fast," said Mordechai. "The informant warned that their captors—not sure who they are—just canceled a deadline and they are planning to execute both of them. And the execution will be televised. What do you have available?"

"Not much," said Levin.

"I know . . . you've got to keep your men on-site. God only knows what's in store for you tonight. And I don't want to engage your reserve. Do we have any mobile units who aren't at the Mount?"

Levin dropped his head to his chest. This was insane. But he didn't have much choice.

"I've got a heavy squad in two armored Humvees on their way here."

"Send them!"

"They've got Bohannon and Rizzo . . . I told them to bring them from the detention center so the Americans could watch the Tent being erected . . . figured they deserved that before we kicked them out of the country. I can't—"

"Send them," said Mordechai. "My authority and responsibility. We need to get there an hour ago. Send them, Avram."

⌒⌒⌒

The Humvee rounded a curve going up an incline—some kind of entry ramp. Buildings were swimming past in the shroud of night. A small, black box, sitting on the floor between the driver and the sergeant, came to life. Lights flashed on and off at its corners and an insistent buzzing split the silence. The sergeant pushed a red button on the top of the box.

"Tiger One. We've made the pickup and we're bringing them to you as planned. Twenty minutes out."

"Plans have changed. Which one is with you?"

"Bohannon."

The silence produced a noticeable firming of the sergeant's shoulders. He pushed himself even straighter in his seat.

"Mr. Bohannon . . . I know you can hear our conversation. This is Major Levin—we met at Miss Nolan's apartment. We have received information concerning your wife and Miss Nolan."

Bohannon's world stopped.

"From what we've been told, they are alive."

Hope!

"We have a source who gave us information that, if true, may lead us to where the women are being held."

They're alive! Thank God—they're alive.

"Sergeant Fischoff, I have no one else to send. We have also been informed that elements of the Martyrs' Brigade, Hezbollah, and other groups are planning an attack on the Temple Mount. I don't have anybody else . . . I can't spare any of our men here. You and your team are to divert from plan. You are to reroute and head for the Citadel at all possible speed. The women are being held in the Citadel—at the top of David's Tower or in an underground cell, we're not sure."

"And the prisoners?"

"You don't have the time to bring them here. You will have to take them with you. Just get to the Citadel as quickly as possible."

The Humvee made a hard left.

"Major Levin," Bohannon called from the back seat. "You said my wife was alive. You know that for a fact, right? So why are we—" He stopped as the probable answer flooded his mind.

"There has been a threat . . . a deadline." Levin's voice was as flat and lifeless as the black box it emerged from. "But the kidnappers just threw the deadline out the window. Sergeant, you must get there quickly. And you and your team, you are on your own.

"Keep the prisoners safe, as best you can. But the women are your assignment. Get there. Find them. There's not much time."

⌒⌒⌒

There were now nearly as many priests and rabbis on the platform as there were soldiers. They moved in what appeared to be random cycles, measuring heights and distances between poles, widths of openings. A score were inspecting the huge bundles of hides and curtains piled carefully on canvas sheets that covered the concrete. Levin walked over to the mounds of coverings that would soon be draped over the poles.

"We were most careful in loading them," said one rabbi to a robed priest. "That is why it took us so long to get here."

"The hides are so brittle, I am fearful they will break apart when we try to open them and fasten them to the poles."

"Yes, they are brittle to the touch," said the rabbi, "but they won't break. Two of the soldiers dropped one as we were loading—one tripped over a stone. There was no crack in it. Nothing broke. We lifted up a corner to look for damage and the hide opened easily."

The priest looked over at the rabbi with a mix of disbelief and wonder. "A miracle?"

"No," said the rabbi, "*another* miracle."

Levin turned his mind back to his defenses. *Another miracle will be if we get away with this.*

2:11 a.m.

Sergeant Fischoff swiveled left into the space between the two front seats and crouched, face-to-face with Bohannon. He placed a hand on the back of each seat to keep himself balanced while the Humvee—now with its lights flashing and a low siren preceding it—rocked through a series of high-speed turns and evasion maneuvers. Bohannon, his hands manacled, a seat belt tight across his hips, was still tossed back and forth on the back seat. Fischoff studied Bohannon with the intensity of an inquisitor and the compassion of a man who probably had his own wife and family.

"If it was me," said the sergeant, "I would go absolutely insane sitting in this truck while other people attempted to rescue my wife from danger. From what I know of you, I have to believe you would make my life very difficult if I tried to leave you in this wagon."

Bohannon began to hope once more.

"Here's what I'll do," said the sergeant. "My orders were to bring you to the Temple Mount. Now my orders are to keep you safe. I'm going to follow my orders. And you are going to make sure that I do."

The driver stomped on the brakes and jerked the vehicle to the right, its back tires in a skid before it straightened out and resumed its headlong flight through the streets leading to the Old City.

"Sorry, sergeant."

Fischoff picked himself off the floor and helped Bohannon back into a sitting position. The sergeant reached into the breast pocket of his fatigue shirt, pulled out a key, and unlocked the manacles on Bohannon's wrists.

"Thanks."

"Okay . . . you need to follow my orders—immediately, completely, and without hesitation or reservation. Do you understand that?"

"Yes, sergeant."

"You will remain behind me at all times. I repeat . . . you will remain behind me at all times, no matter what happens, no matter what we see or hear. Do you understand?"

"Yes, sergeant."

"Do you know how to use a gun?"

Bohannon felt a queer surge of apprehension and power. "No."

Fischoff pulled a nine-millimeter automatic from the holster on his hip. He pushed back a large button just off the top of the gun. "Safety. Push it back to shoot. Then just aim and pull the trigger. One shot at a time. More than that, and you'll never hit anything. Got it?"

Adrenaline swept through Bohannon's body like a river at flood stage. What surprised him was the hunger . . . the lust for revenge. He was stunned, disappointed, when Fischoff put the gun back into its holster.

"Don't even think about it," said the sergeant, "unless something happens to me. If it does, then grab the weapon and do the best you can. There will be six of us on the ground. So, please, try not to kill anyone on our side, okay?"

"Yes, sergeant."

An X-ray machine couldn't have examined Bohannon any more thoroughly than Fischoff did at that moment. Bohannon could feel the sergeant searching for certainty.

"I need your word. Will you obey my commands?"

Bohannon leaned forward, resting his arms on his knees. "Sergeant, I'd give you one of my limbs, if necessary, to go with you. I'd give my own life to save my wife's life. So, don't worry. I'll do whatever you tell me to do."

Fischoff gave Bohannon another hard stare, as if there might be something hidden in Tom's eyes that would help him come to a decision.

"Three minutes, sergeant."

"Right." Nodding his head, Fischoff extended his hand toward Bohannon. "Don't get hurt, or you'll cost me my stripes."

Fischoff swung back into his seat and toggled the radio. "Corporal, you heard our orders, correct?"

"Yes, sergeant."

"Okay, read Mr. Rizzo the rules. If he accepts, keep him on your hip at all times. Our orders are to keep him safe. If he refuses to agree, attach his manacles to the floor rings so that he has to lie on the floor. That's the best we'll be able to do to keep him safe in the vehicles. We're going through the Armenian Quarter. Come up to the Citadel from the south. Turn off into David's Garden and pull up tight against the outside wall. They could be in the dungeon or on the Pinnacle. You take the cellar. Move fast, but smart. Let's go silent." The driver killed the siren and the flashing lights.

Bohannon's mind was traveling as fast at the Humvee. He thought of Annie and Kallie . . . were they . . . okay? He couldn't bear to even fear the worst. That was up to God. Then he felt shame and remorse—was God really with him? Now that he despaired so much? Now that his faith had failed him? Then he thought of the Citadel. And his fear returned. Would there be a fight? Shooting?

"Here, quick, put this on," said Fischoff, handing Bohannon a thick jacket of body armor.

Looking at the armored jacket, Bohannon's mettle began to crack. Did he really have the courage to risk his life, give his life in return for Annie's safety? He always thought that he did. Now he would find out. He thought of Doc, of Winthrop Larsen, and the fear began to live a life of its own in the pit of his stomach. Doc was dead—in a coffin on his way back to the States. Winthrop was dead, blasted all over 35th Street by a Prophet's Guard bomb. Would more die? Would *he* die? Would Annie— no, he couldn't go there.

2:15 a.m.

Clasped to the poles by brass rings, the curtains of the Tent of Meeting now hung from all four of its sides. There were upright poles in heavy brass stands and, connected to the upright poles, the framing wood ran horizontally from pole to pole. It was from these horizontal rails at the top of the frame that the hides now hung down, obscuring the work being done inside the Tent itself as the Sanctuary was erected. The Tent was huge . . . one hundred and fifty feet on each side, seventy-five feet across its breadth.

The pace and demeanor of the priests and rabbis scurrying over the Mount elevated from hurried to frantic as more material was carried inside the enclosure to erect the inner Sanctuary—the Holy Place and, inside that, the Most Holy Place which, in the time of Moses, had been the home of the Ark of the Covenant.

Activity in the skies also became more frenetic, and much louder. Not long after construction of the Tent began, media helicopters flocked toward the Mount, their spotlights searching out visual images to send across the airways. They didn't get close. Phalanxes of military helicopters hunted down every civilian craft that ventured near the Old City and drove them off into the distance—twice unleashing 50-caliber bursts in the vicinity of the more daring pilots. Now Israeli gunships hovered at the four corners of the platform, pairs of helicopters circled around the perimeter of the Old City, and individual choppers continued to flash across the top of the Temple Mount from random directions.

On a regular basis, the whine and thunder of fighter jets could also be heard crisscrossing the sky above.

⌐∿∕∿⌐

The Humvee jumped the curb on a tight, curving street, drove across the grass of a small park, and came to a violent halt, its right front fender intimately close to a long wall of golden-hued Jerusalem stone that towered above their heads. Bohannon pulled on the flak jacket.

"Let's go. Bohannon, you're with me." Fischoff pressed the shoulder mic. "Two-by-two, corporal. Through the gate. Then bear right, to the stairs."

Fischoff squeezed through the right side door. Bohannon stood with the driver by the left fender, conscious of his empty hands as he watched the four soldiers cradle their Uzis in front of their chests.

"You okay?"

Tom looked down into the face of Sammy Rizzo. The wise guy was long gone.

"Scared," said Tom, "but, yeah."

"Remember when we were here last time?" said Rizzo. "Seems like a lifetime ago."

Just south of the Jaffa Gate, the Citadel—commonly but inaccurately called David's Tower—had been planted on the most exposed flank of Jerusalem since long before the time of Herod the Great. Every conqueror had added to this stronghold, which held a dominant view over the Old City—Herod built three massive towers; the Romans expanded and strengthened the walls; the Ottoman Turks added a soaring minaret. Was it only one month ago that Bohannon, Rizzo, Rodriguez, and Doc stood on the parapet of the Citadel, staring across the Old City to the Dome of the Rock and the Temple Mount? Yes, a lifetime ago.

"Weapons check," whispered the sergeant, pulling Bohannon into the dangerous present.

Standing erect, Fischoff was smaller than Bohannon realized. Taut, sinuous muscles defined his arms and legs. The sergeant looked like the kind of guy who could eat nails for breakfast. He looked over his expanded squad and motioned the first two soldiers down along the ancient stone wall. Rizzo, his armored vest slipping and sliding with every step, jogged to keep up with the fast-moving corporal.

Halfway down the wall, the first group stopped. They were on a narrow lane, the Old City wall on their right. Bohannon could hear steady activity on the Hativat Yerushalayim, the main road to his left, traffic winding around the Old City even at this hour.

Fischoff led off at a trot, paused momentarily next to the first pair of soldiers, then moved again along the wall, stopping just short of a narrow wooden door. It was padlocked from the outside.

Fischoff's driver stepped forward, reached into the right thigh pocket of his fatigue pants, and pulled out a stout, but compact, cutting tool. He wrapped the blades around the hasp of the rusty old lock, and squeezed.

Rizzo and his group arrived at the sound of the dull snap. The corporal's group crossed to the far side of the door and crouched against the wall, mimicking Fischoff's group. Bohannon, crouching between the sergeant and his driver, could sense the eye contact between sergeant and corporal. The corporal's hand reached out and opened the door as if a bolt of lightning was waiting to be loosed from the other side.

Fischoff glanced inside, left, along the angle of the open door. Inching it farther open, he tucked his head around for a glance in the opposite direction. They were in shadow, below the lights that illuminated the walls of old Jerusalem. Fischoff nodded his head forward. First the driver moved around Bohannon and the sergeant, slipped inside the door to its far side, and turned his body and his Uzi to cover their backs as they came through the wall. Then it was Rizzo, trailing his team. When Fischoff broke, he didn't stop on the other side of the door as the others had but ran straight and low across the open space and ducked under the overhang of a portico.

Bohannon hesitated.

The ground in the open space, a courtyard in its distant past, was a honeycomb of sinkholes and raised edges, collapsing in some places, sticking up like ragged fingers in others.

The sergeant had raced across what looked like the top of an old wall, maybe twelve inches across, with gaping holes falling away intermittently on both sides. With others running up behind him, Bohannon was forced to move. He sucked in a desperate breath, focused his eyes on his feet, and ran. Fischoff was waiting. His scowl asked the question for him.

"Caught me by surprise," said Bohannon, his voice barely a whisper. "Just a little intimidated by—"

"Let's go," Fischoff hissed. "Down," he said to the corporal, pointing to the stairs, then spun on his heel and led Bohannon and the driver into the dark of the ancient Citadel.

—∾∿∾—

"What's your name?"

"Fischoff."

Bohannon and the sergeant were pressed into a small alcove under the stairs leading to David's Tower, catching their breath, looking for any movement and listening for any sound from above.

"No, your first name."

"Sergeant."

Their whispers traveled inches. Their eyes and ears stretched to unknown heights.

There were two towers lifting a hundred feet from the floor of the Citadel. The far tower was clearly a creation of the Crusaders, as square and solid as the Germanic knights who erected it after the second great European invasion. It was one of the corner battlements of the fortress, an integral part of the walls. Above them a second tower stretched into the sky. This one was also squat and square at the bottom, fastened to the wall of the Citadel by centuries of mortar and old stone. At the top of the wall's first rampart, the tower left the security of the fortress wall and became a round minaret visible throughout the city. At its peak, the spiral flattened out again and supported a square room with balconies from which the imams would call the faithful to prayer.

Sergeant Fischoff looked up at the spiraling tower, then over toward the square Crusader tower. There was a ten- to twelve-foot gap between the square tower and the platform pinnacle of the Islamic minaret. Bohannon watched, perspiration spreading across his forehead, as the sergeant looked back and forth between the two towers. He appeared to be uncertain, choosing his route.

"If it were me," Fischoff whispered to himself, "I'd be in the square tower . . . two men guarding the base . . . the rest at the top. Easier to defend. Easier to escape."

The sergeant stiffened. He was getting ready. He turned his head to the driver. "Stay here. Make sure no one comes out of those towers except us . . . and the women."

He met Bohannon's eyes. "Stay close."

Before Bohannon could respond, the sergeant bolted out of the stone alcove.

⸻

Rizzo expended every ounce of energy as he struggled to keep pace with the Israeli soldiers darting ahead of him, one running past the other, taking point, while his partner mimicked his moves. A few dirty window panes, set high in the walls, filtered the orange, mercury-vapor lights washing the Old City walls, creating a heavy twilight into the corridor under the Citadel. The considerable layer of dust on the cobblestone floor muffled their steps but clogged their throats. Tourists weren't permitted in these winding catacombs—storage rooms and stables for a thousand years—and it smelled like the stalls hadn't been cleaned in that long. Even though there were no other footprints in the dust—at least from this direction—the soldiers paused at every opening, swept each room with their eyes and their Uzis, before swiftly moving on. Rizzo's legs were cramping.

They came to a fork in the corridor. The corporal peeked down both shafts of retreating stone walls, looked at his partner, tapped two fingers under his eyes, and then pointed to the right. Before Rizzo could blink, the soldier was gone and the corporal spun around to face Rizzo, only inches away. Rizzo's eyes bulged as the corporal grabbed his shirt and yanked him nearer. "Close," he whispered.

⸻

Fischoff selected the Crusader tower. Bohannon didn't care. He figured they would be easy targets no matter which stairway they chose. Now much more deliberate, Fischoff placed his back against the stone wall just inside the tower's entrance, then side-stepped his way along the wall, never taking his eyes off the highest point of the circular stairs as they rose out of his view. Bohannon followed suit, two feet behind the sergeant. Before the first step, Fischoff stopped and tipped the barrel of his machine gun down toward the stairs. Bohannon could easily detect the marks of boot prints on the steps—going up. He tensed, set his body, and was ready to run up the steps, but Fischoff's burly right arm barred the way. The sergeant caught Bohannon's eyes, his arm pressing harder into Tom's chest. Bohannon got the message.

The sergeant removed his arm, then reached down to his holster, pulled out the automatic, turned the butt end around to Bohannon, and handed him the gun. Tom felt the cold metal in his hand, but he was now sweating so hard that the gun nearly slipped to the floor. He felt its weight—heavier than he expected. He felt its power, and blood began to beat through his temples. He looked up from his fascination with the weapon. Fischoff had his palm up, toward Bohannon. He tapped his chest and walked his fingers up the stairs. He held up his palm again, then pointed at Bohannon, pointed at Bohannon's eyes, and reached around and touched his own back.

Watch his back.

Spit was impossible, breathing almost as difficult. Bohannon squeezed the nine millimeter in his palm and nodded his head. He was going to get up those stairs one way or another. If it had to be protecting the sergeant's back, fine. But he was going up.

The sergeant swung his head, shoulders, and machine gun around, fixed the uppermost segment in his sight, and started up the stairs.

⸺⌇⌇⸺

Rizzo and the corporal came to the last door in the corridor. The corporal pushed his back against the wall alongside the closed door and looked down at Rizzo, who had done the same. At the first four rooms they encountered, the doors were open, the corporal swept the room quickly, and Rizzo could swallow again. Now Rizzo's heart was racing faster than when he'd been running to keep pace with the soldiers. He placed his hands against the wall for support, bit his lip, and waited for the corporal to try the door. Instead, the corporal held the Uzi against his chest with his right hand. With his left, he reached behind his back, unsnapped the cover on a small holster clipped to his utility belt, and pulled out a small, black automatic pistol. He handed it to Rizzo.

About time, kibbutznik! Rizzo hefted the gun in his hand. *Now we're talking. Let's go.*

The corporal reached down to his left and snapped the safety on the automatic forward. He pointed with his left hand, index finger straight out, thumb in the air.

Armed . . . got it! Rizzo nodded. He was surprised. His hands were steady. He felt calm . . . purposeful.

The corporal returned both hands to his Uzi and turned his attention to the door. He inched to his right, away from Rizzo, closer to the frame. Taking his palm, he placed it tenderly against the wood and pressed. It didn't budge. The latch was on the far side of the door panel. The corporal glanced momentarily to his left, toward Rizzo.

Don't worry about me, buster.

Tapping the wall with his knuckle, the corporal pointed down to the floor. Rizzo stayed put. The corporal moved to the other side of the door. It was a gamble. Rizzo knew the door opened in. He would get the first look into the room. He would be vulnerable. But the corporal would have the full room in view from his vantage point once he threw the door open. Rizzo raised the small automatic and held it with both hands.

Don't kill the kibbutznik.

———∽∿∾∽———

Bohannon followed the sergeant, his back against the wall, his head swinging back and forth, trying to look ahead and behind at the same time. The boot tracks on the steps kept rising above them. They were up four flights of the square tower, about halfway, when they heard the first gunshots.

Bohannon ducked and looked up the stairs.

The sergeant was looking down. The shots came from below . . . then more of them. Tap-tap-tap . . . three more in succession. Then a burst of automatic fire. And the sergeant was racing up the stairs.

———∽∿∾∽———

Fischoff was running like a man possessed, Bohannon right on his heels, running as fast as his legs could possibly pump. Fischoff was younger, in much better shape, and had the training, and soon he was half a flight ahead of Bohannon, taking the stairs two at a time like a hurdler reaching for the finish line. Without pausing for a moment, Fischoff burst onto the upper platform. Bohannon stumbled, looked up, and the sergeant was gone. Left or right? The muscles in his legs ready to ripsaw through his skin, Bohannon reached the platform to the sound of splitting wood.

There was one room at the top of the stairs, occupying half of the upper platform, its door to the left. Bohannon wrapped both hands around the gun's grip and took two long strides toward the door as something crashed against a wall inside the room.

Bohannon leveled the gun, his finger off the trigger, and turned into the room. Fischoff was standing over a shattered table, a terrible look of despair on his face. Tom quickly scanned the room. There was a black backdrop against the far wall, with a design at its center—the Coptic cross with the lightning bolt slashing through on the diagonal. The sign of the Prophet's Guard. In front of the backdrop were two chairs and two video cameras. A small satellite dish pointed out the only window.

Draped over the back of one of the chairs was a piece of cloth—blue cotton with a floral print. Bohannon knew what it was. A piece of Annie's nightshirt. He had seen it too many times. It probably still had her smell. He stumbled toward the two chairs, reached down, and picked up the cloth. It was one of the sleeves and the bottom half of the torn fabric was stained, wet, sticky. A reddish-brown stain ran down the back of the chair.

Bohannon's eyes went wide and a primordial scream boiled up from the depths.

"Oh . . . my God . . . oh, my . . ."

Blood from the cloth now stained his fingers as Bohannon squeezed the fabric.

"How could you! God . . . how could you!"

Bohannon wiped his hand on his pants, leveled the gun toward the black backdrop, and emptied half the clip into the sign of the amulet hanging on the wall.

〜〜〜

As echoes of gunshots reverberated off the stone walls and through Tom's head, Fischoff grabbed his arm and pulled him toward the door.

"C'mon . . . they can't be far ahead."

The sergeant raced from the room, turned right, and was out the small door that led onto the tower's rampart. Bohannon stumbled after him, only half aware of what he was doing.

When Fischoff reached the edge of the platform, he stopped and looked across the gap of open air, and then down toward the ground. "Look!" he shouted.

Bohannon closed his eyes. He couldn't look down.

"They must have crossed to the other tower on those boards!"

With that declaration, and a slight pause, Fischoff hurled himself off the top of the square Crusader tower and onto the muezzin's porch—the balcony from which Islam's faithful were called to prayer—on the Muslim spire. Fischoff landed on the far platform with both boots, his body leaning forward, and stumbled two steps to the wall of the minaret.

Bohannon stood frozen in place, his eyes riveted on the open sky between this tower and the other—probably ten feet, but it looked like a hundred. Annie . . . Kallie . . . could they have gotten across? Impulsively, Bohannon looked over the edge and saw the planks, a long way down. His head started swimming, a current like cold electricity shivered through his muscles, his stomach felt like an airplane in turbulence. He gripped the balustrade. There were no bodies on the ground—yet.

"Move man! Jump!"

Only a heartbeat had passed. Fischoff hesitated for only a moment on the other side, then thrust himself through an opening on the porch and into the minaret's interior.

Annie! The renewed thought of his wife suffering and bleeding somewhere restored the steel in Bohannon's spine. He pushed two steps back, accelerated with all the strength he had gained in his high-intensity bike rides with Connor, and launched himself from the very edge of the balcony, arms flailing, legs racing into that place that had no bottom. Except way down there, ninety feet below.

A split second? An hour? A day? Time stood still for Tom Bohannon as he fought against distance and gravity.

Falling.

His eyes and heart and hope were fixed on the far balcony, coming no nearer. He wished away fear, but fear was flying with him. And neither of them were getting any closer.

He felt the falling, and it was real. His body on a downward arc, not a crossward flight. Panic grasped for mastery, but Bohannon grasped for life, he grasped for Annie, he grasped for that far, stone spiral . . .

He crashed hard onto the stone floor of the balcony with a shoulder-shuddering, knee-ripping thud as the front of his forehead came down and violently kissed the stone. The world blackened, then brightened, then the pain poured through him. Something was probably broken, but he was up before the thought could penetrate his resolve. Stumbling through the doorway into the minaret, he was surprised to find that Fischoff was not that far in front of him. It hadn't been that long. The sergeant was bounding down the circular stairs, but not that far in front.

3:15 a.m.

Colonel Levin took the radio receiver out of his ear as Major Abner Katz ran up to his side.

"We may have a problem."

Levin focused his full attention on the major. "Only one?"

"I sent out two squads of men—one to roam around underneath us and sweep the caverns, and the other into the archaeological digs of the Ophel . . . places where men could hide. The squad that went through the Ophel digs just got back. That's all clear and the troops on that side of the valley are keeping a close watch. But we've lost contact with the squad that went under the Mount. They could just be out of radio contact down there. But . . . I don't like it. I sent twenty men down to look for them."

Now robed priests were carrying golden lampstands past Levin and Katz, who stood just to the side of the Tent's open portal.

I truly can't believe what I'm seeing.

"The reinforcements?"

Major Katz shook his head. "The streets in this part of the city are a mess. With the Jerusalem and Jericho highways shut down completely and most of the roads around the Old City closed to civilian traffic, the streets that are left open are a parking lot, clogged with people trying to get a look at what we're doing here. Those reinforcements have just abandoned their trucks and are on their way to us, on foot, double-time. Shouldn't be long."

The singsong prayers of massed priests and rabbis rose from inside the Tent enclosure. Levin watched as a second tent, smaller, covered with animal skins, rose inside the outer walls. Four priests—led by four singers and followed by four singers—carried a long, golden table down the length of the platform and into the enclosed area. "No . . . it shouldn't be long," Levin agreed. "They'll have to wait for sunrise, but it sounds like they're ready."

⌇⌇⌇

Fischoff cradled the Uzi in the crook of his left arm, his right hand skidding along a thin, metal railing mounted on the outside wall of the descending spiral stairs. Bohannon, on the other hand, discovered that his right shoulder was not responding to the neuron signals of his brain, his right knee throbbed, and something seeped into the corner of his right eye; likely blood, but he had no way to test that theory. The gun held aloft in his left hand, Bohannon lurched down the stairs, out of control, his muscles desperately trying to exert some influence on his runaway body, and failing miserably. And he was gaining on Fischoff.

Fischoff slowed near the bottom of the stairs and stopped at the last step. His face was turned to the doorway leading out of the tower. He didn't see Bohannon glance off the stone wall to his right, or carom against the inside railing to his left . . . didn't see him until Bohannon's rampaging body catapulted past him and hurtled toward the open doorway.

The flat ground at the bottom of the spire accomplished what the circular stairs failed to do. Bohannon's knees buckled and he crashed, sprawling through the door and onto the stone walkway outside.

Fischoff was instantly at his side, kneeling, his back to Bohannon and his attention on the open square around them.

Pushing against his elbows and knees, Bohannon elevated his head and shoulders and looked across the open expanse of the Citadel. It was empty except for shadowy forms that materialized into the corporal, the other two men in his squad, and Rizzo, running toward them from the direction of the front gate.

There was no sign of Annie or Kallie. Bohannon sagged.

"A brown Mazda sedan pulled out of here just moments after we split into two groups. We found a porter outside who saw it go by."

The sergeant spit out a Hebrew word that had the sound of how Bohannon felt. It must have been profane.

"Great . . . there are probably a thousand brown Mazdas in Israel tonight. The shots?"

The corporal looked over at Rizzo, who was bent at the waist, gasping for air.

"C'mon, tell me while we get to the Humvees," said Fischoff, who took off at a gallop, his men in close stride. "Get up, Bohannon," he shouted over his shoulder, "or we'll leave you behind."

As Sergeant Fischoff and his men ran back toward the vehicles, he was already on the radio.

"We missed them. They've taken the women. We think they're still alive."

On the other end of the radio, Major Levin cursed.

"Your assignment is to find those women, and find them alive." The edge in Levin's voice could cut a rock. "What do you know?"

"A witness told us a brown Mazda sedan pulled out of the Citadel. They waited until we split up and entered the fortress. Sir, we think they're headed west. My guess is that they're running for Gaza. Can we get something in the air to track them?"

"Negative, sergeant," Levin's voice crackled. "Everything I have at my disposal is tied up in and around the Temple Mount. You're the closest. If they're headed for the Strip, they'll stay off the major highways. They've got to take either the Thirty-Eight or the Forty-One. Even a brown Mazda, moving fast, shouldn't be hard to spot. I'm sorry, Sergeant, but you're on your own."

Fischoff grabbed the corporal by the shoulder as they ran around the corner of the Citadel and came to the Humvees. "Take the Ashdod Road. I'll be on the Thirty-Eight to Ashkelon. Traffic should be light, but I don't know, with much of the city being locked down. And I don't care. Move, fast. Our only hope is that they are running to Gaza. If so, they're still on the road. If they've gone to ground somewhere else, we're screwed. So get moving. Don't let anything stop you. Run every brown Mazda you see off the road, I don't care. Just find those women."

They piled into the Humvees, but Fischoff stood on the running board and hollered over the roof. "And stay on your radio. I want to know everything that's going on."

―∞∽―

Ten minutes later, the corporal toggled his radio switch. "Nothing yet. Too much traffic."

"What happened at the Citadel?" The sergeant's voice showed the strain of the long night and their empty quest.

"The basement corridor forked about fifty meters in," said the corporal. "Rizzo and I went left. There were four of them in the last room we swept. They were wiring up bricks of C-4. Some well-placed explosives down there could have destroyed half the Citadel."

"But I heard single shots," said the sergeant.

The corporal nodded his head and smiled into the back seat. Rizzo gave him a thumbs-up, but it brought no smile to his face. "We cracked the door and somebody inside started shooting. I shoved it open and there were two, just inside the door, against the wall. I couldn't see them. Mr. Rizzo did. Three shots before anyone could react. Took them both. The others I got."

3:48 a.m.

More Israeli soldiers were coming through the tunnels below the Temple Mount. The Hezbollah commander stepped around the dead bodies of the first squad and addressed his second-in-command. "I don't care what he said. We've got to move now. Send ten men. Ambush them at the crossroads. Then lead the Martyrs' Brigade up the steps." He looked at his watch. "Even if we don't hear from him, ten minutes, then over the edge of the platform."

Without waiting for a response, the Hezbollah commander turned quickly and waved his men forward. The beams of the high-density flashlights, carried by the men behind him, bounced off the walls of the low-ceilinged tunnel as the men ran crouched at the waist up the steep incline. Nearly seven hundred years old, the tunnel had been dug from the foundation of the Al-Aqsa Mosque as a precaution—a way to escape if the infidel Crusaders ever returned. Now it led to a section of the concrete rigged with explosives . . . explosives that would blow the concrete out, onto the platform, and into the eyes of Israeli soldiers. At the back end of this long string of Muslim soldiers were ten who struggled under the weight on an immense burlap bag.

3:55 a.m., Tel Aviv

"What about the women? There hasn't been any word."

Baruk paused before responding. He wanted better news for the American president.

"We received a tip that they were being held in David's Tower . . . to be executed, on live television, if we didn't withdraw from the Temple Mount. Our men got there quickly. Can you believe they have Rizzo and Bohannon with them? But the kidnappers fled before we could capture them. We think the women are still alive, with the captors. We think they are making a run for the safety of the Gaza Strip. Our men are in pursuit. But . . ."

"But you're not sure where they are?" said the president. "Well, maybe this is something I can help you with."

4:26 a.m., Jerusalem

Levin and Katz were at the south end of the platform, near the place where the Al-Aqsa Mosque once stood. They were moving fast, a small squad of men in their wake, when the singing stopped. Levin pulled up and looked back at the tent.

"Now what?"

4:29 a.m., Balata Camp, Nablus, West Bank

The telephone on the table rang. Al-Sadr reached it before the second ring.

"Speak."

He listened, then slapped the handset into the cradle and looked up at Youssef.

"The singing has stopped. Send them."

Moussa al-Sadr opened his own cell phone again and pressed a speed dial number. When it was answered, there was no greeting.

"You know where he is," said al-Sadr. "He won't be there long. This is your mission. Strike at the heart of the Zionists. Go with Allah."

4:44 a.m., Jerusalem

The blast slammed Levin's body backward and drove him to the concrete, but not before he felt a crushing blow to his right side. Gunfire erupted around him, not the heavy thumping of the perimeter fifty-caliber machine guns, but the staccato bursts of automatic weapons. His ears were ringing. His right side failed to respond, so Levin pushed himself up with his left arm. He nearly vomited from the pain in his right side . . . and the sight of Abner Katz, his head half severed from his body by a shard of concrete almost as long as his arm.

The gunfire was fierce in every direction, shouts of *Allahu Akbar!* and the screams of the wounded and dying. Two arms hooked under his armpits and grasped his shoulders, one on each side. The Israeli soldiers had closed ranks and were returning fire as Levin was pulled toward the center of the Temple Mount platform. As he was being dragged away from the raging firefight, he could see two things more clearly. One was a steady stream of Muslim fighters pouring onto the platform from a ragged hole of smoking concrete, surrounding and wiping out the machine gun batteries on the southern end. The other was the heavy trail of blood left behind by his dragged body.

⌒〰⌒

With his hands shackled in front of him, the explosion threw Rodriguez off the hood of the truck and onto the concrete at the platform's edge, knocking the wind out of his lungs. As he struggled to his feet and stumbled toward the front of the truck, a relentless cacophony of rapid arms fire raced across the surface of the platform. All hell had erupted and every soldier nearby was running to the sound of the guns. Except one. One of Joe's guardians stopped short, spun around, ran back to the truck, and tossed him a set of keys. Then he was off again, following his brothers in arms.

Rodriguez removed the shackles from his legs and wrists. For a split second, he wondered what to do. Then a lethal spray of bullets clanged off the metal side of the truck. Without thinking, he jumped up into the small space between the cab and the body of the hauler. Not as exposed, he felt safer. Unsure of what attention he might attract if he took off running, or the response a running man might get from the Israeli soldiers, Rodriguez figured the best course at the moment was to stay put. And keep his head down as much as possible.

From his hiding place, he still had a clear view across the Temple Mount platform, a clear view of the vicious ferocity unleashed on the far side of the concrete slab, and a clear view of the Tent of Meeting, standing in the midst of a raging gun battle between Israeli soldiers and a small army of Muslim fighters who were pouring out from under the concrete at the far end of the platform.

4:59 a.m., On the Ashkelon Road

Bohannon's world was a blur. . . blackness broken by sporadic slashes of light quickly left behind. Since breaking out of the snarled traffic in the city, they were speeding at a manic pace. Jerusalem's suburbs were far behind, the Humvee racing through hills and farmland as the Jerusalem Heights fell away to the Mediterranean basin.

Both Sergeant Fischoff and the driver slipped into silence as reports came in over the radio of the battle on the Temple Mount. But there was no report from the other team. Tom found himself praying that this was good news. He was praying the prayer of the disillusioned, the prayer of the desperate.

God, I don't know why you've left me. I don't know what I did for you to punish me . . . to punish Annie . . . like this. I didn't want this. You called me into this. I thought this was what you wanted. That you had a plan for me. So why has it all gone so wrong? Why are you letting all this happen? What have I done, that is so bad, that you would abandon me like this?

"I will never leave you nor forsake you."

"What?" Tom lifted his head and saw that Fischoff was turned around in his seat, staring at him.

"It's part of our holy book, too," he said. "We got it before you did."

Bohannon's mind—scattered in so many directions—found it hard to focus. "What are you saying?"

Sergeant Fischoff once again swung into the space between the two front seats of the Humvee and crouched in front of Bohannon. "It's in the book of Joshua," he said. "Joshua was one of the greatest warriors, greatest leaders, in Jewish history. But when God first spoke to Joshua, three times he told him not to be afraid, to be strong and courageous. If Joshua wasn't afraid, if he wasn't feeling weak and fearful, why would God have talked to him like that?"

Bohannon stared at Fischoff.

"I looked back at you and I could tell," said the sergeant. "You feel like God's abandoned you. Like you don't even know what to pray. What's the point? Have you been listening to the radio reports?"

"Sounds like some kind of battle on the Temple Mount."

"Yeah, and it's not good. We're getting hammered. And I'm afraid it might be some of my friends up there. I'm worried about them. I want to turn around and go help."

Now the sergeant had Bohannon's attention.

"I was in Lebanon in oh-six. We got chewed up by Hezbollah. They knew our tactics and they ripped us to shreds. Sent us running back over the border. Worst defeat I've ever experienced. Where was God then? When my friends were dying all around me, where was God? How could he let this happen? Why had he forsaken his people?

"I felt just like you do now. I could feel that same kind of despair about what is happening on the Temple Mount right now. But there's one thing we need to remember. We're not God. We don't get to have all of life's questions answered for us before we start. We don't know what God's plan is. How can we ever expect to understand God's plan? But there is something we can understand. And that is what God has spoken to us. We have it in the Talmud. You have it in both the Old and the New Testaments.

"And when God first talked to Joshua—before Joshua ever did anything special, before he ever won any battle—God told him, 'No one will be able to stand up against you all the days of your life. As I was with Moses, so I will be with you; I will never leave you nor forsake you. Be strong and courageous.'" I don't know why either. But we don't always get *why*. What we get is, hang in there. We'll get your wife back, Mr. Bohannon." Fischoff pushed himself back into his seat, facing the windshield. "Just hang in there." He seemed to be talking to himself.

10:41 p.m. Eastern Daylight Time, Washington, DC

Jonathan Whitestone watched the video feed from the orbiting satellite. "You're certain?"

"We're getting reports from the ground as well," said Cartwright. "Our team, and others we have in Jerusalem. There is still fierce fighting—on top of the Temple Mount and in the surrounding streets. Hezbollah and Martyr's Brigade together. Don't know how, but they got inside the Israeli defenses."

"What are the Israelis doing?"

"Orhlon's got nearly the entire army on the move. They will crush whatever opposition they find on the ground in Jerusalem," said Cartwright. "What's more alarming for us are the number of men and the amount of ordnance Israel is deploying to its borders with Lebanon and Syria. And half their air force is in the sky. This could get a lot worse."

"How about the women . . . Bohannon?"

"Our birds are incoming now."

5:10 a.m., Western Israel

They came out of the blackness over the Mediterranean, skimming the wave tops so tightly that sea spray dripped from their undercarriages. Two helicopters flashed across the coastline into a desolate area between Israel and Gaza, south of Ashkelon. They were nearly invisible.

U.S. Army Commander Browne Counsil dialed in his wide-angle helmet display—showing flight info, night vision sensors, and sight system for use with weapons—as the Boeing-Sikorsky RAH-66 Comanche stealth helicopters lifted to one hundred feet and sped inland at two hundred miles an hour.

"Browne, you have any clue how we're supposed to find this needle in a haystack?"

"Sweep the two roads, look for a brown Mazda running like a bat out of hell. Take the Ashdod Road, Pete. And no chatter unless it's required."

Commander Counsil banked to the right and disappeared into the night.

5:17 a.m., Jerusalem

There was no preamble or salutation.

"How many men do you have within arm's reach that you can move right now?"

"Fifty, well-trained, heavy arms," Posner said to his commander, General Moishe Orhlon, Israel's defense minister.

"The Temple Mount is under attack . . . several hundred . . . Hezbollah and Martyrs' Brigade we think. Send the men now. You too."

"But . . . I can't raise Shomsky. He—"

"Forget Shomsky for now. Move. Men are dying."

5:25 a.m., On the Ashkelon Road

"I've been locked on for the last two minutes," Commander Counsil said into the radio. "This is the one. Brown Mazda . . . we've got him. Back me up, Pete."

Counsil was flying his Comanche sideways at sixty miles an hour, keeping pace with the small brown sedan that was tearing down the Ashkelon Road, east of Kiyrat Gat. Counsil's visor display showed him a small bridge coming up in a mile. He turned his nose west, goosed his fourteen hundred horsepower twin turbo shafts, and rocketed ahead.

The Comanche, the Army's latest development in the stealth arsenal of invisible power, was armed with fourteen Hellfire antitank missiles; fifty-six rockets; and a three-barreled, twenty millimeter, nose-mounted mini-gun that pumped out fifteen hundred rounds a minute. Browne Counsil had his pick of how to obliterate the bridge. He hovered, waiting, until the car rounded a distant curve. He set loose a "fire-and-forget" Hellfire missile, programmed to control its own flight to a target.

The small bridge erupted, steel, wood, and concrete flung upward by a growing fireball.

Commander Counsil watched the brown Mazda brake hard, skid sideways, and rumble onto the shoulder of the road, about twenty yards short of the smoking pile of rubble that once was a bridge.

⸺⌇⌇⸺

Bright orange flashed a false dawn over the low, brown hills, then died away into darkness once again. That was all it took. The Humvee was ripping down Thirty-Eight to Ashkelon at over eighty miles an hour and was already daring the law of gravity to keep its tires on the road.

In the flash and the black, the driver was blinded. He remembered seeing a curve before the flash and, with his eyes useless, he willed himself to sense the road under his wheels, the curve in the asphalt, the shifting weight from whatever banking might be in the road surface. He failed.

The Humvee bounced, slamming down hard on its springs. "Hold on!"

In a ballet of high-speed slow motion, the left front of the truck began to fall away into some void. The left front fender caught the ground and dug into the earth, and the Humvee flipped. It wouldn't have been so bad if they hadn't been going so fast. *Maybe we'll just land on the roof.* But the truck continued to rotate and hit the ground again with the front, right side of the cab, crushing the roof and doors into the passenger compartment with a force that buried the right side of the vehicle in two inches of brown dirt and clay. The Humvee sat, suspended, on its crushed right side, until the unseen hand of gravity or inertia continued its rotation and it slowly fell to its tires in an upright position.

The driver looked at his hands—still gripping the steering wheel as if he could somehow still steer them out of this wreck. He knew his left wrist was broken from when the wheel snapped violently on the first crash. Other than that, he was in one piece, saved by the seat belt he habitually wrapped across his chest.

He looked to his right. Sergeant Fischoff was lying drunkenly against the shattered remains of the right door and window. Glass shards protruded from his scalp, and an ugly gash, pulsing blood, ran down the left side of his neck.

The driver unbuckled his seat belt, pried the fingers of his left hand off the steering wheel, rested his left wrist against his chest, and reached toward the sergeant with his right hand, grabbing the sergeant's wrist. There was a pulse, but the sergeant was bleeding out. He wouldn't live long like this.

Twisting painfully further to his right, the driver looked into the back seat.

Bohannon's eyes were wide open . . . staring . . . in shock.

"Listen, sir, we've got to get the sergeant out of the vehicle."

Bohannon didn't move. Didn't look like he was about to move. The right side of his forehead was already shading from scarlet to deep purple, surrounding a golf-ball-size lump. His right arm hung limp from his shoulder—but it was like that from the Citadel

"Sir," the driver said, pumping urgency into his voice. "Sir . . . you've got to help me get the sergeant out of the vehicle. I can't do it by myself. And I can't treat his wound in here. If we don't get him outside now, he's going to bleed out and die. Sir! Do you hear me?"

Bohannon blinked.

Thank, God.

"Let's go . . . grab hold of the sergeant's shoulder and help me pull him out this side. C'mon . . . pull!"

5:32 a.m., Tel Aviv

"Send in the helicopters. Blow them to hell," said Prime Minister Baruk.

"We can't do that, sir." General Orhlon was on the other end of the telephone. "They're too close. The Muslims and our men are fighting right on top of each other."

Baruk stood in the living room of his private residence. This night, he didn't smell the brackishness of the sea or the sweet fragrance of the flowers outside the terrace. He smelled fear. His fear.

"What about the reinforcements?"

"Mr. Prime Minister, the reinforcements are on foot. They're on their way, but our men who were stationed around the base of the Mount are also under attack. It appears Muslim fighters are pouring out of houses in the entire quarter. Looks like Hezbollah and the Martyrs' Brigade, Elie."

Baruk knew what that meant . . . hardened fighters had infiltrated Jerusalem. This was a battle, not a skirmish.

"The Tent?"

"Still up, still protected," said Orhlon, "but I don't know for how long. Abner Katz is dead. Levin is in command, but I've been told he's gravely wounded. Captain Theodore would be the next in command, but no one has found him yet."

"All right . . . I'm coming in," said Baruk. "I'm going to the helipad now . . . be there in twenty minutes. And Moishe, find a way to protect that Tent."

Baruk cradled the telephone and was on his way to the door when his private cell phone vibrated in his pocket. He looked . . . it was Whitestone.

"Yes, Mr. President?"

"This doesn't look good, Elie. There's a helluva fight going on up there. We should call it off."

Baruk's bodyguards were anxious, shuffling around, looking out the window. And they were within listening distance. Baruk would have no privacy now until he was safely installed in Central Command. "I'm afraid not, Mr. President. We must push forward with all our resources. The command has already been given, the action has already been launched."

There was a pause on the other end. Whitestone was measuring his words. This call was not secure.

"You've got a battle raging in the center of Jerusalem," said the president, his voice revealing the depth of his concern. "Isn't that trouble enough?"

"It's our trouble, Jonathan. You know we always take care of our own trouble. We'll deal with it."

5:33 a.m., On the Ashkelon Road

It was cold. He didn't expect the cold. He looked up. Stars were out. But it was cold. He didn't expect the cold. He looked down. The stones on the ground were moving in circles. He looked to his right. A soldier was kneeling over the sergeant; bloody, seeping bandages pressed against the sergeant's neck.

The sergeant must be cold. He didn't expect it to be cold. He looked around. Everything seemed to be moving, but in slow motion. Must be the cold. Off to his left was a moldering, crimson horizon. Something happened there. What happened there—in the cold?

His mind cleared. Annie was out there . . . there was an explosion . . . *she's out there.* Then it fogged over once more.

Bohannon thought he was running. That was the message he was sending to his legs. But, really, his movement was more like a stumbling rumble. A well-intentioned lurching that covered almost as much ground side-to-side as it did forward. But he kept moving, his eyes on the glow, and the smoke, ignoring the cold.

5:34 a.m., Jerusalem

The pole at his back and a soldier by his side held Levin in a sitting position at the corner of the Tent of Meeting. Over the cacophony of gunfire surrounding him, Levin detected the sound of additional gunfire in the distance. The reinforcements, fighting their own battle. They would be too late.

He looked down at the hole in his right side, where his ribcage used to be. Too late. His men, what was left of them, were falling back, converging around the Tent. But there was no cover, no place to hide on the newly completed platform. And his men continued to die around him as the Muslim fighters kept coming, more of them, over the edge and out of the hole in the concrete.

≈≈≈

"How did you get there?" Sam Reynolds was so distraught that he sounded as if he was going to jump across the ocean. "Do you have any idea what's going on?"

Rodriguez moved the wristwatch away from his face . . . another of Sam's gadgets . . . as the gun battle raged in front of him. It looked like the Israeli soldiers were falling back—forced toward the center of the platform by an ever-growing force of Muslim fighters. Rodriguez pressed the button on the side of the watch that activated the satellite phone.

"Yeah . . . I know what's going on here," said Rodriguez. "The Israeli soldiers are getting hammered—Muslim soldiers have fought right through the Israeli positions and they are butchering every Jew on the Mount—soldiers, priests, rabbis, doesn't matter. They are pressing in on the Tent. They're going to get it, Sam. They're going to get it. And . . . there's a group skirting the fighting. They're dragging a large sack—a huge sack—dragging it with them toward the Tent. This is not good."

"Joe . . . listen to me," said Reynolds, a demanding urgency in his voice. "What I've got to tell you is not good, either."

—⁓∧⁓—

Levin held an automatic pistol in his left hand, but didn't have the strength to raise it. All he could do was sit and watch the carnage raging around him.

He saw a group of Muslims, ten men, dragging some strange cargo across the face of the platform, an immense burlap bag. They seemed oblivious to the warfare around them.

Bullets ripped through the hides hanging to his right, splitting open the enclosure wall around the inner sanctuary. The soldier next to him fell at his feet. Levin looked up as the Muslim fighters cleared a path through the few remaining Israeli soldiers. More fighters now joined the men pulling the burlap bag. They lifted it off the concrete. Levin believed he saw it move, but his attention was pulled away. There was no more shooting. A tall, fierce-looking Arab ran over to Levin and kicked the gun out of his hand. Levin thought he heard a squeal as the men passed him with the burlap bag and hurried to carry it inside the Tent.

"We have a sacrifice for your altar, Jew. Something to celebrate the completion of your new tabernacle." The Arab waved to some of his men. "Turn him around so he can watch the sacrifice . . . quickly."

Levin could hear the whomp of the helicopter blades coming close and knew the gunships would soon open fire when it was clear all of his men were dead. But above the noise of the oncoming choppers, Levin heard the squeal, louder, more frantic. Through the Tent's shattered side, Levin could see the entry curtains to the Most Holy Place were thrown aside. The burlap bag was cut open, lying atop the altar.

Trussed up, straining against its heavy rope bindings, a huge sow sprawled across the top of the altar and hung over each side. Several of the Muslim fighters pulled out knives. Some gutted the pig . . . some cut its main arteries. Blood and intestines and entrails defiled the golden altar and spread across the floor of the Most Holy Place, desecrating the sanctuary. One of the soldiers emptied an animal skin full of fluid over the pig's body and another threw a flame into it. Pig, altar, and the coverings of the Most Holy Place were ignited instantly and the fire raced along the ancient, hanging hides on both sides of the Tent of Meeting.

The Muslim leader moved in front of Levin, who was being held at the shoulders by two of his fighters. "Watch your blasphemy burn, Jew. There will never be a temple on the most holy Haram." The leader hitched his thumb toward the growing conflagration. The two fighters grabbed Levin's belt and shoulders and threw him into the raging flames.

⸺⸺⸺

Ali Hassan waved the fighters of his Martyrs' Brigade and those of Hezbollah toward the edges of the Temple Mount platform. Hassan and his aide ducked behind a sandbag wall, their backs to the burning Tent. "This victory will not last long." Hassan pointed toward the west. "Israeli gunships kept their distance while the battle was close, but now they will come."

⸺⸺⸺

Torn between his fears for Kallie and Annie, his grief over Doc's death, and the slaughter he was witnessing, Rodriguez's mind was numb as Reynolds finished his demoralizing report. He gazed blankly across the platform, seeing but not registering the chaos. He didn't know what to do next.

"They set the Tent on fire," Joe said, his voice as lifeless as the sprawled bodies littering the platform. "They hauled something into the Tent and then they set it on fire. Looks like all the Israeli soldiers are dead. I can hear the helicopters coming in now . . ."

"Stay where you are!" Reynolds demanded. "Those gunships see any movement and they may not wait to check your ID."

"Where am I going to go?" he asked. He saw flames rise from the Tent, the fire growing more intense. But his emotions had no life.

⸺⸺⸺

Two black gunships flashed overhead, from west to east, and immediately another pair came roaring out of the north. Hassan risked a look over the sandbag wall. Too many of his men were still in the open and they were shredded by the heavy cannon fire from the helicopters. Those who found refuge in the sandbag bunkers wrested from the Israeli machine gunners were blown out of their safety by one salvo of rocket fire after another.

We won't survive long.

The hair on the back of Hassan's head began to wilt, and he felt a sudden rush of heat against his back. He twisted his neck, expecting to see a crumbling mass of embers. Instead, the blaze that engulfed the Tent of Meeting appeared to be growing—broader, higher, and hotter.

What did we put in there?

A rippling stream of cannon fire flowed across the concrete toward Hassan, reaching for him with its promise of death. He looked once more at the burning Tent then dropped into the hole he had blown in the concrete slab less than an hour before.

5:39 a.m., Tel Aviv

"The Temple Mount is overrun . . . we have over one hundred dead, probably more." General Orhlon's voice wore the heavy mantle of grief and responsibility. "Major Levin, Major Katz are dead. Fighting is still heavy in the streets. The Arabs slaughtered a huge pig on the altar before they set the fire. The Tent is engulfed in flames, and the fire keeps growing. I don't know what the Arabs threw on it."

"What are we doing, General?"

Prime Minister Baruk tried to hold his fury in check.

"Our gunships are pounding the Arabs now . . . they're Hezbollah and Martyrs' Brigade. I have no idea how so many Hezbollah fighters got so deep into Jerusalem."

Orhlon sounded as if he was talking to himself. "We're massing our force for a counterattack on the Mount. Our military is on full alert. Half the air force is already in the air, more pilots are awaiting orders. Armor and artillery are moving to the borders. Our missile batteries are red. Tell me when . . . tell me who . . . and we will crush them."

"So where is Shomsky?" said Baruk. "Tell him to get something ready for the press."

"I wanted to talk to you about Shomsky," said General Orhlon, "but this is not the time. And I don't know where he is."

"Find Shomsky," Baruk exploded. "We can't leave the situation like this. We must regain control of the Temple Mount. Make it happen."

5:41 a.m., Dayr al Qiddis Oasis, Egypt

Two camels got into a loud disagreement, splitting the brittle quiet of the desert night on the plain of Wadi Gerifat along the flank of the Al-Qalzam Mountains of the eastern Sahara. A dog barked in the distance, and another replied from the opposite side of the tent encampment. The men of the Prophet's Guard were home, safe, and slept with the soundness of the secure, including the two who were on guard—now huddled around a moldering fire. Had they been awake, they would not have seen the three black-clad men with the hoods over their heads. They moved like moon shadows on the sand as they closed on the tent in the center of the compound.

The old man stirred in his tent—so little undisturbed rest, so few nights of real sleep for old men. He felt the pressure and knew he had to get up. His bones ached as he pushed off the heavy rug, and he swung his spindly legs off the sleeping platform. A shadow moved to his left.

One of ours—? The question stalled in his mind, supplanted by the surprise of a gloved hand over his mouth, the pinch of a blade to his neck. Another shadow moved—floated to stand right in front of the old man, looking into his mismatched eyes—one brown, one yellow. This shadow pulled the hood from his head and pushed his face to within inches of the old man. The old man shivered in the night. He wasn't cold.

"I'm here to share with you a gift from my father." The man cut the leather strip around the old man's throat and lifted the amulet to his sight—a Coptic cross with the lightning bolt slashing through on the diagonal. "My father wishes you a long life," said the young prince to the leader of the Prophet's Guard, "a long life in hell."

The old man's spine stiffened as the knife at his neck opened his throat from ear to ear.

"Joe . . . are you still there?"

Rodriguez didn't know how much time had passed. He looked at his watch, talking to him from half the world away, and shook his head. Then he realized he was perspiring, heavily. He looked up at the fire on the Temple Mount. He lifted the watch to his mouth.

"Yeah, I'm here . . . I'm still here. Listen . . . the fire is getting awfully hot. And it's spreading."

"What do you mean?" asked Reynolds.

"Well . . . the Tent is still burning—incredibly hot. I can't believe there's enough stuff in there to be burning this hot for this long. But the really odd thing is that the fire is spreading. It looks like liquid fire, like it's flowing out of the Tent and washing over the platform as it continues to burn."

"But the platform is concrete."

"I know," said Joe, wiping the sleeve of his shirt over his sopping face. "But it's burning. The concrete is burning. And it's burning really hot. I feel like I'm getting scorched."

"Look, Joe . . . if the gunships are . . ."

"Yeah, they are." Rodriguez swallowed, trying to get some moisture in his mouth. "They are ripping up the Arab fighters still on the Mount. But there's not many of them. The fire is spreading to the far end of the platform, too. Anybody who's down there is going to get . . . wait . . . wait."

Were it not for the incredible things he had experienced since the day Tom Bohannon first showed him the huge safe in the Bowery Mission, Joe would have questioned his own eyes. But not now. "Sam . . . it's burning down."

"What?"

"It's burning *down*," Rodriguez repeated. "The flames were burning up— from the Tent, from the platform, up into the sky. But now the flames are burning down. The fire is coming from the sky, down onto the Tent, and spreading across the platform."

"Oh . . . my God."

"Yeah, that's right. And it's getting even hotter. I can feel my skin blistering."

"Get out of there, Joe."

"Not on your life," said Rodriguez. "This isn't over. I want to see what happens next."

10:44 p.m. Eastern Daylight Time, Washington, DC

"Maybe we'll get out of this—now that the Tent's been destroyed." The secretary of state sat in a corner of the sofa in the Oval Office, looking at President Whitestone like a man who had lost his last friend. All his work on the Bavarian Peace Treaty lay obliterated on the crest of the Temple Mount.

"Are you kidding, Ollie?" The secretary of defense snapped to the edge of his chair. "There is no way on this green earth that the Israelis will leave the Muslims in control of the Temple Mount. They're going to hit 'em, and they're going to hit 'em hard. They're embarrassed. And by thunder they're gonna make somebody pay. I wouldn't want to be in their crosshairs right now."

A knock on the door, and the president's secretary stepped into the room. "Mr. President, the Israeli prime minister is on the line."

Whitestone and Cartwright were seated across from each other. They passed a cautionary glance—the fate of the Middle East hung on these next few minutes. Perhaps all their fates. "Put him on the speaker."

Silent thoughts and whispered prayers hovered along the curves of the Oval Office as the secretary returned to her desk. Soon the speakerphone in the center of the coffee table crackled to life.

"Mr. President?"

"Mr. Prime Minister," said Whitestone, "I'm here with the secretary of state, the secretary of defense, and the CIA director."

"And I'm here with myself," said Baruk. "Orhlon doesn't want me in the air and my security doesn't want me to move from the house. I feel like a eunuch."

"Mr. Prime Minister . . . Elie . . . I'm sorry for the men you've lost. And, forgive me if I'm being insensitive, but we've got to know what you're planning now."

"Planning? What would you think?" said Baruk, the sound of defiance accenting his words. "We're going to retake the Temple Mount . . . at any cost. This is a terrorist act by those psychopaths in Lebanon. Do you think we will sit back and ponder?"

Cartwright moved closer to the phone. "Mr. Prime Minister, we have solid intel that there is more than Hezbollah behind this action. We think the Brotherhood is behind everything that is happening—including tonight. Are you going to take on every Muslim government in the entire region?"

He looked across the table to the president. No one in that room wanted to break the silence.

"Mr. Cartwright," said the prime minister, "the blood of Israeli soldiers now stains the very place where Solomon's Temple once stood. In thousands of years, nothing has changed. The Arab wants to annihilate the Jew."

The grandfather clock was ticking along the north wall of the Oval Office, its beats measuring the future of peace.

"We will fight," said Baruk, "with everything we have, to stay alive."

"But, Elie, you know what that will mean," said the president. "You need to show restraint, or—"

"Or the deserts will melt. I know," said Baruk. "That is not my concern. My concern is to fight for life . . . even if that means death."

The door pushed open as the president's secretary rushed into the room and came to Whitestone's side. "Mr. President," she whispered, "please, excuse me, sir . . . but King Abbudin is on the phone. He wants to speak to you and the prime minister at the same time."

Whitestone quickly weighed his options.

"Elie, King Abbudin is on the line . . . he wants to get on a conference call with both of us."

The leaders of the most powerful nation on earth looked at each other with shock at the Saudi king's call, and resignation that none of them knew which button to push.

"Carol . . . can you make that happen?"

The president's secretary stepped around the sofas and approached the table. She pushed two buttons. "Mr. Prime Minister?"

"Yes."

"Your Highness?"

"Yes."

She turned to her boss. "You're on," and left the room.

10:47 p.m. Eastern Daylight Time, Washington, DC

"It has been a conspiracy of the Muslim Brotherhood, orchestrated by this once-dead imam, Moussa al-Sadr—founding father of Hezbollah—for his own dreams of jihad, that has thrown the Arab world into chaotic revolution," said King Abbudin, his voice from the speakerphone gritty through the combined connection. "We must not allow the radical Islamists and the Iranians to turn the Middle East into a radiation-poisoned wasteland."

"And what can you do about that now?" snapped Baruk. "My men are already slaughtered on the Temple Mount."

Whitestone knew the future of the world depended on the next answer.

"I will cut the head from the conspiracy," Abbudin promised. "With the support of my brother in peace, President Baqir al-Musawi, I dispatched avengers to remove the threat to Islam—a black plague to wipe out our enemies.

"Yes, much blood has been shed tonight," said the king, "and more will soon be shed to save us all. But, Mr. President . . . Mr. Prime Minister . . . we must not allow the maniacal plans of this man to succeed. It is up to us to keep the peace, to maintain order in the Middle East, throughout the world. I have ordered the soldiers of Hezbollah and the Martyrs' Brigade to withdraw, to abandon their arms and leave Jerusalem. We can rescue peace. We can avoid the conflagration that would destroy us all. It is up to us."

Whitestone and the men in the Oval Office held their breath. "Mr. Prime Minister?"

"Israel will retain sovereignty over the Temple Mount."

"Agreed," said King Abbudin.

Silence sharpened the edge of desperation in the room.

"All right. Perhaps we can step back from the abyss," said Baruk. "But our military will remain mobilized until we are certain that we are no longer under attack."

"Very wise, Mr. Prime Minister," said Abbudin. "Now I must go and ensure that my orders are carried out . . . immediately."

One of the lights on the telephone console was extinguished.

"Thank you, Eliazar," said President Whitestone. "You have saved your nation."

"No, Jonathan . . . I have saved my revenge for the moment when it will do the greatest damage."

5:45 a.m., Balata Camp, Nablus, West Bank

Sitting at the window, Moussa al-Sadr gazed at the glowing sky to the west. "Your men have done well, Youssef. The fire burns bright on the Temple Mount. We have destroyed the Israeli claim to sovereignty. Tomorrow we call on the world to condemn their arrogance, to isolate the Jews even more."

Youssef came up behind his master and looked over his shoulder.

"The Tent has burned for a long time, Holy One."

"Let it burn forever," said al-Sadr.

━━∿〰━━

Three black-clad, black-masked men moved like wraiths through the empty, dusty street.

On padded feet they approached the house, a stout, wooden door on the ground level, windows dark. But on the second floor, light burned in the room at the front of the building. Moving shadows, they climbed the outside staircase and stopped at the upper door. One bent, worked the lock, and edged the door ajar. The sound of voices came from the front room.

Four men occupied the lit room—a cleric in black robes, looking out through a far window, with a huge, muscled Arab at his side and two, large, armed men who looked and acted like bodyguards.

The masked men waited. Two of them had silenced automatics pointed into the room. When the cleric turned from the window, two muffled spits sliced through the room and each of the guards fell dead. A second pair of muffled shots and the massive Arab was driven back against the far wall. Shaking off the surprise on his face and the two mortal bullet wounds in his chest, Youssef managed one, stumbling step toward the assassins, then fell flat on his face, blood seeping from under his body.

Imam Moussa al-Sadr faced his assassins as the three black-clad men entered the room. He raised his arms, closed his eyes, and prepared to sing out *god is good—Allahu Akbar!*—when strong hands grabbed his arms and pinned them to his back and another set of hands grabbed the back of his head and forced a cloth into his mouth.

Al-Sadr opened his eyes. One man in black stood before him. With drama and grace he withdrew the hood. Crown Prince Faisal—eldest son of King Abbudin. Vengeance . . . Sunni vengeance.

Faisal moved so close to al-Sadr's face, their noses almost touched. His breath smelled of chickpeas and garlic.

"You will bleed a drop for every insult," said Prince Faisal.

Al-Sadr felt the knife enter his stomach.

"You will bleed a drop for every offense, every slur you heaped upon our father, our family."

Faisal pulled the knife across al-Sadr's midsection with the precision and purposefulness of a butcher slicing a filet, the hands confining al-Sadr's arms behind his back holding the imam steady.

"You will bleed until you die. And we will sit here, and watch you die. And your last thought will be of the House of Saud."

5:49 a.m., Tel Aviv

The reports from the Temple Mount were getting worse by the minute. Baruk and his bodyguards raced down the steps toward waiting cars.

Three black-clad men moved up along the edges of the driveway, remaining in the shadow of the high hedges. Behind them, the security gate to Baruk's home was closed and disabled, the gate guards dead at their posts. They came to the first of the two turns in the driveway, just before the hedges gave way to open ground.

All three came to rest at the edge of the hedge. They heard the sounds from above . . . running feet . . . slamming car doors. They tensed, but not because they were about to strike. Instead, each man felt the stab of a thin, razor-sharp blade run through his throat, the honed-edge steel pulled across the back of his neck, severing his spinal cord.

Three other black-clad men now moved out of the hedges and away from the limp bodies. They advanced up the hill toward the house.

5:50 a.m., On the Ashkelon Road

Commander Browne Counsil swung his Comanche into a snap turn left, burped the accelerator, and jumped his helicopter to a position in front of, and above, the Mazda sedan as it continued its retreat back along the road. Counsil floated the Comanche down, a lethal feather, to fifty feet off the ground, and held her steady. He was directly over the road. *This is where it gets tricky.* Reveal himself to the kidnappers in the car and put the women at risk, or remain at height—at a distance—to watch and wait. The safety of the women was paramount. He eased the Comanche back up to one hundred feet. "Pete . . . copy?"

"Roger."

"I've got 'em," said Counsil. "Over on Route Thirty-Eight. I'm overhead, spy in the sky. They've turned around, heading back east on the road. Seems a bridge suddenly vaporized in front of them. Go back two clicks and land. I'll materialize when we're abreast of you and get their attention. You get the women."

"Roger that."

"You'll need to be fast, Pete. No dawdling coming over that ridge. Get there and get the women out."

"I'll be there."

Counsil tripped the turbo in the tail and the Comanche rotated toward the east without a sound. As the car passed underneath him, Counsil felt as if the helicopter was adrift on the night. Sixty miles an hour was like standing still. But he used the opportunity to scan the car with night-vision sensors and heat-seeking thermal imaging. Two bodies in the front; three in the back. From the size of the bodies in the back, the one in the middle was a man. But he didn't like the looks of the thermal scans. In one of the women, life was fading. He was about to radio his wingman with the information when a strange sight came into view a hundred yards in front of the escaping Mazda.

It was a white man. He looked like he'd been hit by a train—his clothes were shredded, his body was bloodied, his right arm dangled at his side and swung at its own, incoherent rhythm, and he was lurching over a hillock next to the road. He stumbled onto the asphalt roadway, in front of the oncoming car, waving his left arm back and forth. He was trying to stop the Mazda.

Guy looks like a walking MASH unit.

The driver of the car apparently didn't see this apparition until the last moment. The Mazda went into a skid, across the road, coming to rest straddling the berm on the left side of the road—the oncoming lane.

Mr. MASH Unit took two stumbling steps toward the car . . . and Captain Browne Counsil opened up. He threw on his three, one-kilowatt Xenon Arc floodlights, blinding everyone on the ground, toggled his twenty millimeter nose cannon, and tore up the earth around the front and left side of the car—away from Mr. MASH Unit—and put one, well-placed burst through the car's engine block.

Counsil dropped the chopper. He figured his only hope was to ground the helicopter with all dispatch and try to reach the women before their captors recovered from the sound and fury of his onslaught.

But as those thoughts were flashing through his mind and the Comanche was speeding toward a hard landing, a black Humvee hurtled into the picture from the east, ripped into a controlled, high-speed skid, and slammed its rear quarter-panel into the smoking front end of the Mazda. Bedlam ensued as the two-hundred-million-dollar Comanche slammed into the ground and snapped Counsil's body against his harness.

Without pause, two Israeli soldiers leapt out of the Humvee, Uzis leveled. Right on their heels came a dwarf, shooting an automatic pistol into the sky.

Mr. MASH Unit lurched up to the car, his good arm stretched out in front of him. The dwarf climbed onto the smoking hood of the car, holding the gun in front of him. Counsil could see him screaming at the men in the car. The soldiers ripped open the front doors, pulled two men out, and buried them in the dust. But the women were still in the back seat.

Counsil aimed his spotlights right through the back window of the Mazda, lighting it up like a Hollywood premier. He painted a laser sight on the head of the man in the back seat. But before Counsil could engage a trigger, the man's head exploded.

Arms through a hole in the car's windshield, the dwarf held his smoking gun aimed at a point once occupied by the kidnapper's head.

⎯⎯∿⌒⎯

It was cold tonight. He was surprised about the cold, surprised that he remembered the cold. What was he doing?

He could hear the sirens in the distance better than he could hear the soldier talking to him.

And his arm didn't work.

Funny. Annie was here. In her nightshirt. But the sleeves were ripped off.

Over there, Sammy Rizzo was kneeling in the dirt and hugging Kallie Nolan. Kinda cold for Kallie to be wearing a tee shirt. And with one of Annie's sleeves, all gooey, wrapped around her neck. Funny about dreams. Kallie's eyes were open, but she looked asleep.

Oh, and there was some science fiction flying machine. And it was cold.

But Annie was there. She was smiling at him—holding something up to his head—but tears were running down her cheeks. She said something.

It was cold. But it was all right. Thank God.

5:56 a.m., Saudi Arabia

Dry desert winds pushed against the silk curtains. The king of the Saudis sat cross-legged on the carpet, his back straight, ignoring the support of the large pillows stacked by his side, his eyes as hard as the steel in the dagger he pointed at the other men seated around the carpet.

"Islam is the power of the New World Order," said Abbudin, "and we are the power of Islam. We have ripped control of the Muslim Brotherhood from the Shi'a heretics. Al-Sadr and the old man of the desert are dead. Our teams of black death will soon eliminate the leaders of the Great Satan. Israel will be crippled, ripe for attack. The United States will be leaderless and vulnerable.

"In a few hours, the Muslim Brotherhood will be united once again . . . united behind a purpose, behind a destiny. All Muslims, one-third of the earth's population, solemnly dedicated to the fulfillment of Allah's great prophecy— the restoration of the Caliphate."

"We have extracted our revenge. Now we will finish what we have begun. And you"—Abbudin pointed at each of the men with the curved tip of his dagger and pierced their hearts with his passion—"you will be the princes of the East.

"There is more than one way to wage jihad. Without oil, the West will be powerless. Jihad has begun . . . the Caliphate will be restored . . . and we will never relinquish the Temple Mount. Jerusalem will be ours. We will no longer bow to the Jews or their infidel Christian allies. There is a new Saladin and the lands of our fathers will once again be under our feet."

10:57 p.m. Eastern Daylight Time, Alexandria, VA

A line of limos and SUV escort vehicles pulled into the circular drive of the Alexandria mansion and stopped directly in front of the main doors. A small army of men in suits and earpieces poured out of the cars on both sides, searching the roof, the sky, the trees for any sign of danger.

Jonathan Whitestone stepped out of the presidential limousine and entered Senator Green's home for the private fund-raiser. The president hated this part of the job, but it was necessary.

None of the men in suits saw the three, black-clad, hooded men slip from the darkness of the Virginia woods that ran close to the southeast corner of the senator's house.

5:58 a.m., Jerusalem

Rodriguez watched as the pillar of fire grew in intensity, pouring out of the sky like a flaming waterfall. But he was driven back by the heat.

He retreated through the opening between the cab of the truck and the hauler, grabbed onto a handle at the corner of the cab's roof, and swung himself to the right, landing on the running board, just under the passenger side door. Blocked from the heat by the truck's cab, he continued his vigil, in wonder at this miracle on the Mount.

"Something is happening." He leaned closer to the satellite phone transmitter in his wristwatch. "Are you still there? . . . The fire has stopped. . . . No, I don't mean it's gone out. It's stopped. It's not coming down and it's not going up. . . . No, I am not kidding. It's standing still. The fire is standing still. . . . Yes, it's still burning. But it's just hanging there in the air. It's not moving at all. . . . Yes, there are flames. And they are big. And hot. But they are not moving. They are just—"

A spine-shaking, crashing and yawning, as if the earth were ripping itself open in some primordial birth process, attacked his eardrums and drove splitting shards of pain behind his eyes. Joe may have screamed; he couldn't tell. The thunder of rending earth grew, not only in volume, but also in mass, overwhelming his senses.

Right in front of him, the fire lifted up the concrete platform of the Temple Mount—lifted it straight up, about twenty meters. The fire then fully engulfed the top, bottom, and sides. The whole thing was blazing, a cauldron of rampaging flames.

And then it exploded.

Chunks of flaming concrete pounded into the far side of the truck, one crashing through the driver's side window. Rodriguez hung on desperately as the truck rocked wildly back and forth on its haunches.

He momentarily lost sight of the Temple Mount, but as he pulled himself back to a standing position on the running board, Rodriguez saw a sight even he had trouble believing. The pillar of fire was still pouring out of the sky, but the Tent had vanished. A horrible, groaning rumble came up out of the earth, and the pillar of fire was sucked down into a gaping, flaming hole where the Temple Mount once stood.

Caught in the vortex, the truck slid sideways toward the burning abyss.

10:58 p.m. Eastern Daylight Time, Alexandria, VA

Both men were on secure cell phones, Whitestone talking to the secretary of state and Cartwright talking to his deputy director of Middle East affairs. But Cartwright was getting a more detailed picture of what was happening on the ground.

"The whole thing is gone, *again*? What are the Israelis doing? . . . Okay. Call if anything changes."

The CIA director flipped shut his phone and turned to his boss. Whitestone looked older. His face was ashen; his hair disheveled from where his hand held his head. His eyes were blinking and darting from place to place in Senator Green's private office.

"Mr. President . . . are you all right, sir?"

The telephone nearly fell from his hand as Whitestone leaned against the desk at his side. "Shin Bet has men rushing to Baruk's residence. They haven't been able to contact the prime minister or his security detail for the past ten minutes. The last communication they had was twenty minutes ago and Baruk said he was on his way to the helipad. He was leaving Tel Aviv for Jerusalem."

5:59 a.m., Jerusalem

Rodriguez squeezed out every ounce of strength he could muster to hold on to the truck. He struggled to turn his body around, his back to the Mount, and was debating what the more foolhardy decision was—stay with the sliding truck or jump and run.

And then everything stopped.

The noise of the fire, the heat, the groaning death of the Temple Mount, everything stopped in half a heartbeat.

Rodriguez hung from the door's handle and tried to control his breathing so he wouldn't hyperventilate. He pulled himself upright and turned around to look once more.

Through the shattered windows of the truck, Joe realized that night had passed. The sun was rising in the east, the sky over Jerusalem pinking in the distance.

And a pillar of smoke hung over the yawning grave that once was the Temple Mount.

31

FRIDAY, AUGUST 28

Jerusalem

It was Rizzo who convinced them.

Now he sat alone, in a shaded corner of the Garden Tomb, surrounded by fragrant flowers, but numb in his grief. Tom Bohannon, his right arm snug in a sling, walked over to the bench, sat down next to Rizzo, and put his good arm around Sammy's shoulders.

"It's time," said Bohannon.

Rizzo turned his head, the lenses of his thick glasses fogged by his tears, and looked toward Bohannon's voice.

"Okay . . . it's okay." Rizzo slid from the bench and managed slow, heavy-footed steps down one of the many paths in the lovingly tended grounds called the Garden Tomb, just off the Nablus Road, near Jeremiah's Grotto and the Damascus Gate leading to Old City Jerusalem.

Ronald Fineman had talked to his friends who ran the Garden Tomb to gain access to the gardens, but the memorial service was Rizzo's idea—one he pursued doggedly, overcoming every other barrier and impediment. "Kallie would want it this way. She loved this city. She would want to be remembered here."

So they gathered, before Kallie's body was flown back to her family in Iowa, to pay their respects in Jerusalem, the place where Kallie Nolan lost her life, but had lived her life to the fullest. Rabbi Fineman was there to lead the service. Kallie's friends from the Garden Guides, from the university—her former roommates—were joined by Tom and Annie Bohannon; Joe Rodriguez and his wife, Deirdre, who flew in the day before, accompanied by Sam Reynolds from the State Department. At Tom's request, even Brandon McDonough joined them from Ireland, to honor Doc's life as well.

Tom followed Sammy down the path toward the center of the Garden Tomb, what many believe is the place where the body of Jesus Christ was buried following his crucifixion on Golgotha. The tomb first came to the attention of a famous British general, Charles Gordon, in the late nineteenth century. The site, and the tomb it encompassed, fit so much of the description about Christ's burial place—and place of resurrection—that the land was purchased in the late eighteen hundreds by the Garden Tomb Association of Great Britain and, over many years, turned into a verdant garden of reverent reflection for thousands of visitors.

In the center of the garden, near the large first-century cistern, the rest of the group waited for Sammy and Tom. In their midst was a plain, wooden casket, draped with an American flag and covered with flowers.

Bohannon stood close behind Rizzo. Tom's eyes were red. His knees buckled. But he would be there if Sammy needed him.

Rabbi Fineman stepped up to the casket.

⸺∿∿⸺

An hour later, Rabbi Ronald Fineman welcomed them all to his home.

He called it the *Seudat Hawra'ah*, the meal of condolence—one of the oldest, most important, and most meaningful traditions of the Jewish people. As determined as Rizzo was to have the service, Rabbi Fineman was determined that all who attended the service come to his home for the Seudat Hawra'ah.

Bohannon was grateful for the food. And it gave them all time to talk.

Kallie's Jerusalem friends congregated in the kitchen and dining area but, one by one, members of the team found themselves in the shade of a trellis in the small garden alongside Ronald Fineman's home. The rabbi and Brandon McDonough were already in the garden, huddled together under the blooming wisteria as the others escaped the house and the sun. Only the buzzing of flies, and the whispers coming from Fineman and McDonough, disturbed the silence. Until Tom asked one of the many questions that nagged his mind.

"It appears there were several teams of these black-hooded assassins," said Sam Reynolds. He was sitting in a cushioned chair, his feet propped up on the edge of a large planter. "I don't know how Baruk survived—they breached the security of his home and came darn close to killing him. And Baruk's chief of staff, Chaim Shomsky, is missing and hasn't been seen since that night. But they didn't get close to the president. The Secret Service shot all three of them before they came near the senator's house."

"But who would try to assassinate the president of the United States and the prime minister of Israel, both on the same night?" asked Bohannon, who sat across a small table from Annie, in the opposite corner. "Who has that kind of power . . . that kind of reach?"

"Remember I told you about the new leader in the Muslim world?" said Reynolds. "It all doesn't add up yet, but we believe radical Islam is behind these and other attacks."

Joe and Deirdre sat on a bench, side by side. "Al Qaeda?" asked Joe.

Reynolds turned to his right, shaking his head. "No . . . Al Qaeda appears to be fading. There's a lot I can't talk about, but . . . well . . . we see the Muslim Brotherhood's hand at work throughout the Middle East. And your guys with the amulets seem to be involved, too."

Annie's chair screeched along the flagstone as she shoved it back and stood to her feet. "God help us. Aren't we ever going to be rid of these people? Why can't you guys wipe out the Prophet's Guard and give us our lives back?"

"But—" Reynolds only got out the one word.

"But nothing," Annie snapped, crossing half the distance to Reynolds. "You and the president and all his power have been nothing but bystanders, watching from the sidelines as we . . . as Tom and Joe and Sammy . . . risked our lives, our families, chasing after the messages on the scroll. We need—"

"They were never after the scroll." Another voice entered the conversation.

Rizzo stepped into the shade under the trellis. Again, Bohannon was struck by the devastating change. Rizzo carried his grief in every contour of his face. There was little life left in his eyes. He looked like an old man.

Dressed in black, head-to-toe, Rizzo walked up beside Annie, took her left hand in his, and looked up into her face. It nearly broke Tom's heart.

"We were wrong," Rizzo said. "They wanted what the scroll, the mezuzah, pointed to. And it wasn't the Temple or the Tent. The guys who got me out of the monastery—the Temple Guard guys—they told me what this is all about. They showed me." He held Annie's eyes. "I think it's why so many have died. Why so many more may die."

Rizzo rubbed Annie Bohannon's hand in both of his. She looked directly into his face.

"It isn't over," said Rizzo. "What they're after . . . they'll never stop."

Annie reached out her right hand and caressed Rizzo's cheek. "Then you and I will stop them, Sam. You and me, Tom and Joe. We can't live the rest of our lives like this, running in fear from these killers. If God's hand is in this—and I believe that with all my heart—then he's called us to be in this to the end. No matter what it is that they want."

Rizzo took a deep breath. He held Annie's hand, and her eyes, locked in an embrace. "They want to control the world," he said. "And they think they can use God's power to do that. That's what they're after."

For a moment, silence came back into the shade under the trellis.

"I don't understand," said Deirdre. "What do you mean, use God's power?"

Rizzo turned his head to the left. "They're looking for a weapon."

"I know." Rabbi Fineman stood up, followed by McDonough.

McDonough picked up a large sheet of paper that had been laid out between him and the rabbi as they talked. He held it up in front of him. "I traced these images off the cover of a sarcophagus in Jeremiah's tomb." On the sheet of paper were two large, angelic beings, their wings upraised, flaming swords held aloft in their hands. Between the angels was a huge tree. Below the angels and the tree was a shepherd's staff.

"I know what they're looking for," said Fineman. "The most powerful weapon in the history of man."

"And I think I know where we need to look," said McDonough.

AUTHOR'S NOTE

While *The Brotherhood Conspiracy* is a work of fiction, there are several plot elements that are based on fact.

Details about the Tent of Meeting are biblically accurate up to the point when the Tent disappears from the pages of recorded history. The last reference to the Tent of Meeting, or Tabernacle, that traveled with the Hebrew exiles through the Sinai Desert is written in 1 Kings (8:4) when Solomon went to Gibeon and gathered up the Tent and its furnishings prior to dedicating the Temple on Mount Zion. There is no mention of the Tabernacle in the Jewish Tanakh after the destruction of Jerusalem by the Babylonians in 587 BC.

─────

The Temple Mount in Jerusalem is a platform, supported by a series of arches built by Herod the Great. The Mount is a formation of karstic limestone which has eroded over time by water, creating a honeycomb of cisterns, tunnels, and caverns. Other than the unofficial diggings of Charles Warren in the nineteenth century, there has been virtually no archaeological study of the space under the Temple Mount platform.

─────

The Muslim Brotherhood, for most of its seventy-five years a little-known but powerful network, came to worldwide attention in the aftermath of the Arab Spring and the overthrow of Egyptian despot Hosni Mubarak. Now the ruling party in Egypt's nascent parliament and the home of new president Mohammad Morsi,

The Muslim Brotherhood is, in fact, the oldest, largest, and most influential Muslim organization in the world. Founded in 1928 by an Egyptian teacher who preached a more pure and devout form of Islam, the Brotherhood's motto makes its intent clear: "Allah is our objective; the Qur'an is our law, the Prophet is our leader; jihad is our way; and death for the sake of Allah is the highest of our aspirations."

The Brotherhood's reach and presence is global. It is a major funding source for the terrorist group Hamas. The Holy Land Foundation (HLF), a U.S. fund-raising arm for The Brotherhood and Hamas, was indicted in federal court in 2004 of a fifteen-year conspiracy to raise funds for a terrorist organization. In 2008, the HLF and five individuals were convicted of 108 counts of tax evasion, money laundering, and funding a terrorist organization. The HLF raised over $12 million in the United States before it was shut down.

⸺∿∿⸺

Imam Moussa al-Sadr is the founder of Amal, the military arm of al-Sadr's Movement of the Disinherited, and the forerunner of the terrorist army, Hezbollah, that now controls the government of Lebanon. Al-Sadr and two companions disappeared in 1978 during a trip to Libya to meet with Colonel Muammar Qaddafi. Thirty years later, the Lebanese government indicted Qaddafi in the death of Imam al-Sadr.

⸺∿∿⸺

On July 20, 2006, an Irish farmer digging peat in a remote bog at Faddan More, in north Tipperary, close to the town of Birr, uncovered a book of psalms dating back to the late eighth century. Known as the *Faddan More Psalter*, the book is an illuminated vellum manuscript encased in an unusual leather binding. Fragments of papyrus were discovered in the lining of the Egyptian-style leather binding. This potentially represents the first tangible connection between early Irish Christianity and the Middle Eastern Coptic Church.

⸺∿∿⸺

In the Irish county of Meath, outside the small town of Loughcrew, is a pair of hilltops overlooking the Boyne River Valley on which were erected the largest complex of passage tombs in Ireland. These sixteen tombs are between five and six thousand years old, older than the Egyptian pyramids. The largest of these passage tombs is Cairn T and within its rounded burial chambers are a series of stones with megalithic decorations. Cairn T is also called the tomb of the *Ollam Foldah* . . . the Old Prophet. There are some who claim the stone carvings in Cairn T depict the flight of the prophet Jeremiah and his scribe, Baruch, from Egypt to Ireland and locate the burial place of Jeremiah within the tomb. In the smallest, furthest burial chamber of Cairn T, the ceiling contains six-thousand-year-old stone carvings that look as if they were completed yesterday. During the vernal and autumn equinox, people gather at dawn to watch sunlight enter the chamber and illuminate the decorated stones within the tomb. And the key to Cairn T is indeed available from the pastry shop at Loughcrew Gardens.

〜〜〜

Other items: American Egyptologist Charles Edwin Wilbour (1833–1896) was all that has been portrayed here, and more . . . St. Anthony's Monastery is the oldest inhabited Christian monastery in the world, being continually occupied by monks since its founding in 356 AD . . . All five kings of Saudi Arabia are sons of the first king, Abdul Aziz al Saud . . . Krak de Chevaliers is a spectacular Crusader castle in the Syrian foothills of the Alawite Mountains . . . Marine One helicopters do perform the "President's Shell Game" maneuver as they fly . . . The stealth Boeing Sikorsky RAH-66 Comanche helicopter was designed to be the world's most advanced helicopter. Nearly seven billion dollars was spent on the program, and two prototypes constructed, before Boeing and the U.S. Army canceled the program in 2004. There is apparently no truth to the widely believed rumor that Comanche helicopters were used in the U.S. attack on Osama bin Laden's compound in Pakistan, offered up as the reason for why it was so important to destroy the one that crashed . . . And you can buy—once in a while—$5 tickets to baseball games at Yankee Stadium.

Apart from basic facts and associated research, *The Brotherhood Conspiracy* is a product of the author's imagination. Any "errors of fact" are a result of that imagination.

ABOUT THE AUTHOR

Terry Brennan's twenty-two-year career in journalism included:

- Leading *The Mercury* of Pottstown, Pennsylvania, as its editor, to a Pulitzer Prize in Editorial Writing;
- Serving as executive editor of a multinational newspaper firm—Ingersoll Publications—with papers in the United States, England, and Ireland; and
- Earning the Valley Forge Award for editorial writing from the Freedoms Foundation.

In 1966 Brennan transferred to the nonprofit sector and served for twelve years as vice president of operations for the Christian Herald Association, Inc., the parent organization of four New York City ministries, including The Bowery Mission.

He now serves as chief administrative officer for Care for the Homeless, a New York City nonprofit that delivers medical teams to serve homeless people in shelters, soup kitchens, and drop-in centers. Two of his adult sons and their families live in Pennsylvania. Terry and his wife, Andrea, and their two adult children live in the New York City area.

ALSO BY
TERRY BRENNAN

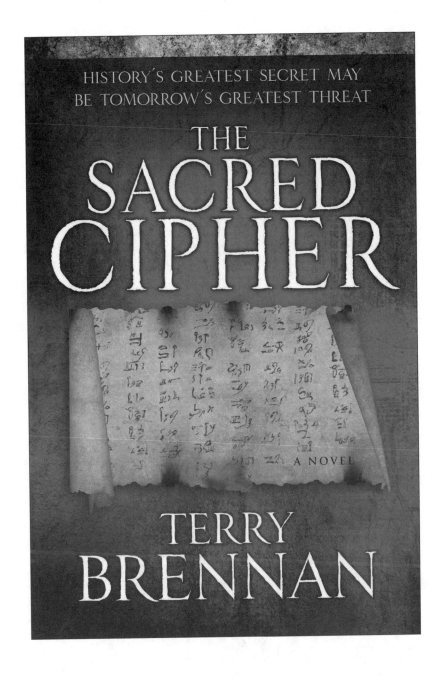

HISTORY'S GREATEST SECRET MAY
BE TOMORROW'S GREATEST THREAT

THE
SACRED
CIPHER

A NOVEL

TERRY
BRENNAN